What people are saying

The Wistful and the Good

G. M. Baker

Cuthbert's People, Book One

Stories All the Way Down
Bridgewater, Nova Scotia

First published by Stories All the Way Down, April 2022

This is a work of fiction. The characters and events are the product of the author's imagination. Any seeming resemblance to real persons or events is a product of the reader's imagination.

ISBN: 978-1-7780663-0-6

For Anna

1 The Ship

Elswyth sat on the clifftop looking out over the bright sea. There was a steady onshore breeze blowing, stinging her eyes and tossing her hair out behind her. She refused to wear the wimple that should have covered her head and neck, for young men's eyes would follow her hair as it bounced and swayed and danced. Young men's eyes were a novelty and a delight. Not so long ago, a child's smock had hung from narrow shoulders straight downward to the ground. But now a woman's dress flowed over curves like the tide flowing over smooth stones. Young men's eyes followed the curves. Whenever she walked through the village, the young men would pause in their tasks, like seagulls hanging on the wind, eyes hungry for something beneath the surface of the wave.

Nor was she shy about looking at the young men. In the autumn, when the harvest had called every able body, man, woman, child, noble, free, and slave, into the fields from dawn till dusk, she had gloried in their broad backs, the flow of their muscles under the skin, the salt sweat of their tanned faces. And in the quiet of the evenings, she had found herself delighting in the thought of lying beside this one or that in the soft new-cut grass, and of the rasp of a calloused hand upon soft flesh.

But she was not for them. She was a thegn's daughter, and promised long since to an ealdorman's son. Young men's eyes had no right to follow her. Her thoughts had no right to stray to hard hands or soft grass. There could be no starlit tryst on new-mown hay for her.

But the eyes of the young men were not her only delight. From where she sat, her eyes could follow the great curve of the horizon, the restless boundary between sea and sand below, the roll and swell of the tide, the curve of the sea grass, bent before the wind. These too were a delight, though the same blustering wind tried to tear her embroidery frame from her fingers and whisk away her threads to catch among the bracken and the gorse.

For the hundredth time she glanced upward, and this time, at last, she saw it. A flash of white, far out in the band of haze between sea and sky. A sail. Her frame and her needle fell into her lap as her eyes yearned outward toward a horizon that was empty once again.

This is how it is when you first see a sail. It will appear for a moment when the ship crests a swell and the light catches the sail just so. And then it will be gone, perhaps not to be seen again for minutes, or perhaps never again. Few eyes would have caught that first flash, or known it for what it was. But Elswyth knew, and in that moment of recognition her breath grew still and her heart raced as the world grew large around her.

Elswyth loved ships, every rope and spar, every plank and sail. She loved the smell of the pitch that lined the seams. Her eyes followed the curves of a ship. Her hands longed to touch, to follow the rise of the curving prow, the round fullness of the stern. She loved the way a ship cleaves to the swelling of the waves, its urgent energy under the force of wind or oar, its rise and fall as it mounted and drove from crest to trough of the ocean swell.

And she loved the young men who sailed in ships, with their strange voices, their hard, strong hands, their red sea-weathered faces, their sheepskin jackets stiff with salt and smelling of both land and sea and the marriage of both. She loved the tales they told, of wild rocky northlands with their soaring peaks and deep fjords, of the sun-scarred south, where winters were green and summers brown, and men and women rested on the great verandas of stone-built palaces in the heat of the day. Everywhere they travelled, it seemed, was sharper, more vivid, more extreme than Northumbria, the soft country she was born to with its low hills, cool summers, and damp winters.

Once, as a child, she had asked why they came here at all, to which the answer was, "For trade, my darling, and to see the pretty girls." At which she had pouted and said, "But you always leave us behind!" And they always would leave her behind, for her fate lay elsewhere, in the ealdorman's hall in Bamburgh. As the wife of Drefan of Bamburgh, she would rule over a great hall and host kings at her table. And yet, one glimpse of a sail and her heart was soaring, over the horizon and away.

Again a flash of white. She rose, letting her embroidery frame fall into the work basket at her feet. She shaded her eyes as she strained at the horizon. A square white dot danced into view along the line between sea and sky. She took an anxious step forward, careless of the nearness of the cliff edge. Her right foot caught her work basket and sent it tumbling over the cliff face toward the distant sands below, threads of green and gold and blue scattering to the winds.

What was it? Anglish, Pict, Norsk? It was a Norsk ship she longed for. But it was also Norsk ships her father feared. The ship she longed for was a knarr, a broad-bellied trade ship. The ships her father dreaded were longships, ships of war. Nothing but a knarr had ever come to their beach. Elswyth had never seen a longship. But the news was that a dozen Norsk longships had raided the holy island of Lindisfarne two weeks since, murdering dozens and carrying off much treasure and many slaves. Her home in Twyford was only a day's ride south of Lindisfarne and her father, like every coastal thegn kept anxious watch for Norsk ships, though no other made his daughter his sentinel.

She longed for a knarr, for not only would a knarr bring wine and gemstones and silver—to trade for the dull necessities produced by her father's manor—it would also bring new songs, old friends, and tales of Spain.

Ah, Spain! Her heart was full of the young men who sailed to Spain, who got drunk on the wines of Spain, who lounged on verandas with the dark girls of Spain. Was this a ship that had been, that would go, to Spain? Did it carry men who had been, who would go, to Spain? For a moment, all the longing in her heart was fixed on Spain.

The sail was plainer now, no longer disappearing into the haze along the horizon, and sometimes she could glimpse the line of the hull. Whether it was a longship or knarr, she still could not be sure. But she was certain of its course now. By the quarter it came from and the line it sailed, it was coming from Norway, and it was heading for their beach.

"Anything on the horizon?" her father asked.

She had heard him coming up along the cliff path while her eyes had stayed fixed on the horizon. She could always tell his footsteps. An old wound made him favor one leg and she could hear it in his steps, a slight scuffing as his right foot rotated mid step.

"There," she said, pointing at the square white dot that at that moment danced into view along the line between sea and sky.

"Where?" he asked, cupping his hands around his eyes as he gazed out over the sea.

4

"You won't see it yet, Father," she said. The holy island of Lindisfarne itself could have floated by half a mile off their beach and her father would not have seen it. But Elswyth could see a ship long before anyone else could make it out among the glare and the shimmer of the distant light.

"Is it coming this way?" he asked.

"Yes," she said. "It was over there the first time I saw it. Now there. That heading will bring it to us."

"Is it Norsk?"

"I can't quite make out the shape of the hull yet. But coming from that quarter, who else would it be?"

"Just one ship?"

"I've only seen one so far."

"Longship or a knarr?"

"I'm sure it must be Uncle Harrald," she said, straining her eyes to see if the ship was broad or narrow. But the ship was too far off.

"He did not come last year, child," her father said.

"Not a child anymore," Elswyth said, automatically.

"He has come spring and autumn every year since you were a bairn. But last year not at all. And not this spring. He never did come in high summer. By this time of year he should be in Spain."

"I can see the hull now, as it crests. I do think it is his ship. It must be Uncle Harrald."

"You're sure it's just one ship?"

She searched the horizon again, shading her eyes against the glare of the bright sky and the sting of the onshore wind.

"I see no other ships," she said.

"Then if it is not them, if it is a longship, I can at least meet them strength to strength," her father said. "Today you have proved yourself a good sentinel, child."

"Not a child."

"I will go down and call the men from the fields. Run and find me as soon as you are sure of who it is."

He bent and kissed her on the top of her head. She turned and embraced him swiftly, her soft cheek brushing against his stiff beard. She was alarmed, suddenly, and she could feel a touch of panic in her father as he pulled her to him.

"If it is a longship," he said, "tell the first man you see and send him to tell me. Then go to the hall and get your mother and your sisters and the other women and get them up the road as fast as you can. And find someone to ride to Alnwick with the news."

"I'll ride myself," she said.

"No child."

"I'm not a child. I can ride as fast as anyone, and it saves time if I don't have to find someone to go, and tell them the message, and then tell them again because they didn't listen properly the first time."

"I need you to help your mother."

"Why take a man from your battle line when I can take the message?"

"Even if you are not a child, the road to Alnwick is not safe for a woman riding alone."

"There hasn't been a brigand seen on that road in four years, Father."

"Aye, but it was a poor harvest, and these are famine months, until the next harvest is in, for any man who did not take proper care. There are desperate hungry men about."

"If I meet one, I will shout out that there are vikingar chasing me. The fox does not steal the wolf's supper."

"I don't have time for this argument."

"No, you don't, Father, so don't be stubborn."

Her father raised his eyes and implored heaven with outstretched arms. "Alright, you may ride. But since you are not a child, for Cuthbert's sake, put your shoes on."

Elswyth might wear a woman's dress, but she still went bare-foot like a child. She did not like her feet to be parted from the earth, or to have the bother of taking shoes off every time she wanted to put her feet into the sea or the river.

Her father hugged her and kissed her on the top of her head and then set off running down the cliff path. He had a strange gait as he ran, every tenth step becoming a skip, as if he were a child. And she knew that he winced with that step.

2 The Unsuitable Child

Edith, Lady of Twyford, had never lost a child. She knew no other woman over thirty who could say the same thing. She had five daughters living and a sixth child making her awkward and clumsy. But there are other ways to lose a child besides death.

In her fifth year, Elswyth, her eldest daughter, had disappeared and had not been found for a week. Then a Norsk trader who had called to pick up a shipment of wool returned to the beach with Elswyth perched on the prow, full of the glow of adventure, and oblivious to the agony her absence had caused to her parents, her family, and the whole village. They had suspected that she had stowed away on this ship, for her disappearance had been noted shortly after it departed. Some had even whispered that she had been kidnapped. The Norsk were known to trade in slaves, and Edith, who had herself been born a slave, had feared that Elswyth would end up a novelty in the markets of Cordoba.

And though she had never gone so far again—Edith had never again let any ship, pack train, or farmer's wagon depart the village unless her hand was on Elswyth's shoulder—Elswyth, now fifteen and on the cusp of marriage, was still lost to her much of the time. Today she was up on the clifftop somewhere, having persuaded her father that he could free a man for the fields if he let her keep the watch. She had taken her work basket with her, promising Edith that she could work on her embroidery and keep lookout at the same time. "It would be so boring just staring at the sea all day," she had protested. "I'd fall asleep if I didn't take something to do. I'll work on my embroidery and just glance up now and then." But this was nonsense. Edith knew well that Elswyth could stare at the sea day and night and never grow tired of it.

None of Edith's other daughters seemed so anxious to be away from her. Daisy, the youngest, was in her arms, spitting out the milk porridge that Edith was shoveling into her mouth in hopes of completing her weaning. Daisy was growing sharp little teeth and Edith was desperate for a respite before the child within her arrived. Daisy would not even leave her mother's breast, let alone her hall and her heart.

Poor mad Whitney, the next youngest, a child of blissful love and eternally restless feet but neither speech nor understanding, was running in circles around the hall and would soon collapse exhausted into Edith's arms and then fall asleep in the dust at her feet. Whitney would run long, but never far.

Moira, chatty Moira, was with her grandmother, learning to spin and gossiping endlessly as she did so. What need had Moira of distant lands when she found so much gossip—and so many to share it with—all within sight of the hall?

Diligent Hilda would be on her favorite bench beside the hall, where the light was best, her needle busy in her hand, a growing strip of impeccable embroidery declining from her hands as she worked, oblivious to Whitney's endless circling, to the dogs and chickens that wandered about, to the coming and going of the slaves, to all the din and bustle of the village. What need had Hilda of wandering, who never raised her eyes to the horizon?

But Elswyth, her eldest, her favorite, her image, her source of greatest joy and heartache, the child of whom she prayed in secret, whenever sickness came to the village, "God, if you must take any, don't take her." That child had her eyes, her thoughts, her heart ever over the horizon and away.

Elswyth had a beauty that any young woman might envy (and that poor plain Hilda did most grievously envy), a ready wit, a positive glut of charm, the ability to draw attention to herself and to excite affection in the coldest heart (even Hilda loved her). She was to be married after the harvest to Drefan of Bamburgh, the son of an ealdorman, who had doted on her like a big brother and had shown her great care and affection all through their childhoods. And yet Elswyth had a wistful heart, always consumed with longing, a longing that could never be assuaged, for it had no one true object. Give Elswyth wings and she would long for gills. Give her silver and she would long for pearls; sunshine and she would long for rain; autumn and she would long for spring; spring and she would long for winter. Elswyth would live a life of wealth and honor in Bamburgh Hall. She would have a noble husband and bear him fair and healthy children. She would lack nothing that any woman of sense could desire. And yet her heart would ever break with wistful longing, and sometimes it almost made Edith weep to think of it.

Her reverie was disturbed when Attor, her husband, thegn of Twyford, appeared, hurrying awkwardly down the path that led to the cliff top. Attor had grown too old to run for pleasure.

"Not again!" she called out to him as he shuffled by.

He turned aside from his path and came to her. "She says it may be Norsk,"

"That's what she said Wednesday. And last week. You nearly terrified those poor fishermen, meeting them on the beach with twenty spears. It will be months before we taste cod or lobster again."

"She has better eyes than mine," Attor replied.

"And greater fancy," Edith said. Since the raid on Lindisfarne, every scrap of sail, every floating log, every breeching whale or dolphin, had been taken for vikingar.

"Still, better to be safe," Attor said. "I will go call the men."

Edith put two fingers in her mouth and whistled loudly. Three boys came scampering at the command.

"Run to the fields and tell the men that the thegn summons them," she told them. She held out a hand to her husband so that he could help her rise. "You should not use that girl as a sentinel."

"There's not a better set of eyes in the village."

"That may be, but she is to marry Drefan after the harvest, and I've much to do to make a lady of her yet. Can you imagine if, the day after she marries Drefan, Lady Cyneburg finds her in the mud behind Bamburgh hall, barefoot, playing pickup sticks with the slave children?"

"Cyneburg loves her."

"Everyone loves her. That is her curse. But Cyneburg loving Elswyth and Cyneburg thinking Elswyth fit to succeed her as lady to the ealdorman of Bamburgh? That is a very different thing. For that she must be a lady—and not just when it pleases her. Cyneburg has not forgotten who she is. She has not forgotten that I was born a slave. There were days I washed her feet and served her meat, and she has not forgotten that, I promise you."

"You're a lady now," Attor said. "And Elswyth always was."

"But she looks more like those who serve in Bamburgh than those who rule. So in her dress, in her manner, she must be more a lady than any of them, than Cyneburg herself. But what

12

is she today? A shoeless child pining for sailor men. And it is you giving her leave to do it."

"It frees a man for the haying."

"And is the haying worth losing her marriage over?"

It was an old argument between them. Not a week went by without Edith asking her husband if some adventure or indulgence was worth losing Elswyth's marriage over.

"She'll not lose the marriage," Attor said. "Drefan's smitten."

"Smitten?" Edith said. "Of course he's smitten. But what has smitten to do with the marriages of nobility?"

"I was smitten," he said, placing one arm around her and pulling her to him so he could kiss first her, and then Daisy, upon the head. "Still am."

"And what advantage did you have by it? It cost you thirty hides that Elene of Hadston would have brought you, your brother's friendship, your mother's love."

"My mother loved the children."

"She loved Elswyth because everyone does. She loved Hilda because she looks like her. She never loved me or forgave you. Blood debt or not, Kenrick and Cyneburg won't throw so much away if they don't think Elswyth suitable."

At that moment, the unsuitable child came tearing down the path from the clifftop, bare feet flying, hair streaming behind her.

"It is Norsk!" she cried as she ran towards them. "It is Norsk, but I think it is Uncle Harrald. It is a knarr for sure. But perhaps I should ride to Alnwick anyway, just in case."

"Ride to Alnwick?" Edith said.

"Father said I could ride to Alnwick if it was vikingar. To give the alarm."

"Well you can't," Edith said. She turned to her husband. "What were you thinking? We would not have seen her for a month if you had given her leave and a good horse."

"Of course you would," Elswyth said. "Of course, it would be rude to ride to Alnwick and then not call on Uncle Leofwine and Uncle Osgar, and Eglingham is so close that I would have to go there too. But I would only be gone a week at most."

"And four men taken from the fields to escort you."

"No. Father said I could ride alone."

"Just to give the alarm," Attor protested. "Thegn Wigberht would have sent you right back with an escort."

"If he could catch her," Edith said. "You are not leaving this village, miss, till the ship comes to take you to Bamburgh after the harvest. And by then you must have your wedding dress complete."

"But—"

"If the ship is Norsk," Attor said, "then I must certainly meet them with spears, whether you think it is Harrald or not." He who had never flinched in the battle line wanted no part of war between his wife and daughter. He hurried off, with his awkward gait, to organize the men who were beginning to stream in from the fields.

"You don't really think I would ride away for a month and miss Uncle Harrald and Uncle Thor, do you?" Elswyth asked her mother.

Edith looked at her daughter. Elswyth's appearance provoked a frown that expressed not simply annoyance, but a deep and vexing puzzle. Elswyth was a lovely young woman, plump in the bosom, round in the hips, with a mane of glossy black hair. Her face was the image of Edith's own. It was the face that Edith had once seen staring back at her from a still pool, when she was a slave and her face had been the whole of her fortune. It was a wholly Welisc face with not a trace of Anglish in it. On Edith, who had been born to Welisc slaves on the manor where she was now lady, that face had been enough to catch the eye of an Anglish thegn's son. On Elswyth, Edith believed, it was a face

14

that might have caught the fancy of an Anglish king, if only the opportunity had presented itself.

Elswyth was clad in a summer dress of green linen with brooches befitting her rank, and a decorated belt with heavy copper terminals shaped like the heads of herons, which she wore high to emphasize her bosom. Yet she was barefoot like a child, and there were at least a dozen sticky burs clinging to her skirts and a posy of assorted and drooping wildflowers stuck behind one of her brooches.

"Where are your shoes?" Edith asked.

"Why would I wear shoes in the middle of summer?"

"Because you are no longer a child. A respectable noble-woman wears shoes on her feet, winter or summer. And a wimple on her head."

"There's a ship, Mother."

"Where is your work basket?"

"It's Norsk! I can tell by the shape, by the way it sails. I'm almost sure it's Uncle Harrald."

"I'd be glad if it was," Edith said. "But he has not come in two years. Wrecked and drowned, like as not. Such is the fate of sailors."

"Of course they are not wrecked or drowned," Elswyth said. "Uncle Thor would never let them be wrecked or drowned."

"Uncle Thor is just a man. I know you loved him, darling, but you are a woman now and you have seen quite enough of death to know that people die, no matter how much we love them."

"I know," Elswyth said, looking downcast for the moment or two that was all her nature was capable of. "But not Uncle Thor. Not Uncle Harrald either. You'll see. It's their ship. I know it is."

"Well then go put your shoes on and make yourself pre-sentable to receive guests." Edith yanked out the posy of flowers that drooped behind Elswyth's brooch, and threw it on the ground. She bundled Daisy into Elswyth's arms while she pulled the sticky burrs out of Elswyth's skirts. Then she took the baby back from her grown daughter and said, "And put on a wimple too. You should not be parading your hair in front of sailors at your age."

"Not till I'm married, Mother. You promised!" Elswyth replied. But she said it over her shoulder as she ran off so that she was gone before Edith had a chance to respond.

"Well, you've wasted enough for one day," Edith said to Daisy after Elswyth had disappeared from view. She wiped the child's face and flicked the bigger lumps of porridge off the front of her smock, then surrendered the bowl to a small dog that had been nosing about hopefully.

In a year, Elswyth would likely have a baby of her own and Edith would be a grandmother. Would Elswyth find all her wistfulness assuaged, all her longing recompensed, in the urgent suck of her firstborn child upon her breast? Edith prayed so.

She walked around to the side of the hall to where Hilda sat, exactly where Edith had known her to be, on a bench against the wall of the hall, bent over her needlework. Hilda did not look up as her mother approached.

"Your sister is seeing ships again," Edith said.

"Okay," said Hilda, not looking up, her fingers not pausing as they guided her needle in its swift and agile passage through the cloth.

"Take her, will you?" Edith asked, thrusting Daisy in Hilda's direction.

Hilda finished her stitch and secured her needle in a fold of the cloth, then folded the cloth neatly and placed it on top of the neat rows of skeins in her work basket, the colors ranked according to the order prescribed by God and revealed to mortal women in the rainbow. Only when this was done did she look up, rise, and take Daisy from her mother, positioning her carefully so that the remnants of porridge should not transfer themselves from Daisy's smock to her own dress. There were several splotches of porridge on her mother's dress. Hilda flicked them onto the ground then wiped her finger clean on the last clean spot on Daisy's smock.

"Sit down, Mother," she said.

"I've been sitting. I'm sick of sitting. I hope it is a ship this time. It would be nice to have company."

"Unless it's vikingar," Hilda said. "Vikingar are not good company." Daisy was squirming in her arms and reaching out for her mother. Hilda turned so as to face Daisy the other way, but the child simply squirmed around in her arms and reached for her mother again.

"It's not vikingar." Edith said. "Why on earth would vikingar come here? We don't have hoards of gold, like the monasteries, and what did we ever do to offend God?"

"You and Father…" Hilda began.

"Not that again, darling."

"Brother Alun says that virginity is a pearl without price."

"Your father and I did get married, thank you very much."

"Afterwards…" Hilda retorted. It was a point of endless contention for Hilda that while she had been conceived in wedlock, Elswyth had not.

At twelve, Hilda was already taller than both her mother and Elswyth. But where Elswyth was plump and round and buoyant from her restless feet to her mounds of glossy hair, Hilda was straight and narrow and anchored. If Elswyth was too slow to give up childish things, Hilda had packed them neatly in a basket and long since put them away among the rafters of the hall. Hilda had a wimple on her head and shoes on her feet.

"Did she get any work done at all, or did she spend all morning looking for ships?" she asked.

Edith closed her eyes, remembering. "She didn't have her work basket when she came down," she said.

17

"She threw it over the cliff, I bet," Hilda said. Elswyth's work basket seemed to have more misadventures than mere inadvertence could account for.

"Nonsense," Edith said. "But remind me to tell her to fetch it later."

Daisy began to squeak and struggle more ardently in Hilda's arms.

"You stay with your sister for a minute," Edith said, rolling her neck and stretching her arms and shoulders.

"I saw father called the men out of the fields again." Hilda said.

"He's afraid that the one time he doesn't, it really will be vikingar."

"If he does it every time, he won't get the hay in before it rains," Hilda said.

"Don't tell him that unless you want to find yourself with a pitchfork in your hands," Edith replied.

"If anyone should be made to pitch hay, it's Elswyth," Hilda said. "It's her fault if they are late, calling them out of the fields every other day for a ship."

Daisy, seeing that her mother was not going to take her, was squirming towards the ground, and Hilda obliged by placing her in the dust at her feet. The small dog, which had finished all the porridge in the bowl and followed the scent of what remained on Daisy, started licking Daisy's face and smock, which delighted her, and the two of them were soon rolling on the ground squealing and yipping. Hilda started to rub her hands, as she always did when she was deprived of her needle or threatened with heavy work. They were delicate hands, with long slender elegant Anglish fingers, quick and intelligent with a needle, and the thought of ruining them with farm labour alarmed her. Any beauty that God had granted to Hilda was in her hands. But it was not the gift of possessing beauty that he had given her, but that of making it.

"If it's company, we'll need two score loaves at least," Edith said, "and three casks of wine."

"There's only two left."

"More mead, then. And the good beer. A pig or a sheep. Turnips, carrots…"

"Why are you telling me? We have slaves."

"But first we'll need the fires lit. Then the trestles and benches out of storage…"

"Let Elswyth help. I'm only halfway finished my dragon and I need to get it done today so I can start on the swans tomorrow."

"Your dragon will keep. Go fetch Moira and catch Whitney her next time around. I want you all together in case Elswyth's ship is actually landing."

Hilda opened her mouth to protest but Edith cut her off. "Just go!"

Hilda stormed off to obey, shoulders hunched in indignation.

Oh, the coming and going of ships! Without it they would be so much the poorer, for much of the manor's trade moved by ship. Without it they would lack for half the news that came their way. There would be fewer songs, fewer stories, fewer visits by the people she loved. And yet, that coming and going of ships could take away, just as it brought. It was the coming and going of ships that had taken Elswyth away from her once, and she could never look at a ship again without thinking that, as children came to her, so too must they leave. Elswyth would go soon. Only to Bamburgh. But go she would. Go she must. And Edith would weep at her going.

Edith looked down at Daisy, still blithely playing with the small dog, "You won't run off and leave Mother alone, will you pet?" she said. But she would. They all would. It was the way of daughters. It was the way of ships.

"St. Cuthbert, pray for me," she said.

But then, where had Cuthbert's aid been when the vikingar had sacked Lindisfarne, his very shrine and holy place?

She bent to pick up the child, feeling the need to soothe her, though Daisy was wholly unperturbed.

"Don't worry," she said, stroking Daisy's hair. "All will be well. All will be well."

3 Leif

Leif, son of Harrald, stood in the prow of his ship and gazed at the low green coast of Northumbria. It was so different from the steep fjords of his home. There, every bay and inlet had a distinct character and shape so that a man with the knowledge would never doubt where he was or where he was going. But here the coastline was a low rolling bank of green, as indistinct as a fogbank almost. And it was more than two years since his eyes—boy's eyes then, man's eyes now—had looked on it.

There was the estuary, with the village just behind it. There the small cliff with the beach below it, a beach that stretched on for miles north and south. These were his landmarks, but they could be the landmarks of a dozen places on this vast sameseeming shore.

He glanced back at Thor, seated by the tiller. But if he were off by a hundred miles, Thor would say nothing until they were beached on some unknown shore. Then he would look around, stroke his beard, and ask, "So what have you learned?"

Leif looked at Eric, standing ready for the order to lower sail. No sign from him either. It would only amuse Eric to see Leif fail.

His ship. In a sense, perhaps, it was Leif's ship. It was his to command, for this voyage at least. But it was his father's ship, and no man just made captain was ever more willing than Leif to hand his ship back to its former commander. His father had been kidnapped by vikingar—vikingar who had twice raided Leif's village while the men were away at sea. The vikingar had killed the old men and boys who had tried to resist them. They had stolen women, and gold, and most of the trade goods the clan had in store, and, in the second raid, they had taken his father prisoner, demanding a ransom, either gold or the secrets of the clan's trade.

The knarr he commanded—his father's ship, more than forty feet from stem to stern—sailed with less than a quarter of its hold full—the few trade goods remaining to them. But below his feet, lashed under the fore-deck, was a chest that contained his clan's last hope. A treasure worth, if tales were true, a jarl's ransom and more among the holy men of Northumbria.

It had been a smooth voyage. He had made every sacrifice. He had placated every god. Surely, therefore, Odin, Thor, and Ran would not let Loki deceive his eyes and cast him up on the wrong beach. But it was too late for such doubts now. The beach was approaching. The people of the village—hopefully his Uncle Attor's village, as he supposed—were assembled on the sands to greet them. Forget grand navigation now. He would look a greater fool if he holed the ship on a rock, cracked her spine by hitting the sand too hard, or slopped back into the tide by losing way too soon. Get safely onto the sand and then worry about being on the right beach.

And so he did not pay much attention to the faces of the people waiting on the beach, did not notice that the men had shields and spears in their hands and waited in battle line, the women and children kept back behind them.

He judged the moment and ordered the sail down. The ship nosed gently onto the sand, and the men were over the side to secure the ship on the beach. It was only then that any of them realized that they were facing a line of spears.

"Uncle Attor!" Leif cried, searching along the line of men for the face of his uncle-by-oath, Attor of Twyford. He found him, but Attor was squinting up at him as if he could not make out his face. "It is me, Leif, son of Harrald," he cried, hoping that he was remembering his Anglish correctly. "Put up your spears. It is me."

Two figures came toward the ship. One was Attor, walking slowly, peering upward as if he were half blind. The other was a young woman, black hair flowing in the wind, who plunged past his startled men toward the side of the ship. Seeing no threat in her, Leif paid her no attention, but kept his eyes on the slowly advancing Attor. He glanced around at his men, who had re-treated back to the water. They had gone over the sides without weapons and the men they faced outnumbered them and had both shields and spears. "It is me, Leif, son of Harrald," he cried again. A woman, pregnant and holding a child in her arms, hur-ried toward the hesitant Attor. Leif recognized her as his aunt-by-oath, Edith, Attor's wife, Lady of Twyford. He called out to her, but she was whispering to Attor. Light sprang into Attor's face and he cried out, "Leif, is that you? Come ashore lad, come ashore."

Relieved, Leif turned to make his way amidships where the sides were low enough to jump over into the water. But as he turned he saw that the young woman with the flowing hair was now wrapped in Thor's arms, embracing him. She seemed tiny, childlike, in Thor's embrace, but then, most people seemed childlike compared to Thor's massive frame. As he came up to them, she broke the embrace and asked Thor, "Why do you have blood on your face?"

"It is the blood of the horse blot," Thor said, responding to her in Anglish. Leif understood well enough, but immediately felt tongue tied, too embarrassed to try to speak the young woman's language in her presence.

She was an astonishing creature. She seemed of the Welisc race rather than Anglish. Her head was bare and her hair unbound, though it was the custom of Anglish women to wear a wimple that covered their hair and their throats. She was very youthful in her face, and slight of stature, yet shapely in her figure as few women he knew. Her green linen dress was wet to the waist and clung to her legs. Her feet were bare, though he saw that she had shoes in her hand. She was as lively as she was beautiful and it was hard to say which was the greater part of her allure. From face to figure, he hardly knew where to look at her.

"Horse blot?" she asked Thor.

"Leif sacrificed his horse to appease the gods. He used the head to set up a nithing pole to curse our enemies, and we ate of the flesh and marked ourselves with the blood to show honor to the gods."

"You have enemies?"

"Aye, lass. All men who prosper have enemies."

"Where is Uncle Harrald?"

"Leif commands this trip. It's his news to give," Thor replied.

"Leif?" she said, turning toward him for the first time. "Is that you? You're so much taller—and you're practically covered in blood!"

This was true. Like Thor, Leif's cheeks were streaked with dried blood. But Leif's arms, his sea-jacket, and his leggings were covered in it as well. He had not wanted to stint the gods with his sacrifice, or be stinting in placing the marks of it on his person. When the rest of the crew had marked themselves much more sparingly, he had felt a little foolish. But washing off any part of the sacrificial blood before the voyage was over would have brought the worst possible luck, so he had left it where it was.

The young woman stepped towards him, holding out her hand in greeting. "Don't you remember me?" she asked.

He did not. She was a creature entirely new to his experience. She might have been a selkie or a swan maiden.

"*You remember Elswyth, Attor's eldest daughter,*" Thor said, in Norsk.

"Elswyth?" he replied, searching her face for some resemblance between the girl who corresponded to that name in his memory and the young woman before him.

"*I grew up,*" the swan maiden said. "*Do you like?*" She did a complete twirl for his inspection. She spoke Norsk with complete confidence, if imperfect diction. He turned his eyes away from her face and figure, trying to remember his duty.

"*Lady,*" he asked, "*why does your father meet us with spears?*"

"*Norsk raided Lindisfarne last month,*" she replied, "*Or maybe it was Danir. But don't worry. I knew it was you. I told them so as soon as I saw the sail. But where is Uncle Harrald?*"

"I am sure your father wishes to know that too," Thor said in Anglish.

"*Well, come ashore, then.*" Without warning, she put her hand in Leif's and led him toward the rail of the ship. The touch of her hand filled him with desire and alarm. He remembered his father's rules of trade—never interfere with the women of the men you trade with. It leads to nothing but trouble. He pulled his hand away from hers and vaulted over the rail into the water.

There was a splash beside him and she was there, her skirts billowing around her in the tide so that he could see her calves, palely refracted through the seawater.

Thor lowered his huge frame gingerly over the rail. He was awkward in his movements and a little slow, and he gave an

"Ooof" as his boots splashed into the shallow sea. He was growing old, which Leif, in his youth, would have thought impossible. Elswyth turned and looked at Thor with concern also, as if the same thought had occurred to her in the same moment.

Attor and Edith had come down to the tideline with their daughters and stood ready to greet their visitors. He could no more have put names to the other daughters than he had been able to do with Elswyth. Two stood beside their mother, while a small girl with a blank blissful face ran around them in circles, her bare feet slopping in the wet sand, her untidy yellow hair flying behind her. Each of them had grown out of whatever memory he might have had of them.

Elswyth led Leif and Thor onto the dry sand. Attor strode forward and greeted Thor with a hug. Then he inspected Leif, commented on the size he had become, and embraced him too. But all through Attor's inspection and greeting, Leif could not turn his attention from Elswyth. Thus he witnessed a whispered conversation between Elswyth and her mother.

"What do you think you were doing boarding the ship?" Edith hissed.

"I went for news of Uncle Harrald."

"Not your place to do so."

"But I always…"

"You're not a child anymore."

"Then why is everyone still telling me what to do?"

"Because you didn't learn it when you were a child!"

"It is not polite to quarrel in front of guests, Mother."

Edith replied to this only by fiercely shaking out and beating down Elswyth's sopping, sand-grimed skirts. But this violent grooming was cut short when Thor turned to greet Edith. Edith dumped the child she was carrying in Elswyth's arms and went to hug Thor. This left Leif once again face to face with Elswyth. He tried to look away, to spare her from the embarrassment of his having overheard her mother's scolding. But Elswyth seemed

26

entirely unembarrassed by it. "This is Daisy," she said, turning the child to face him. "She wasn't born the last time you were here."

Leif reached out a hand to touch Daisy's cheek. Daisy strained to reach his beard.

"*Can I hold her?*" he asked.

Elswyth looked at him, startled, as if she had not heard such a request before and for a moment he feared that she might have misunderstood him—that he might have insulted her in some way. But she smiled—her smile was like dawn over a fair sea, gladdening the heart of a sailor—and handed Daisy to him.

Daisy laughed and tried to catch at the strands of his thin beard. Leif was immediately embarrassed that the child was drawing Elswyth's attention to his boyish chin.

"I have a sister," he said. "Same age. Likes to pull my beard too. Tove would like to play with you," he added, addressing the child. He kissed Daisy on the forehead then gasped as Daisy grabbed his nose and twisted.

"She likes noses," Elswyth said. "Ears. Teeth. She tried to grab my eye once. It hurt for a week."

"Tove likes to pull hair. She is strong. It hurts." He disengaged Daisy's fingers gently from his nose.

"I see you are making a friend of my daughter," Attor said as he joined them. Daisy held out her arms to her father, who took her then promptly turned and handed her on to Edith.

Attor then looked around, puzzled, and Leif followed his gaze.

"Why are your men all still standing in the sea?" Attor asked.

"Why do your men stand glaring with spears in their hands?" Thor asked in reply.

Attor turned and chastised his men. "Put down your spears. These men are friends." Turning to the Norsk, he said, "Come ashore, come ashore before you ruin your boots. You are friends here. Friends always."

Both Anglish and Norsk did as he told them, but while the Anglish put down their shields and spears, they did not change the grimness of their faces, and as the Norsk came ashore, the Anglish stepped back as many steps to maintain the distance between them.

"I'm sorry," Attor said. "I can command their hands, but I cannot command their hearts. Any Norsk ship will be met with spears in Northumbria these days." And then he told them that two weeks before a fleet of longships had landed on the holy island of Lindisfarne and the raiders had killed many monks, looted the riches of the monastery, and taken many slaves. Lindisfarne was the holiest site in Britain and one of the richest as well. All along the coast, people watched in fear, and unwary Norsk and Danir had been beaten and killed in York and other towns. A chill came over Leif's heart as he heard the news, for not only did it tell the ruin of people he had loved, but he saw in it the ruin of his own hopes as well.

"We know this place well," Thor said. "We have traded with the holy men many times. They valued our trade, for the materials for the making of their books."

Attor looked at him. "So you knew the place, knew how wealthy it was, knew it was not guarded, feeling itself under the protection of God and St. Cuthbert."

"You can't think we did this, Uncle," Leif protested. "We are traders. We are not vikingar. You cannot think it was any of my kin."

"No. But I counsel you not to boast of knowing the place. People are asking what guided the vikingar to that spot, how they found it, out of all the coast of England. Some say God himself guided them there, to punish us for our sins. Others think secrets have been told, and they suspect any man who trades with Norsk or Danir. I have heard ugly things behind my back in the market at Alnwick."

"So if it were known we traded there, they would say we betrayed the place, even if we did not raid it ourselves," said Thor.

"We do not tell the secrets of our trade," Leif protested. "My father forbids it. Only our most trusted friends know where we sail or who we trade with."

"Aye," said Thor, "and where is the gain for us to tell these secrets? We'd only lose our trade."

"There was more taken from Lindisfarne than you would make in a lifetime of trading," Attor said.

"It was not us," Leif repeated. "We have no great fleet. No longships. We have two knarr to carry on our trade. My father is a sworn friend to the jarl of the holy men. My father would not break his oath to any man."

"I know you didn't do it," Attor said. "But others here do not know you as I do. They will only see Norsk, and they hate Norsk now. And remember, we are Cuthbert's people. Lindisfarne is Cuthbert's place. His shrine and his burial place. Every one of Cuthbert's people feels this raid like it was a spear in his own heart."

Leif looked at the faces of the Anglish, at the tight expectant grip in which they held their spears. Having seen that the Norsk were unarmed and that their thegn greeted them as friends, it could not be fear that made their faces so grim. And if it was not fear, it must be hate. Their spears, he understood, longed to pierce Norsk hearts.

"But you can vouch for us, Uncle," he pleaded.

"I could, and I will if need be. But this is no time for a man in Northumbria to claim a Norsk or a Danir for a friend. A thegn was beaten in a tavern in York for drinking with a Danir. The Danir was killed."

"That is not good for trade," Thor said.

"It's not," Attor said, "But tell me of your father, lad. Where is he, and why do you sail here out of season and with a ship so lightly laden?"

Leif began to reply but was soon lost for a word and turned to Thor.

"We too were raided," Thor said. "Harvests have been poor and the weather foul. Foolish men have lost their ships and their livings, and there has been much evil in the halls of kings. Second and third sons, left without lands or lords. We are too many for the little land we have that can be farmed. So men go viking, for food or land or wives or gold or slaves. Half the women of our kin have been taken. Our warehouses and our gold looted. Many men killed. Houses burned. Harrald was taken captive, for ransom. It is the secrets of our trade they want from him, or a sum of gold. But they have taken our gold already, and we will not give up the secrets of our trade. We will not betray our friends, nor can we give away our livelihood."

And at these words, Leif felt his heart grow colder still, for he saw that their news and Attor's were of a piece. His father taken by men who demanded the secrets of his trade. Lindisfarne raided by men who must have been in possession of those very secrets in order to bring such a fleet to such a spot— under the very gaze of the great fortress of Bamburgh, and yet just beyond the range of its swift aid. It cannot have happened by chance. The vikingar had to have had the knowledge. How had they gained it? His people could not have been the only clan who traded there. And yet, so soon after his father was taken by vikingar, vikingar had acted on this knowledge. What tortures would his father have suffered before he would have yielded such a secret or betrayed such friends?

He felt a woman's hand in his. He looked and saw that it was Elswyth's. She looked up at him with stricken eyes. Clearly the same thought was in her heart. She shook her head, and such was her power that he accepted her reassurance, blind though it was, and some small thaw came over is heart, like a touch of noonday sun in the dark month of marrow sucking. But then he recollected his duty and disengaged his hand from hers.

He remembered his mission. "We want to bring our people to live in Britain," he said. "We come to look for a home, and to raise my father's ransom."

"But how will you raise the ransom," said Attor, "since all your goods are taken?"

"We saved a few things," Thor said. "All we have left is in the ship."

"Enough for a jarl's ransom?"

"Not of ordinary goods. But Leif says there is one item that may raise the gold we need, if we can find the right man to sell it to."

"Books," said Leif. "We have books of your holy men. Your holy men are rich. They will give much gold for books."

"Books?" Attor asked. "Not books from Lindisfarne? I heard the vikingar destroyed the books there, rather than stealing them. How could they have come into your hands?"

"No, Uncle, these books have been in our possession for two years, and they do not come from Lindisfarne. We hoped to sell them there. We only came here first to learn their value from you, so that we could demand a fair price from the holy men."

Attor shrugged. "I know nothing of this trade," he said. "But lad, I do not think you will find a lord in all Britain that will give refuge to a Norsk clan these days. And I don't know how you are to find a man in Britain to sell your books to—books of all things—without getting yourselves killed."

4 Eric

Attor declared a formal feast for that evening, so that Anglish and Norsk would be bound in the most solemn bonds of hospitality. Eric, who was next in command after Leif and Thor, was placed in charge of unloading the ship, while Attor ordered his men back to the fields and the women and children back to the village and their tasks.

There was much grumbling at this. The men were reluctant to leave the women and children in the village, closer to the beach and the Norsk. At last they agreed to go if Hogni, Leif's cousin, was given to them as hostage. Hogni went with them. He looked very green, though, in true Norsk fashion, he made no outward sign of fear, and showed no reluctance to obey.

Edith wrapped Elswyth's arm in hers and led her back to the hall to begin work on the feast.

"Leif's grown into a handsome young man," Edith said, as they walked.

"Oh, yuck!" Elswyth said.

"You don't think so?"

"Too skinny. And his beard is ridiculous. I could practically count the hairs on his chin."

"Well I think he looks very nice. And his beard will grow in."

"It's orange! Besides, you know who I like. I've told you often enough."

"Eric?"

"Uh huh. That's what a sailor's supposed to look like."

"He's a bad lad."

"I know," Elswyth said with relish.

"I'm not sure you do know. You should stay away from Eric."

"Mother! It's not like I'm going to…"

"No, but you've grown up since he saw you last. He was giving you the eye on the beach, if you didn't notice."

Edith was not on steady ground warning her daughter about the perils of seduction, having raised herself from slave to lady by that very device. But, unlike Hilda, Elswyth had reached a truce with her mother on the subject. "If you can seduce the king, and get him to marry you," her mother had said to her, one winter evening by the fire, after more than a little mead, "I will not say a word against you. You will have done as well by it as I did. But sailors and plowboys will only bring you ruin, no matter how much you like the smell of them." Elswyth should have blushed at this, but she had had a little mead herself and she had only giggled at it.

"Eric can give me the eye all he pleases," Elswyth said.

"Darling it really is time for you to start covering your hair."

"The wimple is too hot for summer. It makes me itch."

"You will get used to it if you wear it every day."

"Not till I'm married. You promised I didn't have to."

"You were twelve at the time."

"Still counts."

"Yes. I don't break my promises, however much I regret them. But I can still give advice. Drefan would not be pleased to see a ship full of Norsk leering at you."

"Then Drefan needs to start leering at me himself," Elswyth retorted. It was a sore point that, of all the young men she knew, only the man she was to marry did not seem to notice that she had become a woman.

"Drefan has better manners than a sailor," Edith replied.

Elswyth said nothing. She had seen Drefan leer at plenty of young women. But her mother did not want to hear anything said against Drefan. Drefan was an ealdorman's son. Besides, Elswyth liked Drefan. She liked his broad muscled form, his full dark beard, his hair, his hands, his swagger, his easy conviviality. She wanted nothing more from him than that he should at last stop treating her like a little sister. But until Drefan was willing to look at her as a woman, she was happy to let Eric's eyes confirm what Drefan's eyes refused to see.

"Anyway," Edith added, "be nice to Leif. I don't understand why you girls were always so cold with him. He's a nice boy. And he is bearing a terrible burden now, with his father being kidnapped. So, be nice to him, won't you?"

"I don't mind being nice to him," Elswyth said. "But still. Yuck."

And then, judging the moment ripe, she said, "Oh no, Mother. I think I've left my shoes on the ship!"

"Really?" Edith said, turning on her in exasperation.

"Well, I'm not used to wearing them on the beach. I must have taken them off to go aboard and then forgot them."

"I don't—" Edith began. But what was the point? "Oh! Just go and get them. But hurry back. There is work to be done!"

"I will, Mother, I promise."

Elswyth ran.

Edith closed her eyes to pray, "St. Cuthbert give me patience. And save her from the charms of ships and sailor men."

***

"Ves heill, princess," Eric cried when he saw Elswyth coming. Eric was nine parts to Thor's ten in every dimension, which made him taller and broader than any man you were likely to meet in a week's ride in Northumbria. He had begun calling her princess long ago when she was a child of seven or eight summers and he a beardless youth on his first voyage. When Elswyth lay abed dreaming of sailor men, of cresting the swells of the boundless ocean in the arms of a sailor man, of lounging with a sailor man on a veranda in the heat of the day on the baked plains of Spain, it was Eric's face she saw, Eric's arms that enclosed her, Eric's broad chest that she rested her head upon, the roughness of Eric's sea jacket she imagined against her cheek.

"Ves heill, field mouse," she responded. Field mouse was the humblest creature that her childish tongue had been able to summon in retort, and they had been princess and field mouse to each other ever since.

She clambered aboard and went to embrace him. His arms slid intimately around her, and stayed there. "Well, you grew up," Eric said.

"You didn't," she said, noticing how his embrace lingered after she released her hold on him. He was looking down on her with a look she had imagined seeing in his eyes when she was younger. She returned his gaze and he did not look away in confusion as she had seen other young men do. As a child she had pursued him with guileless flirtation and he had laughed at her. Now he looked down at her with a look that said, well, here we are, both grown up now, and for a moment she thought that his mouth was about to descend on hers. Her mother had been right—he had noticed the difference in her. Here at last was a man who not only noticed, but was prepared to show that he had noticed. But though she had become used to eyes being

36

upon her, this lingering touch was something new, and though she had thought of it often, had wondered if a hand or an arm so placed, and with such an interest, would feel different from an ordinary embrace, to experience it, so unexpectedly, for a moment confused her.

But then the pressure at her waist slackened and he laughed and said, "If I grow any more, I'll be a dormouse."

"Where's Thor?" she asked.

"Gone off along the beach with your father and Leif. They take council while squabs like you and me are left to our labor. How did you escape the kitchen?"

"I just came for my shoes. I forgot them before."

"Kept them for you," he said, reaching behind him to where he had stowed the errant shoes neatly in a niche. She took them from him and somehow his hand seemed to linger on hers as he handed them over.

She withdrew from him and perched on the rail of the ship, setting her shoes down beside her. "Thor said you were raided," she said. "What was it like? Did you fight them?"

"I was at sea. Both times. We sent out only one ship after the first raid, which is why we have not been here in two years, but both times I was on the ship."

"So who did fight them? Was it just the women and children at home?"

"The first time, the old men and the cripples tried to stand against them, but they were killed."

"I'm so sorry."

Eric shrugged. "They were a burden to the people anyway. It was right that they should sacrifice themselves. I suppose they were glad to be able to die in battle. That way they may merit Valhalla, which is more than many of us will have a chance to do."

"Well, I think it's terrible."

"Do you want me to go on? Or are you not brave enough to hear it?"

"Of course I am! Just because it makes me sad does not mean I'm not brave enough to hear it."

Eric smiled at her. How could a man tell such a tale and smile? Harrald had always been so honorable. Thor was so loving. But these were virtues she had known and admired in other men. In her father she knew both, though in him they were softer, somehow, less grand than the singular virtues of Harrald and Thor. But Eric was not like any man she knew. He was a man who said, with every stride and glance, come, know me if you dare. She pouted at him, refusing to be drawn. Eric's smile turned to a grin. He shrugged, and then suddenly grew grim.

"The next year Harrald stayed at home with half the men. There was talk up and down the fjords of vikingar and landless men roaming about. And there was murder and treachery in the king's hall. He thought he had enough men with him to make any vikingar think twice. But when we returned from our spring cruise, we found the vikingar had come again, better led and in greater numbers.

"My wife was among the women they took. She fought them. Gouged the eye of the one who took her and half bit his ear off, so I'm told by one who saw it. He threw her against a rock. She hit her head and she died. He cursed her for dying and threw her body in the fjord."

"Oh, Eric!" Elswyth cried, hopping down from her perch and embracing him. "How awful. I'm so sorry. I didn't even know you were married."

"Just last year," he said, holding her to him tightly. "We had been promised to each other for many years, but she had just come of age. She was a good girl. I was becoming fond of her."

Again she found his embrace uncomfortable. He seemed to be taking more than comfort from it.

38

"But what happened to Harrald?" she asked, withdrawing from him and perching herself back on the rail again.

"He did not leave the village after the first raid," Eric said. "He sent his ship out with Thor in command last year, and then Leif this year, since he was of age. When the second raid came, he defended the retreat to the refuge until all the women and children they could save were hidden. But he was taken.

"When our ship returned, we found most of the village burned, the goods mostly gone, the dead lying on the beach or floating in the fjord. That was a sight to chill you, lass."

It chilled her indeed. Yet still there was a smile behind his eyes as he regarded her. Was he untouched by the cruelty of life? Or was it all bravado? Was the man who could tell such tales with a smile the stoutest of hearts, or the coldest?

"And here we have had Lindisfarne sacked," she said. "People say that God has abandoned us. That the vikingar are a punishment for our sins."

"Did your kings and lords make their sacrifices? Horses? Cattle? Dogs? Slaves? It is always blood with the gods."

"That's horrible! We don't do that."

"Then what do you expect?"

"Our gods are not like that. The old gods, maybe. Not the new God. The monks say the new God is the sacrifice himself and we must not make blood sacrifices anymore. My granny still kills chickens to keep off the frost, but I don't think it works and the monks say it is wicked."

"Our gods are not like yours. I have spoken to your monks about it, and I think they expect more of your Christ than any god can deliver. Odin is subject to the Norns as much as any man. You make no sacrifices, yet you expect endless bounty from your Christ. It makes no sense, princess. He who expects his lord's bounty must give his lord due service. It is no different with the gods. How could it be?"

Elswyth did not know the answer to this so she changed the subject. "So now Leif is your captain? Does he even know how to sail?"

"He's a good ship handler. He has the gift for navigation."

"But is he a leader of men?"

Eric looked at his boots a moment. He shrugged and said, "He has Thor." Then he stuck his jaw out a little and said, "And after Thor, he has me."

"He just seems like such a boy."

"He's anxious to please. Always was. But he's steady enough. You know him well enough. You played with him when you were kids."

"Leif? No. I never played with him."

"I thought you liked sailor boys."

"I like sailor men," she said, incorrigible flirtation flying to her tongue even as she grew uneasy under his steady gaze.

He was silent, simply looking at her, his eyes moving over her slowly and methodically while a half smile, half mocking, half hungry, played on his lips.

"Oh, Princess," he said, his eyes still surveying her. And then he spoke, slowly and quietly, so that the men working around them could not hear it. "You are not for the likes of sailor men. Why, if you were a village girl, a sailor man might lead you by the hand and find some low spot among the dunes. There he would lay you down, and whisper sweetly to you while he unclasped the brooches that hold your dress, unbound the belt from around your waist, unwrapped the linen that bound your bosom. And then he would lie with you, while the ocean beat upon the shore nearby, the waves and the gulls and the seals all full of din to cover any cry you made, and for a while, all the cares of life would go blowing in the wind, and there would be only joy and peace.

"And a silver shilling for your trouble," he added, with a grin.

She hopped down off the rail and crossed her arms over her bosom, scowling at him.

"But you are Attor's daughter," he said, "and all the sailor men here are bound by Harrald's rules of trade. Do not lie with the women of the house of any lord we trade with. The price is the gauntlet, and it is run on dry sand, and may the gods swiftly receive any man who stumbles. So no sailor man here will take you by the hand and walk with you to a low place in the dunes, or unclasp your brooches or loosen your belt."

"Well, I didn't know you were all such cowards," she said, but inside she felt a little ashamed and a little like a child reproached. She would have been furious at him for his smugness and his teasing, had she not imagined his hands busy at the clasps of her brooches as he spoke, had not felt the belt running between her back and the sand as it was withdrawn, had not heard the gulls' sharp cry and felt the rush of the wind and the sting of salt in her mouth.

"I have to go," she said. "I promised Mother I'd be right back."

She vaulted over the side into the sea, clambered up out of the water, and started to run back toward the village.

"Hoy! Princess!" Eric called after her. "Do you want your shoes?"

She turned back to him, scarlet cheeked. He threw the shoes to the sand one by one, and stood on the prow smirking as she bent to retrieve them. She did not look up at him, but ran straight back to the village without looking back.

5 Lady of the Hall

There was not enough time to do anything properly. The ovens were cool, so new bread could not be baked. They made fry bread instead. There were not enough hours to spit-roast a sheep or pig, so they boiled meat in pieces, the butcher hacking a ewe into chunks that went straight into cauldrons, still bloody and warm, so that the blood frothed on the surface of the water as the meat boiled. They hacked up the last of the spring harvest of turnips and carrots and threw them into the cauldrons with all the barley and onions and sage they could lay their hands on.

At every turn it was the last of this and the last of that, and still weeks before the harvest. It was not quite desperate. There was still a little grain in the barns, and a few dried beans in the store houses, and oil and salt, and the hens were laying well, and the woodlands were not foraged out. But crops had been poor for the last two seasons: blight in the corn, hail knocking down the bean rows, cutworms in the cabbages. Edith, knowing that it was her own kin that would be first to suffer in a famine, was strict in forbidding anything to be harvested before it was full grown, and in making sure all that was harvested was preserved and stored properly, and that nothing was wasted, from field to table. Thus she was better prepared than many women might have been to feed guests that year. But it was a grim thing for her, all the same, to see the bottom of so many baskets and barrels while the days were still so long.

Edith's grandparents had been born in Powys. They were taken in a raid by Mercians along with several of their village, then traded into Northumbria and bought as a job lot by Attor's grandfather. Her mother always claimed that they had been nobles in Powys, but Edith had never seen any sign of noble bearing or skill in her mother or father. They might have been freemen in Powys, but they were slaves in Northumbria and knew all the privations of slavery. In the lean times, Edith had lived on acorns and dandelions and felt her belly pinch, till the harvest was in, and then she had spent days bent under the autumn sun gleaning the fields, getting her bread one grain at a time. She had not seduced the first son of the estate for the sake of idleness, but in hopes of a son with Anglish blood who would enjoy his father's favor and gain a place in his household among the men who never dined on acorns, no matter how long the summer dragged and how empty the larders became.

She had won far more than this. Calculation had grown to affection long before he had finally laid her down beneath the harvest stars, and she had seen affection returned, in his look, and in his gentleness, even as he stripped her clumsily, and then stopped to gaze at her in a kind of wonderment. He had struggled so helplessly with the thong of his own trousers that they both wept with laughter, until she rolled on top of him and undid the knots. And then their mutual conquest became not conquest at all, but an alliance and an understanding.

Afterwards, doubt had assailed her as he lay panting beside her in the grass. Would he now rise, shamefaced, pull a coin from his pocket, and trot away, tying up his trousers as he went, without a backward glance? But he had grunted and sighed and turned his face to her, lifting a hand and cradling her cheek as he said, "Oh dear, my mother will not be pleased."

"Mine will," she had said. And they had both known then, and they had laughed till their sides ached, naked under the stars.

It was only later that she had come to understand the limit to what she had gained. Her act was not the act of a respectable woman. By the time that Attor had won his battle over the marriage, there had been a cradle standing beside them in the hall as they had made their promises. God had forgiven her, for he had sent her healthy children. Some said Whitney was a punishment, but Edith did not believe that. Whitney was a God-touched child, a creature of almost unalloyed bliss. A burden and a treasure, but never a punishment. But these signs of God's favor had done nothing to give her respectability. Hilda hated her for it. If God was extracting a penance from her, it was Hilda's reproach. Elswyth did not feel that way at all. But that was almost worse. Elswyth had wheedled the story out of her, and expressed delight at it. And Edith was certain that that delight had never entirely left Elswyth's heart.

But if Edith had not gained respectability, nor had she learned idleness. The habit of work was too far ingrained in her ever to be extinguished by rank. She commanded where once she had served, but she was cousin to half those she owned, and if any word of envy was ever to be spoken among her kin, she would not let it be envy of idleness. But in truth, idleness never tempted her. She burned with energy and would have burned up in anxiety and discontent if there were not always work to be done. In becoming lady of the hall she had found contentment in the gift of an infinity of work to be done.

Not so the child conceived beneath those stars. Elswyth had all her mother's energy, and her looks, but she had her father's wistful heart. Perhaps, Edith sometimes thought, it was the stars themselves that were to blame for this. There was none of that wistfulness in diligent Hilda or chatty Moira, both conceived in a bed under a firm roof. Nor was it any part of Whitney's strange, blissful madness, and Daisy seemed set to be another Moira. No, the wistfulness was all in Elswyth, and, in Edith's heart, this was a greater worry even than Whitney's madness. Elswyth or Hilda would provide a place for Whitney in their households, for both of them loved her. No, it was the wistfulness of her star-begotten child that ached in Edith's heart.

Yet it was hard for Edith to resent that wistfulness entirely, for without it, she would not have the husband she had, nor the children she had, nor the promise that no matter the harvest, none of them would feel their bellies pinch as she had. But that wistfulness had to be tamed. It was too wild a thing to let run free. She had tamed it in Attor, and she was determined to tame it in Elswyth as well.

The only yoke she knew to lay across the shoulders of wistfulness was labor. Elswyth was least the skylark and most the hen when she had work to do. And while she genuinely had no talent in her fingers, she was capable of diligence, and cheerful enough in her work until she was distracted. Once she was married and installed in Bamburgh hall, her duties would more than fill her days, and she would grow happy in them, especially when her children came. But Drefan of Bamburgh was a practical young man. He would happily forgive the Welisc side of Elswyth's blood if he believed that she would be an asset and a credit to him. But if not, the marriage would not take place.

Not that Elswyth would lack for suitors. There was something about her, something beyond her beauty, that brought young men to her like seagulls to a plowed field. But no other suitor could promise what Drefan of Bamburgh could provide.

Attor's family had never accepted his choice of wife. If Attor's father had not died at Christmas, just as Elswyth had begun to make her presence in the world obvious by the swelling of Edith's belly, Attor might never have been allowed to marry her at all. But as lord of the manor he was free to choose who he would, and he had chosen her. Even so, his mother, Lady Edmunda, had been bitterly opposed, and had wrung every kind of concession from Attor. Edmunda had softened a little with time, charmed by Elswyth and pleased to see her likeness in Hilda, but Attor's brother, Fyren had never reconciled, and had left the estate to take up service in Bamburgh.

If Attor were to die—were he to contract a fever, were a plague to pass through the district, were a blade to slip and a wound to fester—Fyren would lay claim to the manor, and Edith and her daughters could expect little sympathy from him. Certainly, he would make no effort to secure good marriages for Elswyth, Hilda, Moira, or Daisy. If he could find a way to cast Edith back into slavery, she did not doubt he would do it.

If she had conceived a son, it might be different. If he were old enough, when his father died, to have completed his military service, he should be granted the manor in the course of things, and if he were not old enough, Edith might have been allowed to manage the manor herself until her son was of age—though even of this she, being slave born, could not be entirely certain.

But with Elswyth married to Drefan, all such fears would be put to rest. Even if the manor fell to Fyren on Attor's death, there would be room in Elswyth's hall for her mother and her sisters, and the sisters of the lady of Bamburgh would not lack for suitors. But if Drefan were to find some reason to refuse her, then the displeasure of Bamburgh would descend on Twyford and another thegn's son, no matter how much he might desire Elswyth for a bride, might think twice before offering marriage to a woman spurned by Bamburgh. And a man who cared so little for Bamburgh's friendship as to take the risk might not have the resources or influence or even the willingness to find good matches for Elswyth's sisters, or the courage to take Whitney under his roof.

And so it was Edith's business, for the sake of all her children, to make sure that Drefan found nothing to object to in Elswyth, no reason to fear that she would fail him in either the private or public duties of marriage. So, even though she knew that Elswyth had left her shoes behind on purpose, and then dawdled on the beach when she went to retrieve them, leaving others to do the work that should have been hers, Edith decided that Elswyth should be lady of the hall for the feast that night.

She found her daughter forming loaves for the fryer. She was standing beside Mayda and their heads were together, joining whispers to giggles. Mayda was Edith's niece, the youngest child of her oldest sister, a slave like all her kin. As girls Elswyth and Mayda had played together, and they had been hard to tell apart, save that Mayda's hair was kept close cropped. Alone they were still liable to descend into giggles and gossip, but in the hall Mayda knew her place. There she served in silence and kept her eyes down. Edith waved Mayda away before she spoke to Elswyth.

"It is a shame you did not have a chance to stop and talk to the sailors while you were fetching your shoes," Edith said drily. "But you will entertain them tonight. You will be lady of the hall. Your father will need a peaceweaver tonight, and in that much at least, I have confidence in you. I've been on my feet all day, and my back is sore."

"Oh, thank you, Mother," Elswyth said, dropping the dough she was forming and throwing her arms around her mother, sending up a small cloud of flour. There was something shamefaced about her, despite her pleasure, or perhaps because of it, and Edith saw it and smiled at it. Sometimes an undeserved privilege is the sharpest form of rebuke.

"You should go and sit down," Elswyth said. "Put your feet up."

"And are you going to supervise the whole feast as well?" Edith asked.

Elswyth paused and looked at her, a little shamefaced still. "I can," she said, "if you need me to."

Edith considered for a moment. The responsibility would do Elswyth good, but her daughter still had no idea of half that needed to be done. Hilda could have done it, with a shrill crispness that would have left everyone fuming long before it was time to serve. Under Elswyth's direction they would work twice as hard with hearts twice as light, but half of it would be left forgotten and undone. Besides, the thought of sitting by while the work went on was intolerable to Edith. The child in her made her awkward, but never tired. Sitting still through the entire feast was going to be torture enough for her. It was impossible for her to go and sit now, with so much to be done.

"Walk with me," she said, "so I can send you if I need someone to run, and so you can learn how to keep this all going. Making sure the food is hot and served on time, and the drink does not run out, these are all part of weaving the peace of a hall. They are just as important as charm and song and preserving honor. And I don't care if you will have half a dozen housekeepers when you are Lady of Bamburgh. If you don't know what is needed, they will rob you blind."

6 The Peaceweaver

Her father was waiting for Elswyth when she emerged from the sleeping house after dressing for the feast. Her hair was loose about her shoulders and she wore a light linen dress that conformed to her figure. Her father looked at her with a touch of discomfort in his eyes that she had seen more and more as she had matured.

"Are you sure you are ready to do this, child?"

"Not a child."

"Alright. You are a fine peaceweaver. I know that. But you have not had to weave such a peace as this."

"I may have to when I am Lady of Bamburgh."

"That is what your mother said. But listen—Leif and Thor and I have discussed it, and we agree: least said, soonest mended. Everyone knows what happened, so let's not bring it up again. Let's just have food and drink and song and hope they remember they were once friends."

"Alright," she said. "I'll remind them that we are friends."

"Are you really sure you're ready to do this?"

"You always ask me that, and what do I always say?"

"That's what worries me sometimes. But come on. Everyone has gone in, Leif and his men included, and I don't want to leave them alone in there together for too long."

They went together to the back door of the hall. Edith was waiting for them just outside. She looked at Elswyth with pursed lips, then tugged Elswyth's belt down towards her waist and smoothed out the madder on her left cheek with a licked thumb.

"Is your back really that sore, Mother?" Elswyth whispered. Her mother's assault on her wardrobe was so routine that there was no profit in protesting it.

"Don't you worry about me," her mother replied. "Keep your mind on your task." But then she pulled Elswyth into a quick hug, pecked her on the cheek, and whispered, "Make your father proud."

It was still quite light outside, and so it took a moment for her eyes to adjust as they entered the hall. Elswyth walked beside her father, with her mother behind her and to her right, with a hand on her shoulder to show the delegation of authority from mother to daughter.

There was barely enough light inside the hall. Because of the heat, Edith had had only one fire laid, its smoke drawn up to the smoke hole under the false roof above. There were rush lamps too, in hooks on the walls and on the posts that supported the rafters. But the light got lost among the soot-blackened thatch. The faces of the people were ruddy in the dim light of fire and lamp, and they were many, and they were grim. But as Elswyth entered, every shining eye in every grim face fell on her, and she felt her power. The smile that played on her lips only served to draw the eyes more avidly towards her.

Elswyth greeted the company, and then carried the feasting horn to her father. Mayda came to her side with a jug and filled the horn with mead. Elswyth then offered it to her father, saying "Take, Lord, and drink." Her father took the horn, drained it, and handed it back to her. Then he turned to the company and said, "Let us feast well, for we are old friends come together in peace."

The invitation to feast should have been greeted with cheerful approval, but tonight it was met with silence. Elswyth turned to glance at Leif and Thor and Eric, all sitting stone-faced on the guest benches, and wondered how they must feel under the hard eyes of the company.

Attor then bid the company stand for the blessing and when it was said, bid them sit again. This was the last thing that it was the lord's part to say until the formalities were over. Now it was the lady's part, and her first task was to introduce the guests.

Elswyth went to them and, placing a hand on the arm of each in turn, said, "This is Leif, son of Harrald; his first man, Thor, son of Lars; and his second man, Eric, son of Thor; and the men who follow them. We know them well. There is not a man or woman here who does not wear or own something that they bought from them in trade. We all have some piece of silver in store that we got from them in trade for our goods. They are our friends. Harrald, their jarl, is oath-brother to my father, your lord. They are kin by oath to all of us. We have feasted with them many times. We have drunk with them, exchanged tales, learned games and crafts. We trust them."

There was some murmur from the back of the hall that might have been the words, "In Cuthbert's privy we do." A wave of muted agreement followed it. Someone on the free men's benches was testing the water. Elswyth fancied she knew who it was, but she had not heard the words distinctly enough to call him out. Still, she felt a little cold at that moment. This was indeed not such peaceweaving as she had done before. It was, in many ways, easier to mend a hot quarrel than this cold, sullen dislike that wanted a quarrel, and looked only for an occasion to start one.

She turned to Leif and said, "You are welcome, Jarl, in this hall, as a cousin is welcome among his own kin. Drink with us. Eat with us. Tell us your story."

It was Leif's turn now to speak, but he made no movement to rise. She turned to face him, and for a moment their eyes met. She saw no fear in him. He seemed to be pondering, calmly, as if he cared nothing for the silence and the eyes fixed upon him. But while he might endure it, the silence was unbearable to her. She took three steps toward him, held out her hand, and said, "Rise, Jarl, and tell your tale. In the order of things, we are required to hear it before we are allowed to drink. Speak then, before we all die of thirst!" She ended this with a flourish and a pantomime of parched desperation, which drew a low ripple of laughter from some of the crowd, though many others remained silent.

Leif, at least, was wakened to life by this. "Thank you for your welcome, Lady," he said. "Your words are…"

"Gracious…" she whispered to him, realizing he was struggling for the proper formula.

"Gracious and…"

"True."

"Your words are gracious and true. Your family and mine are long friends. My father loves you as a daughter."

"My father loves you as a son," she replied. Their eyes were now fixed on each other.

"He does indeed," Attor said at this, breaking the lord's customary silence.

"Tell your tale," Elswyth said, still eye to eye with Leif.

"Aye, Lady, I will."

The trouble was, there was little in Leif's history that Attor had thought it wise to tell in the hall. To speak of a cargo of monkish books would draw instant suspicion. To speak of seeking a new home, instant opposition. And to speak of the raids they had suffered, instant suspicion that they might themselves have taken to raiding to restore their fortunes. So all Leif could offer was a bland catalogue of journeys made, none of which were specific, for he would not name the men he traded with nor the cargos he carried for them. The only virtue in this was that it presented little trouble to his unsteady command of Anglish. The vice was that the hearers sensed omission in the tale, and deceit in the omission.

"You forgot the part about sacking Lindisfarne." It was the same voice at the back of the room, but a little louder than the speaker had perhaps intended, for Elswyth heard it distinctly.

She heard her father rise from his chair. She spun around and glared at him. She was the peaceweaver. His part was to listen and to give judgment, should judgment be needed. Hers was to weave the peace. He looked at her, saw the determination in her face, and slowly sat down again.

Elswyth turned back to the crowd. She was quite certain who had spoken. It was Snell. It was always Snell when words were muttered at the back of the hall. Snell was a young freeman. He had inherited two hides of land and had added two more to his holdings. One more and he would rise to the rank of thegn. But two bad harvests in a row had blunted his progress and soured his mood.

Least said, soonest mended, her father had said. But it was not for her father alone to decide how much should be said. Free men were entitled to have their say. But to mutter to your neighbors in the back of the hall instead of standing and saying your piece before the whole company, that was dishonorable and cowardly. Still, from the sounds of the murmurs that had followed Snell's words, there were many in the crowd who agreed with what he had said. She could see it in their faces, in their taut shoulders and stiff necks.

Least said, soonest mended? Not tonight. "Sorry, Father," she whispered under her breath. She plunged into the crowd. She pushed between rows of backs, men and women scrambling to pull themselves closer to the tables so she could pass by. Cups were overturned, hands got in the butter, knees got banged on trestle legs as she barged through. She came to Snell. He sat still and looked at her. He knew that he was caught, but he did not hide his face. He looked at her square on. He was a hard man to shame. If no man in the village had ever looked at her quite the way Eric had on the ship that afternoon, Snell had come closer than any other. Whenever she would catch him at it, he would not blush and turn away rapidly, trying to pretend he had not been looking. No, he would hold her eye for a moment and then slowly raise his hand and touch his forelock. He was a man always willing to test the very bounds of insolence. "One more hide of land," that look seemed to say to her. "One more hide and there will be no more tugging of forelocks, and I may look where I please."

"Why are you seated so far from the fire, Snell," she asked him. "You are a man of four hides. One more and you will qualify to be a thegn! You have done so well, and so young! You should be at the front, next to the fire. Come up with me now. I will find you a place."

This was not at all what Snell had been expecting, nor any of the people who sat by him. He stared at her a moment, furious, fearing he was about to be shamed. Yet how can any man refuse when he is asked to sit nearer the fire? "Aye, Lady," he said, dropping his eyes for a moment. Then he rose and followed her between the rows of sullen backs. The people were silent and compliant when Elswyth passed, but a certain amount of grumbling followed the passage of Snell's more substantial frame. Already they thought him not quite so fine a fellow as he pushed past them toward a place of greater honor, not as careful with his elbows as he should have been in that tight space.

Someone would have to give up a place to make room for Snell by the fire. Elswyth chose Æscwine, an old man of three hides. Three only, but all earned in battle, while Snell's four had been inherited or bought for silver. In age and honor, Æscwine was far more deserving of a place by the fire, but he was a dear and indulgent man who had entertained her so often as a child that he felt like an uncle to her. It would grieve him, but he would not refuse her.

"Dear Æscwine," she said, squatting down before the old man and placing a pleading hand on his arm, "won't you please move down and give Snell your place?"

Æscwine looked at Snell sourly, and then back at Elswyth. "Since you ask it, Lady, I will," he said. Elswyth bobbed up and kissed him on the cheek—a sign to recompense him for lost honor. "Thank you," she whispered in his ear. And then she stood and ordered everyone on that row of benches to move down one place, except Peada in the middle, who she told to go and take Snell's old place in the middle of the other bench. All this commotion, and the dishonor to Æscwine, caused more grumbling against Snell, but Elswyth was not finished with him.

"While everyone else is moving to make a place for you," she said to him, "come and meet our guest." She took him by the arm and led him to the guest benches, motioning Leif to stand as she did so.

"Leif, this is Snell. He is one of our most prosperous young freemen. Did you know that he inherited just two hides from his father, but now, by hard work and shrewd trading, he has four, and it will be five soon, I'm sure, if this harvest is better than the last. You must have a lot in common, you are both men of trade."

"Greetings, Snell," Leif said, extending his hand.

Snell looked round at Elswyth, his face thunderous. He did not take Leif's hand.

"Didn't you have something you wanted to ask Leif?" she said.

"No, Lady," Snell said, his voice deep in his throat, his cheeks starting to flare a little, for all his lack of shame.

"But you did! Something about Lindisfarne?"

The shuffling and complaining and scraping of benches in the hall ceased at the word Lindisfarne. Elswyth could hear her father's sharp inhalation of breath, but she ignored him. It must be said before it could be mended. She was convinced of this now.

"No…"

"Go on, ask. Leif has nothing to hide."

Snell, seeing he was trapped, remembered his pride. He drew back his shoulders and straightened his back.

"We want to know," he said, "was it you who raided Lindisfarne, killed all those monks, took all them slaves and all that treasure?"

"It was not," Leif said, looking at Snell very steadily. "We only heard of this raid this afternoon. It grieved us greatly to hear it." His hand was still outstretched toward Snell for a hand-shake.

Still Snell refused to take the extended hand. Elswyth pushed Leif's hand down and stepped between them.

"Do you know the story of when I stowed away on their ship?" she asked. Of course they did. Edith had never let it be forgotten. But it was a good story and they were going to hear it again. "When I was a little girl, I took a bag of apples, three loaves of rye bread, and my favorite doll and hid under the deck in Uncle Harrald's ship. Silly me, I forgot to take any ale. Anyway, two days out into the sea, Eric found me. I was so afraid they were going to punish me. But Uncle Harrald did not even scold me. He gave me cakes and sweet wine and a blanket to sleep in, and then he turned the ship around and rowed three days back against the wind to bring me home.

"I sulked the whole way home, even with the cakes and sweet wine. I wanted to go to Spain. I know now that Uncle Harrald could have taken me there and sold me to a caliph. A pretty girl is worth a lot of money in the slave market at Cordoba. But he took me home. Father wanted to give him silver to cover the cost of a week's lost sailing time, but Uncle Harrald would not take it. He said, 'A man does not take a reward for returning his brother's child.'

"I was still angry with him for bringing me back, but when I heard him say that, I loved him very much all the same because I knew he was my proper uncle. And Leif is his son. And the first thing he did when he met us on the beach was to ask to hold Daisy. And he didn't mind at all when she pulled his nose. You were all there. You saw that. That is who these men are. Not vikingar, but traders—and not just traders but old dear friends."

"Aye, but…" Snell began, and then stopped, unsure now of the mood of the room.

"But what?" she asked. And then, without waiting for an answer from Snell, she turned to Leif. "Have you ever been to Lindisfarne?" she asked.

Once again Leif paused, and the pause was far longer this time. She sensed the tension rise in the room as he delayed. But he seemed unmoved by it. He glanced at Attor, but Elswyth did not turn to see how her father responded. Thor's eyes were on her, but she kept her gaze on Leif.

"Have you ever been to Lindisfarne?" she repeated.

"Yes," Leif replied. "I visited there when I was a boy. The holy men welcomed me."

"So you knew the place. You had seen its riches?"

"Yes."

"I think what Snell wants to ask is, did you tell anyone? Did the vikingar learn about it from you?"

At this there was a strong murmur around the hall. Snell turned and looked at them. If he had had the courage to ask the question himself, he might have won them back, might have earned his place by the fire. But his chance had passed. They belonged to her now. He took a step backward, but Elswyth took hold of his arm and held him there.

Again, Leif paused. And then: "We told no one."

"Snell wonders why we should believe you," Elswyth said.

Leif waited a moment, glancing at Snell. Snell said nothing to either own or disown the question.

"We would lose our trade. Anyone can sail a ship. We know men from Faroe to Cordoba. We know what they have to sell. We know what they want to buy. Because of this, our holds are always full. We know where a cargo will fetch the best price. We know where to get that cargo at the lowest price. We do not tell these secrets."

"Is that the only reason?"

Leif looked at her again. Another long pause. She knew exactly what she was asking for, but she knew she could not prompt him, and she stood, gazing into his face, trying to will the words onto his tongue.

"No," he said at last, a slightly quizzical look in his eye, as if he were trying to follow where she was leading him but was not sure of the direction. "We value our friendships. My father is oath-brother to your father and to other men that we trade with. Men trust us with their trade, and with their gold, because we are oath-kin to them. The gods would surely send storms to drown us if we broke these oaths."

"You understand this, don't you Snell," she said. "You don't betray the men you trade with, do you?" Half the men he traded with were in that room. "You don't short your weights or clip your silver? You will answer to God that there is no straw in your wheat or water in your mead?"

"Yes," Snell replied. "I am an honest man."

"Is that why your father brought me home instead of selling me to a caliph in Cordoba?" Elswyth asked, turning back to Leif. "Because he is an honest man?"

Leif paused again. Unhurried in the midst of a hall in which all were again silent, and every eye was on him.

"He did that because he loved you," he said, eventually. "But he would have done the same for any child of Attor's people, because of his oath-brotherhood with him."

Elswyth beckoned Mayda to her. Elswyth held the feasting horn to be filled and Mayda poured the mead. Elswyth offered the horn to Leif, saying, "Drink, Jarl, and be at peace with my people."

Leif took the horn and drained it.

Mayda refilled it and, in dead silence, Elswyth turned and offered the horn to Snell.

"Drink, and be joined in friendship," she said.

Snell looked at her stiffly, uncertainly. Her hand was still pinioning his wrist.

"Will you not be the first to drink?" she asked Snell. "Do you think the honor should go to another? I do admire a man who will not claim an honor he does not think is his due." And then she smiled at him, radiantly, sweetly, pleadingly, and slowly lifted his hand toward the cup.

He dared offer her no resistance. He took the horn in his hand and she released his wrist. He looked briefly around the room. The faces were blank, expectant. There was nothing in their faces that gave him courage to refuse. He put the horn to his lips and drained it. He handed it back to Elswyth, his eyes glowing at her with a mixture of shame and lust. She handed the horn off to Mayda and then took Leif's hand in one hand and Snell's in the other and placed them in each other's grasp, so that they had no choice but to shake hands.

When the handshake was done, she took Snell's hand in hers again and raised it high, as if he had been some conquering athlete, swiftest in the race or strongest in the throw. She led him back to the place she had made for him, sat him down, and congratulated him on his honor so that by the time she had done with him, the men around him were slapping him on the back and congratulating him and the unmarried women were trying to catch his eye.

The cup was then passed to all the free people present. All drank, Elswyth making sure that Æscwine was next in honor. The bonds of hospitality were sealed. To think that all the old love and friendship between Anglish and Norsk had been restored would be foolish, but violence now would break the sacred laws of hearth and hospitality and bring grave dishonor to anyone who offended. It was a peace woven with poor thread, but she thought it would be strong enough to hold. Snell, she was certain, at least, would not be muttering at the back of the hall or creating discontent in the fields, not for some days at least.

Her part complete, Elswyth returned to her place by her mother's side. Edith took her hand and squeezed it, then leant near and whispered, "I wish Drefan had seen you do that. I know I find a lot to complain about, but you were born to be lady of the hall."

"Thank you, Mother," Elswyth said. "I learned that trick from you." Sometimes an undeserved honor is the sharpest form of rebuke.

7 Tears and Song

It was time for the presentation of gifts. After a little prompting from Thor, Leif approached the lord's dais.

"Lord Attor," he said, standing before the thegn, "allow me to present my gifts."

Leif then took out two leather packets and presented one to Attor and one to Edith. Attor unwrapped his, and took out a splendid knife with a carved bone handle and a gleaming blade.

"It is pure steel," Leif said. "No iron core."

Attor tested the edge with his thumb, and accidentally drew a bead of blood, which pleased him greatly.

Edith's packet contained three combs. Edith thanked Leif profusely for the gift, saying something disparaging about daughters and tangles. She embraced him and kissed him on both cheeks, which left Leif flustered and tongue-tied. How Norsk of him, Elswyth thought as she watched. A hall full of hostile faces did not move him, but a kiss on the cheek and he was all at sea!

Leif had begun to return to his place, but then he stopped, turned back, and stood in front of Elswyth. He reached into his jacket and pulled something out. He slipped it into her hand and whispered, "Thank you." In her palm there lay a beautiful comb, obviously part of the set that he had presented to her mother—he must have slipped it into his jacket just before he rose to present his gifts. The comb was smooth and stiff, with straight teeth and an intricate pattern carved on the handle with the head of a dragon in the center.

"Thank you," she whispered in return, quite touched by the gift, for all that she knew it was stolen from her mother's portion. She smiled at him. He turned away immediately and hurried back to his place, as if he were afraid that she too might rise and kiss him on the cheek.

Attor then presented Leif with a gift of a richly embroidered tunic. "From my daughter's hand," he said. The daughter in question was Hilda, though he forgot to name her, and Hilda, who was sitting almost unnoticed on the step of the dais, glared daggers at him, knowing which daughter would be assumed.

Elswyth then called for the meal to be served, and, her formal duties complete, she sat down and found she was trembling. She had crossed her father's plan for the evening, and she knew that she would hear about it eventually. Attor was slow to scold, but he did not forget. She was already rehearsing what she would say—that it was the wrong plan. That the people had not been satisfied. What she had done had worked, hadn't it? But she was also conscious of what might have happened if her gambit had not worked, if Leif had not found the words that she had trusted him to find. There might have been mutiny. There might have been bloodshed. And she would have been the cause of it.

But this was deeper trouble than her conscience knew how to accommodate. When she offended, she was used to making amends mostly by the sheer exuberance of her charm. And what did it matter how amends were made, if the offended party forgot the grievance, and was welcomed back into the circle of her friendship? For, with Elswyth, her sins never made her the outcast. Rather it was those she offended who became the outcasts, until forgiving her allowed them to return to her circle of friendship. Their desire to forgive her was always more urgent than her need to be forgiven. She did always wish to be forgiven, but it was a wish so easily granted that the privation of that longing left no mark on her. She never suffered for the forgiveness she sought. It was always too readily given. And so the anguish of that moment swiftly passed, and she was soon on her feet again and making her way around the room, making sure everyone's plate and cup were full, and drawing laughs and smiles from them wherever she went.

Once the meal was eaten and the slaves had cleared the tables, it was time for song and story. Wanting to favor neither Anglish nor Norsk, Elswyth chose an old Welisc song that she had learned from her grandmother, translating it from Welisc to Anglish as she went. The result was a rather stumbling performance in which she frequently was at a loss for the right word. Hilda, sitting at her father's feet, awaiting her turn to sing, counted every stumble. But the stumbles didn't matter. The company laughed with Elswyth when she wanted them to laugh, cried with her when she wanted them to cry. When she wanted them to listen in rapt silence, they listened in rapt silence. When she wanted them to pound on the tables and shout, they pounded on the tables and shouted.

Leif, as chief guest, went next. He told a simple and brief tale, translating also as he spoke, from Norsk to Anglish. As soon as he got stuck for a word the first time, Elswyth, quite unconscious of any proprieties and moved only by sympathy, rose, crossed the hall, and sat on the table in front of him, prompting him whenever he got lost. He was not a gifted storyteller, and when he was done, there was hardly a note of applause. But Elswyth took Leif by the hand and led him into the center of the hall, where she curtsied and made him bow. This drew a fresh round of applause, a little louder this time, for no one wished to lose her friendship. But their applause was obedient rather than heartfelt, and Elswyth was embarrassed for Leif. She pulled him close to her and stood tiptoe to whisper into his ear. "You did well. Don't mind them."

She led him back to his seat. Then she returned to the center of the hall and said, "Let the cup go around again, and then my sister, Hilda, will sing."

Hilda should have been in bed, like the other children. But she had protested so aggrievedly at what she claimed was unjust favoritism to Elswyth that her father had been convinced to allow her to attend, and to sing. Hilda had chosen a long song, but she made up for that by singing it very fast, almost stumbling over the words, which came out in great rushes between sharp hurried breaths. It was an Anglish song. Hilda knew no Welisc or Norsk. She knew the song perfectly, never getting a single word wrong, never pausing for a moment to remember, and she was convinced that this perfection of memory would make her song more admired than Elswyth's imperfect effort. But she never expressed any word to fit its meaning. To her, the song was nothing but a task to be accomplished, a credit to her account in her ledger. She had no thought to entertain, only to demonstrate, only to score the point and extend her lead.

Poor Hilda. Except with the needle, it was her fate to do everything correctly and nothing well. She had one true gift, embroidery, and it consumed her. She could see nothing of the art in any other craft. As she rushed on, her high childish voice shrill and breathless, people around the hall ceased to watch or to listen. Conversations broke out here and there until Hilda was singing amid a general hubbub. Elswyth saw tears start to form in the corners of her sister's eyes, though her voice never faltered and her pace never slackened. Elswyth wanted to jump on the table and shout at them all to be quiet, but she knew that Hilda would be devastated to be helped or interrupted by her sister. Anything she did would send Hilda into a rage of weeping and whirling fists. And so the tears kept running down Hilda's cheeks as she kept grimly singing, still more than a third of the song to go.

Then Thor rose from his place on the guest benches and walked round into the middle of the hall. Half the conversation in the hall ceased as he moved. He said nothing, however, ignoring everyone around him, and slowly lowered himself until he sat cross-legged in front of Hilda and gazed at her with perfect attention. Hilda rubbed the tears out of her eyes, never pausing in her singing as she did so, and from that point she delivered the rest of the song solely to Thor, her voice dropping until it was just loud enough for him to hear, though the whole hall was now silent, their eyes fixed on Thor.

The instant the last word was sung, Hilda ran and fell into Thor's arms, bawling her eyes out. Elswyth let her be for a minute, then crossed the floor, kissed her on the top of her head, and said, "Bedtime."

Hilda kissed Thor on both cheeks, hugged him again, and then leapt up and ran from the hall. Not one note of applause followed her, for it was Thor who had seized their attention, not Hilda.

Thor struggled to get back to his feet. He held out a hand to Elswyth to steady him as he rose, and it took all of her strength to do it.

"Are you alright," she asked him.

"Just old," he said. "No cure for that, lass."

"Thank you," she said, keeping hold of his arm as she guided him back to his place, though he seemed to need no further steadying once he was back on his feet.

Thor sang next and held the whole hall as enthralled by his singing as he had done by his listening. Resent his blood though they might, they could not resist him as a storyteller. All the while the cup went round and round. By the end, Elswyth's charm, Thor's grace, and the cup's warming influence had done as much as could be asked of them. If the people did not depart the hall feeling warmly toward the Norsk, they at least felt bound to them in hospitality and no longer feared that they might be murdered in their beds. That was enough, that night, to keep the peace.

Though she had only sipped lightly, each time the cup had come to her, Elswyth was muzzy headed by the time she tumbled into bed, pushing Hilda over to make room, for her sister had sprawled out diagonally across the bed, as if to deny Elswyth a place to sleep.

Hilda's eyes glowed fiercely in the light of the guttering rush lamp that Elswyth had used to light her way to bed. "You don't get to tell me when to go to bed," Hilda whispered fiercely, as Elswyth lay down beside her. But Hilda's chin was quivering. And then Hilda suddenly dissolved into weary tears, and Elswyth wrapped her arms around her sister. After a moment, Hilda's arms went around her in return, and she wept silently in the embrace until she fell asleep.

8 Thor

Thor was an object of awe and fascination for children wherever he went. Despite his size, they quickly perceived the genial affection in which Thor held all creation, and children in particular. Elswyth had loved him from the first time she met him at the age of three. Ten minutes after she had first set eyes on him, she had climbed first onto his knee and then up his thick arm until she perched herself in triumphant possession on his broad shoulders.

She had been an only child then, Hilda being but a growing roundness in her mother's belly, leaving Elswyth the sole object of every hope and every indulgence. This, combined with her natural charm and confidence, had meant no place or person or occasion had been barred to her. She had perched herself on Thor's shoulders through feast and trade talk and on long walks through woodlands and over clifftops and along the seastrand, laughing with delight when he would reach up a great hand to steady her and break into a run, scattering seagulls before him like a wolf among a flock of sheep.

It was Thor who had filled Elswyth's head with the love of ships. It was Thor who told her tales of Spain. Had Edith only realized how much Thor's tales had nourished Elswyth's wistfulness, she might have forbidden her to speak to him. But Edith had been so delighted herself, so honored that a man such as Thor should pay so much attention to her child, should be so entranced by her, that no thought of the consequences had entered her head. Edith had been a young woman then, on the cusp of nineteen, and her hair had barely grown out of the close slave crop that she had worn all her childhood. She took Thor's interest in Elswyth for proof of all she had hoped and believed Elswyth to be, for she had hoped and believed that she had conceived a woman fit to be the consort of kings, and Thor, though he had not the rank, had every other attribute of kingship. Thor had been the first and greatest of Elswyth's conquests, the first hint of her ability to seduce the world. He who loved all children loved her as he loved no other, save those born to him, and even then, if his daughters had seen Elswyth perched on their father's shoulders, seen the joy on their father's face at having her there, they would have felt themselves usurped.

Though she called him "Uncle," he was to Elswyth almost another father—a far more romantic father, a broader, bolder, bigger, brighter father than the one who had given her life and love and sustenance and doting indulgence all her days.

She found him the next morning, sitting upright, with his legs wide apart, his feet firmly planted, his arms folded sternly across his chest. His eyes were closed and he was letting the morning sun fall directly upon his weathered face and his gold-and-silver beard. She crept silently up to him, leaned over, and planted a kiss on his cheek.

Thor did not move or speak, but remained impassive, with the warming sun full on his face.

"Who kissed you?" she asked.

70

"The fairest child in Northumbria, I'll warrant," the old man said.

"If you would open your eyes, Uncle Thor, you would see that I am no longer a child."

"What? It was not Daisy then who kissed me? Who then? Whitney? Moira? Or is it Hilda who claims she's reached a woman's age?"

"Oh, Uncle Thor. Am I not your favorite anymore?"

Thor opened one eye and looked at her. She stuck out her bottom lip at him.

"Don't fret, lass," he said, "you are still my favorite. Becoming every man's favorite, I reckon."

"They like me well enough," she said.

"And so they should. I see you've grown to a woman sure enough, lass. And an able one. You did well last night."

"Did I?"

"You know very well you did."

"I thought I did. But sometimes I think I've done well and then Mother tells me I didn't."

"Did you not see your mother's face? She was proud of you."

"Well, that's a nice change."

"Less than you think," he said.

"Where's Leif?" she asked.

"Still in his bed. He'll make a fine jarl in the afternoon, that lad. But Odin help the clan in the morning."

She laughed and sat down on the bench beside him. "I like the morning," she said. "If you start at first light, who knows how far you can go by evening?"

"Why, he who knows the wind or the tide or the state of the road and the stamina of his horse. They know it to the mile."

"Oh, Uncle Thor, you know what I mean."

"Elswyth!" came a commanding cry.

"How many day's sailing to Spain?" Elswyth asked, ignoring her mother's voice.

"Go when you're bid," Thor said.

Elswyth stuck out her lip at Thor and turned to give an exasperated look over her shoulder at her mother.

"What?" she demanded.

"Since you are just sitting there, you can come and help fetch the breakfast."

"I thought you did not want me to be a kitchen maid."

"I want you to be a good ealdorman's wife," her mother said, laying a basket on the table. "That makes it your business to see that the food gets on the table, and there's no better way to do that than to set to and carry it. Mayda's bringing the bread. You fetch the honey pot and put some of those mushrooms in a bowl."

Elswyth turned back to Thor, but the old man had closed his eyes and was sitting impassively as before. She would get nothing more out of him until she did as her mother had asked.

"Where are you going in such a thunder," her father asked her when she met him in the doorway of the hall.

"Mother is making me fetch and carry," Elswyth complained.

"That woman has powers no man can match!" Attor said, and he bent and kissed her fondly on the top of her head.

Breakfast was almost done by the time Leif stumbled out of the guest house, blinking blearily at the sunshine. He was scruffy and bedraggled and dressed in a dirty sea jacket and trousers. There was something at once comic and tragic about the scrappy strands of hair that were struggling for life on the rocky promontory that was his chin. Elswyth could not help smiling at him. Their eyes touched, and his flitted away.

"Ha, he wakes," Attor cried when he saw him. "Young men love their beds, Thor, even when they've no company."

"Never was a lad saw a sunrise from his tenth year to his twentieth," Thor grumbled. "A man has only to rise with the sun to steal a march on a boy!"

"Pay no mind to them, Leif," Edith said. "You are a guest here, and you may rise at any hour you choose."

Elswyth raised an eyebrow at her mother, scandalized that Leif should be allowed to lie in idleness while she was made to fetch and carry.

"Come and eat," Edith said. "Try the mushrooms. Elswyth picked those herself, didn't you my dear? Went all the way to Foxton wood for them."

"Yes, Mother," said Elswyth, rolling her eyes. "It was such an adventure!"

Leif sat down at the table, which contained the remainders of a large breakfast: a broken loaf, a half empty honey pot with a sticky spoon, a basket with one apple in it, a bowl with a handful of mushrooms in the bottom, and a milk pitcher. He picked up the pitcher and his face fell when he discovered that there were only dregs sloshing in the bottom. He poured the last of the milk into the bottom of a mug, looking very disconsolate.

Edith said immediately, "Elswyth, go and fill the pitcher for Leif, and fetch a new loaf as well."

Elswyth turned to the hall door and shouted, "Mayda, fetch some more milk."

"She'll be feeding the pigs by now, and she will not hear you calling," her mother said. "Go like I asked you to."

"I want to listen," Elswyth protested.

"Then hurry back so you won't miss much."

Elswyth rose and stalked huffily towards the hall door. She was certain that Leif watched her as she went, but when she glanced back, he was listening to the conversation that was going on between her father and Thor.

Elswyth hurried to the kitchen and returned as quickly as she could, bringing a fresh pitcher of milk and a new loaf, still warm from the oven. She dropped these down in front of Leif.

"Thank you," he said, when she laid them before him.

She ignored him. She had been reduced from lady of the hall to fetching and carrying, while her mother, at least, was still treating Leif as chief guest. She was not willing to engage with him on those terms.

Her mother was pressing Thor for news of his family. Something about a youngest daughter married and a newest grandson born.

"Have you been to Orkney lately, Uncle Thor," she asked, interrupting her mother's conversation.

"I've been to Orkney," Leif said.

She ignored him. "Have you," she insisted to Thor.

"Aye," said Thor.

"I have heard that there was a sheep born there with three heads. Did you see it?"

"No, lass."

"Did you hear of it? Is it true?"

"I dunno, lass."

"Norvel says he saw it, but I don't think I believe him."

"Can't say, lass."

"It's nonsense," said Leif. "A sheep cannot have three heads."

She ignored him.

Thor turned to Attor and said, "Your people were not so pleased to see us last night."

"It is quite mad what has been happening since Lindisfarne-," her father replied. "I just heard from a man last week that there was a Pictish trader and his crew beaten up by a mob near Jarrow. Two of them died and their ship was burned with all its cargo."

"Foolish waste," Thor said. "If you kill a man, why burn his goods? No profit of his blood if you do that."

"No one's thinking much, these days," Attor said.

"Not safe for us to travel inland, then?" Thor asked.

"No," said Attor. "Had you planned to do so?"

"We had hoped to sell the books at Lindisfarne," Thor said. "But we cannot do that now. We know men in York, and I know there are many of your holy men there."

"You are lucky you came here first instead of going to Lindisfarne. You would have found nothing there but an angry fyrd."

"We wanted your advice. We have traded with the jarl of the holy men, but he would not make an oath of brotherhood with us, as you did, but only friendship. He said he could make no such oath with heathens. Also, we hoped you could help us find a home here."

"Have you been to York, Uncle Thor?" Elswyth asked.

"I've been by the river way," Thor said, "But I didn't go into the town."

"Why ever not?" Elswyth demanded, scandalized at such an opportunity lost.

"Did our business by the riverbank," Thor said. "No need to go further."

"But you're going now?"

"If we can."

"Take me with you."

"Hush, girl!" her mother scolded. "As if we'd let you on board a ship again! Take some of these things to the kitchen, and then see to your embroidery. I want to see a span's width before noon."

"I want to talk to Uncle Thor," Elswyth protested. "It's been two years since I've seen him. I want to hear his adventures."

"There's work to be done," her father said, dusting the remains of his breakfast from his hands.

Leif stood, a guilty look on his face, his cheeks still stuffed with food.

"Sit, lad." Attor said, "We three must talk our trade talk."

"Come on, Elswyth," Edith said, "We must leave the men to their business."

"I want to listen." Elswyth's tone suggested that her mother was either hard of hearing or soft in the head.

"Come on," her mother replied. "We start listening to their business and next thing, they'll want to listen to ours. Then it will be all listening and no doing and then what will become of the world?"

"Father…"

"Produce a span by lunch," her father said, "and we'll see what time Thor has for stories this afternoon. Now be a good girl and run along with your mother."

Elswyth blushed deep red. She could feel the warmth of the blood in her cheeks and feel it pricking at the roots of her hair. Such a childish dismissal would have angered her on any day, but today she felt her father had reduced her to a child in front of…well, in front of Uncle Thor, who might well have been persuaded to take her to York. And, yes, in front of Leif besides, when that untidy boy was invited to sit in council while she was dismissed.

"If I am to produce a span in a morning," she said to her mother, "I want no sharp words about the quality. To do these things properly takes time." She turned on her heel and began to stalk toward the hall door.

"Here," her mother called after her. "Take these things."

She turned back to the table, stamping her bare feet in the dust, no longer caring how dirty they got. Her mother loaded her arms with basket and pitcher. While she was being so burdened, she caught Leif looking at her out of the corner of his eye. She scowled at him and he looked away.

"Bye, lass," said Thor, with a touch of sympathy in his voice.

Elswyth wanted none of it. She turned once again and stamped across the compound to the hall.

9 The Books

What Edith did not know and Elswyth had forgotten was that Elswyth's embroidery basket had last been seen sailing over the cliff face towards the sands below. So, several cross words having been exchanged, Elswyth was sent to look for it. The best hope was that it had made it all the way down the cliff to the beach below. If it were hung up somewhere on the steep cliff face, it would probably be irretrievable. So to the beach she went, in a foul temper, but on the way there she met Leif on his way to the ship.

Last night they had been jarl and lady, with the affairs of two peoples in their hands. But this morning they had both been treated like children. Both felt the embarrassment of it, and neither wanted to say a word to the other. Yet neither could they prevent their paths converging without one obviously waiting while the other passed, and that seemed absurd and embarrassing as well. So each kept walking at their original pace until they came, at exactly the same moment, to the point where their two paths converged, and one had to give way to the other.

Leif stopped, leaving the path open to Elswyth.

She wanted to stalk past him in silence and let him watch her flounce away, but silent sulking was not one of her gifts. Instead she stopped too and demanded, "Where are you going?"

He paused—paused as she has seen him do in the hall, in moments of doubt or danger. Not freezing in fear, but seemingly its very opposite. A moment of stillness, of calm consideration. It infuriated her. "To the ship," he said, at last, "to fetch a book to show your father."

All her bad temper vanished at the word "book".

"You have to show me," she said. "I have never seen a book."

He paused again.

"It is none of your business if I am supposed to be doing embroidery," she said.

"It's not that," he said.

"Then what?"

His pause. His damnable pause.

"Didn't I help you in the hall, last night?" she said.

"Yes, Lady. I thank you for that." Then yet another pause, and he said, "At one point I thought you were trying to get me killed."

"I was trying to get you not killed."

"Yes," he said.

"And here you are, not killed."

"Yes, Lady."

"So you owe me, for not being killed. Show me the books."

"Your father is waiting for me."

"Leave Father to me."

He was not willing to openly refuse her and so he shrugged and said, "As you wish, Lady."

"Right, let's go."

She set off along the path through the dunes, which was only wide enough for two if they walked arm in arm. He fell in

80

behind her. After a few steps she turned and, walking backwards, she said, "You can call me Elswyth if you want." She then turned and walked forward several paces before turning again and saying, "My friends call me 'Elsy,' but I don't like it much, so don't do that."

"No, Lady," he said.

"Hilda couldn't say 'th' for the longest time, so she called me Elsy, and then everyone started doing it, to tease me. But you are a guest, so you must not tease me. It is Elswyth, to you.

"Yes, Lady."

"Can I call you 'Leif,' then?"

"Yes, Lady."

"You don't really get how this works, do you Leif?"

"I can call you Elswyth if I want to," he said.

"Exactly, Leif."

"Thank you, Lady," he said.

She turned and looked at him, half outraged, half laughing. "I said you were not to tease me!" she said, throwing her arms open in exasperation.

***

The tide was well out and the ship stood high and dry on the beach. Eric was supervising as the men scraped her bottom of weed and barnacles. He caught her eye as she approached, but the look on his face was entirely grim. Did he regret what he had said to her the previous day? Did he fear she would complain about it to Thor or to Leif? She could not read either of these things in his face. It was her presence itself he seemed to resent. In any case, she gave him no acknowledgement, nor did he make any acknowledgement to her beyond an unfriendly scowl.

"Wait here while…" Leif began, but she already had a leg over the rail in the low part of the ship and was aboard before he could finish the sentence. He climbed up after her. Under the foredeck, protected from the rain and the sea spray, a large chest was lashed between a pair of cleats. He went to it and opened the heavy lid. From inside the chest a rich smell of oil and new leather emerged. Elswyth leaned in, inhaling the smell and running her hands over the upright spines.

"Is this a book?" she asked, meaning the whole chest.

"There are six books," Leif said, crowding her away from the chest as much as he could without touching her. He bent and lifted out one of the leather-bound volumes.

"It is like a small chest inside a larger one," Elswyth said. "What is inside the smaller one?"

"I'll show you when we get back to the hall," he said. "I don't want to keep your father waiting."

"Just a peek, now," she pleaded, her hands reaching for the shining leather with its encrusting jewels, "in case Father won't let me stay."

He hugged the book to his chest and turned away from her, avoiding her hands. She realized that not only did he not want her touching the book, he did not want her touching him either.

"Fine," she said, resentfully. "But it wouldn't hurt to give me just a peek."

Leif said nothing, but turned and dropped over the side, still clutching the book to his chest.

Elswyth turned and glanced at Eric, who looked at her, grim faced. She stuck her tongue out at him, but he only glared back and shook his head. She dropped over the side and followed Leif up the sands.

Attor rolled his eyes and gestured heavenward when he saw Elswyth accompanying Leif back to the hall with the book. But he did not send her away. Leif laid the book down on the table in the sunshine. Attor looked it over, running gentle and reverent hands over the new and gleaming leather and inspecting the precious stones with an expert eye. He made no move to open the cover.

Elswyth watched her father's hands with burning envy. The desire to run her hands over the warm leather, to feel the cold hardness of the colored stones, to caress the luster of the gold filigree, was hard to bear. As keen and avid as her eyes might be, she was also a creature of her fingertips. To be denied touch was to be denied knowledge. But she realized how much depended on these books for Leif, how much anguish he must feel until their value was known and a buyer identified. And so she stood back and watched as her father made his inspection, her fingers twisted together behind her back to keep them from reaching out.

Leif too was seething with impatience as Attor's inspection continued. At last he could be silent no longer.

"Open it," he said, "the true beauty is inside."

Attor raised an eyebrow in Thor's direction.

"I did not think such things were worth more in trade than the stones and the metal," Thor said. "But Leif says your holy men value them highly and spend much labor to produce them."

Attor frowned. "It's true they spend a pretty penny on cow skin," he said. "Puts up the price of leather." He turned back the heavy cover of the book. Its leather binding was still new and not yet supple. It creaked and groaned as he opened it. Inside there was a loose sheet of parchment covered with writing. Attor lifted the loose sheet without curiosity and looked at the page beneath. The entire page was covered with a delicate and intricately drawn picture of a man sitting at a writing desk. Behind him was a cupboard filled with books. A large volume was open upon the desk and the man's hand held a pen that was copying new letters into the great book. It seemed as if his hand wrote automatically, for the man's eyes were not upon his work but stared straight out of the picture. Upon his face was a beatific smile and about his head was a halo glowing golden in the sunlight. The room in which he sat was bright with light and richly furnished. The picture was surrounded with an ornate border full of detail, color, and lively line.

Elswyth could not help leaning in. She grasped her right wrist with her left hand to keep herself from reaching out to touch. As she strained forward, she pressed up against Leif's side as he too gazed at the picture. For the first time, he did not draw away at the touch of her.

"Is this the image of your God?" Leif asked.

"I do not know," Attor replied. "Perhaps it is the man who wrote the book."

"Turn the page," Leif urged.

Attor did so, first rubbing his fingertips on the seat of his trousers, so as not to dirty the pages. The new page bore in its top left corner a large and colorfully decorated letter. Elswyth knew it was a letter, for she had seen half a dozen lettered things in the village. There was a dagger of her father's with letters on the blade, letters on the doorpost of the hall and on a couple of the houses, letters on the great stone cross in the center of the village, letters on a silver goblet that had been a wedding present to her mother. The rest of the page was filled with smaller letters, inked in black, and standing tight together in rows like men in a shield wall. There were more letters on that page than she had seen in her whole life.

"Is this a rune of power?" Leif asked. "What are these words that are written beside it?"

"Do you think I read, lad?" Attor said.

"I thought all Anglish people could read."

Attor laughed. "Do you think I have time for such a thing? Only monks read, and they devote their lives to the study of it."

Leif's face fell. "I had hoped to learn its secrets," he said.

"What for?"

"My family has much need of magic."

"If books contained a magic against vikingar, Lindisfarne would have been well defended," Attor said.

84

"But maybe they didn't have these books," Elswyth said. "Maybe each one has a different magic."

Attor looked at Thor and asked, "How did you come by such a thing?"

"Leif came back from Lindisfarne telling us stories of these books, and the value the holy men placed on them. Two years back, Torvalds was trading with a Danir, and the Danir offered him this. The Danir asked little more than the price of the stones and the metal. Torvalds remembered the lad's story and took a chance."

"Well done then, lad," Attor said. "You've a trader's head on your shoulders. But if the Danir did not know its value, then he stole it. And so again, there is no charm against vikingar here."

"If there is no magic in them, Uncle, are they still worth something? Will they raise the money to free my father?"

"I do not do any trade in books," Attor said, chewing pensively on his bottom lip. "But I do not think this book alone will pay your father's ransom."

"But I have more than one," Leif said. "I have a great chest full. I have five more books. Will that be enough?"

"I don't know. Books are not like bales of reindeer hide—all the same price. Some are prized more highly than others, I believe."

"Gospels," said Leif. "Gospels are the most prized. I learned this from the monks. But I did not learn how to tell a gospel from another sort of book. Is this a gospel, Uncle? What is the value of six gospels?"

"I have no means to reckon it," Attor said.

"The monk would know," Elswyth said.

"You have a monk?" Leif asked eagerly. "Is he one of your slaves?"

Elswyth laughed. "Monks are not slaves," she said. "But we have one visiting, because Kendra is a prophet. Or maybe she is. Remember, Father?"

"I'd forgotten about him," Attor said. "But you're right. If anyone here knows the value of these books, it will be the monk. Go fetch him."

10 The Monk

Brother Alun of Monkwearmouth had been elated when his abbot had told him that he was being sent to Twyford. Twyford was the village where, according to Bede, Archbishop Theodore had, in the year of grace 684, convened a synod with King Ecgfrith that had led to the summoning of Saint Cuthbert from his hermitage on Farne Island and made him Bishop of Lindisfarne. To visit a place of such historical and spiritual significance had seemed to him a great honor and privilege, and his abbot had impressed upon him that if prophecy was to be found in Northumbria in this age, this village, of such auspicious memory, was a more likely place for it than most.

But it had all proved a great disappointment. Twyford proved to be a very ordinary coastal village where all memory of the blessed synod held there seemed to have faded (the thegn had said that his father might have mentioned it once). The supposed prophet that it contained proved to be a dying old woman. Many in the village assured him that Kendra of Twyford was certainly a prophet. She seemed more likely to be a simple madwoman. Yet in the ravings of the mad, some said God spoke, and in the madwoman's final words, who could say what oracle might come? She spoke of those long dead as if they were living, which her son and daughter took to be a sure sign that she saw ghosts and spirits. News of this had reached the Abbot of Monkwearmouth, and in these days in which prophecy was so much needed and so little to be found, he had sent half the monks in the abbey out across the countryside to hear and judge the words of every country prophet and madman from the Tees to the Tweed. But so far her words had been of nothing but pain and petty hatreds, sickened cows and palsied sheep and ungrateful children—all of which might be taken as evil omens, by those who looked for them, but to his ear they were nothing but the bitter commonplaces of earthly life.

Kendra was remarkably old for a countrywoman—some said over sixty—and had three children living, and God knew how many grandchildren and great-grandchildren. Her face showed the marks of the pox and of famine and of half the other ills of the world, but still she lived, though emaciated and bedridden. Nuns and queens and noblewomen might sometimes live longer, but for a peasant woman her age was remarkable, which gave all the more credence to the notion that she might be a prophet, even if only in her last words. And so Brother Alun sat beside her while she woke, prayed with her when she seemed lucid, and listened dutifully when she rambled. The hut in which she lay was rank and choked with smoke from a small fire that seemed to him entirely superfluous in the summer heat. Her neighbors and her descendants would come and sit with her, when their work allowed, so that the hut was often crowded, and pervaded by a wondering sadness, a kind of pent-up mourning, like milk spoiling in the pot before anyone was ready to drink it.

He missed the light and air of the scriptorium and the privacy and intimacy of the books. Yet he cherished his obedience as a gift from God, and therefore accepted this trial as a penitential service and attended hour upon hour for some hint of prophecy in the old woman's ramblings. His only respite was when she slept, and though she slept often, the boundary between her sleeping and waking was hard to discern. She would seem to be dozing and then blurt out some piece of bitterness or affection, eyes suddenly wide and staring. And then a moment later seem asleep again. She had slipped into this state, the most tedious part of all his vigil, and he was well sunk into the telling of his beads, when Elswyth stuck her head through the door flap and said, "Father wants you. Can you come or is she prophesying?"

"Rulers are not a terror to good works," the monk said, not turning his head to look at her.

"Huh?"

"If your father summons me, it must be for God's purpose. If He intends to speak prophecy through this woman, no doubt He will wait while I attend to the demands of those rightly placed in authority over me."

"Okay, but did she?"

"I cannot pass through the doorway while you are standing in it," the monk said.

"Oh, right," said Elswyth. She withdrew and turned her back to the doorway to let him emerge. She knew from experience that he would stand stock still and look skyward or at the ground rather than look in her direction, so he was not likely to emerge from the hut if she stood looking at the doorway.

She heard him cross the threshold, then stumble, cry out, and land on his face. She did not turn to look at him.

"You can't even look at me from behind?" she asked, not turning around.

"I have explained the discipline of the eyes to you," he said, grunting as he picked himself up off the ground.

"But you look at Kendra. And Denegyth. And Collibe."

"They present no temptation to me."

"So when I am old and ugly, you will look at me?"

"If I live so long, I expect I will be beyond all such temptations."

"But it's okay for me to look at you?"

"You are not under vows. Though no Christian should look on anything that is a temptation to them."

"Well, I'm sorry, but I am not even a little bit tempted by you, Brother Alun, so why don't I walk behind you so you don't stumble and fall again. Or should I get a boy to run ahead of us with a stick to drive any pretty girls out of your path?"

"If I keep my eyes on the path, I shall neither stumble nor fall," the monk said. "Though I wish you would not tempt me to sharp words."

"I'm behind you now. You can open your eyes and walk toward the hall, safe from my Blodeuwedd charms. And before you ask, yes that is one of Granny's stories. A woman made from flowers, the fairest ever seen."

"Your grandmother is a sterling woman, but more than half heathen. And no creature made by man can be fairer than those made by God. It is because I am sinful that I may not look at you. God made you as you are for his glory, not my torment."

"Well, be sure to thank him for me," Elswyth said.

"Thank him yourself," the monk replied, "but also pray that your beauty not be a stumbling block to others." And with that he started towards the hall, his eyes fixed steadily on the path in front of him.

"So, is Kendra a prophet?" she asked as they walked. "Did she tell you why the vikingar attacked Lindisfarne?"

"She does sometimes speak as if with angels," the monk said, "but she says nothing to help any living man. If she has learned anything from the angels, she has not the wit to speak it, or I have not the wit to understand."

"Have you heard prophets before?"

"No."

"My Granny hears them all the time."

"She must be a rich woman then, beloved of kings and bishops."

"So you are saying Granny is a liar?" she asked, teasingly. She had long since ceased to put much stock in her grandmother's stories, though she faithfully pretended to believe every word of them. Her mother's mother was the most beloved of all her relatives, and the source of all she knew of the Welisc side of her blood.

"More than half heathen, and therefore more than half in error," the monk said. "She wants for instruction more than good will, I believe. Do you not have priests who visit regularly to instruct you?"

"We had one last year."

"What did he preach about?"

"I don't remember. He ate all the blackberries. My mother was furious."

"Your bishop and his priests should be visiting the people, but they sit in their minsters getting fat."

"We hardly ever see a monk either."

"We are sworn to stability of place, yet it seems we travel more than the bishop's priests who are responsible for the laity. Everywhere I have been on my journey I find instruction on modesty and chastity to be sorely needed."

"What do you mean?"

"Young women going about with their heads uncovered…"

"Mother said I did not have to wear a wimple until I was married. Left here, not right, unless you want to go to the pigpens instead of the hall."

The monk corrected his path and walked on in silence.

"Don't you want to know why Father called for you?"

"He will tell me in his time."

"You're going to have a shock."

"I thank you for warning me."

"I can tell you, if you like. But only if you look at me."

"The warning is enough."

And after that she could think of nothing else to say to him until they arrived at the hall, where the monk stopped dead in his tracks when he saw the two Norsk standing around the table with her father.

"Told you."

"I thank you indeed for your warning," he said, half turning in her direction. "I think it is better you did not tell me more."

"They won't bite," Elswyth said. "They are old friends of ours. I thought you might even know them."

"By God," the monk said, "I think I do remember the old man. Hard to forget a man that size, and I think we bought hides and indigo from him when I was in training at Lindisfarne."

"That's Uncle Thor, and he's a sweetie."

"But a heathen. And he would have known of the wealth of Lindisfarne."

"It wasn't them, I promise. Go and greet them. If you don't, I will, and then you will have to suffer to look at my behind."

"I will go, because of your father's command."

Elswyth followed him as he stepped forward again towards the table. But before he reached the men waiting there, Leif turned and saw him, gave an excited cry of recognition and rushed towards him crying "Brother Alun! My friend!"

The monk shied at seeing the young Norsk come rushing at him and darted backwards, stumbling into Elswyth, who was close behind him, knocking her over and then falling over her.

Leif immediately offered his hand to the monk, who shied away from him again.

"Don't you know me, Brother Alun?" Leif asked. "I am Leif, Harrald's son. When I was a boy, my father left me as hostage with your holy jarl, as credit for your goods which he carried to Canterbury. He wished me to learn your ways. What goods you have to trade. What goods you desire. You showed me the Gospel book. From you I learned that a thing of hide and paint can be more valuable than gold and jewels."

Elswyth picked herself up and dusted the dirt off her dress, but the monk stayed on the ground, looking up at Leif uncomprehending.

"Is it because my beard has come?" Leif asked. "I had no beard when you knew me." He gathered up his thin beard in one hand and placed one finger of the other beneath his nose to cover his wispy mustache.

A laugh almost burst from Elswyth's mouth at this gesture, but it seemed to work, for a look of comprehension came over the monk's face.

"I remember," he said. "We showed you our treasures. What fools we were to do that! What fools we were to trade with heathens!"

He still did not accept the hand that Leif extended to him. But Attor offered him his hand and helped the monk to his feet.

"We gave a fair price for your goods," Leif said. "My father would never cheat any man."

"Leif speaks truly," Attor said. "Come, Brother Alun, I need your judgment on something."

The monk came forward hesitantly but when he saw the book lying on the table his eyes lit with love and his hands stopped trembling. He opened the book, not pausing to examine the workmanship of the cover. Inside he came upon the loose sheet that Attor had replaced where he found it. He did not even glance at the rich picture on the first page of the book, but instead laid the loose sheet on the table and began to read it aloud in a language that Elswyth recognized as Latin, the language a visiting priest had used in the Mass.

Elswyth watched in fascination, forgetting the book for a moment. The sheet from which the monk read was a marvel in itself. She had heard it said that books were made from calf skin, but the sheet that the monk was reading seemed stiff, and gleamed a lustrous yellow, almost white, in the sunlight. It was marvelously thin, so that it seemed the light might shine right through it, and she had certainly never seen a piece of leather so stiff, so thin, or so luminous as this. By what process could this transformation have been achieved? And then, by what process were the black letters inscribed on it. What paint or dye could inscribe so fine a line?

She did not understand the words that the monk uttered, but the Latin had a foreign lilt and ring to it, that somehow spoke of ancient places and warm skies. Brother Alun seemed to realize that he had an audience, for he ceased to mutter the words and began to proclaim them like a bard telling an old tale in some distant place where this tongue was the language of hearth and hall.

"What is he saying, Uncle?" Leif asked anxiously. "Is this some magic?"

"I think it is Latin, the monk's own tongue," Attor said. "All writing is in their language."

"No," said the monk, pausing in his reading, "there are books written in Anglish also. Secular works. And no, I do not make magic. This is just a business letter."

"What is 'secular'?" Leif asked.

"Not holy," the monk said.

"But this book is not secular?" Leif asked. "This is a holy book. A Gospel. A book of great value. See how beautiful it is. I am certain it is a Gospel."

The monk did not reply at once. He bent over the loose sheet again and resumed reading, saying each word aloud as he ran his finger along the lines. When he had gone halfway down the page he looked up again and said, "No, not a Gospel."

11 Not a Gospel

Deep dread came over all those assembled at the words, "Not a Gospel." It seemed the ending of all hope for Harrald and for Leif's whole clan. But the monk had produced this judgement without even looking at the book. Leif took the monk by the arm saying, "Never mind that sheet. Look at the book."

The monk shied away from him so sharply that he stumbled, and threw out a hand to Attor for support.

"Step back, lad," Attor said to Leif. "Give him room to look at it properly." He then guided the monk to a stool and pushed the book in front of him. "Do not be afraid," he said. "Leif does not mean to harm you. He only wants to know that the book is valuable."

"It is not a Gospel," the monk said again.

"Look at it, I beg you," Leif implored him.

The monk reluctantly nodded his consent, and opened the book. Elswyth sidled in beside him, to get a better view. The monk responded by pulling the hood of his habit over his head so as not to catch sight of her in the corner of his eye. He gave hardly a glance to the brilliant picture on the first page but turned to the next. Here again he ignored the beautiful decorated letter and began to run his finger along the close packed lines of small letters, speaking aloud in the Latin tongue. Elswyth desperately wanted to ask how the letters corresponded to the words he was reading—how many letters made a word, and how letters made words at all—but she bit her lip and kept silent for Leif's sake.

It soon became clear that the monk intended to sit and read substantial portions of the book. He turned page after page, running his finger along line after line, though keeping it suspended above the pages so as not to dirty them. He muttered the Latin words to himself, and, as he did so, a kind of peace settled over him, and there was a joy in his mutterings. Leif contained himself in silence while the monk read. Elswyth was silent too, not wishing to draw any attention to herself for fear of being sent away. Thor was patience in the form of flesh, but Attor soon grew restless as the monk's voice went on. But then Brother Alun's joyful muttering changed to a sharp cry of dismay and the monk's eyes were fixed in agony upon the page that he was reading.

"What is it?" Leif asked, moved by the monk's distress, and afraid that Brother Alun might have discovered some flaw in the books that rendered them valueless.

The monk looked up at him, tears in his eyes, "The saint writes here that in the ancient days, whenever a general sacked a city, those who fled for refuge in the temples of the pagan gods were not spared, but suffered the same fate as all others in the city. But here he writes that when Rome itself was sacked, in his own time, many took refuge in the churches and the basilicas of Christ, and they were spared by the barbarians who sacked the city. And here he writes," the monk continued bending his head over the book again, "'Whoever does not see that this is to be attributed to the name of Christ, and to the Christian temper, is blind; whoever sees this, and gives no praise, is ungrateful; whoever hinders any one from praising it, is mad. Far be it from any prudent man to impute this clemency to the barbarians. Their fierce and bloody minds were awed, and bridled, and marvelously tempered by Him who so long before said by His prophet, "I will visit their transgression with the rod, and their iniquities with stripes; nevertheless my loving-kindness will I not utterly take from them.'" You see what the saint says. Christ saved those who took refuge in his churches."

"Your God is indeed merciful," Leif said, "for our gods give victory in war, or defeat if they are angry, but they do not protect the weak. It is a man's job to protect his kin from the enemy, and the gods may give him victory if he pleases them. But the gods do not protect the defeated."

"Your gods could not protect," the monk replied, "for they are demons. This is what the saint has written, that those who took refuge in the temples of the pagans were not spared. But those who took refuge in Christ's churches were protected, by his power and mercy—the power and the mercy he now withholds from us. Your people sacked Lindisfarne, and Christ did not protect us. Even when the brothers sought refuge in the chapel, he did not protect them. We have sinned, as many have said, and God has abandoned us. He has sent the vikingar to punish us for our sins. His mercy has gone out of the world."

"Your gods are no better than ours, then," Leif said. "Odin did not protect our village when the vikingar attacked us and kidnapped my father. All gods are fickle."

"No," Brother Alun said, "our God is constant. It is we who are fickle. It seems to me that among the pagans, it is men who are constant, in their lust and greed and anger, and their gods fickle. But with Christians, it is men who are fickle, failing in chastity and charity and peace, and God who is constant, punishing our sins and rewarding our virtues. Only in this way can I reconcile what the saint has written here with what happened at Lindisfarne. But how can I aid a pagan, knowing that Christ has made the pagans his instrument to punish us?"

"Is there not a story," Attor asked, "about a Christian who helped a pagan, when none would care for him? The pagan was robbed and left by the side of the road and the Christian helped him."

"No," said the monk, "it was the other way around. It was the pagan who saved the Christian—except that it was not a Christian but a Jew, and the pagan was a Samaritan."

"Really?" said Attor. "Why would a Christian tell a story about a pagan helping a Jew?"

"Christ told the story to remind us that even the pagans can be merciful."

"If there is a mercy I can do for you, Brother Alun," Leif said, "name it. I will do it if I can, if you will only help me to save my father."

"But what do you ask of me?"

"First," Attor said, "we need to know if the books have value."

"Oh, this book has value," the monk said. "As a book, its value is second only to that of the Scriptures. And since it may show us how Christians may find safety from the ravages of pagans, it may have particular value in our times."

"If the book is not a Gospel," Elswyth asked, "what is it?"

"It is a book of St. Augustine: *The City of God Against the Pagans.*"

"What is a pagan?" Leif asked.

"You are," said the monk.

"I am Norsk."

"Norsk are pagans. Pagans are not Christian. Pagans are vikingar."

"I am not a vikingr!" Leif said. "It is true that I am not a Christian. My people honor Thor and Ran and Odin. But we are not vikingar."

"If you honor Thor and Ran and Odin, you are pagan," the monk said.

"So this book is against me."

"Yes."

"How can it harm me? Has it magic against me?"

"Magic?" the monk said. "That is a superstition of the pagans. The books will not harm you. If you are harmed, it will be Christ himself who punishes you."

"My people have been greatly harmed since this book came into our possession. If I must make some sacrifice to appease your Christ, I will, since I am on Christian land. Uncle, I have no animals with me. Can you sell me one for the sacrifice?"

"Christ has no need of your dead animals," the monk said.

"Then what am I to do to appease him."

The monk looked up sharply at Leif. "This is something you truly wish?" he asked.

"Yes. Yes. It is not good to be at odds with any god, especially among his own people."

"If you truly wish to appease Christ, there is a way."

"What must I do?"

"Reject your pagan Gods and accept baptism."

There was a moment of silence. Everyone gathered there was aware of the enormity of this suggestion. Leif took a few steps back from the table and turned toward the sea, toward his home. He reached inside his tunic and pulled out the amulet of Thor that he wore around his neck. A man who rejects his gods is a vikingr indeed, a man without home or kin.

"Oh," said Elswyth. She had come to his side, feeling his anguish. She pulled his hand down so that she could see what he was holding. She pulled off the chain that was around her own neck and laid on his palm her own amulet, still warm from her bosom. "Look how much alike they are," she said. Indeed, his was a silver amulet, rich with curling line, a bar and a cross piece making the shape of a hammer. Hers was a cross, also silver. Only the shape and position of the cross piece differed between them, and their size and decoration were almost the same, as if they had been made by the same hand. The difference between them was so small, and yet the difference they betokened was vast. He looked down at her, so eager, so open-faced. Would he abandon his gods for her? He might have done so indeed, but for his duty. But if he made himself the enemy of Odin, Thor, and Ran, how could he hope to return the ransom money safely across the sea to his home against the anger of the gods? He turned and looked pleadingly at Thor.

"A man must be true to his gods as he is true to his kin," Thor said. "It is one thing and the same."

"But can't he be a Christian in Northumbria and a pagan in Norway?" Elswyth asked.

"No!" the monk said. "Christ is Christ everywhere. Only among the pagans do each people have their own gods."

Thor too shook his head. On this Christian and pagan were agreed.

Leif looked down again at the amulet that Elswyth had laid on his palm. The cross was symmetrical. The boss in the middle was a perfect circle and the arms extended out like the four points of the wind. The ends were flared and rounded so that their circumference conformed to the arc of a greater unseen circle. He had a notion for a moment to raise it and press it to his lips, for her sake. But what sign would that be to the men who stood about him? What sign would it be to his gods? He folded his hand around it and handed it back to her.

"Perhaps," said Attor, "We should return to the matter of the price. Perhaps that will be easier to agree upon."

The monk picked up the letter and resumed reading aloud where he had left off. When he was finished, he said, "Where did you steal it from?"

"We did not steal it," Leif said, struggling to tame his impatience at the monk's accusations. "My uncle took it in trade from a Danir."

"The Danir stole it then," said the monk.

"What does the letter say?" Elswyth asked.

"It is addressed to the Bishop of Utrecht, who bought the books, thanks to the generosity of his patron, Charles, King of the Franks," the monk replied, turning his eyes to her, and then guiltily glancing away.

"Does the writing say how much the Bishop paid for the books?" Leif asked.

"The price is not mentioned."

"I'll warrant it was not the Danir that took them," Thor said, with almost meditative slowness. "It must have been some Frisian bandit that took them on the road. He sold them to the Danir because he dared not try to sell them in his own country. He must have been disappointed that the Danir would give him no more than the value of the stones."

"These books belong to the Bishop of Utrecht," the monk said. "They must be returned to him."

"They are my property," said Leif. "If this Bishop wants them, he must pay for them."

"You have no right to possess them," the monk said. "This letter proves whose property they are."

"A man owns what he can keep," Leif said. "They are in my possession therefore they are my property. Is it not so, Uncle?"

"Of course it is," said Attor.

"No," said the monk. "A man holds his property from God under the law." He turned to Attor and said, "These books are the property of the Bishop of Utrecht. This vikingr should not have them. You should take them from him and restore them to their rightful owner."

"You will not rob me, Uncle," Leif cried.

"Of course not, lad," Attor said.

Leif turned to the monk. "These books are mine. Any man who wants them from me, must fight me or pay my price."

"The question," Attor said, before the monk could reply, "is what that price should be. That is what we want to know from you, Brother Alun."

"The price should be nothing," the monk said. "No vikingr should have profit of his theft. I will tell you nothing to help thieves and murderers." He rose and started off back towards the hut where Kendra lay dying.

"I'll go after him," Attor said. "Perhaps I can still persuade him." He hurried after the monk.

"Take time to change that one," Thor said, watching him go.

"But we don't have time." Leif said. "My father suffers in his captivity. I must get his ransom quickly. What do we do now?"

"Trust Attor," said Thor. "And put that book back safe."

Leif picked up the book, closed its cover, hugged it to his chest, and began to walk rapidly down the path to the beach. Elswyth began to go after him, but Thor called her back. "Let him be, lass. He's got troubles enough."

"I won't trouble him, Uncle," she said. "I just want to look at the book." She turned and ran down the path after Leif.

12 The Rules of Trade

Elswyth caught up with Leif as he came to the edge of the sand, and put her hand on his arm. He turned and looked at her.

"Where are you going with the book?" she asked.

"I am going to put it back in the chest in the ship where it will be safe. I will set men to guard it. I fear that Brother Alun may try to steal it."

"He won't," she said. "He's too afraid of you. He would not dare go into your ship. I don't think he would touch anything belonging to a vikingr."

"I am not a vikingr," he said. "Why do you call me that?"

"I'm sorry," she said. "I shouldn't have said that. I was just teasing."

"I know of Norsk who go viking, and Danir and Svíar as well," he said. "We were attacked by vikingar ourselves. But we are not all vikingar."

"They are considered evil by your people?"

"A man who goes viking exposes his whole family to vengeance," Leif said. "If a man is an outcast, how else is he to

103

get his bread? But we don't like them. They are bad for trade. We don't like to be taken for them. That is very bad for trade. This is what my father has always taught me: trade depends on trust. You must deal fairly with those you trade with. You must treat them as you would your kin. You must not steal their cattle, or tell their secrets, or take their daughters to your bed. Treat them as you would treat your brother, and they will treat you as a brother. That is why my father swore an oath of brotherhood with your father, so that there might be trust between them as between kin. Is it not so with your people also?"

"Of course it is," she said.

"Then why does that monk think that I should give the books to the Bishop of Utrecht? He is not my brother. He is not kin to my kin. I have no duty to him. My uncle got these books in fair trade from the Danir."

"But the Danir did not know their value."

"My uncle was not kin to the Danir. He was not bound to him by any oath. Why should he tell him their value? He had no duty towards him. And if the Bishop of Utrecht could not take proper care of his property, what is that to me, or to my uncle? Was the man who took them kin to the Bishop? If so, that is his shame, not mine. By what right does Brother Alun say that the books are not mine?"

Elswyth stood with her head on one side for a moment, considering the question. The sea breeze blew her hair across her face. She divided it with her thumbs and guided it over her shoulders. "The monks teach us that all men are brothers," she said. "They say that we should treat every man like kin because we are all brothers in Christ."

"I know of your god, Christ," Leif said. "The monks told me of him. He is like our god Balder, a god who dies. His death is caused by Loki, who you call Satan. But we are not brothers to Balder, for the gods are their own people and they are not kin to men."

104

"The monks tell us that all Christians are kin to Christ."

"That is a strange teaching. Does that mean that all the Anglish people are kin? Does it mean every Anglish man has a duty of vengeance for those who died at Lindisfarne?"

"I don't know." The question had not occurred to her before, but she saw that it was a good one, and her brow furrowed as she pondered it.

"But does it mean that Anglish think all Norsk are kin?" Leif continued. "Does it mean they think they can fulfil their duty of vengeance for Lindisfarne on any Norsk, even if they are not kin to the vikingar who attacked Lindisfarne? Your people need to know that not all Norsk are kin!"

"But we don't practice vengeance like you do," Elswyth said. "We do wergild. So much for a hand. So much for an eye. So much for a freeman. So much for a slave."

"I remember. My father admires this system. It is a trader's system, not a warrior's system. It prevents feuding, and feuding is bad for trade. But still, a man's kin must pay the wergild he owes if he cannot, yes?"

"Yes."

"But is it his blood kin that owes the debt, not the whole Anglish people?"

"Of course."

"Then not all Christians are kin, despite what your monks say."

"I suppose not."

"Then how can that monk think that I am bound to treat the Bishop of Utrecht as if he were my kin? Does he believe that because my father swore an oath of brotherhood with your father that I am now kin to the whole Anglish people, and to the Franks as well? Such oaths apply only to the blood kin of those who swear them."

She frowned. "Oh bother it, I don't know. Does it matter?"

"I want to know so that I know whether the Anglish think they have a right of vengeance against me. I want to know if I must appease your Christ. I want to know if the Anglish will give me a fair price for my books. I want to know because I want no quarrel with gods or men."

She put a hand up to shade her eyes, for he was framed by the glare of sea and sky. She had no answer to his question. "I don't want a quarrel with you either," she said, "so let's not."

He melted towards her then, because she wanted him to, and it was heaven's gift to her to command friendship at her whim.

"I want no quarrel with you either, Lady."

"Elswyth. Don't quarrel about that either."

"I want no quarrel with you, Elswyth."

"Good," she said, coming to him and reaching out her hands for the book. "Can I see the book again?"

He stepped back.

"I'm not going to steal it," she said, impatiently. "You and I are oath-kin, aren't we? I won't rob you. I only want to look at the pictures."

He stepped away from her. She looked at him with wounded impatience.

"If what you tell me is true," he said, "then Brother Alun feels himself to be kin to the Bishop of Utrecht."

"Monks all call each other 'brother,'" she said.

"Then he will try to recover his brother's property."

"He won't rob my father's guest. He is bound by hospitality like any man. He has eaten and drunk at my father's table. And he heard Father say he would not let you be robbed. And anyway, he's too frightened of you to try to take it from you."

"I suppose you are right."

"Of course I am," she said, advancing on him and trying to pull the book from his arms. "Now please let me look at the book."

But here her confidence in her powers was misplaced. She had advanced too quickly.

"No!" he said.

She let go of the book and stood looking at him in perplexity. She was not used to having young men refuse what she asked. "You are very strange people, you vikingar," she said.

"I know my own property," he replied, walking away toward the ship. "If you do not, then you are the vikingr."

"Is this the courtesy your father taught you?" she called out to him across the sand.

He turned again and looked at her.

"I only want to look," she said, plaintively. "I have never seen a book before. It is so strange and beautiful. Please show it to me."

The first time that Leif had been a guest in Attor's hall in Twyford, he had eaten in the kitchen with the other children, where he had been teased by a dark Welisc-looking girl that he had taken for one of the cook's children, and tried to ignore. After the meal he and the other boys had crept into the dark corners of the hall and listened to the bards and storytellers. She had been there too, bright eyes in rapt attention to all that went on round the fire, like any other child. It was only later, when he found her monopolizing Thor's attention, and making Eric play games with her, that he had realized that she was the thegn's daughter.

Her power to attract and hold the attention of adults, and even older children, to have their faces light up at her presence, to have them lay aside their tasks happily to entertain her, and to smile wistfully after her when she left them, infuriated him, for he had no such gifts. He was the child of whom much is expected, but whom no one but Thor seemed to take any delight in teaching. And for as long as their visits lasted, this girl stole Thor from him.

The last time he had been there he had been granted the privilege of sitting at the table in the hall with the men and their wives. His place had been a very low one, far from the fire, but he had been at the table, in the same room where his father and Thor had sat with Attor and his chief men, and he had watched as the great men sat together at the high table, eating the best meat, drinking the best wine, sharing the secret talk of men. He had been allowed a cup of mead, and when it was empty, he had contrived to get it filled again, twice. Afterward, when he was being sick outside the door, she—a slim dark coltish girl then, all hair and limbs—had swept by him with a gaggle of followers, and had laughed at him.

In short she had infuriated him then, and she infuriated him now. She seemed to have no responsibilities of any substance, and those few she had, she neglected. Her father was impossibly weak and indulgent towards her, and she was contemptuous of her mother. And yet, she had an untamed kindness about her that would flash out of nowhere like a rogue breeze that can put a ship on its beam on a calm day. More maddening still, she could put on the full responsibilities of adulthood at a moment, as easily as she might put on a dress. In the hall last night she had played the lady with great boldness and assurance, sweeping away her father's timid plan for the evening, and drawing the whole sullen company into something almost bordering on merriment by sheer force of will, beauty, and charm. But in the morning, that lady was gone, and the petulant child was back, as if she had all along been a bold child playing dress up, though playing it so well that the whole adult world, himself included, had been deceived and charmed.

And yet she was no child. She was a woman. He was aware of her as a woman in a way that he had never been aware of any woman before. Despite all the burdens that were on his shoulders, despite his family's tragedy and his father's peril, his thoughts returned again and again to her hair, her mouth, her bosom, her limbs. He wanted nothing but to lead her away to some secluded spot among the dunes and lay her down. But it was more than that—far more. In his mind he had already made her wife, mother to his children, lady of his longhouse, and companion of his old age.

Madness of course. The rules of trade stood against it. His understanding with the Lady Sibbe back in Norway stood against it. Her undoubtable understanding with some rich thegn's son stood against it. Her certain indifference to him stood boldly against it. Her childlike unworthiness stood against it. He would require a far steadier companion in the trials that were to come. Sibbe might be no such beauty as Elswyth, but she was far steadier in temperament and the alliance the match would bring would be essential to any hope of his clan's recovery—if, indeed, Sibbe's father would still consider the match worth making, now that his family's wealth was gone and its numbers cut in half. Besides, Elswyth was half Welisc, and looked wholly so. The Welisc were a people fit only for slavery, as Elswyth's irresponsibility showed. To return home with such a wife as this would bring only contempt, and she would be treated very cruelly by his people—by the women in particular.

And yet, her mouth, her pleading mouth, her irresistible mouth.

"Very well," he said.

13 Angels and Valkyries

Leif walked towards Elswyth again, longing and foreboding making his feet unsteady. She ran to meet him, beaming, and took hold of his arm. She pulled him along a path that led toward the cliff face. "We can't go back to the hall," she said, "or Mother will find me. And we can't go to the ship because that is the first place she will look. But I know a place she won't find us soon."

She led him to a place above the tide line, under the lee of the cliff, and out of sight of both the village and his ship. There was a large low flat rock here that chance or design has surrounded with several smaller stones so that it resembled a table surrounded by stools. Several much larger boulders, from some ancient fall of rock, masked the small enclave from the beach, forming an area of privacy not unlike a hall in size or shape. It was just the sort of private place that he had imagined leading her to, and he could not help wondering if she had led him here for the purpose he had daydreamed of.

"This is my banquet hall," she said. "Here I rule over all my sisters. Hilda tried to claim the lord's place from me once, and I had to hold her down and twist her ears until she swore me her allegiance. Now you shall be a guest at my table and sit at my right hand."

In all his life he had never felt relief and disappointment in such exquisite conjunction as when he realized that she really had brought him here just to look at the book. She was a child hiding from her mother; not a woman seeking seclusion with her lover. A terrible wistful sadness came over him at the revelation, though he would have fled from the place at once if she had shown him any hint of carnal intent. He suddenly wished to be anywhere but in her company.

"Put it down here," she said when they reached the table.

He laid the book as she had directed him. She sat down in front of it on a long narrow stone that played the part of a bench to the table.

"Sit here beside me," she said, putting her hand in his arm to guide him into place. But this time he resisted the pull, broke his hand from hers, and moved away.

"Where are you going?" she asked, looking round at him.

He had not been going anywhere except away from what seemed a far too intimate seating arrangement. But then he saw something on the sand and went to it, stooped, and picked it up.

His back was to her, so Elswyth could not see what he had found. She got up and went to him. "What is it?" she asked, putting her hand on his to pull it down so she could see more easily. His hand held a skein of bright blue embroidery thread.

Her eyes grew wide when she realized that he had discovered a skein from the work basket that she had kicked over the cliff the day before. With anyone else, she would have laughed, careless of what they might think of her carelessness. But, somehow, with him, she was embarrassed by it, and therefore immediately vexed with him for having discovered the evidence of it.

"That's mine!" she snapped, trying to snatch it from his palm. But as she was about to grab it, he closed his hand around it.

He would not have done this with anyone but her. Honor, courtesy, and his native desire to please, would have had him return the find at once to whoever declared ownership. But she had bewitched him, cajoled him, bent him to her will—and he smarted at it. She had made him powerless and in her moment of embarrassment, he saw the chance to claim back some of the power she had taken from him.

He turned to shield the thread from her with his body and lifted it out of her reach while he examined it. "This is fine-spun lamb's wool," he said, turning again as she dodged round him, trying to grab it from his hand. "This blue was not made with heather dyes. This is expensive stuff. Do you know what price a skein like this will fetch?"

"Yes," she said, furiously, tears pricking in the corners of her eyes as she grabbed for it. "Give it to me." Her body brushed against his as she reached up after it, grabbing his arm to try to pull it down so she could reach the thread.

"Is it yours?"

"Yes." She abandoned her futile attempt to pull down his arm, stepped back, and glared at him. The memory of her body remained against his. He did not understand her anger or her embarrassment, but he was heady with it. He had found a chink in her armor.

"Why did you leave it lying on the sand?" he asked.

"What do you care. I tell you it's mine. Give it to me!"

He glanced around and spotted a splash of yellow a few yards off. He stuffed the first skein inside his jacket and crossed the sands to where the second skein lay. She raced him for it, but he got there first and snatched it up. Then they both saw a skein of crimson and this time she got there first, snatched it angrily from under his reaching hand. His hand fell upon hers for a moment, before she snatched it away, leaving another memory that would linger on his palm for days. Then he spotted a skein of green and beat her to it, stuffing it in his jacket with the rest.

In any contest such as this, Elswyth had no hope against Leif's size, strength, and speed. She glanced around her furiously, trying to identify the next target, but she saw nothing. She faced him, angry, embarrassed, a little afraid, and yet unbowed. "They're mine," she insisted.

"My salvage," he said.

Then she spotted her workbasket, lying overturned a few yards away. Rather than sprinting for it, she circled him, holding his eye with her angry glower as he turned to follow her. Once she was between him and the basket, she sprang for it. But he did not contest the find, for as she had turned him, he had spotted something bright tangled in a clump of seaweed, and took a few quick steps to retrieve it. It was an unfinished strip of embroidery with the needle still dangling from the end of the thread. She turned from retrieving the basket and froze when she saw it in his hands. Her face turned scarlet and she could not keep tears from her eyes.

Oh, why did he who loved her, who was obliged to her in courtesy in every possible way, rejoice to see her tears? What spiteful god had maddened him thus? "This is child's work," he said, examining the embroidery. And then he realized that it could not be. She would not be upset unless this inferior thing was of her own making. He understood his trespass then. He had seen a part of her that she was not ready to show him. He had seen some part of her weakness. He turned ashen with shame. He tried clumsily to conceal his crime, to give her some cover for her nakedness. "One of your sisters must have dropped it here and forgotten it," he said.

114

She flew at him and snatched it from his hands. He made no resistance to her.

"What do you know about it anyway?" she demanded.

"It is my business to know the price of goods and reckon the quality of work." He was aware of too few virtues in himself to let those he had go undefended. "Perhaps it was spoiled by the water," he added—another impossibly clumsy attempt to excuse her.

"It wasn't spoiled by water," she said, feeling the fire in her cheeks and hating it, hating him for provoking it. "It was spoiled by me. So now you know that I'm useless at needlework."

"It doesn't matter..." he began.

"Of course it matters," she snapped at him. "Does it matter if you run your ship up on sand or rocks? This is my work. This is what a lady is supposed to be able to do, and I can't. I should be able to keep the tension constant and the stitches even. But I can't, and I hate it. My hands are too swiving stupid."

He stood looking at her for a moment, remorse flushing over his face. He looked at the hands that she cursed. They were to him all that a woman's hands should ever be. He loved those hands. He wanted to take them in his own and press them to his lips. Remorse, abject and complete, flooded over him. He pulled the loose skeins from his jacket and held them out to her. She snatched them from him. Another memory of her finger's touch was imprinted on his palms. In instinctive grief and submission he fell on his knees before her and bowed his head.

"Forgive me," he pleaded. "Forgive me, Lady. I don't know... I am so sorry... I should never." He trailed off, unable quite to form the words to describe the crime of which he accused himself.

Elswyth was startled by this. She had been angry, for no man but her father had ever teased her in this fashion before, and her father's teasing had had none of the proud display of power that she had glimpsed in Leif. That experience had been wholly new, and quite alarming. But this sudden collapse into remorse was more startling still, and her heart went out to him at once.

"Oh," she said, embarrassed to see him so abject, "It's all right, really. I'm sorry I got so upset. It's just, I hate my embroidery. And I kicked my basket off the cliff when I saw your ship, so my Mother is angry with me about that. So I was embarrassed when you found it."

He raised his head and looked at her. "I should never have questioned your right to it," he said.

"I suppose it is salvage, technically," Elswyth said, wanting to be generous to him; wanting, desperately, that he would get up off his knees. "I lost it. You found it. Isn't that the law?"

"It is not courtesy between friends, between kin," he said. "It was not how my father behaved when he found you among his cargo. He returned you to your father. I should have returned your goods to you in the same way."

She went and held out a hand to him, bidding him rise. He rose as she bid him, though he avoided taking her hand.

"Friends," she said, pleadingly.

"Of course," he said, blushing. He was under her thrall once again. His attempt to break through the bars that held him had only left him more securely imprisoned.

"Can we please look at the book now?" she asked.

And what could he do then but go where she bade him go and sit down where she bade him sit, beside her, hip to hip?

They sat together as she directed. Elswyth opened the book and began to turn the pages.

He showed her the picture on the first page of the book, a picture of a monk or a priest in rich robes. She gave a small gasp of delight at seeing it and turned her head to smile at him a moment, in the shared knowledge of beauty.

"Look at the colors," he said. "Look at the nobility of the face."

"Oh, look," she said. "See, there is a bird in the tree outside his window. How pretty it is. I have never seen a bird with such colors. Show me more."

There followed several pages with nothing but rows of neat black letters, one above the other. She tutted in frustration and began to turn the pages so quickly that he was afraid that she might damage them.

"Where are the pictures?" she demanded, turning to him.

"Let me find them for you," he said. He began to turn the pages slowly. It was awkward, for she was so close beside him that it was difficult to use his right arm without brushing against her.

Fortunately, he soon came to another picture page. This time the picture was of a city. It was a tall and compact city, built in white stone and surrounded by strange trees. It seemed that the city was built on a beach, for it was surrounded with sand, yet the sea was nowhere in sight.

She poured over the picture, giving a little cry of delight every time she discovered a new detail. Her head was bent near his. Her hair smelled like a meadow in summertime. Then suddenly she turned to him, grasped his arm, and said, "Have you been there?"

"No," he said. To her, it seemed, his seafaring gave him a knowledge of all wonders. The truth was that the places he had been all seemed very alike to him. Their coasts, beaches, rocks, trees, all familiar. Their people not so different from his own, alike in manner and way of living. The Anglish holy men, with their books, their stone houses, and their strange teachings, were the most exotic creatures he had met in his travels. But even they were men like other men, who worked and traded and laid a good table for their friends. But no, there was one creature stranger still—this small quick dark girl, so full of delight and impatience. He did not want to confess to her how ordinary his travels were.

"I think it is not an earthly city," he said. "I think it is Valhalla. See the strange warriors, and the Valkyries in the air." He pointed to the pictures of winged men who floated over the city.

"Angels!" she exclaimed. "They are angels. The monk said that the book was called *The City of God*. This must be God's city. It is peopled with angels. Isn't it beautiful? Quick, turn the page, perhaps there is a picture of God himself."

Their shared delight, and the practical necessities involved in two sets of eyes looking at the same picture, drew them closer and closer together until she was nestled into his right shoulder and her left hand rested unconsciously on his knee. Neither noticed how close they had become, for their minds were all on the pictures, the scenes they portrayed, and how one might reach such countries. Questions and stories flowed from them like water from a snow-fed spring in April. They lasted for a good hour in this state of eternal present in which there were no angry mothers or imprisoned fathers, no ransoms to be won or dresses to be sewn, no joinings and no partings, no lust or longing, no frustration or debate.

This happy state was shattered by Hilda, who announced her presence with a loud and accusatory, "Found you!"

Elswyth looked up at her. "Go away, pest," she said. But the spell was broken and she was suddenly aware that her hand was on Leif's knee and his arm was around her back and her hair was intermingled with his beard as they both leant over the book.

"Were you kissing?" Hilda asked indignantly.

"No. Go away." Elswyth eased herself away from Leif, who was shuffling away from her just as fast in the opposite direction. The thought of kissing him had not occurred to her. She glanced at him, at his mouth, and wondered about it. Oh but that ridiculous scrap of beard!

"Father sent me to find Leif, not you," Hilda said. "Mother's really peeved, though," she added with evident relish.

"Your father summons me?" Leif asked.

"Yes. You are to come and see the monk. And Father said to bring the book."

"Thank you for the message. I will come at once."

"Were you kissing Elsy?"

"No. I was showing her the book."

"Elsy can't read."

"There are pictures, idiot," Elswyth said. "Not that you would appreciate them."

"I like pictures," Hilda said. "Maybe Leif would like to hide in the play hall and show them to me this afternoon."

"No he wouldn't" Elswyth said firmly, fearing that Leif would volunteer to do just that.

"Why? Am I too young for 'looking at pictures'? Does he only want to 'look at pictures' with you?"

"Don't you have work to do?"

"Don't you?"

"I've been doing it," Elswyth said, triumphantly, producing her embroidery basket, which had lain forgotten on the sands for the last hour.

"Liar," Hilda said. "You've been kissing, and I am telling Mother."

"Lady," Leif said, stepping in front of Hilda so that she had to look at him rather than Elswyth. "I have not kissed your sister. On my oath, I have not. I have been showing her the pictures in the book. I would be happy to show them to you as well, as soon as we are both free to do so."

"Has she been doing any embroidery?"

"Not while I have been with her, no." Leif was not made by the gods to be a discreet third party in a battle between sisters.

"Liar," Hilda said, looking around Leif at Elswyth.

"Mother sent me to find my basket, and I did," Elswyth said.

"Then you stayed here 'looking at pictures' with Leif. I'm telling Mother."

"If you do, Leif won't show you any pictures."

"He just said he would."

Both sisters glared at Leif. Leif paused and reflected while they glared at him. "I will keep my promise, Lady," he said to Hilda after a while, "but tattling is dishonorable."

"So is lying," Hilda retorted.

They both turned to Elswyth.

"Okay, you want to know?" Elswyth said. "I came here to look at the books because I didn't want Mother to find me. I might not get another chance to look at them and I didn't want to miss it. Leif found the basket and collected the threads for me. I wasn't looking for it."

"I knew you were lying."

"I said I was. Don't rub it in."

"I made that shirt Father gave you," Hilda said to Leif.

Leif turned and looked at Elswyth questioningly.

"I never said I made it," Elswyth said.

"I thought your father meant… That is why…"

"My embroidery is much better than hers," Hilda said.

"Yes it is," Elswyth said. "I wish you could make my dress for me. You'll have enough for six dresses before it is time for you to marry."

"You're supposed to do it yourself," Hilda said.

"I know. And I will. But while Leif and Thor are here, I want to look at the books and the ship and hear the stories. You can too, if you want to. But please don't rat me out."

Hilda wavered. "You promise I can look at the books?" she asked Leif.

"I promise."

"Okay. I won't tell Mother. For now."

"Thank you," Elswyth said, and she ran forward and kissed her sister on the cheek. Then the two sisters each took Leif by an arm to lead him back to the hall.

"What about your basket?" Leif asked.

"Bother the basket," Elswyth said.

"Bringing the basket will please your mother," he said.

"Nothing pleases her," Elswyth growled. But she ran back and picked up the basket.

14 The Making of Marriages

Attor had succeeded in persuading the monk to help them sell the books, arguing that Leif's only other option was to pry out the gold and jewels in the covers and scrape down the pages to sell them for scrap, a prospect that so horrified the monk that he had no choice but to assist in their sale into Christian hands. However, there was considerable debate about how the sale was to be conducted, for it was not safe for Leif to go to any monastery in Northumbria, and he was unwilling to send the books with a demand for payment, fearing that other holy men would feel, as Brother Alun did, that Leif had no right to them, and therefore would not send gold in return. Finally it was decided that Brother Alun would write a letter to his own abbot in Monkwearmouth describing the books and naming a price for them. Attor would then send Heorot to take the letter and return with the gold, a journey that was likely to take a week, especially if the abbot required time to raise the money.

This plan required the making of ink, since there was none of it in the village. Elswyth's request to help with the making of it was rejected on the sensible grounds that if the monk refused to look at her, her presence was not likely to speed the work. Leif, it was decided, would render any aid the monk required, and Elswyth would return to her embroidery.

She sat down next to Hilda on Hilda's usual bench by the hall, where the light was good. Elswyth could not help noting, with frustration, that Hilda's work proceeded much more quickly than her own. It was simply a matter of practice, she told herself. Hilda had picked up a needle when she was four years old and had not put it down since. She was a graceless child, she had few friends, and there was a plainness about her that suggested that she would have to content herself with few suitors in the years to come. And yet, her skill with the needle could not be denied. Hilda would never enchant a room with a song. She would never set a table that doubled the pleasure of the meal. But her needle would execute wonders. How could she begrudge her sister this one gift? Wishing to appease her conscience, she said, "After the letter is written, you should ask Leif to show you the books."

"He doesn't want to," Hilda replied sulkily.

"He said he would. He won't go back on it. There are some wonderful patterns in them. You could copy them in embroidery."

"You don't want me to."

"I didn't. I'm sorry. There's no reason why you shouldn't."

"I don't want to."

"Why not?"

"I'm not going to be alone with Leif in the play hall. I don't want to kiss him."

"Neither do I. But you could go to the ship. He keeps them in the ship."

"I don't like the ship."

This scandalized Elswyth. How could Hilda care so much for beauty and yet not see the beauty of the ship? "You don't like the ship? The ship is wonderful!"

"Someone would have to lift me into it. I don't like that."

"Not even Uncle Thor?"

"No."

"After he was so wonderful to you yesterday? You were weeping in his arms."

"I was tired, that's all."

"You should have gone to bed then."

"Shut up! I don't want to talk, I'm busy."

"You're not afraid of them, are you?"

"Everyone is afraid of them, except you and Father."

"And Mother, and Whitney and Moira and Daisy."

"Whitney is mad, and Moira and Daisy are babies. No one else likes them."

"You just hate everybody."

Hilda did not refute this claim. Silence reigned for some minutes before she spoke again.

"Do you want to marry Leif?"

"Because I was looking at a book with him?"

"I still think you were kissing."

"I'm going to marry Drefan. You know that."

"I think you want to marry Leif," Hilda said, eyes fixed on her stitches.

"You want me to sail away to live in Norway? That would suit you, I suppose."

"No!" Hilda said, vehemently. "You're so stupid some-times."

"Maybe you want to marry Drefan."

"No I don't!" For the first time, Hilda paused in her work and looked at Elswyth, so great was her indignation.

"What's wrong with Drefan?"

"He likes you. They all like you. It's not fair. I want someone who likes me."

"Someone will. Just wait till you grow up. They'll all like you too."

"Not as much as they like you. It's not fair. I'm the one who looks Anglish."

"It's not as much fun as you think, having men staring at you the whole time. You'll see."

"If you don't like it, you should cover your hair," Hilda said, tugging on a corner of her wimple.

"If you want them to look at you, you should uncover yours," Elswyth replied, tugging Hilda's wimple askew so that a lock of her mouse-brown hair escaped and glowed dully in the sunlight.

"No." Hilda tucked her hair back into place. "They won't stare at me like they stare at you. They'll say, 'How neat your stitches are! How straight your seams are!'"

"I'm sure they'll stare at you plenty."

"I don't want them to."

"Really?"

"It just causes trouble. Father will find me a nice husband. Mother says he will."

"Well of course he will. Mother will make him. Mother probably won't be happy until Father finds you an ealdorman to marry."

"Father found Drefan for you the year you were born," Hilda said, mournfully. "He hasn't found anyone for me yet, and I'll be of age soon."

"You should be glad he is taking the time to find the right boy."

"I heard him telling Mother that he was going to talk to Edris about Baldwinn for Moira."

"Baldwinn is too young for you."

"He should find someone for me first, before doing Moira!"

"Well, finding someone for Moira is easy. All she needs is a man with ears. He's taking more time to find someone just right for you."

"Because there isn't anybody right for me?"

Elswyth sighed. Hilda's self-pity was impenetrable. She returned to her former ploy. "You should go and ask Leif to show you the books."

"I don't want to! And I don't believe you care about the books either. I think you just want to kiss Leif!"

Elswyth, didn't answer this. The truth was, Hilda had put the thought of kissing Leif into her head. It hadn't been there before. Now it was. Despite his ridiculous scrap of beard and near barren upper lip, his mouth was in her thoughts. That brought thoughts of Drefan. Drefan was, after all, the man she was supposed to think of kissing. He was a man she had thought of kissing, more and more over the last year. Drefan had kissed her, of course. She had kissed him. But never on the mouth. Never as she had found herself—at Hilda's prompting—thinking of kissing Leif. And so, a little remorseful, she set herself to imagining Drefan's mouth on hers. And while she thought of this, she worked on the embroidery that would adorn the dress in which she would soon marry Drefan, and suddenly the work seemed pleasing to her, and she wanted to make it well enough that it would be pleasing to him also. She began to think that if he were to ride into the village now he would draw her aside, to some spot behind the hall, and touch his mouth to hers.

Of course, it would be a bad thing if he came now. It would be hard to explain to him about Norsk trading holy books so soon after Lindisfarne. The raid would have been an affront to Drefan and his father, the monastery being under their protection, almost within sight of their walls, and a place which they visited often and where they had many friends. No, it was better that Leif's business should be concluded and Leif away to ransom his father before Drefan came again to Twyford. And so she thought of Drefan's mouth and wished for his absence, but wished also for his coming later, after Leif's ship had sailed, and looking at her at last as Eric had looked at her, as Leif too had looked at her, in his more shy and courteous way.

She had no notion that Leif felt anything for her. He desired her of course, though his reluctance to touch her, to even let their hands brush against each other, contradicted the desire in his eyes. She knew the meaning of an eye that lingered. But lingering eyes had become such a familiar part of her experience that she had come to regard it as an ordinary feature of young men, without any individual significance. It was the men whose eyes did not linger that were the oddity: the monk, who admitted desire and was at pains to avoid it, and Drefan, her intended husband, who was entitled to desire her and yet could look at her and never show it, who seemed not to have noticed her transformation into womanhood, and continued to treat her as a child at every visit.

Drefan was four years her senior—quite enough to prevent any friendship developing between them in childhood. Drefan was always friendly, mockingly gallant, and slightly condescending, in a big-brotherly sort of way. He would often tell her stories of Bamburgh and its estates, and would talk easily of the time when they would be married. But he never seemed to look at her with desire. He never tried to be alone with her, never arranged to sit close to her, never brushed against her or let his hands stray. He seemed to regard their impending marriage as a natural and happy event, but without any urgency or desire for the wedding night or any of the things that pertained to it.

But while this had increasingly offended her pride, as the attributes of her womanhood had crept upon her, it had not caused her any anxiety about the appropriateness or eventual happiness of the marriage. She was confident enough in herself to assume that he did want her, and would show his desire, when it pleased him to condescend to do so. Every young man she knew confirmed, with longing stares and furtive glances, that she was desirable. Drefan was simply a man of greater rank, greater honor, and greater discipline than they, who would not idly betray his desire with dishonorable glances or errant hands. Besides, she too maintained the same reserve. To Drefan she presented the face of friendship and the face of fealty due to his rank, not the face of desire. Her eyes, her hands, made no more trespass than his. Her situation was not at all what her mother's situation had been. Her marriage to Drefan was promised. She had no more need of seduction than he did.

And if Drefan did not desire her, why visit as often as he did, why talk of their marriage and the lands of which she would become lady with such affection and ease? Whatever the promises their fathers had made to each other, nothing in the law required either one of them to marry against their will. If Drefan did not want her, he did not have to take her. If she did not want Drefan, she did not have to accept him. But for all the wistfulness of her heart, it had never occurred to her that she might refuse him.

She was aware, too, that her marriage would complete the work that her mother had begun. She was grateful to her mother for that—grateful that she had been born noble rather than slave—and quite content to return the favor by making a marriage that would secure the position of her mother and her sisters against any threat of a return to slavery.

It was an odd thing, she acknowledged, that when she thought about what would have happened had her mother not seduced her father, that she always saw herself, exactly as she was, born a slave, gotten on her mother by a different father. Why not see herself, exactly as she was, gotten by her father on Elene of Hadston, the woman he had been promised to before Edith seduced him? Well, because that girl would have looked like the tall, fair-complected, rather plain-featured Elene of Hadston, more or less; certainly nothing like Edith the small, dark, beguiling kitchen slave. Hilda might have been born to Elene, exactly as she was. Would she, Elswyth, then have labored to bake Hilda's bread, to fill her cup, to wash her feet and comb her hair? Oh, Mother, you saved me from that! How can I do less for you?

She looked forward to the marriage contentedly enough, therefore. Drefan was a good man—gallant, kindhearted, industrious, confident, brave. If she was not consumed with longing for him, neither did she have any dread of his marriage bed—the ordinary fears of maidenhood, of course—but no fear of cruelty or indifference. She would be the Lady of Bamburgh, and Bamburgh was a fine manor possessed of fair fields and woods. There were countless pleasures there. She would want for nothing. Her children would want for nothing.

And she would travel! As ealdorman, Drefan would make an annual progress around the district, which encompassed sea-coasts, islands, rich valleys, and high moors. And they would go to York, when summoned by the king. And the king would visit them, in his annual progress, and she would set a table for the king, sing for the king, present her children to the king.

None of this was Spain. But it was more than any kitchen slave would ever have seen. It was more than all but a few of the luckiest women in Northumbria would ever see. (And perhaps—but do not let the thought dwell!—perhaps one day, as their years grew on and thoughts of the soul's care became more pressing, perhaps, if Drefan should feel the weight of sin upon his conscience, perhaps she might whisper in his ear the thought of pilgrimage!)

And while her thoughts now played with the idea of Leif, with the thought of Leif leading her to a hidden place among the dunes, of Leif's hands withdrawing the belt around her waist, unwrapping the linen that bound her bosom, of the rasp of those calloused hands upon the softness of her flesh, of the sting of salt and the cry of gulls and the surge and fall of a ship before the wind—sweet St. Agnes, where did that thought come from! —she knew this all for the fancy it was. She was to marry Drefan. The embroidery she worked was for the dress she would wear to marry Drefan. Leif was a friend. A friend about whom she entertained impure thoughts, perhaps. A friend who perhaps entertained impure thoughts about her. But was that so unusual? He was not her first impure thought—Oh! Eric!. She guessed she was not his. Nor was he the first to have such thoughts about her. Those were legion. One did not marry because one only ever had such thoughts about one man or one woman. One married to purify those thoughts for one man or one woman. And she would marry Drefan, and he would think pure thoughts about her, and she him, and they would enact those thoughts upon their marriage bed, and would live happily and have many children, all of whom would live, for she would birth them easily, as Granny and her mother had.

***

She kept her head down and persevered in her work and was making some steady progress with stitches that were not too badly botched, until out of the corner of her eye, she saw Leif leave the kitchen and go trotting down towards the ship. Her feet wanted to jump up and follow him, but she schooled them, though she could not school her eyes, and her needle paused as her gaze followed his long lanky form as he trotted down the path to the beach. It was not till he was out of sight that her eyes consented to turn again to her work and her fingers started moving again.

Presently she noticed him coming back up the path, not loping his time, but walking with his head down and one hand held to his temple. As he approached, she could see that there was blood between his fingers.

131

15 Blood and Vengeance

"Watch my basket," Elswyth said to Hilda as she leapt up from her seat. She ignored Hilda's indignant reply and ran to Leif, pulling his fingers away to inspect the wound. There was a gash on his temple that was bleeding freely.

"Put pressure on it," she said.

"I was," he replied, putting his hand back in place over the wound.

"Come to the kitchen. We must put some honey on it to stop it from festering."

She led him to the kitchen as if he were a child. The monk looked up when she came in. He was startled to see her, and his hand darted up to pull his cowl over his eyes. Unfortunately, the hand that darted up was holding a candle. He yelped when the candle burned him, dropped it, and then patted out the flames that had started to catch in his cowl, singeing his bare hands.

Elswyth stepped quickly to pick up the candle before it set fire to the rushes on the floor. "Perhaps I should wear a bell around my neck so you can hear me coming," she said.

The monk did not reply, but looked sheepish and hunted around for a water bucket in which to cool his singed hands.

Elswyth took the honey pot down from the shelf and made Leif sit on a bench while she slathered the wound with enough honey to stop the blood from flowing. Then she ripped a rag into strips and used it to tie a bandage in place around his head to keep the honey on the wound.

"Who did this?" she demanded, when she was satisfied that the bandage would stay on.

"Boys throwing stones," he said with a shrug, as if the wound had come as no surprise to him.

"How many?"

"Two I think. Hiding in the dunes."

"This high?"

"About that."

"I know who they are, the little vermin. I'll fix them."

She stormed out of the kitchen and returned a few minutes later dragging two boys by the ears, which she was twisting fiercely. They screeched horribly, but though they were almost as big as she was, neither made any attempt to escape her, knowing what lashes they would suffer if they offered any resistance to their thegn's daughter.

"Apologize," she said, forcing them to their knees in front of Leif.

"Do not make them kneel to me," Leif said, getting to his feet. "If they are men, let them stand. If they are children, let them go."

She looked at him with surprise. It was the sort of thing she expected Thor to say, not Leif. She let go of their ears. They looked at each other, each wanting to know if the other wanted to run. But they did not run. They stood and faced Leif.

"You are freemen's sons?" Leif asked.

"Yes, sir," they muttered, eyes downcast.

"Your fathers broke bread and shared a cup of hospitality with me in your lord's hall," Leif said. "You have broken the laws of hospitality. Your thegn will want vengeance for my blood that you have spilled. With you, this is done with money. What is the wergild for drawing the blood of a lord who is your lord's guest?"

"More than their fathers can afford," Elswyth said. "The only way they could pay would be to sell themselves into slavery. Or sell these two."

The two boys looked very pale.

"There is always the old way," Leif said. "Simple vengeance. Man to man. Blow for blow. No need to tell your fathers, or the thegn. Would you prefer that?"

The two boys looked at each other, then turned back to him and nodded shyly. Leif struck the first, an open-handed blow to the ear that knocked him down but did not draw blood. The boy bit his lip to hold back tears and struggled to his feet. The other had tears already starting in the corners of his eyes, which he clamped firmly shut. Leif gave him the same blow, sending him sprawling. He struggled to his feet like his friend, cuffing tears from his eyes as he did so.

"Quits?" Leif asked.

"Quits," they said, looking at the floor.

"If we are at quits, look me in the eye."

They slowly raised their eyes to his and held them there.

"You bore my vengeance bravely," Leif said. "Shall we be friends?"

They looked up at him and nodded wordlessly.

He held out his hand to each in turn and they shook it, then stood gawping at him, with no idea of what to do next.

"Get out," Elswyth snapped at them.

They turned to go.

"Waes hael," Leif said to them.

They turned. "Waes hael," they whispered, and then turned and fled.

"That will be all over the village in the time it takes to sing Sext," the monk said.

"No," Leif said. "They broke hospitality. That is a serious matter, even among the Anglish. They will not boast of it. Besides, we are friends now. To shake a man's hand and call him a friend is as good as an oath, and no boy wants to be known as an oath breaker."

"Why do young men make friends with their fists?" Elswyth asked. She was curious, for she had seen it many times before.

"No man wants a coward for a friend," Leif answered, as if there were no mystery to it at all.

The monk, meanwhile, having cooled his singed hands and righted his equipment, had returned to his task. He held a bronze bowl suspended over a smoky tallow candle so that the flame of the candle gutted and flickered, and the oily smoke licked up under the corners of the bowl before rising into the gloom of the roof. He had jammed the rim of the bowl into the cleft of a stick and used it as a handle to hold the bowl over the flame.

"What are you doing," Elswyth asked him, circling behind him to avoid further accidents if he should look up and catch a glimpse of her.

"Making ink," the monk said.

"With a candle?"

"I am collecting soot. The soot of tallow is good for ink making."

"How long will it take?"

"Some hours to collect enough soot. Then I will boil it in flax oil and add a little glue, to make it bind properly."

"The day will be gone before you are finished," Leif complained.

"Writing is not a swift craft," the monk replied. "All must be properly prepared if the work is to succeed. Is it not so with your art? Must you not prepare well before you set to sea."

"Yes," Leif said, "but when our need is urgent, we put to sea as quickly as we can."

"But like any sailor, you must wait upon the tide, and I must wait upon my candle."

"If it takes this long to make enough ink for one page, how long does it take for a whole book?" Elswyth asked.

"At the abbey we make ink in large volume, from willow bark or oak galls. That process takes many days, but it supplies all the ink we need for a year. But to make a little ink quickly, this is the best method I know."

"There's soot all over the kitchen," Elswyth said. "Wouldn't it be quicker to collect that?"

"Candle soot is better," the monk said. "If my work is not of Abbey standard, the abbot may not believe the letter comes from me."

"I'll get more candles," said Elswyth, and she quickly rounded up five more candles and various small metal vessels to act as soot catchers, and soon she, the monk, and Leif were all seated at tables gathering soot as fast as they could with both hands. The monk sat at a table by himself with his back to them. Leif and Elswyth sat opposite each other.

It occurred to Elswyth that she could just as easily call Mayda or one of the other slaves to come and take over her candles so that she could return to her embroidery. But it was very pleasant to sit across the table from Leif and watch the light of the gutting candles play on his features. Even his scanty beard looked more attractive in this light. They did not speak, but each watched the other, and was aware of the other watching them. It seemed such a comfortable thing, a thing that felt familiar, somehow, though it was entirely new.

Once she said, "Does it hurt," meaning the wound on his head. He knew at once what she meant, and shrugged and gave a small smile of pleasure at being asked.

Once he shifted his position and his leg brushed against her dress under the table. He shifted again, so that he was no longer touching her, and she found herself wishing that he had left his leg where it was. She half wished to move her own leg to let it rest against his, but that would have been a different thing—a deliberate act where his had been an accident. She began to remember his arm around her back, her hand on his knee, as they had sat together looking at the pictures, and thinking how comfortable, how natural it had been. And her thoughts went once again to kissing, and, as she looked at his mouth in the candle flame, she found herself wishing that they had.

Her mind did not run as his did. In his thoughts he had already laid her down, explored her, mastered her, possessed and occupied her. Her longing, as yet, was just for a touch, a brushing of leg against leg, an arm around the shoulder, a brush—the lightest brush—of lips upon lips. Her thoughts had not yet led him to a bed of straw beneath a dome of stars. As a traveler, she relished every step of every journey, every flower in every hedgerow, every bird in every tree, every wind that sighed and stream that babbled. She had departed on a journey, without ever having intended to. She was meandering with no clear idea of her destination or any urgency to reach it, nor any thought at all of what she might be leaving behind.

And yet, when she caught herself thinking of his mouth— the mouth surmounting that jutting chin with its ridiculous scrap of orange beard—she was astonished at herself. It was not the attraction of sailors, with their hard hands, husky voices, and far-sailing ships that surprised her. Such thoughts were for her an old companion. It was the particularity of the desire that was new. If Eric had long been the image that had given body to the idea of a sailor, a bold far-voyager, she had long since got over any infatuation with Eric himself. But this so-slight lingering on the thought of Leif's kiss was stunningly particular, not a sailor's kiss, but Leif's kiss. Leif's kiss in particular.

After this realization came to her, she avoided looking at his mouth again but kept her gaze on the two guttering candle flames that she was teasing at the point of extinction, torturing their soot from them.

When they had enough soot, the monk mixed it with oil and the other ingredients and hung it over the fire to boil. He then asked for a goose feather. Elswyth went to find one, and Leif went with her, not because the task required two, and not because she had asked him to, or because he had asked if he could. It just seemed to each of them perfectly natural that they should go together, chatting easily as they went. They had fallen into ease with each other.

They returned with several specimens and the monk selected one and asked for a knife. Leif handed him a small knife—the tool for which he had gone to the ship earlier. The monk had sent him for it long before he needed it because Leif had been pacing endlessly and it had been driving the monk to distraction.

"I could have given you one just like it if you'd asked," Elswyth said when she saw it.

They watched him make the delicate cuts in the quill to form his pen and to make a few experimental strokes to test ink and pen.

"Are you ready to write now?" Leif asked.

"I suppose this will have to do," the monk said, sniffing somewhat disconsolately at both the pen and the ink. And then he glanced up at the window, said "Excuse me," and rose from the table. He made his way to the door, tripping over a bucket and walking into the doorpost because he kept his eyes on the ceiling to avoid looking at Elswyth. He stepped outside and was gone.

16 Granny

For a moment Elswyth and Leif were held entranced by the practice marks that the monk had made on the surface of the table. Leif touched one with his finger, which came back black and left a smear. He sniffed the ink and then touched it to his tongue, grimacing at the taste.

"Let me taste," Elswyth said, taking his finger in her hand and touching it to her own tongue.

"That's awful!" she said.

"I suppose it is not meant for drinking," Leif said.

"Granny would make it a medicine for something, I bet," Elswyth said.

"Where has the monk gone? To the latrine?"

"Oh, I know where he's gone," said Elswyth. "I'll show you. It's kind of interesting. But I think I'd better put the pen and ink away first. The slaves will be in here soon to start making dinner."

Elswyth found a safe place for the monk's tools, and then took Leif by the hand and led him out to see what the monk was doing. They found him kneeling before the great stone cross in the center of the village, chanting in Latin.

Leif wanted to interrupt him and get him back to his work, but Elswyth put a hand on his arm and said, "He prays eight times a day. He even gets up in the middle of the night to do it, though some nights he sleeps through and is all upset with himself in the morning. I think in the monastery there is someone whose job it is to wake them up to pray in the middle of the night. He asked the watchmen here to do it, but they forget. Anyway, it's no use disturbing him. He won't do anything until he gets to finish."

"He prays, but he makes no sacrifice? I don't see what good can come of it. Do you all do this?"

"We all say our prayers, of course, morning and evening. We pray to Ælfflæd and Cuthbert. I pray to Agnes, of course. And if a priest visits we have the Mass."

"Who are Ælfflæd and Cuthbert and Agnes? I thought you only had one god, the one you call Christ."

"Not gods, silly, saints."

"What is a saint, then? Are they like an elf or a dwarf or a troll?"

"No no. Oh, how can I explain it? A hero, I suppose. Only a holy hero. Ælfflæd and Cuthbert are our own saints— Northumbrian saints, I mean—so they are our special patrons and they look after us."

"And Agnes?"

"Oh, well, all girls pray to Saint Agnes."

"But why?"

Elswyth pursed her lips and flushed a little. "She is the patron of virgins," she said.

"A god of virgins?" Leif said. "This is very strange to me. We have Freyr, who is goddess of fertility. Women sacrifice to her to get children. But a goddess of virginity is strange indeed, for every people has need of fertility and increase."

"Well, if you say the right prayers on her feast day, Saint Agnes will help you find a husband."

"That is good service I suppose. But your husband was found for you long ago. Why do you still pray to her then?"

"I don't know. I like her, I think. She was a girl like me. And she was a martyr— they tried to make her a whore, but she refused and they killed her."

"You have strange heroes. Are you certain Brother Alun does not work magic?"

"The priest says that in the Mass he makes bread and wine into the flesh and blood of Christ. But Granny says you can't work magic with just words. You need blood or stool or something with sap in it, or a feather, or…well, all sorts of things really."

"It is the same with magic among my people," Leif said.

"You should come and meet Granny, while we're waiting," Elswyth said.

"Your father's mother?"

"No, Father's mother, Grandmother Edmunda, died three years ago. Granny is Mother's mother. Granny Hunith."

"Was she not in the hall for the feast? Why was I not presented to her then?"

"No. She won't come to the hall. She is still a slave. All the rest of the family are still slaves—Grandmother Edmunda made Father promise not to free any of Mother's kin if he wanted to marry her. Granny Hunith used to be her maid, until Mother ensnared Father. That's what Grandmother Edmunda called it—ensnared. But she hated her after that—Granny Hunith I mean. She didn't like Mother much either, though she always loved me—though she loved Hilda best, because she looks so much like her. But she hated Granny Hunith. She said she had egged my Mother on to seduce my Father—which I don't think is a bit true because Granny doesn't much like Anglish. So Grandmother wouldn't let Granny be her maid anymore. So even though Mother was Lady of the Hall, Granny Hunith actually had harder work to do. Anyway, she still lives with the slaves, and they all love her and take care of her now she is old. Mother wants her to live like a lady and wear jewels and take her meals in the hall. Father wouldn't mind. He never promised to treat her like a slave, only to keep her a slave. But Granny won't. She thinks the slaves and the free people would both resent her if she did. But we make sure she eats like us. We take her sweet cakes and wine all the time. Well, Mother does, and Moira and I do. Hilda doesn't. Hilda likes to pretend she's pure Anglish, so she pretends Granny doesn't exist. Would you mind if your children were not pure Norsk?"

"My people get wives from many lands," he replied. "We take them in battle or in trade. There are never enough women. Great men take many wives and concubines. And many women die in childbirth. Ordinary men are left with no one to marry."

"I suppose you could say Father got Mother in trade. My great-grandfather bought Granny from a Mercian, after all. Mother pops babies out with no trouble at all—like shelling peas, she says. And we've all lived, so far. Granny was the same. I have so many aunts and uncles. I expect I will be the same way."

***

Granny Hunith, was an elderly woman. Edith had been her last child and she was well past her sixtieth year, though no one seemed to remember when she was born, and if she knew herself, she was not telling. Hunith and Kendra had disputed for several years over which of them was the elder, for it was some distinction to be the oldest woman in the village. Kendra's impending death would secure Hunith her supremacy, an event she looked on with a mixture of triumph and regret.

She was sitting on a bench outside her hut, a spindle busy in her hands while she watched several small children—offspring of Elswyth's Welisc cousins—playing in the dirt at her feet. She was dressed in rough-spun brown like a slave, though underneath she wore fine-spun linen, so as not to itch from the wool. She had the face of an aging well-tanned cherub, framed with long grey hair that her various daughters and granddaughters, noble and slave alike, kept immaculately combed for her.

The children leapt up and ran to attach themselves to Elswyth's skirts when they saw her coming, begging for the nuts or apples that Elswyth usually had with her when she came to visit Granny. But today she had forgotten to bring anything, so she kissed each of them on the cheek and sent them away.

"Hello, Granny," she said as they approached. She and Leif were hand in hand, though neither had consciously offered a hand to the other.

"So you've brought your swain to see me at last, Elsy," Hunith said.

"No, Granny, this is Leif."

"Help me up, young man," Hunith said.

Leif offered her his hand and she pulled herself to her feet. She did not let go of his hand, however, but held him with one hand while she inspected him with the other, testing the muscle in his arm and forcing open his mouth so she could inspect his teeth. She lifted the corner of his bandage and made him bend over so that she could smell the wound.

"It's fresh, Granny," Elswyth said. "It wouldn't smell yet. I bound it with honey so it would not fester."

Hunith nodded. "Well, he's fit," she said, when she had completed her inspection. "Very tall. Tall men are good in battle, but it can be hard work birthing their babies. Big babies could get stuck inside a wee thing like you."

"I'm not having his babies, Granny."

"Waiting till the wedding, then? You are taking her on faith, young man? Don't worry, we're a fertile lot, and we birth easy."

"I'm not marrying him, Granny. I'm marrying Drefan. Don't you remember? This is Leif, the captain of the Norsk ship on the beach."

"Norsk? You still remember the old gods, young man?"

"We honor Odin, Thor, and Ran."

"And what of the Christ, then?"

"I will give no offence to your Christ, in his own country."

"Good lad. Will you be taking Elsy back to Norway, when you marry?"

"I am not marrying your granddaughter, Lady."

"Lady? You're not in the hall now, young man. I'm not an English lady, and I won't hear it said. You heed me?"

"Yes…"

"You should call me Granny, since you are marrying Elsy."

"He's not marrying me, Granny. I'm marrying Drefan. You would have met him several times already, if only you would come to the hall when he visits."

"I'll not go to the hall, and Drefan of Bamburgh will not come down to the slave huts to visit me. But this young jarl of yours, he comes to see me when you ask him to. He regards the whole of you, not the half. He will make you a good husband."

"But I'm not marrying him, Granny. Stop being dense. I know you're not really."

"She has a temper, this one," Hunith said, still holding on to Leif's hand. "But she has a good heart. Do not beat her. She will disobey you sometimes, but she will be sorry for it. She has a good heart, and beating would only turn her sour."

"I would never beat her," Leif said.

"You will be a good husband. She will be a good wife. She can't sew, but she will entertain your guests and take good care of your children."

"Granny…"

"You may tell your mother I approve the match," Hunith said, dropping Leif's hand and taking both of Elswyth's hands in her own. Then she pulled Elswyth close and whispered. "Come to me before your wedding night. I have a salve that will make things easy for you, and herbs to put in his food, and a charm for under the pillow."

"I'm sorry, Leif," Elswyth said. "Sometimes she's lucid as a bishop and sometimes she's just dotty. This must be a dotty day. Let's go and see if the monk has finished his prayers."

Elswyth kissed her grandmother goodbye. Leif bowed to her and thanked her for receiving him. They turned and walked back toward the hall, her hand falling into his again, without either of them noticing.

Hunith sat back on her bench, picked up her spindle, and watched them go, a contented smile on her face. She could always tell when the weather was changing, long before other people noticed the sun come out or the clouds roll in.

17 Drefan

Attor's messenger, Heorot, was dispatched for Monkwearmouth at first light the next morning. At about noon, Drefan of Bamburgh, Elswyth's intended husband rode into the compound before the hall with two companions.

At nineteen, all trace of youthful gangliness was gone from Drefan's form. There was nothing in his face or figure that suggested work not yet completed. His shoulders were broad, his beard was full and rich, his dark hair fell heavy to his shoulders. He wore red trousers of fine lambswool and a green tunic over a linen undertunic with embroidered cuffs.

Drefan was everything Edith thought that a nobleman should be. Attor, her husband, certainly was not. But then, if he had been, though he would probably still have laid her down beneath a haystack, he might not have married her. He would have acted honorably. There would have been silver for her trouble, and when she cropped, a marriage would have been arranged with a freeman, and she would have become a freewoman, and Elswyth would have been a freewoman also, for no man of

149

honor would wish to see his child a slave. But there would have been no marriage. There would have been no Hilda, no Moira, no Whitney, no Daisy, no whoever it was she now carried before her wherever she went. Not them, but another man's children, and, of course, she would have known those children as she knew her own, and loved them as she loved her own, for they would have been her own. Yet it was impossible to imagine that her own could ever have been any but who they were. And certainly none of those freeman's children, nor yet Attor's unacknowledged bastard, could ever have contemplated a marriage to Drefan, heir to the ealdorman's seat in Bamburgh—heir, indeed, to the kings of Bernicia of old.

A truly noble character must be infinite in grace and honor, and yet there must also be a certain hauteur to a truly noble spirit, for without hauteur, there could be no true condescension. How could those above behave with grace and honor to those below without hauteur? What was noble condescension, after all, but this—that height comes down to lowliness and does not abhor what it finds? The very hauteur of the noble spirit honors the lowly, for it says, you are low and I am high, and yet, in your lowliness, you are deserving of grace. The eagle may converse with the wren, and so honor the wren. But if the eagle cowers in the thicket when he sees the shadow of the falcon, he ceases to be an eagle. And if he is not an eagle, he does no honor to the wren.

Attor had raised up Edith. But he had lowered himself in doing it. He had lost his hauteur, become too easy, too familiar, too soft with those he ruled. He had stepped down even as he had raised her up, thinking it would make it easier for her, never imagining that it would rob her of half her victory. Perhaps she loved him better as a man for doing so. Perhaps it had indeed made it easier for her, for the step from slave to lady of the hall is steep indeed. But she felt always that in her climb she had missed the top step.

Drefan would make no such stoop for Elswyth. He would not lower himself to her. He would reach down and lift her up. And Elswyth, in her turn, would make that step with ease, for she had, when she chose to show it, all the grace and competence of a great lady, the hauteur of a great lady also, even if it was shown before it was earned. She would be Lady of Bamburgh, wife to an ealdorman of Northumbria, peaceweaver to a hundred estates, and she would dine with kings.

The embroidery on Drefan's tunic was Hilda's work, and this pleased Edith greatly. Hilda's work was as fine as that of most grown women, so there was nothing to fault in it at all. Still, Drefan knew it was a child's work, and wore it anyway— proof of his willingness to condescend. He had always been gracious to her children.

The young men who rode with him, his cousins, Drang and Earh were similarly handsome and well dressed. All three were armed with silver-hilted swords in decorated leather scabbards hanging from similarly decorated belts.

They came in at a walk, for they had met with Attor on the road as he was returning from the fields for lunch. Drefan and Attor were chatting, Attor walking beside Drefan's horse. Edith could not help but smile at her husband, much as the contrast grieved her. He was dressed in old brown trousers and a simple peasant smock and his face was red from the sun. His boots were clarty and stained, and he had a battered old hat on his head that would have shamed a freeman. It was Attor's way to lead by example rather than by fiat, and at haying and harvest he worked as hard as any freeman or slave. How else, then, would he have dressed for the fields? She herself was dressed not much better, for she led the work of the hall the way he led the work of the fields. It was not in her to be more haughty than her husband. With her daughters, it was another matter. They must dress to be the consorts of eagles, and both Elswyth and Hilda did so with pleasure, though only Hilda could be relied upon to

151

keep her dress as clean at the end of the day as it had been at the beginning.

Yet still it grieved her to see Attor, in his filth and sweat and plain garments walking at Drefan's stirrup, though Drefan himself gave no sign that he noted the distinction.

Drefan swung down from his saddle when he saw her and hurried as he came to embrace her, to save her steps as she came to meet him. "Edith, you look well," he said, taking a moment to admire her swollen belly. He had begun to call her "Edith" last year, after having called her 'Lady' all through his childhood. It had shocked her, the first time it had passed his lips, but she understood. He was a man now, and son of an ealdorman, and entitled to condescend.

"Attor tells me you have guests," Drefan continued. "We heard rumors of a Norsk ship seen along the coast and my father sent me to see that all was well."

"All is very well," she said. "But I am glad you came all the same. Elswyth will be delighted to see you. There is but a quarter of a year to go and you two will be married. You must be excited."

"I'll not wish the summer any shorter," Drefan replied. "But I look forward to autumn with special delight this year."

"As does she, I know."

"Where's Hilda?" he asked. "This tunic she made, the bishop thought it very fine and asked who my needlewoman was. We had a laugh when I told him it was a girl of ten."

"Twelve," Edith said.

"Is she? But it's a better story if I say she's ten. If I tell it three more times, I'll make her seven!"

"But you should tell her what the bishop said. She'll be delighted."

"I mean to. Is she near? Ah, here she is," he finished, for Hilda, ever alert for the sound of praise, had come around the corner of the hall—not running, but walking as swiftly as dignity would allow.

Drefan bowed to her and she curtsied to him—he was formal with Hilda as he was with no one else, knowing it pleased her and put her at ease. "Did you hear me tell your mother," he asked. "The bishop loves your embroidery. I think you may soon have a commission for a stole—though the poor man has other concerns these days."

"A commission?" Hilda asked, her face whitening and her eyes darting as if she feared he was teasing her and she was about to be laughed at.

"Certainly, Lady. You don't think I would wear second-class work do you?"

"No, Lord."

"Then I expect the commission will come in the week. Make him pay, and then make him wait. Patience is good for the soul, he tells me."

"How much?" Hilda asked, immediately practical at the thought of earning money in her own right.

"Oh, Lord, I don't know. But I know a woman in town who knows this trade. I'll ask her and send someone to let you know."

"Did you hear that, Mother?" Hilda said, turning to Edith. "I'm getting a commission."

"Maybe," Edith said. "Don't count your chickens just yet. As Drefan says, the bishop has other things on his mind since Lindisfarne. Now, go and tell Mayda we have three more for lunch and then fetch your sisters. You can ask your grandmother too, though I know what she'll say."

"Mother!" Hilda protested, indignant at having her moment so abruptly curtailed.

"Just go," Edith said. "Elswyth's already gone to the beach to fetch Leif and Thor." Hilda went, for obedience was part of her protest against the injustice that was her parent's preference for Elswyth. She did not go happily, but she went.

"Here's Elswyth now," Edith said, having turned toward the beach in hope of seeing her.

Drefan turned and looked along the path that led to the beach, where Elswyth, Thor, and Leif were approaching, Elswyth hanging on Leif's arm.

"Who's that with her," Drefan asked, an edge coming into his voice.

"Oh," Edith said, "that's Leif with Elswyth, and Thor behind."

"She seems very familiar with him," Drefan said.

"Oh, those two are like brother and sister," Edith said, placing a hand on his arm. "They have been for as long as Leif has been coming here with his father. And when I say brother and sister, I mean they are either quarreling or conniving, but quarreling most of the time."

"You're sure?"

Edith laughed. "What? Are you worried about Leif? Don't be. The day they came, I said to Elswyth that Leif was starting to look handsome. The first word out of her mouth was 'Yuck!' I told you, brother and sister."

And, as if to confirm Edith's words, Elswyth raised her head and noticed them and at once disengaged from Leif's arm and came running to meet Drefan, beaming.

"Drefan!" she said, coming up to him breathlessly. "How wonderful that you've come." She reached out two hands before her. Drefan took her hands but then drew her to him, looked into her face for a moment and then bent down and fixed his mouth on hers.

18 First Kiss

Edith was startled, for she had never seen Drefan and Elswyth kiss before, had not supposed they ever had. She watched as Drefan's hands disengaged from Elswyth's and went around her back to draw her closer to him. She was sure that Elswyth was startled by it as well, but as Drefan continued to hold her, continued to work his mouth against hers, Elswyth seemed to relax into it, and her arms went around him in return.

"Now, you two. Calm your horses," Attor said, laughing awkwardly.

Drefan released Elswyth, but his eyes did not immediately return to her face. He looked up at Leif and Thor, both of whom had stopped a few steps back, not approaching nearer while the kiss lasted.

Elswyth glanced a moment at Leif, and at Drefan's inquiring stare, and then she reached up a hand and pulled Drefan's mouth back down on hers. The men all looked away from the kiss, but Edith watched it, fascinated.

"Did you miss me, then?" Elswyth asked when the second kiss ended. Her face was flushed and there was pleasure and surprise mingled in her appearance.

"How could I not rush to you on a day so splendid as this?" Drefan said, gallantly.

"The weather has been splendid all week," Elswyth retorted.

"Ah, but I was…" Drefan began, but then stumbled seeking a gallant quip, and finished lamely, "…busy."

"Well, if you were busy, then of course I forgive you," Elswyth said, "Though I missed you terribly."

"Did you? I'm glad."

This time, Drefan's eyes lingered on Elswyth rather than rising to look at Leif again.

Edith felt a glow of pride in her daughter then. Clearly Drefan's kiss had caught her off guard, yet she had recovered her composure almost at once and had managed to both tease and flatter him, and had picked him up when he stumbled in his banter. It was masterfully handled. Yet she could also see in Elswyth's face that inside she was still reeling from the surprise of the first kiss.

Seeing that it was safe to look again, Attor came forward and said, "Well, Drefan, that ship you came to investigate, she is Norsk indeed, but just a trade ship. This is her captain and his first man. Come and greet them." He beckoned Leif and Thor forward. "Leif, son of Harrald, this is Drefan, son of Kenric, and his cousins, Drang, son of Tredan, and Earh, son of Piers. Drefan is heir to Bamburgh, and soon to be my son-in-law. Leif, and his father before him, have traded with us for many years. I am oath-brother to his father, which makes him oath-nephew to me."

"And oath-cousin to me," Elswyth said, keeping her eyes fixed on Drefan.

Leif stepped forward and offered Drefan his hand.

Drefan ignored it. Slowly he walked around Leif as if he were inspecting a cow at the fair. Then he did the same thing to Thor.

"How long have they been on your beach?" he asked Attor. "The news we heard said the ship was seen three days ago."

"Three days, aye," Attor said.

"They have been on your beach three days? Does it take so long to unload their goods and load yours?"

"They are my guests. We have been friends for a long time."

"But a good guest stays three days. No more. That is the custom. To stay longer is to presume on your host's pantry. So surely they will sail with the tide?"

"My wool production is delayed. Half my spinsters are with child."

That was a lie, and Attor made a poor job of telling it. Edith was surprised, for her husband was not given to lying. But she remembered that Attor wanted nothing said of the books in Leif's cargo, and it was because of the books that Leif and Thor could not leave their beach. That this would mean having to choose between Leif and Drefan had not occurred to her, and it surprised her that, when the moment came, Attor had chosen Leif.

Drefan did not seem to have detected the lie. He was not looking at Attor. He was looking at Leif, who had withdrawn the hand he had offered and was standing impassively, returning Drefan's gaze. Then Drefan looked away from Leif to examine Thor again.

"Which is the captain, again," Drefan asked Attor, "the oak or the sapling?"

"I am captain," Leif said, extending his hand again.

"You are Norsk, yes?" Drefan said, addressing Leif directly for the first time.

"We are Norsk."

"Heathens then?"

"We honor Thor, Odin, and Ran."

"You know what the heathens have done at Lindisfarne?"

Lindisfarne. Edith grew cold at the mention of the name. That holy place was now a name of dread. She looked at Elswyth, anxious to warn her daughter, if eyes alone could give the warning, that Drefan could not be shamed out of his anger as she had shamed Snell in the hall. But Elswyth made no motion to speak or to intervene. She was looking at Leif, with seeming confidence, though Lief was for a moment silent, pausing as Edith had noticed him pause before.

Then, without any betrayal of emotion, Leif said, "I learned of it from my uncle Attor. It saddens me. My people are traders. Now all Norsk are feared in Anglish lands, and that will ruin our trade."

Drefan's face curled into a sneer. "Ruin your trade, will it? Well, that is a tragedy. Let me tell you what it has meant to my people. What it has meant to me. I had a tutor, Father Billfrith. I served him poorly as a student, but I loved that old man. After many years of service to my father's household, he retired to Lindisfarne last year, where he promised he would pray daily for my soul. I am told that they found his body in the scriptorium. The vikingar had cut out his heart and his liver and daubed the books with them."

"I know nothing of that," Leif responded. "I weep to hear of it."

"What do you trade in, then? Slaves? Women? Boys?"

"Anglish wool is the finest in Europe," Leif said. "It is a cleaner trade than slaves. It does not need to be fed, nor does it soil the ship."

"If I were to look among your cargo, would I find tapestries and alter cloths, gold and silver crosses? Altar vessels set with precious stones? All such things as were the wealth of Lindisfarne?"

"I have seen the whole of their cargo," Attor said. "There is no monkish stuff among it. I have it in my storeroom if you want to see."

Edith had been thinking how proud she was of Leif for the way he handled Drefan's enquiry. Leif, or rather, Leif's father, whom he represented, ranked no higher among the Norsk than Attor did among the Anglish. It was right that he should be humble before Drefan. But it was also right that he should stand up for himself, and that he had done. But it astonished her to hear Attor again lie to Drefan, a lie more direct, more provably false than the first. Did his falseness seem so plain to her only because she knew the truth? Could Drefan really be as blind to it as he seemed? It was a lie that could ruin all if it were discovered. And there were so many ways it might be discovered. This was not her husband as she knew him, and it chilled her. He could not possibly have thought through what might come of it before he spoke. It was his cursed wistfulness, reawakened for Leif's sake. She glanced at Elswyth and saw that the same thought was in her daughter's head. But both understood that it was too late now to change the course that Attor had set.

Elswyth went to Drefan then, hugged him, laid her head on his shoulder, and said, "I'm so sorry. I remember Father Billfrith. You introduced him to me. He was a lovely old man. He taught me the story of Ruth. Do you remember? 'Intreat me not to leave thee, or to return from following after thee: for whither thou goest, I will go; and where thou lodgest, I will lodge: thy people shall be my people, and thy God my God'. I loved that story."

Drefan's eyes dropped from Leif's face then and looked down at Elswyth with a very genuine look of affection and gratitude.

"But Leif would never do anything like that," Elswyth continued, holding his attention by her look. "He is friends with our monk. Did you know we have a monk? Only for a little while until Kendra dies. But he's so funny. He won't look at me and he keeps falling over his feet because he won't look where he is going. But he's a lovely man too, really. And he and Leif are friends—old friends, for they met years ago. Why, the monk visits the ship, when he can."

"Visits the ship?" Drefan asked. "Why should he visit the ship."

It seemed to Edith then that Elswyth had gone too far in her praise of Leif's friendship with the monk, and she held her breath a moment fearing that her daughter would stumble for an answer. But Elswyth's answer came swiftly and surely, compounding her father's lie.

"They are friends. They drink beer and tell stories, I suppose, like you men do with your friends. You and Leif should be friends too. You both like beer and you both have such good stories to tell."

Drefan looked down at her.

"Please," she said, smiling so winsomely that it would be impossible to deny her. (Oh, Hilda, if you could only learn one tenth of that art!) "If we are to marry," Elswyth continued, "you cannot hate my friends."

She had won him over. The wren had stormed the eyrie and submitted the eagle to her will. Drefan turned to Leif. "Your pardon, Captain. You took me by surprise, I confess. We don't think much of Norsk in Northumbria these days. But if my lady vouches for you, I must take her at her word. A word of warning to you though. Be away as soon as your cargo is loaded, and do not put in to any other beach in Northumbria or you will certainly end up with a sword in your guts."

"I am aware of the danger," Leif said, extending his hand once again. "I thank you for your welcome."

"Did I say 'welcome'?" Drefan asked. "I don't recall. But welcome, Captain." He gave Leif a hearty slap on the back, but did not shake his hand.

"And you, sweet Goliath," he said, turning to Thor. "Welcome also." It seemed as if he thought of slapping Thor on the back, but then thought better of it. Neither he nor Thor extended a hand to the other, and Thor responded only with a nod.

"He does not speak Anglish?" Drefan asked, turning to Elswyth.

"Of course he does," Elswyth said. "Don't you, Uncle Thor?"

Thor replied only with a nod.

"And I speak Norsk," Elswyth went on. "Did you know that? I learned it from Uncle Thor and the other sailors. I speak Welisc too. I would like to get the monk to teach me Latin, but he won't be here long enough, and besides, he won't look at me. Would you like your wife to speak four languages?"

"As long as she scolds me in one I don't understand, and praises me in one I do," Drefan said. Then he grinned and bent down, lifted Elswyth off her feet, and extracted another long kiss from her, drawing her tightly into his embrace as the kiss continued, until Elswyth squirmed in his arms and dropped her chin to bring the kiss to an end.

When he released her and put her back on her feet, he turned and looked at Leif again. Leif's face was stoic. Of course it was, Edith thought, for Elswyth was like a sister to him if she was anything.

Then Drefan released Elswyth and turned away from her.

"Come, Captain," he said, clapping Leif on the shoulder again so hard that Leif almost staggered. "Show me your ship. I hear you Norsk are fine shipbuilders."

"Lunch is on the table, Drefan," Edith said. "Won't you sit and eat with us, and with Leif and Thor."

Drefan turned and bowed to her. "Forgive me, Edith," he said. "But I have eaten already. I stuff my saddle bags in the morning with enough to last me to evening, but then I eat it all before noon."

"Drang and Earh, will you join us?" Edith asked, seeing that the two young men were looking wolfishly at the table.

"Oh, they are as bad as me," Drefan said. "Come on, cousins. Let us go see this ship."

Edith noted both surprise and disappointment on the faces of Earh and Drang. Drefan was lying too. He had never refused lunch before in his life. He was simply unwilling to break bread or share a cup with Leif.

Drefan turned to Leif. "Captain, you won't mind if we delay your lunch a while?"

"Of course not," Leif said. "I would be proud to show you my ship."

"And Goliath, too."

"Thor," Elswyth said. "He's my uncle Thor, and I love him, and I want you to be polite to him."

"Then I shall call him Thor! Come, Thor, show me a ship so mighty that it can float your vast frame."

Thor again merely nodded.

"Let's go then!" Drefan said, and began to walk toward the beach, beckoning the rest to follow.

19 Haystacks and Plowboys

Elswyth started to follow Drefan toward the beach and the ship, but Edith called her back.

"What is it, Mother?"

"Wait a moment." Edith put her hand on Elswyth's arm and they watched as the men walked off together toward the beach, trying to sort out among themselves who should lead and who should follow, who was guide and who guest, who lowly and who high, and who among the high wished to have whom among the lowly to speak with. It was odd to watch how they spread out across the compound as they tried to sort themselves out, and then the process of deference and urging by which they worked out who should go before another when they came to the place where the path narrowed.

When they were well out of earshot, Edith turned to Elswyth. "Have you lain with Drefan already?"

Elswyth's face registered surprise rather than guilt. "No. Why?"

"He kissed you like you had."

"We haven't. I'm not lying."

"I believe you. You looked startled."

Elswyth frowned. "He didn't have to do it like that, in front of everybody."

"He hasn't kissed you before?"

"On the cheek. On the forehead. On the top of my head."

"Those don't count."

"No."

"So that was your first kiss?"

Elswyth's eyes glistened at the question. "I suppose," she said, defiantly.

Edith came and hugged her. "I'm sorry," she said. "It shouldn't have been like that. But then you kissed him back."

"I wanted him to look at me instead of Leif."

"I saw that. I told him he had nothing to be jealous about. I told him you and Leif are like brother and sister."

Elswyth stepped back from her. "We are not," she said. "Just because you treat him like a son does not make him my brother."

"You don't mean?"

"Don't mean what?"

"You're not..."

"You're as bad as Granny."

"What did she say?"

"Never mind. It doesn't matter. I like hearing sailor's stories. I like looking at the books. That's all."

"You're not upset with Drefan, then?"

"The only reason I was ever upset with Drefan was because he kept treating me like a little girl."

"You got your wish then."

"Yes..." But here Elswyth grew wistful. "I just wish... What was the first time Father kissed you?"

Edith smiled. "Pentecost, after the feast. He came into the serving kitchen looking for more wine. He was very drunk. I was whipping cream for the pudding. He stumbled and I caught him. We looked at each other—we'd been looking at each other a lot since Christmas—and I saw a look in his eye so I tilted my head back a little and he took the hint."

"What was it like?"

"Sour. He was very drunk. And then he burped."

Elswyth giggled. "Oh, Mother, that's awful. At least Drefan was sober. I just wish it hadn't been…"

"I know. I'm sorry about that. But at least you know he really wants you now."

"I suppose. You don't think he just did it because…"

"Because Leif was there? No. I'm sure not. Maybe it took Leif being there to make him want to show it."

"You think so?"

"Of course. Oh child, they all want you. You know that. I was that girl once. I remember."

"Sometimes I wish I wasn't."

"I know, believe me. It's harder when you are a slave, and every man thinks he can have you."

This clearly came as a shock to Elswyth. Edith watched her face work a moment. Elswyth knew, of course, what it was like for every man to want her. But every man on the manor knew well that he could not have her. It had not been so for Edith, and now, it seemed, Elswyth understood.

"How awful, Mother. You never told me."

"Your father put a stop to it. I think maybe that is when he started to notice me. I mean, notice more than my figure and my face. He rescued me from under a plowboy behind a haystack. After that… Well, by autumn, I was under him behind a haystack."

"Mother! The plowboy didn't…"

"No. Your father didn't give him the chance, thank God. I bit the plowboy's lip and he boxed my ears for it and then your father pulled him off me and gave him a kicking. The wergild for assaulting a thegn's kitchen slave isn't much, but he didn't have it, so your father made the plowboy sell himself into slavery to raise it. After that, the rest left me alone. But darling, you understand, don't you? No one would ever lay a hand on an ealdorman's wife, nor any of her kin. No matter what might happen to your father... When you are Drefan's wife, your sisters will be safe."

Elswyth turned and hugged her mother. "When you used to say 'safe', I thought you just meant from Fyren. From losing the manor. You never told me about that."

"Not a thing to tell a child. But you are not a child now. I needed you to know."

Elswyth broke from her mother's embrace. Dabbing her eye with her sleeve, she said, "I should run down to the beach and make sure they are getting on. Drefan's in a mood, and I can help keep him sweet."

"No," Edith said. "Let them be. We want them to make friends, and they won't do that while you are around. It's their way. Young men will test each other. They will push and boast and even fight, and come out of it firm friends. But not when there is a woman in the middle. A man will never court his friend's woman, but he will never stop courting his rival's woman. So let them become friends before you put yourself between them. Your father will keep them from coming to blows. Besides, all Leif's men are there, and Leif is not going to start something, no matter how stroppy Drefan gets. When your sisters get here, we should all eat together and then leave the table to the men when they get back."

Elswyth frowned. She did not like to be left out of any conversation.

"You are a fine peaceweaver, my darling," her mother said. "But you have to learn to leave men be sometimes. They need to talk their own talk, just as we need to talk ours. Besides, you have a great deal of embroidery to do if your dress is going to be ready for your wedding day. Enough of looking at books and listening to stories. You have work to do. If Drefan decides to stay for dinner, you can sing and tell stories this evening. But this afternoon, give Leif and Drefan a chance to get to know each other. They are both good young men, and Drefan has dined with many a Norsk before this business at Lindisfarne. But if you are around, it will just be more showing off and bluster. Have your lunch and then—I can't believe I am saying this— take your work basket up on the cliff out of the way and get on with your work."

Edith turned to look for her other daughters and saw that Hilda, Daisy in her arms, was standing close behind her, glaring at them.

"Oh boy," said Elswyth, looking at her sister's grim face. Hilda had a gift for hearing more than she was supposed to and it did not serve her well.

Elswyth took Daisy from Hilda and beckoned Moira and Whitney to take their places at the table. Edith beckoned Hilda to her. "How much of that did you hear? And what part of it has you so upset?"

"The plowboy," Hilda whispered.

"Oh, sweet love, don't worry about the plowboy. He's long gone."

"But if something happens to Father... Uncle Fyren does not like us, because we are half Welisc, even though I don't look it at all."

"You will be quite safe, pet. Drefan and Elswyth will not let anything happen to us. No matter what Fyren does, you will never have anything to fear from plowboys."

"This one ought to be a boy," Hilda said, rubbing her mother's belly.

"Maybe it will. I dream it is a girl, but it kicks like a boy. But it doesn't matter. Drefan will keep us safe. Besides, why should anything happen to your Father? He's healthy as a horse."

167

"Elsy didn't like it."

"Didn't like what?"

"The kiss."

"He took her by surprise is all."

"She didn't like it."

"She didn't like that he did it like that in front of everyone."

"She didn't like it," Hilda repeated, stubbornly.

"She kissed him back, pet."

"Do I have to get married?"

"Do you want to be a nun?"

"Maybe…"

"What's upset you, really? Drefan or the plowboy?"

"The plowboy…" Hilda whispered, wrapping her arms around her mother and putting her head on her shoulder.

"Your father will find a good man for you to marry, and he and his kin will protect you and your children."

"I meant what the plowboy did to you."

"But he didn't, dear. Your father stopped him."

"But if he hadn't…"

Edith had no answer for this but to draw Hilda into a tighter embrace. But that moment of comfort did not last long, for there was a violent collision against their legs as Whitney—as avid for hugs as Elswyth was for conversations—threw herself into the embrace and beamed up at them blissfully. Hilda kissed her mother then bent and kissed Whitney before taking her place at table. Edith and her daughters ate in silence for a while. Even Moira kept silent, aware that some cause of somberness had come over her mother and her elder sisters. But it was not in Moira to restrain her tongue too long, and soon she began to gossip again and soon they were all talking and laughing, and even Hilda and Elswyth were affectionate and merry with each other.

20 The Price of Virginity

After lunch, Elswyth did as her mother suggested, carrying her embroidery basket up the cliff. She had not made much progress on her embroidery, however, before her mother came laboring up the cliff path.

"Drefan wants to take you riding," she said.

"Mother! Why did you climb all the way up here yourself? You could have sent Moira."

"I'm not an invalid. And I wanted to talk to you."

"What about?"

"Drefan. I don't know what's in his head."

"He's taken me riding lots of times."

"But he's never kissed you like that before."

"You mean you think…"

"I don't know what to think. He won't hurt you. I know that. But I know what you think about me and your father, and I want to tell you—" Here Edith paused to swallow before continuing. "My darling, you don't want to end up with a child that hates you the way Hilda hates me."

"She doesn't hate you. She was just crying in your arms about the plowboy."

"I am the only mother she's got. When she needs to weep, she comes to me. But she hates who I am. She hates what I did."

Elswyth snapped the head off a buttercup and set it floating on the breeze. "She wouldn't be a thegn's daughter if you hadn't done it. She'd be a slave and never have had a needle in those precious hands of hers."

"I think she imagines she would have been the daughter of your Father and Elene of Hadston."

"How horrid of her!"

"Have you never imagined having someone else for a mother?"

"How could I? We look just the same."

"But Hilda doesn't. She'd be pure Anglish if it wasn't for me. And your daughters won't all look like you. I'm just saying, you have no cause to give yourself the same grief I suffer."

Elswyth stopped to consider this. It had not occurred to her that Drefan, whose treatment of her until today had been so chaste, might suddenly desire to lie with her. But nor had it occurred to her that he would kiss her with such hunger as he had done. And now that her mother had put the thought into her head, she could not laugh it off. She had for so long wanted him to show signs of wanting her. She had craved proof of ardor. They were to marry because of a promise that their fathers had made long ago. But she longed for what her mother had had—a marriage born of passion and affection. A passion irresistible, enacted beneath stars behind a haystack. It might be sinful in Brother Alun's eyes, but to her it seemed to have a purity to it—a dignity not to be found in two old men shaking hands over the fate of a little boy and a baby girl. But today? And if today, would that be proof of ardor or an act of jealous possession?

She plucked another buttercup and set it free on the wind. And then another thought came over her, part dread and part exculpation.

"I can't lose him either," she said.

Now it was Edith's turn to fall silent.

"Why should you lose him?" she replied after a moment, but there was doubt in her voice.

"But what if? What if he expects? What if I refuse?"

Edith was silent again for a moment. She came and lowered herself gingerly down to sit beside Elswyth. She looked at her daughter, and then turned and looked out to sea. After a moment's anxious contemplation, she said, "You must be careful not to lose him. Would you mind so terribly if—"

Elswyth felt her heart stop. Could her mother really be asking this? And yet, was this not exactly what she had longed for?

"It's not that I would mind, Mother…." But some part of her did mind, though what or why it minded she could not quite express to herself. "But I wouldn't want my daughters to hate me."

"Oh," said Edith, embracing her daughter, "I'm sure they wouldn't. I'm sure they wouldn't. Forgive me. I shouldn't have said anything."

"But if he did, Mother, what would we do then?"

"If he refused you? If he refused you, and then your father died, and the estate went to Fyren? I suppose I would go to a nunnery. They would take me in and help me find husbands for your sisters. And they would take care of Whitney when I died. Or I could marry again, though I don't know if I could bear to lie with another man, or if I could find a widower willing to take us all in, especially Whitney. It would be no trouble to find a husband for you. But, my darling—" Here Edith paused and looked at the ground. "My darling, there is something you don't understand."

"What, Mother?"

"I have never said this to anyone," Edith said, husky voiced, as if she were a child, ashamed and yet defiant. "It could lose us the marriage if I said it too soon. But when you are married to Drefan, you will get your morning gift. Land, money, horses, cattle, slaves, all your own, to do with as you please. Far more than your father's estate. I have been planning for so long to come to you and beg you to buy your grandmother, and Mayda, and all the rest of my kin from your father. Then you could give them their manumission and land to settle on."

Elswyth's eyes grew wide at this. "Oh, but of course, Mother! Of course I will. But will they want to leave? They all seem happy here."

"Because I make sure that they do not go hungry, that they are not worked to death, that the women are left alone. Why do you think your father does not go hawking? Why do you think we have not given you a horse fit for a lady? Because the money goes to keep them from misery. But if Fyren were thegn, it would be different. Hilda loves to tell me that virginity is a pearl without price. But I know the price of virginity. Twice I have had thegns try to buy Mayda from us. And I know the difference between the price they will offer for a kitchen maid and the price they will offer for a concubine. I know the price of virginity in Northumbria today. I know it to the shilling. I can't tell Hilda this, not yet. But I could never have kept my virginity. All I could do is choose the thegn who took it."

"Oh, Mother, I never knew."

"I never wanted you to know. Not till you were grown. Not till you had the wealth to make a difference. But you understand, don't you? Only Drefan's morning gift will be enough. Your father can sell them, but by his oath to his mother he cannot free them, and to sell for less than they are worth would be the same thing. You must buy them all, at full price, so that your father can keep his honor and his oath. Only Drefan's morning gift can provide such wealth."

The weight of this settled on Elswyth's heart.

"But you will still need people," she said.

"And we will buy the people we need with the money that you pay for our kin. I know where I can find a family of Picts, so that I can keep them all together. I know we can't run a manor without slaves, but my kin, your kin, will be free."

"Then I really cannot lose him," Elswyth said.

"You really cannot lose him," Edith replied. And then she put her arms around her daughter and tried desperately to keep tears out of her eyes.

They remained in each other's embrace for a moment, each with their thoughts a whirl of anxiety, hope, and desire. And then Edith, having fought back the tears that had been rising, said, "Well you better hurry along. I'm sure I'm worrying about nothing. I told Gwilym to saddle Spotty so he will be ready for you when you get there."

***

Spotty was an elderly pony that Elswyth shared with her sisters. Elswyth had been complaining for two years that she had outgrown Spotty, but her mother had scoffed at the very notion of letting her have a swifter mount. Over the hills she would have been, she reckoned, and never seen again. Elswyth had complained bitterly at the injustice of this judgement. Only now did she understand the true reason, and it filled her with a renewed affection for Spotty. It was Elswyth herself who had given the pony his name, sometime in her seventh summer, when the pony had been sprightly and hers alone, and its grey coat spotted white had seemed to demand no other name. But now, the coat, the pony's age, and his low stature all made Spotty look vaguely ridiculous beside the tall horses of the young men. Drefan grinned at her when he saw her ride up on Spotty.

"Don't forget that you promised me a proper horse for a wedding present," she said, smarting at his grin.

"Oh, I intend to see you properly mounted," he replied.

173

She blushed at this and stuck her tongue out at him.

"It should be today, if only your mother would consent," he added.

This time it was she who was stuck for a riposte. Now she felt absurd on Spotty's back beside Drefan on his tall stallion, Sherwyn. The horses of Drang and Earh were almost as tall as Sherwyn, and so they looked quite a comic party as they rode out of the village. Spotty, in natural deference to the superior animals, took up the rear of the party. Elswyth, anxious for his dignity as much as her own, tried to urge him forward so that she could ride beside Drefan, but Spotty knew his place in the order of creation and refused to budge from it.

A few minutes outside the village, two young women were waiting for them. One was Willa, the oven keeper's daughter. She was a few years older than Elswyth and a classic Anglish beauty, flaxen haired and as plump as any man could wish for, for her father's trade kept his family's table well supplied in good years and bad. The other girl was Elwyna, who had not, to Elswyth's eye, any reason to hope for a husband above her station, but who followed Willa's lead in all things. It was well known that Caflice was in love with Elwyna, and Caflice had shown enough prowess as a hedger and a thatcher that his living was secure. Elwyna should have been very happy to have him. But there she was, waiting by the roadside for the young thegns to ride by.

A year ago, Elswyth had seen Willa hop up onto Drefan's saddle, in this very spot, where no eye would have seen them, had that eye not been deliberately following and spying. Elswyth had burned with fury for days after witnessing this scene, until she had heard Drefan speak of Willa with such contempt that she had thought he could not possibly have desired her. Still, the thought of her mother's tryst beneath the stars, and the subsequent disappointment of Elene of Hadston, was not far from her mind whenever she saw Willa. No, it was not impossible that she could lose Drefan.

The meeting was not one of chance, nor was it Willa's initiative that had brought the two of them to this place, for Willa said, "What took you so long?" to Drang as he hauled her up ahead of him in the saddle. She made this ascent with practiced ease, while Elwyna struggled clumsily to get up in front of Earh.

Drefan turned in the saddle and looked back at Elswyth as if to ask if she wanted to come up and ride on Sherwyn, tucked into his belly in the same way that the other girls were mounted.

Well, it was clear now what was in Drefan's mind. Willa and Elwyna were not the women they would have chosen to take for a picnic and conversation. Nor would they have arranged to meet them in secret if their intent were innocent. Not beneath stars behind a haystack would her moment come, then, but under a blue sky in the greenwood. But did that matter? Was one less romantic than the other? It did not feel so. But would her daughters hate her if she did?

She pretended not to have seen his invitation, and he turned forward in the saddle, and led the party forward again.

"Where are we going?" she called out to him.

Drefan turned in the saddle. "You choose," he called back, a little sourly.

Was she to choose? Had he not chosen already? Or was that what he wanted of her, more even than her virginity, her choice?

"Then I choose Longhoughton," she shouted. But why make her choose at all? Surely he did not plan that they should reach Longhoughton.

She had not read the situation wrongly in any particular. After they had only gone a mile or two, the young men brought their horses to a stop in a clearing full of high grass and wildflowers. Drang and Willa wandered off in one direction, Earh and Elwyna in another, and Elswyth and Drefan were left alone together.

He looked at her, as she had long waited for him to look at her, not with jealousy or possession as he had by the hall, but with affection and wonder, looked at her as her father must have looked at her mother once, behind a haystack, under the stars. Proof of ardor then, not jealous possession after all. Did this excuse her? Did it absolve her of her mercenary motive, her need to keep the marriage at all costs? If she lay with him in this mood, it would be for affection only, not for the ransom of her kin. She looked into his face again and saw there all the ardor she had longed for.

21 The Cusp of Womanhood

The day was warm and a slight breeze rustled the high canopy of leaves above them. The grass all about them on either side of the narrow path was near waist high and full of wild flowers. The sky above them, where it showed through the canopy, was very blue, and the sun made the leaves of the canopy glow a brilliant green. Birds chirped and cricket sang. A rabbit passed by, getting quite close before he noticed them, and then scurried away, embarrassed at having almost disturbed the lovers.

They were both curiously aware of all of this, though the gaze of each was focused on the other. And yet, to each of them, the place mattered. It had to be a place of joy, a place of dignity, a place of happy memory. Drefan gazed at Elswyth for a long time, then turned his eyes away and looked around, assuring himself that all was as it should be for the moment to come. Elswyth looked around, too. She looked for some misshapen tree, some cleft stone by which she would be able to remember this spot, by which she would be able to return to it in wistful remembrance, so that she might one day bring a daughter, on the cusp of womanhood, to whom all must be explained, and say, "This is the spot. Here you were made. Do not hate me for it."

She had been waiting for his initiative, but, now that this moment was upon them, he made no move toward her. Perhaps he considered that he had already made the first move, when he had kissed her before the hall in front of her parents. Perhaps his desire now was that she should take a step toward him. Perhaps his pride demanded this. Perhaps his courtesy granted this privilege to her. Or perhaps this was for him, for all his experience, a moment as uncertain as it was for her.

A man marries later than a woman, and thus there is a time, in the life of a young man of means, when he is prey to a pretty kitchen slave, to a buxom oven keeper's daughter. Drefan need hardly have lifted a finger to have such as Willa, to have such as her own mother had once been. Elswyth did not doubt that he had lain with such as these. She was resigned that he would not come to her a virgin.

And yet, he did not look at her now as if this were some routine pleasure taking. And her mother had been right—he did not behave to her now as he had when Leif was present. Then he had expressed an easy and familiar possession. But now he stood opposite her with a look on his face that spoke tenderness, uncertainty, even a kind of reverence.

God makes many kinds of lovers. Some couple with greedy haste. Some with easy laughter. Some with submission yielding to conquest. Some with slow awe. Elswyth had expected easy laughter, for her mother and father were lovers of that kind. But Drefan was not such a man. With any but her he would have been a man of greedy haste. But he was not so with her, for the truth, which she could never have guessed, was that he was in awe of her. That he was worthy, by blood and birth and courage, of the most beautiful, the most lively, the most charming, the most enigmatic woman between Tyne and Tweed, he had no doubt. That she was that woman, he alone had the experience to know. In accompanying his father on the ealdorman's progress around the district, he had met every thegn's daughter of note, several of them pretty and accomplished young women. But none were like Elswyth in his eyes.

She was beneath him. He did her honor to raise her. Yet in his eyes she was the pearl beyond price. She was his, not because he was worthy of her, but because she must have a husband, and no man was more worthy than he. She was both beneath him and above him, and the contradiction made him shy.

Seeing him hesitant, and charmed by the adoring look she saw in his face, she took a step toward him, her skirts rustling as she moved through the tall grass. She stood before him and offered him her hands, which he took. He had fine strong hands, though not rough like Leif's. Sword and spear shape a hand differently than rope and oar. The grip in which he took her hands—small hands, shaped by spindle and needle and idle wandering—expressed both strength and gentleness. She looked up at him and tilted back her head, just as her mother had done in the serving kitchen so many years ago. But the mouth that descended to meet hers was not sour. There was no belch. His breath was sweet, and, unlike the kisses he had given her before, this one was gentle, even tentative. It was as if he remembered that he owed her a first kiss, with all the hesitant enquiry that a first kiss demanded.

The result was not entirely satisfactory. Perhaps a first kiss can never satisfy once its place has been usurped in the grand order of kisses which must constitute a courtship and a marriage. It was a fourth kiss pretending to be a first, and so lacked both the charm of the first and the ardor of the fourth.

Still, there was much more to the great arc of their coupling, the coupling which would last till death, than an imperfection in a single kiss. She was not going to spoil the far greater first that was now before her by pouting about the imperfection of a single kiss. She kissed him again.

Imperfect still. But what art is mastered at the first attempt? Diligence is required for perfection in all things, and surely the diligent pursuit of perfection in kissing would be less laborious than the pursuit of perfection in needlework.

Try again.

The third kiss was better, perhaps. A little better.

But they were here for more than kissing. If there was imperfection in the kisses, did that mean there would be imperfection in the greater conjunction as well? She stepped away from him and cast her eyes down. Let him take this for coyness. Was not coyness part of this, a proper and a necessary part? If she were too bold, surely that would spoil it for him. Oh! Had the kisses been as imperfect for him as they had been for her? Oh! How was one to know such a thing? She turned and looked at him again, searching his face for signs of satisfaction. Should there be perfect knowledge between lovers? Did they who became one flesh also become one mind? Did he know her doubts? Did he sense the imperfection of their kisses? And in the moment of consummation, would the whole of her mind be laid bare to him? And if it were, could she bear to show him all that she held there?

He lay down on his back among the long grasses and held out a hand to her, inviting her to condescend to him. She lay down beside him, leaving a little distance between them, a comfortable distance for holding hands and gazing at the glow of the forest canopy and talking softly of the things that courting couples talk of.

But neither spoke. Voluble as they both were by nature, the impending moment hushed them. He turned his head to look at her face, sunlit through a fringe of wildflowers as she gazed upward toward heaven. Welisc she was, in every feature. An inferior breed. And yet he had long fancied that there was something of the fair folk about her. Nonsense, of course, but could it not be that those conceived in field and forest might have some touch of the fey about them? Might she and he, this day, conceive another such child as this?

Her hand found his and he took it lightly, his thumb gently caressing her palm.

"No one would see us from the path, would they?" she asked.

"No one is like to pass this way," he replied. "Besides, Sherwyn would give the alarm if a stranger approached him."

She could hear the sound of their horses champing the grass nearby. The closeness of any creature, particularly a creature so much a part of her childhood like Spotty, made her shy. But Drefan was emboldened by her question, for he thought that she would not have feared discovery if all she thought they were to do here was to stare at the sky. He rolled toward her and placed a hand on her belly, propping his head up with the other hand as he looked at her. He had to beat down a patch of daisies that stood between her face and his and popped back up, insubordinately, as he tried to brush them aside. On the third try he pinned them down with his elbow and they both laughed. The thumb—just the thumb—of his left hand slowly caressed her belly as his hand lay across her.

22 Promise and Pleasure

It was the simplest of caresses, and yet Drefan's thumb inscribing small circles on her belly was a touch of such intimacy, such easy familiarity, that Elswyth found her chin quivering and could hardly catch her breath.

"Did your father ever tell you how we came to be promised to each other?" Drefan asked.

"I never thought to ask," she said. "I was just always promised to you. I don't even remember when they told me. I don't remember ever not knowing."

"You know that wound your father will not talk about, the one that makes him limp a little? My father fell in the battle line. Actually fell, I mean. He tripped over a rabbit hole. Your father stood over him. It only took a moment for the shield wall to close again, but in that moment a Pictish spear found your father's thigh. My father won't speak of it because he is embarrassed for having tripped. Your father won't speak of it to save my father embarrassment. Or so my uncle told me, last year, when I got him drunk. My father wanted to reward your father for saving his life. But it could not be gold or land, for that would mean confessing to the trip—such rewards, and the act that merits them, must be announced in the hall. But your father had a daughter—a baby—you. And so my father said, let your daughter be married to my son. And so they agreed. My mother was not pleased. You are a slave's daughter, after all. Half Welisc. And your father is not the most important thegn in the district, nor the richest, nor the wisest of councilors."

"Hey…"

"He's a lovely man, your father. I like him a lot. But does he think of the affairs of the kingdom, the affairs of the district, from one Pentecost to the next?"

"No, but…"

"Not the sort of man whose daughter marries an ealdorman's son."

"No. But aren't I the sort of woman who marries an ealdorman's son?"

"In beauty, sure enough," he said. "In charm. In song. In peaceweaving."

"But I bring neither land nor lineage into the alliance."

"No."

"But you will marry me anyway." This she said primly, with confidence.

"I was four years old when the promise was made. I'm like you. I don't remember being told. I've just always known I was going to marry you. I think I remember holding you, all swaddled up and sleeping, and being told, 'This is the girl you will marry, Dreffy,' and kissing you on the forehead. But maybe I don't really remember it. Maybe I have just been told about it so often by soft-hearted women that I think I remember it."

"You never told me that before," she said, laughing at the thought of it. "It's sweet. Why didn't you tell me?"

"I wanted you to think me a great warrior, a captain of men."

"Well I do! So why tell me now?"

"I want you to know that I shall love our children."

He could not have said anything that would have pleased her more, and if he had kissed her then, and begun to undress her, all would have been as they both anticipated. But he was still shy. He still felt the need to prove his worthiness to her, to prove that she was his choice, not merely his father's.

"Your uncle Fyren has served my father in his household all these years," he said. "They have become fast friends, and your uncle has given my father noble service. He has more than earned a reward."

He paused but she said nothing. Her uncle's name never brought cheer to a conversation.

"Your uncle does not approve of your father's marriage," Drefan continued.

"You mean he does not approve of my mother."

"He does not think it wise that Welisc blood should be mixed with Anglish, especially not in the ranks of ealdormen and kings."

"There have been Anglish kings that took Welisc wives. Saxon and Jutish kings as well."

"I have said that to him. But he has tales in which the offspring of such unions come to grief. You would think to hear him that if any lord ever lost a battle it was because he had a Welisc mother."

"You are going to marry me, aren't you?" she asked, suddenly alarmed.

Her alarm emboldened him. Anything that was fey about her would care nothing if they married or not. Now he saw that she did care. But it remained to prove that he cared also.

"My father would not break a promise," he said. "Not without cause, and neither you nor your father have given him cause to break it. But he has reminded me that, under the law, his promise is not binding on me. No man or woman can be forced to marry against their will. If I wanted another, he told me, he would not object to my choice.

"But I told him I was content as things stood. Why should I choose another? Why should I want another in my hall? Why should I want another in my bed?"

And then, feeling justified at last, he leaned in, moved his hand from her belly to envelop her breast and pressed his mouth eagerly on hers.

The kiss was not awful, the pressure of his hand was not cruel, yet she found them both somehow irksome. She was not afraid. At the moment of conjunction, it was not maiden shyness that afflicted her. But she discovered that she was offended by the clumsiness with which this had all been arranged. If they were to come to this moment by seduction rather than marriage, could he not at least have put some more thought into it? Why, above all, did he have to bring his cousins along with whores on their saddles? Her father would not have had his friends rutting trollops on the other side of the haystack when he laid her mother down.

She pushed him off her and wriggled out from underneath him. She did not get to her feet. That would have seemed too final a rejection. She needed time to gather her thoughts.

"Are you all right?" he asked. "I wasn't too rough, was I?"

"No, no," she said, annoyed. Could he not see that she needed a moment?

He had been offered the opportunity to put her aside. He had even been encouraged to do so by his father, and by his mother too, she guessed. Lady Cyneburg would not have done it cruelly. There was no cruelty in her. But she wanted the best for her son and she would never believe—would never believe until it were proved to her—that the daughter of a Welisc slave could be the best wife for Drefan. Elswyth had long known that she would have to prove herself to Lady Cyneburg. It was the spur her mother used whenever Elswyth slacked or fell short in her preparation. But that the promise on which her mother had so long relied was in such jeopardy, now that its moment of completion was so close at hand, was something she had never guessed at.

Marrying Drefan had never been a hope or a possibility to her. It had been a fact, a fact as natural as that autumn must follow summer, as firm and undoubtable as anything that is learned before the age of reason. Her wistfulness had, by turns rebelled against it and imbued it with languorous anticipation, but she had never questioned it. But now, it seemed, it depended upon Drefan's pleasure alone. Had he brought her here to demand that pleasure? But why? Why try to force from her by blackmail something she had been ready and willing to give for affection alone? Had she been able to guess at his shyness, had she known the awe in which he held her, she would have known it was not this. But he was the son of an ealdorman. It was his brash confidence that she admired most about him, and she was still too young to see behind it.

But if he was so confident and masterful, why should she be less so? Had she not longed for this, dreamed of this, seethed in frustration that he has shown no desire for this? And here was the desire she had longed for. Why quail before it now? And if what she desired also served her duty to her family and her kin, why question his intentions? Surely where duty and desire meet, there should be no hesitation. She rolled toward him, pushed him onto his back, and kissed him. She the master; he the supplicant.

If he had had the patience to let her set the pace, to let her work through her reluctance at her own speed, had let her decide where hands might go, when belts might be undone, when brooches might be unclasped, then she might have found her way through the sense of irksomeness that had descended upon her, might have found her old desire, found her way to pleasure, and delivered to him the pleasure he sought from her. But he did not. He received her kiss, but then with sudden and impatient ardor, rolled her on her back, his hands greedily grasping, hunting urgently for her brooches and her belt, his mouth so firm upon hers, his tongue so greedy, that she had to gasp for breath.

For months she had longed for him to want to kiss her with this passion, for his hands to seek out the womanly parts of her, but when it came there was no pleasure in it. It was not that he hurt her. Greedy as he was, firm as his grip on her was, it was pleasure he sought, not pain. She sensed that his wanting was not mere jealousy. He wanted her genuinely, wanted her affection as much as her body. He was trying to suck the affection out of her, like sucking the yoke out of a bird's egg. And for so long she had wanted this from him. But the affection that she had been so willing to yield, if ever it should have been asked for, would not come. The fault did not lie in the kiss, nor in the mouth that gave the kiss. It was simply, inexplicably, bewilderingly, the wrong mouth.

She pushed him off her again. It took a moment for him to stop and release her, and when he did he looked down on her, hurt and confused, his pride injured. Had he not proved his worthiness to her, though it was her worthiness that, by the world's measure, was in doubt?

"We've still two miles to Longhoughton," she said.

"Longhoughton?"

"We were going to Longhoughton."

"I don't know what you meant by 'going to Longhoughton,' but I meant this."

"Well I meant going to Longhoughton. And I intend to go. You know my mother never lets me go anywhere."

"She let you come riding with me. She knows what 'going to Longhoughton' means. She 'went to Longhoughton' herself, didn't she?"

"Don't you talk about my mother like that!"

"You do."

"Well I shouldn't, and I'm sorry I ever did."

"You don't want me?"

"I want you to take me to Longhoughton."

"I'm trying. It seems like you don't want to go."

"I don't intend to go to my wedding with a round belly," she said.

"Many a girl does," he said, roughly, looking up at her from his bed in the meadow. "Some think it right that a girl should prove herself capable, to give her husband assurance of an heir."

"You will have to take my fertility on faith," she said, "for I will not add two spans to the labor of my embroidery." She smoothed her dress and tugged her dignity into order.

"Your mother never produced a son," he said. "Fyren says that is the Welisc in her."

"Are there no men in Powys then, if Welisc women never birth sons? Where do they get fathers for their daughters?"

"Still, if your mother could not produce a son…"

"If you put a baby in me today, you would not know if it were a son or daughter until spring. What are you going to do—put a bun in the oven of every thegn's daughter from Tyne to Tweed and marry the first one to pop a boy?"

"Don't you want me?"

"Of course I want you. I just don't want this." Here she indicated the disturbed grass. This was a lie. She had longed for this. It was not the trampled grass that was at fault. "Can't you court me for more than an hour before…"

"Court you?" he said, leaping to his feet. "Is it not enough that I consent to the bargain? I must court you now?"

"Am I wrong to want to be courted? Don't I deserve it? Are you going to marry a girl you don't even think deserves to be courted?" She was trembling as she said this. Was she throwing away her future, her mother's safety, her sister's prospects, the freedom of all her Welisc kin? Was she putting all their lives in the hands of chance just because a kiss seemed irksome?

He turned his back and began to walk away from her. Had this not been courtship? What more did she want from him? She should be grateful that he regarded her at all! Why must he do more to please her? And if he must, what more?

She did not guess his thoughts. Was his turned back a rejection? Or was it because she had shamed him and he needed a moment for contrition to call forth grace in him? Was this the desperate moment in which her last remaining chance to fulfill her duty was to run after him, collapse before him in the grass and bid him condescend and enter her? If it was, the rebellion was too strong in her. She strode to Spotty's side, grabbed the pony's mane, and threw her leg over his back. "I'm going to Longhoughton," she called, not looking round to see how he responded. She kicked the pony's sides and Spotty jolted reluctantly forward. She turned his head round to the path, not looking back to see if Drefan followed her.

23 The Bonds of Hospitality

Drefan did follow her, though he let her get almost out of sight before he hopped up on Sherwyn and cantered easily after her. "It's not safe for you to ride off alone," he said gruffly when he came up beside her. He dropped Sherwyn down to Spotty's pace, and they rode along in silence together until they came to Longhoughton.

They spent several hours there, visiting people that they knew. They were a popular couple—Elswyth for her charm and beauty and Drefan because of his good humor and the fact that he would one day be their ealdorman. People were so pleased to see them individually that they scarcely noticed that they barely spoke to each other or looked in each other's direction from the time of their arrival to their departure.

But as the afternoon wore on, Drefan cast an eye at the declining sun and said, "We'd best be heading homeward if we don't want to be stumbling in the dark."

They said their goodbyes and mounted.

"Let's return by the sea path," Elswyth said.

"That adds near a mile to the distance."

"We have time," she insisted. "It is near midsummer and evenings are long."

They mounted their horses and made their way through the village to the track that led to the sea, a mile distant. It was hardly a track in places, but she knew the way and she and Spotty took the lead with Sherwyn and Drefan following docile behind.

They arrived at the coast at a point where the track descended to a beach beside an inlet that was protected from the sea by broad expanses of rock to the north and south. There was a narrow break in the rocks, enough to allow a ship to pass. Two small boats were hauled up on the sand above the tide line, turned upside down to keep them from filling with rainwater. Just above the sand there was a dilapidated hut, not lived in, but used by fishermen when they worked their catch. Beside the hut were rows of rough wooden drying racks, but there were no signs of fishermen or fish. It was a wonderfully lonely place, and Elswyth stopped and shook out her hair in the brisk breeze that blew in from the sea.

"I've always thought this would be a wonderful spot for a village," she said, as Drefan drew up beside her. "It is such a perfect place for boats."

"No decent water," Drefan said, glancing around. "And your father would not thank you for creating a rival to his trade."

Elswyth took a deep breath. "I like the smell of it."

"That's because there is no village. Bring in people, latrines, pigs, chickens, horses, a tanner, a smith, all the other trades, and it will smell just like Twyford or Longhoughton."

"We could live here, just the two of us. Then it would not smell like a village."

"It would as soon as I took my boots off," he said with a laugh. "But an ealdorman cannot live off in a corner. We shall live in Bamburgh, right in the middle of things."

"I wish the tide was out," she said. "We could go home along the sands."

"You can get all the way to Twyford along the sands from here?" Drefan asked, with a sudden quickening of interest.

"At low tide, yes. You have to pass the Bally Cars and the Marden Rocks, but at low tide it is all open. With the tide high like this, though, you can't pass the headlands. Besides, Spotty doesn't like crossing the rocks. They're too hard on his poor old feet. So we'll have to take the path above the beach."

She turned Spotty's head and urged him forward again following the path that petered in and out of existence in the margin between the forest and the sand. The land rose slightly as they rounded Seaton Point, fell again as they skirted the broad deserted bay below Foxton, and grew steadily higher again as they passed the Marden Rocks and climbed the hill that became a cliff above the beach at Twyford. The village, lying in the lee of the hill, was hidden from them, but from quite a long way off they could see the ship lying on the beach. There was water all around its keel in the high tide, almost enough to float it off. Elswyth's heart was instantly afloat. She transported herself to the prow of the ship, waving goodbye to her sisters watching from the sand while Leif, Thor, and the Norsk men pushed the ship into the sea. Where was she going? What did it matter?

She was startled by a sudden thudding of hooves as Drefan spurred Sherwyn past her and cantered upward to the top of the rise where the view of the ship was best. There he reined in and stood staring down the hill and across the sand at the ship. She urged Spotty forward, but, on a climb, that made no difference to his pace. Drefan was still staring fixedly at the ship when she came alongside him.

"Isn't it beautiful?" she said.

"What?"

"The ship."

"Tell the people of Lindisfarne that those ships are beautiful," he replied.

"That ship is a knarr, a trade ship. See how broad she is in the belly. The Norsk warships are slender. Vikingar would use a longship, not a knarr."

"How do you know so much about Norsk ships?"

"I live in a trading village."

"We should not be trading with Norsk. All it accomplishes is to let them know where our riches are, and where our defenses are weak."

"Not trade with Norsk? I can show you five things you are wearing that come from the Norsk trade. Your boots are trimmed in reindeer hide. Three of the jewels in your belt, for certain, and perhaps a fourth as well. Your sword is made from Svíar iron. That Frankish wine you like is carried in Norsk ships, and whale oil for your lamps…"

"If that's true, I'll do without all of it, and find better of Anglish make."

"You would like Leif, if you took the trouble to know him," she said. "He has been so many places, and has stories of the sea. The two of you could sit over a jug of ale and tell tales till the candles burned down. And you should see the things he has in his cargo. He has books with such wonderful pictures. You never saw anything like them."

"I care nothing for books. Waste of time and good cowhide."

"He gave me this comb," she said, pulling the comb out from the pouch that hung from her belt. "It's red deer antler, and it's beautifully made. Look how even the teeth are, and see how delicate the pattern is that is carved in the handle. It is interlace, like our art, but the patterns are different, and look at the dragon head in the middle. Isn't it wonderful?"

She held the comb up for his inspection. He reached down and took it from her, and scowled at it in the ruddy light of the declining sun.

"He gave you this?"

"Yes."

"Why?"

"He is a guest in the hall."

"Then he should give gifts to your father. To your mother. Why to you?"

"I was lady of the hall, for that night. Mother was tired because of the baby. He gave me this to say thank you," she said, and then she cried out "Don't!" for Drefan was bending the comb between his two hands, pushing in the middle with his thumbs.

He paused, the comb poised on the point of breaking. "He has no right to give you gifts," he said.

"If you break it I won't speak to you," she cried, reaching up vainly. Between Spotty's short stature and her own, she could do no more than tug on the corner of his tunic. There were tears in her eyes, and that just made her more angry. "Give it to me! Give it to me!" she shouted, beating on his knee with her fists.

He looked down at her, his face grim. Then he scowled, and with a sudden jerky motion, he handed the comb back to her.

She cuffed the tears out of her eyes and inspected the comb for damage. The teeth were all intact and the patterns on the handle were unhurt. She put it safely back into her pouch.

"Mother said you would have been proud of me, if you'd seen me. Everyone was angry with the Norsk, because of Lindisfarne, even though they have known them forever and they had nothing to do with it. But I got them to be friends again. Mother said I was born to be lady of the hall. She said you would have been proud of me."

The tears were back in her eyes. She couldn't help them. Drefan looked down on her for a moment, and then he dismounted and held a hand up to her to help her dismount. She looked at his face and saw contrition there. Normally she would have scorned the hand he offered, but now she accepted it and slipped down off Spotty's back to stand before him.

"I'm sorry," he said. "I've been a brute. Everyone's out of sorts over this business at Lindisfarne."

"It wasn't them."

"No one knows who it was. All we know is it was Norsk."

"Or Danir. Either way, it wasn't them."

"I know," he admitted. "A boy and an old man. Not the type to go viking. That Eric, maybe. But not the boy and the old man."

"Then why were you such a beast to them?"

"When your father finds his sheep killed, does he ask which wolf did it?"

"No, but he knows his own dogs did not do it. Leif and Thor are friends. Old friends. They are part of the family."

"All right, I believe you."

"Then when we get back, will you shake Leif's hand and break bread and share a cup with him?"

"Do you know what you are asking?" Drefan looked at the ship and then at her. "I rode to Lindisfarne with my father as soon as the news came," he said "It would turn your stomach to see what we saw there. The dead unburied, their wounds laid open, breeding flies. Those who lived abused my father for not protecting them. I did not think that was just. Who thought they needed protection from the sea? They built on that island to seek protection from the land. And hasn't my father pushed back the Picts whenever they became troublesome? But my father took the abuse to heart. His anger against the Norsk and the Danir is like a flame that consumes him. And you want me to go back to him and tell him that I broke bread with a Norsk? That I shared a cup with Norsk? That I shook hands with Norsk? That I bound myself in hospitality to Norsk?"

"Leif's own village was raided by vikingar. If it was the same people who raided Lindisfarne, he would stand beside you in battle and fight them. I know he would."

"But I could not find an Anglish thegn who would stand in battle line beside a Norsk, especially not in a fight against Norsk. Every man would expect treachery at every blow."

"Harrald brought me back when I stowed away on his ship when I was five. I've told you that story. He and my father swore an oath of brotherhood. That makes Leif and Thor and all of them oath-kin to me. Don't think of it as breaking bread with Norsk. Think of it as breaking bread with my kin."

"Girl, I can't. Not with Norsk. Not this year."

She crossed her arms and turned away from him, walking a few paces nearer to the cliff edge.

"Was I unkind to you today?" he asked, after letting her stand thus for a minute.

She turned and looked at him, and then down at the ground.

"Did I frighten you?"

"I know you would not hurt me," she said, still looking at the ground.

"I would protect you against the world," he said.

She looked up at him. "I know you would," she said.

He came to her slowly. She raised her face to him and their lips touched in a tiny hesitant kiss. A proper first kiss.

She looked down again. She did not want another kiss until she understood how she felt about this one, and she seemed to be feeling everything in the world all at once—fear, relief, delight, doubt, joy, sorrow. And wistfulness, oh, such a churning wandering wild-hearted wistfulness, though for what she could not tell.

"I was unkind," he said. He sat down on a grassy hillock. "I've known you so long as a child. I knew we were going to marry. I knew that I was going to take you to my bed. But you were still a child, and I could not think about it. I tried to think about the woman you would become, not the child you were. But it was confusing, so then I tried not to think about it at all. And you became a woman, and I still did not know how to think about it. And then today I saw you, and, well, suddenly it seemed I was free to want you."

"And so straight to bed?"

"I'm sorry."

She believed him. He was as ardent now as he had been before, but ardent for forgiveness.

"I'm sorry too," she said. "You took me by surprise, and that put me out of sorts." But that was a lie, and it sickened her. She cast her eyes down. "No, that's not true," she said. "I knew what 'going to Longhoughton' meant. I knew as soon as I saw Willa and Elwina. I should have turned Spotty around right then. But I didn't, because I thought I wanted...I thought I wanted you to lay me down in Foxton wood."

"I thought you did too," he said, but then he too sickened on the lie. "I hoped you did," he amended, sheepishly.

"But I'm not a Willa, or an Elwina," she said.

"Of course you're not."

"Maybe if you had taken me there alone... But with them there... It made it..."

"I can take you there tomorrow. If you want to. Just the two of us."

"It's not how I want to win a husband. You're right. It's how my mother did it. And I know I'm marrying above my rank, just like she did. But I want a proper wedding night. Do you understand? Can you wait?"

She went and sat down beside him on the hillock and wrapped her arms around his left arm. He bent toward her and pecked her on the top of the head.

"You deserve a wedding night," he said. "I don't care what Fyren says, or my father, or my mother. I want you, for my bed and for my hall."

They sat in silence for a moment.

He asked, "Do you want me to be a big brother again, until after the harvest?"

"No," she said, laughing and kissing him. "I want you to pant with desire for me every hour. I want to spurn you with my toe when you try to kiss my feet. I want you to be my puppy and my slave." She was lying again. She knew it but she could not help it, for all the bitterness it brought to her tongue.

"I wish we could sit here a while," he said. "I would try to kiss your feet and let you spurn me with your toe. But those clouds are only thickening and if we stay any longer, it will be pitch black without the moon and we will stumble off the cliff and kill ourselves."

"Just promise me one thing," she said.

"All right."

"Shake hands with Leif, and break bread and share a cup with him."

He growled softly. "Why must you make me?"

"I want to know that you will both keep the hospitality of my father's hall."

"Very well. If I must. To please you. But you must promise to say nothing of it to my father. But come on, you must get up on Sherwyn with me. It will be faster and we are losing the light."

This was not true. It would not be faster. They would still be constrained to Spotty's pace, for they certainly could not leave him behind. But Elswyth consented anyway, because she wanted to be at peace with him, wanted to feel his arms around her in gentle affection. He threw a leg over his horse and then reached down a hand and pulled her up. He urged Sherwyn forward, and Spotty fell in behind. She took one look behind at the ship, stark against the shimmering of the twilit water. Drefan's arm tightened around her, and as they rode on it seemed to grow tighter still. She squirmed and protested, but it made no difference. He would slacken his grip for a moment when she asked, but it would tighten again almost at once so that she could hardly breathe. As they neared the village, he began to hum an old tune under his breath, a sad little ditty of love gone wrong. As he sang the song, his grip grew even tighter until she cried out in pain. She elbowed him in the ribs and he let her go. She slipped off Sherwyn's back and glared up at Drefan.

"You hurt me," she said.

"I was afraid you were slipping off," he said.

"I wasn't slipping off."

"I'm sorry. It felt to me like you were."

"Well, I wasn't" She took Spotty's reins to lead him to his stable through the gathering darkness. Turning back to Drefan she said, "Remember what you promised."

24 Dolts and Oafs

Drefan kept his promise. There was no feast that night. Drefan had told Attor and Edith that they should do nothing special to mark his coming. He gave the excuse that he had come without notice, and everyone's barns were near empty in a hard year. But in obedience to his promise, he asked that Leif and Thor join them for the evening meal, and there he shook Leif's hand and broke bread and drank a cup with him, thus binding them both in the bonds of hospitality.

He did it without humor. The cup did not go round again. There was no telling of tales, no singing of songs. It was mostly uncomfortable silence, which both Edith and Elswyth in turn tried to fill, but without success.

Everyone went to bed early and as Edith lay beside her husband, cupped inside his body while his hand gently stroked her swollen belly, she whispered, "You lied to Drefan."

"We agreed Bamburgh should not know about the books."

"I thought you meant we would not send news."

201

"I did. I had not thought he would come. He's usually hunting up Wandylaw way this time of year. But I suppose not, after Lindisfarne."

"So why?"

"I wasn't sure how he would take it."

"But he's your…"

"I know. But Harrald brought my daughter back to me. So I will keep Leif as if he were my own."

"I hate that they quarreled."

"The quarrel was not on Leif's part. Not that I blame Drefan. I'm not so fond of Norsk myself since the attack on Lindisfarne. But Lindisfarne is practically under Kenric's walls. It will grieve him not to have defended it, though he could not have known. He will be boiling to put sword to Norsk flesh, and Drefan will have heard him raging. But Leif is kin, and kin comes first."

"At least Drefan broke bread with him tonight."

"Aye. Her doing, I reckon."

"I suppose…"

There was an uneasiness in her voice that he detected. "What grieves you then?" he asked.

"I just wonder what they did all afternoon."

"Longhoughton, visiting, she said."

"They were not back till near dark," she said. "Drang and Earh said they rode off and left them—and they were smirking when they said it. And she was vexed when she did get back. She was uneasy all evening."

"Was she? I didn't notice."

How little the man noticed, Edith thought. Indeed, his poor eyes alone could not account for it.

"She plays the lady well. She is a peaceweaver. It is an art practiced on men. If she convinced you, maybe she convinced him. But I could see she was uneasy, with him or with herself."

"You said she was vexed about the kiss. I couldn't watch."

"It was her first. She didn't want it like that. But there was something else that made her uneasy when they came back."

"You don't think they..."

Edith rolled over to face her husband.

"I don't know. She won't talk to me."

"He wouldn't hurt her."

"Not on purpose. But he's an oaf sometimes, though I shouldn't say it."

"So am I."

"No," she said, smiling at him. "You're a dolt sometimes. Never an oaf."

"But you think they..." Then he frowned. "They wouldn't."

"We did," she said.

"That was different..."

"How?"

"She has no need," he said. And then he frowned at his own words. "Sorry, love. I shouldn't..."

"I never pretended anything else," she told him. "Not that I didn't fancy you, you know. Not that you didn't fancy me. But you're a dolt sometimes."

"But not an oaf?"

"That's why I had to start it."

"But she has no need to start it with him," he said.

"Doesn't mean she didn't want to. Doesn't mean he didn't start it either."

"Well if they did, why was she vexed?"

"He's an oaf. And if they did, she would have been frightened, no matter how much she wanted it. It's easy to make a quarrel when you are afraid of what you want."

They lay looking at each other in the gutting flame as their rushlight consumed the last of its oil. Attor's features moved from wondering to shame to tenderness.

"Were you?"

"What?"

"Frightened?" he said. "Of me?"

"Terrified, and yet not. You're not an oaf."

"Should I speak to her?"

"No. If it's done, it's done. She'll come to me when she's ready. And if it's not that, you'll just vex her more."

"Should I speak to him?"

"What would you do if he says they did?"

"It was done without my leave."

"You would demand the wergild? From the son of your ealdorman? From the man she is to marry? If she complained, it would be different. She'd not keep quiet if he had hurt her. Whatever it was, it wasn't that. He's her safety, love. She couldn't do better. And she'll knock the oafishness off him, given time."

"I hate to think about it, is all. She's still a child to me, though I know she ain't. And she's mine to protect still. Not his, yet. I'd stick a knife in him, ealdorman's son or not, if I thought he hurt her."

"I know," she said. "Go to sleep now, pet. I'll know in the morning if anything happened."

Edith rolled over again, and he rolled back to embrace her. She settled in the crook of his body and listened to his breathing until he fell asleep. Still, sleep would not come to her. Her design had been fifteen years in the making and she had believed that Elswyth was entirely happy to play the part that Edith had meant for her. But now Elswyth's obvious disquiet troubled her. Had she not one daughter now, but two, who hated her?

There are more ways to lose a child than death. There are more ways to lose a child than ships.

25 The Hedgehog and the Gannet

When Elswyth woke, in the very first hints of predawn light, she heard the sound of harness and the blowing of grumpy horses and emerged from the sleeping house to find Drefan and his cousins already mounted.

"You weren't going to say goodbye?" she asked him.

He looked down at her from Sherwyn's back. She was dressed only in her thin linen sleeping smock, which clung to her body, and she saw his eyes survey her. For a moment she found herself wanting to say, "Get down off your horse and come to bed." She had never stood so near naked in the face of such naked lust, and for a moment it seemed only proper to succumb to the moment. But she said nothing, and Drefan turned his head with a frown and said, "Business to do. Can't waste the light. Thank your mother again for me."

"Alright," she said.

He kicked Sherwyn to a walk, but then reigned him in again and turned back to her to say, "Goodbye."

"Goodbye."

"I'll visit again."

"Soon?"

"Soon."

There was a dullness in the way he spoke the word that made it unconvincing. His visit might come soon. It might not come at all.

Drefan urged Sherwyn forward again. Drang and Earh, bleary-eyed and yawning, fell in behind Drefan. They saluted her silently as they rode past, their eyes running over her lazily, as if they did not think she could see where they were looking.

She watched them ride out of the village, none of them turning back to glance at her with affection or regard, and in that moment she hated them, all three. The feeling made her wretched. Of course Drefan wanted to leave. It was not because she had disappointed him. His remorse over that had been genuine. But she had turned his moment of remorse against him, used it to make him do something that offended his honor and would surely offend his father, should he hear of it. A fine piece of peaceweaving that. Was it an injury that time would soften? Or had she shown him something of herself that would fester in his heart? Would a man so used still wish to marry?

She went back for her lambskin and went to bathe. She did not bathe in the river as she often did, but crossed the low ford and made her way to a sea cove on the south side of the river, away from the beach, where she could bathe in the sea unseen by any early-rising male eye. Sea bathing would make her hair stiff, and she would have to rinse it in fresh water to restore its bounce, but the violence of the waves against her flesh, and the sound and smell of the sea were both calming and invigorating in a way the river was not. She waded out until she was almost floating, letting the swells lift and toss her about as dawn swallowed up the stars one by one.

A deep sadness welled up in her. She was not given to melancholy. Her wistfulness was ever hopeful. She was a creature of physical delights. The sea, the wind, the ground beneath her feet, the world at her fingertips, all the light and dance of the natural and human worlds, the taste of sweat on her tongue, even the sharpness of her needle and the color and lush smoothness of her embroidery threads—these all delighted her in a way that had never seemed exhausted or capable of exhaustion. But now this sadness came, and she found she was adding to the ocean with her tears and wondering if the whole salt ocean was not made of centuries of maiden's tears, all weeping for they knew not what.

The mood passed, and she half waded and half swam back to the shingle, dried herself with the lambswool, taking less pleasure than usual in its roughness and its smell and the warmth it brought to her skin. The great mysterious sadness had left her, but it had left in its place a dull grumpiness, a sense of being out of sorts with the world and everyone in it. Hoping to find some solace in the one man with whom she was never out of sorts, she rinsed her hair and dressed hurriedly before seeking out Thor, her hair still damp about her shoulders.

She found him in his accustomed spot, saluting the rising sun. She did not tease him or play guessing games with him, as she usually did. She simply seated herself on the log beside him and slowly let her head sink sideways until it rested on his shoulder.

"I should like to be a monk," Thor said, after she had remained silent in this posture for several minutes.

"No!"

"You dig the garden. You say words to the gods for other men, and they give you gold for it, and silver, and land. You live in a great house, safe against the wind and the rain. There is food always on the table."

She raised her head and looked at him to see if he was in earnest. "But you would miss the sea," she said.

207

"The sea that buffets me, that chills me, that strains my sinews and cracks my bones?"

"The sea that takes you to Spain and Orkney and York and Cordoba. The sea that takes you where the sun bakes and the ice flows, where it isn't always damp, and low, and green."

"I have seen all those things. And I am growing old. Too old for this life. I should very much welcome a stable home among rich fields and fine herds. I would say words to the gods day and night for such a bounty."

"I think you would have to change gods. No lord in Northumbria will pay you to say words to Odin."

"Gods are fickle. Should a man be more constant than the gods?"

"You should be a monk," she said. "Then when I am the lady of Bamburgh I could be your patron and give you gold to talk to God for me, and I could ride out to see you any time I wanted to."

"Nay lass," Thor said, "If you came there, all the monks would be looking at the sky and tripping over their feet. Then I would have to spend all my time in the infirmary mending their broken bones."

She giggled. "Well then, I shall wear a wimple and put ashes on my face to make me ugly. It would be so lovely to have you nearby.

Thor laughed. "Nay, child. It is but a wish. I have my part to play, as we all do. My duty is to Harrald and to Leif and to the clan. Much evil has come upon them, and my leaving would only make things worse. I have roamed the world long enough to know that it is right to grow where you are planted, unless the gods say otherwise."

In all her life it had never seemed so disagreeable to her to grow where she was planted. She sighed and said, "I want to go, and I can't. You want to stay, and you can't."

"The hedgehog dreams of the sky while the gannet longs for his nest."

"Do they?"

"Who can say? Perhaps each is content as they are. Perhaps we are the only ones who are discontented."

"Just you and me?" she asked, wistfully, leaning against his broad arm.

"Aye, lass," he said, laughing, "just you and me in all the world. The rest are happy as lambs in clover."

"You scold in the nicest way, old man."

"You are growing too wise for my tricks, it seems."

"I don't feel very wise."

"What grieves you, lass? It is not like you to be melancholy."

Elswyth gave another sigh, not for dramatic effect, as she sometimes did, but because it welled up in her, irresistibly. "I have my part to play, like we all do," she said. "My duty is to my mother and my father and my sisters and my kin. I have hardly roamed the world at all, but my leaving would only make things worse."

"Worse, lass? What troubles have you? You've a bonny man who fancies you and can keep you very well. It would be a long day's sail to find a lass, or her mother, that did not think you blessed. And you will roam far enough in his company, when his time comes to be ealdorman."

And then Elswyth realized that she could not tell her sorrows even to Thor. "I'm sorry," she said. "My troubles are nothing to yours. Nothing to Leif's. I shouldn't be sad like this. I just feel…"

Here she paused, waiting for Thor to ask what her feelings were, hoping that when he asked she would find an answer. But Thor shifted where he sat, seeming to move away from her slightly.

"Do not add to his burden," he said.

"Who? Leif?"

"Aye."

"But I'm not adding to his burden, am I?"

"He must go. You must stay. Do not make that harder."

She bristled at this. "I don't know what you mean."

"How often have you sought his company?"

"I like looking at the books. I like the ship. I like the stories."

"Aye, and you like the man."

She laughed. "I like all you sailor men."

"Then choose another to tell you stories and show you the ship."

"Like Eric?"

"Aye."

She frowned at this. "I don't think I like Eric anymore."

"Been giving you cheek, has he?"

"I think he was just teasing."

"You give no heed to him."

She was offended now. "You don't think I know better?"

"I knew the child. I hardly know what you are as a woman."

"Well, I'm not that." She stood and stalked a few paces away from him.

"I'm glad you are not wanton," He said. "But even the chaste are not always wise."

"You scold less kindly now, old man."

"You've grown too fond. Just let him be."

"Even if I did like Leif, that is my problem, not his."

"Oh, child. Can you not tell?"

She turned back to him, indignant. "Tell what?"

"When a young man likes you?"

"They all like me. It's starting to be boring."

"Lass, can you not spot one salmon in a school of herring?"

"Leif? Half the time I think he is avoiding me."

"The rules of trade, lass. And they are his rules now. If the crew thinks he does not follow them himself, they will not follow them either, and then we shall be dining in Hel's hall. Then you will have vikingar on your beach for certain. Do not add to his burden."

"I can't talk to anyone it seems."

"You can talk to me, when you've a mind."

"I'll come to you next time I want to be scolded, old man." She turned her back on him and stalked away.

26 Slave and Cousin

She did not see Leif all morning, except at breakfast, where they hardly spoke to each other. From the reserve with which Leif treated her, she guessed that Thor had had similar words with him. This set her wondering exactly what Thor might have said about her, what feelings Leif might have admitted to having towards her. For all that she had thought of kissing him, even thoughts of lying with him, she had not fully realized how much she had come to enjoy Leif's company, how much it pleased her to see him approach, how much it ached to be apart from him, how natural it felt to slip her hand into his. Their friendship had not begun face to face, but side by side, in the shared pleasure of the books, and their fascination with the monk and his arts. She wanted to protest that it was nothing more than that, a friendship based on shared interest, but now that she sat by the hall diligently working away at her embroidery—sharing the bench with Hilda—the thoughts she had of him were not of things done side by side, but face to face.

213

"Are you still going to marry Drefan?" Hilda asked, after they had worked in silence for a while.

"Of course I am."

"Then why are you so angry with him?"

"Who says I am?"

"I have eyes. I can see things."

"You're imagining things."

"I still think you want to marry Leif."

"Will you stop with that? Anyway, I was thinking, once I am married to Drefan, I can arrange for you to marry Drang or Earh."

"No thank you."

"Why not?"

"Drang and Earh lie with trollops."

"So did Drefan," Elswyth said.

"With Willa," Hilda said. "I see things. I'm not stupid."

"All right, yes, with Willa."

"Is that why you are angry with him?"

"He's done with Willa," Elswyth said. Of that much she was certain. Willa had been passed on.

"Does Leif lie with trollops?"

"How should I know?"

"Mother says sailors always lie with trollops."

"How would she know?"

"She was a trollop," Hilda said, with a vehemence that defied contradiction. "That's how she got you. That's how she ensnared Father. That's why no one likes me—because my mother was a Welisc trollop."

Elswyth was about to give several other reasons why no one liked Hilda, but she bit her tongue and said, "I hate it when you say things like that. Besides, she wasn't a trollop when she had you. She was properly married to Father. I'm the one who got made under a haystack."

"Have you been a trollop?"

214

"No," Elswyth said, but she said it quietly, without the vehemence the word deserved, and she felt her cheeks grow hot.

"Do you want to be?"

"No!"

"I still think you and Leif were kissing."

"We weren't."

"You want to, though."

"I'm marrying Drefan. You've seen me kiss Drefan."

"I saw. You didn't like it."

"Of course I liked it."

Hilda turned and looked at her. "Mother says I'm not to call you a liar," she said.

"I'm not…" Elswyth broke off. "What makes you think you know?"

"I'm not stupid. I may not be pretty, but I'm not stupid. You didn't like it when Drefan kissed you."

"Oh, leave it will you?"

"I would miss you if you went with Leif," Hilda said, grudgingly, half whispering.

"I know you would. I would miss you too. But I'm not going with Leif. I don't want to go with Leif. I am going to marry Drefan. I'll see you all the time. If I arrange for you to marry Earh, you could live at Bamburgh and you'd see me every day— If you want to see me every day."

"Of course I do."

"You don't act like it."

"You're so stupid sometimes," Hilda said again.

"Well," said Elswyth, exasperated, "At least I'm pretty."

This created a gulf that neither of them cared to cross, so they lapsed into silence.

At about the third hour of the morning, Elswyth saw the monk walk through the village on the way to the beach, tripping and falling when Mayda surprised him by emerging from the corner of a hut just as he was passing. Elswyth laughed to herself, and found herself surprised to note that Mayda, despite having her hair cropped close around her ears, was also pretty enough to cause the monk to avert his eyes and fall over his feet. But then, of course, as her mother had just told her, two thegns had offered a concubine's price for Mayda, a price that might have been accepted in another hall. It might well be accepted in this hall, were Fyren in possession. Or Fyren might take her for himself. But still, it did not matter, for she would buy Mayda, once she had her morning gift. She would buy her and set her free and then Mayda could grow out her hair and find herself a freeborn husband. If Drefan should return.

As Mayda passed where Elswyth was sitting, they looked up at each other, then at the figure of the monk disappearing over the dunes. They began to giggle, and the more they tried to stop the more the giggles came.

"What are you laughing at?" Hilda demanded, supposing that she must be the butt of whatever joke it was.

They both turned to her. Elswyth tried to form an explanation, but the giggles came all the harder. Hilda turned scarlet.

"No, no, we're not laughing at you," Elswyth said.

Hilda put her head down and pulled her needle with furious tugs, her cheeks still the color of sunrise.

Mayda bobbed and carried on with her errand, but as she was leaving, Elswyth suddenly threw her embroidery down into her basket, jumped to her feet and embraced Mayda.

"Lady!" Mayda exclaimed, startled.

"Call me Elsy, cousin."

"I mustn't!"

"I won't tell."

Mayda's eyes went to Hilda, who was looking at them, wide eyed.

"She won't tell either," Elswyth said, furiously.

"I will if I want to," Hilda said.

"She's your cousin too."

"I'm Anglish! And if she doesn't call you Lady, I will tell. You can twist my ears all you like, but I'll still tell."

"May I go, Lady," Mayda begged.

Elswyth ran her hand over Mayda's close cropped hair, black like her own, and likely as full and lovely, were she permitted to grow it out. Elswyth whispered, so that Hilda would not hear. "One day you will call me, Cousin, or Elsy, or whatever you like."

She released her, and Mayda bobbed a curtsey to her, and then to Hilda, before running off, red cheeked.

"I'm telling," Hilda declared.

"Telling who? Mother who was a slave? Father who married a slave? Tell on me if you like, but if you try to tell anything on Mayda, I'll pour the monk's ink all over your precious embroidery."

Hilda responded to this by picking up her basket and stalking off to a different bench at the other end of the hall. Elswyth resumed her own place and looked wistfully out toward the beach where the monk had gone. The monk, of course, was going to the ship to read the books. Elswyth smarted a bit at the thought of the books being open while she was not there to look at them. Of course, the monk valued the books for the words, whereas she loved them for the pictures. If she wanted to see more pictures—and there were five more volumes that she and Leif had yet to explore—that really had nothing to do with the monk. It would be between her and Leif, and, for today at least, her conscience was bound to Thor's plea to leave Leif alone. Yes, other sailor men could tell her tales and show her the ship. But only Leif had custody of the books. And it was only Leif's company she craved. To look at the books without him would be to rob the experience of half its joy for only he seemed to love them as she did. And so she stayed where she was, and kept her needle moving until her neck grew stiff and her fingers started to cramp.

Close to noon a small boy passed by, running helter-skelter toward the beach, and presently returned with the monk hurrying behind him. Presumably Kendra was awake and speaking and the monk's duty called him to her bedside. Or perhaps she was dying at last and he was summoned to hear her last breath. The desire came over her to rise and cross his path, to see if she could make him stumble. But her conscience rebuked her and she stayed where she was. As he approached, the monk evidently caught sight of her out of the corner of his eye, for he pulled his cowl up over his head as he hurried on, but he did not pause or stumble.

Mayda reappeared shortly afterwards to set the outdoor table for lunch. They almost never ate in the hall in the summer, unless it rained or there was occasion for a feast. It was a grim lunch. Everyone seemed to be out of sorts. Hilda was still furious at Elswyth and spent much of the meal staring daggers at her. Elswyth tried to engage Leif in conversation on ordinary matters—nothing suggesting spending time together, just general civil chit-chat—but he would not engage. His efforts to avoid even catching her eye seemed to rival those of the monk, so that she began to wonder if Leif would start to insist on taking all his meals alone, as the monk did. Elswyth, treated her mother's attempts at conversation in the same way. When the joyless meal was over, she picked up her embroidery basket, meaning to resume her seat of the morning. But then she spotted Leif, who had left the table early, sitting on a log on the height of the dunes, alone, looking out to sea.

Suddenly she was angry. If anyone had asked her what or who she was angry at, she could not have given a sensible answer. She would have snapped at them, angry for being asked. But whatever the transgression and whoever the transgressor, it was the sight of Leif sitting there alone that brought it welling up in her, and she stalked off towards him, fuming.

"Did Thor tell you not to talk to me?" she asked, as she came up to him.

"Yes," he said, turning to look at her and then turning away.

"Who is jarl, you or Thor?"

"I am jarl. He is my councilor. I listen to him."

"What did he say?"

"He reminded me of the rules of trade."

"The rules of trade say you cannot talk to me?"

"No."

"Then why?"

He paused. She expected his pauses now. She knew she could wait him out.

"Can you look at me while you think about it?" she said, moving to stand in front of him.

He raised his eyes and looked her in the face. For a long time he did not speak.

"Well?"

"Thor thinks I want more from you than talk."

"Do you?"

"What do you want from me?"

"I want to see the books."

"You may do so."

"I want to look at them with you."

"Why?"

"Because I want to talk about them. I want to talk about them with someone who loves them as much as I do."

"Thor fears that will lead to other things."

"Do you?"

Again a pause. But he did not take his eyes off her face. "Yes," he said, at last. "Don't you?"

"No," she said. She had thought the word was true when it formed in her mind, but she knew it was false when it came out of her mouth. She looked away from him.

"Well I do," he said.

"What is it you want, then? Do you want to take me to a low place among the dunes and lay me down and undo the broaches that hold my dress?"

He did not answer, but his eyes moved away from her and he looked out towards the bright sea.

"You've done it before, haven't you? It's what sailors do. It's what Norsk do."

"We do not take any woman against her will," he said, still staring at the sea.

"There were many women raped in the village at Lindisfarne," she said.

"It was not us who raided Lindisfarne," he said, turning his face back to her, suddenly flushed.

"It was Norsk."

"Some Norsk rape. Some Anglish rape. I bet some Welisc rape too. We do not rape. One of my father's men raped a girl in Spain once. My father killed him and gave his body to the girl's father to mutilate. We do not rape. It is bad for trade. And my father does not like the company of such men."

"And do you? Do you like the company of such men?"

"No." And then he looked at her quizzically and said, "Has any of my men insulted you? Put a hand on you? Name him and I will kill him."

She thought of Eric, with his over-long embraces, his undressing of her with eyes and words, the canny calculation of opportunity and desire that she had seen in his face. Had he merely been teasing her? Or, if he had seen something different in her face, would he indeed have led her among the dunes and laid her down? And once he had laid her down, would he have let her up again, as Drefan had done?

She had been silent too long, and boast had turned to suspicion in Leif. He rose to his feet. "Name him and I will kill him."

She laughed. "No one has said a word to me," she said. "They're just like you and the monk. They won't even look at me."

She turned and stalked away, still fuming.

***

Edith watched her go. She had seen her talking with Leif and knew a quarrel when she saw one. She had hoped to find Elswyth ready to talk about what had passed between her and Drefan the previous day, but she sensed that Elswyth was in no mood to be talked to. There are other ways to lose a child besides death. There are other ways to lose a child besides ships. You can lose a child even while she still sleeps under your roof and eats at your table. You can lose a child by showing them any part of yourself that is not a mother. By showing them any rival to your love for them. By asking them to sin for you, however great the cause.

What Edith ached in her heart to know was, had Drefan asked Elswyth to lie with him, and if she had done so, had it been of her own desire, or because Edith had asked her to. And yet, how infinitely would it compound the breach between them if she were to go to Elswyth and demand to know. Did you make yourself a whore, as I asked you to? It had not seemed what she was asking when she revealed her full design to Elswyth. She had thought only of her cause, of her mother, of her kin, of Mayda, of keeping Mayda from degradation. But as she had lain beside her husband, and heard him so innocently fret over Elswyth's innocence, the full understanding of what she had asked of her daughter had come over her. There are more ways to lose a child than death or ships.

What made this estrangement worse was that it was clear that Elswyth's discomfort was not with her mother alone. She had quarreled with Drefan, whether Drefan knew of the quarrel or not. And she had quarreled with Leif as well.

In some sense, it relieved her mind to see that Elswyth seemed as vexed with Leif as she seemed to be with Drefan. Did that suggest that she was angry with both of them for quarreling with each other? Did her mood of the evening mean that she had not been able to soften Drefan towards Leif? Did her mood of the morning mean that she had not been able to move Leif? Had she perhaps been scolding Leif for not being more submissive to Drefan, as Drefan's rank demanded? Had she been jealously defending the right and honor of the man she was to marry? Had the last angry exchange that she had witnessed been Leif proudly refusing to bend, and Elswyth, exasperated, storming off in anger? Oh God, let it be that, she prayed. Let it be that Drefan never asked her to lie with him. Let it be that Elswyth never understood what I asked of her. Let it be that she has forgotten it. Let it just be a quarrel between two stiff necked young men. But if it were that, why did Elswyth, as she passed her mother on the way past the hall, glare at her as well?

27 Fear and Consolation

Wishing to be alone, Elswyth collected her embroidery basket from the hall and made her way up to her clifftop perch to get on with the embroidery for her wedding dress. Slowly, as the hours passed, sun and birdsong, wind and cloud, sea and sky, leeched the anger and the melancholy and the sadness out of her, so that when she heard footsteps coming up the path from the village, she was not immediately vexed at the interruption, but hoped for the company of someone who might provide comfort without enquiry. Her father would have suited her purpose at that moment, but it was not her father's distinct gait she had heard, and she was about to turn and look when she realized that she recognized the gait already. She turned just as the footsteps ceased, and saw Leif. He froze in his tracks and looked away, clearly surprised to find her here, and unsure whether to continue.

"Your pardon, Lady," he said.

"Oh, don't start that again!"

"Your pardon, Elswyth. I will go another way."

223

He turned to leave, but she found she could not bear to see him go. Their quarrel, after all, was not really with each other, but with Thor, who seemed to think neither one of them was capable of discretion or restraint.

"Don't go," she said. "Come sit down beside me."

He stood still where he was, a dozen yards away.

"Just to talk," she said. "You look like you need to talk to someone."

This seemed to move him, for he came towards her. She made room for him on the rock and he sat down next to her, his hip against hers. He no longer wore the bandage she had used to cover the wound on his head. There was a line of small scabs on his temple, edged by pink and delicate skin. She felt an almost irresistible urge to stroke the wound with gentle fingers.

"The weather is turning," he said.

"What is it like to ride out a storm at sea?" she asked, "Is it fearful or is it exciting?"

"It is hard work," he replied.

"You do not fear storms then?"

"We do not seek out storms," he said. "We do not sail when the weather threatens. But if a storm comes when we are at sea, we ride it out."

"And you are not afraid?"

"Why do you speak of fear?" he asked.

"I am kept so awfully safe," she said. "Sometimes I just want to be terribly terribly frightened. Is that silly?"

"What would you put at risk, to be so frightened?" he asked. "A broken bone? An adder's bite? A wound that will fester? The loss of an eye? Alone in the sea with no sight of land and your body chilled so you cannot swim? Or perhaps the death of someone you love?"

"You are a terribly serious man, aren't you?"

"I have to be."

"But I don't?"

"Aren't you?"

"Serious?"

"Yes."

"Oh, I don't know. Should I be? Would you like me better if I were?"

"No."

Without noticing, she laid her head against his shoulder. He noticed, but he let it remain there.

"Drefan says that in battle he is not afraid."

"Has he been in a battle?"

"He led his father's household men to put down a band of cattle thieves. They killed four of them and the others ran away."

"Not a real battle then? He boasts that he was not afraid of cattle thieves? I wonder how he would stand in a North Sea gale."

"So you have been in a storm, a real storm?"

"More than once." He glanced sideways, searching her face for signs of admiration.

"Which is more fearful, do you think—a battle or a storm?"

"In either battle or storm, I suppose, a man must do his work without flinching, or else he and his comrades will perish. Those who are afraid are those that don't have work to do."

"Are you afraid, now that you must sit here with no work to do?" she asked, turning her face towards him.

"You want to hear me say that I am afraid?"

She laughed. "No, of course not. I'm only teasing."

"I am afraid."

She placed her arms around his arm and rested her head on his shoulder again. "Tell me what you fear," she said.

"I fear for my father."

"You will raise his ransom," she said.

"I fear he is already dead."

"No."

"I fear he has been tortured. I have seen men who have been tortured. The pain never leaves them. Their bodies never regain their strength. Death soon finds them."

"I'm sure he hasn't…"

"You are kind, but you cannot know."

"No. I don't know what else to say."

"Say what you fear. Say what I cannot say."

She looked up at him sharply. "Really?" she asked.

He closed his eyes and nodded. "Really."

"I fear your father betrayed Lindisfarne."

He wept. She put her arms around him and held him and he did not resist her embrace.

"I fear that they tortured him until he told them, and then they killed him," she said, feeling the full weight of her obligation to him. And then she felt the tears welling up in her own eyes.

She had never been close to Harrald the way she had to Thor and Eric, though she had loved him from afar after he had returned her to her family, for the truth that she had admitted to no one, even herself, was that Eric had not stumbled upon her in her hiding place, but that terror had driven her from it, terror and thirst and squalor and darkness and separation from her family that had all been more than she could bear. She had not come out of her hiding place. Her pride had been too strong for that. But she had made sure to be found, had shuffled and banged and sighed when Eric had passed near. Pride had not kept her from throwing herself weeping into Thor's arms the moment she was discovered, and gazing in terror at Harrald while they discussed what to do with her, for fear he would not take her home. But there had been no real debate about the matter. Harrald had turned the ship around at once, and had praised her for her pluck, shown her how to wash and change her garments (for she was rank and filthy after three days in her hiding hole), given her cakes and wine, and treated her like an honored guest all the way back to her father's beach. He was never a man to sit her on his knee and tell her stories or to suffer her to run her fingers through his beard as Thor did. But as she had grown older and had learned more and more of what that detour had cost Uncle Harrald, and what anxiety her parents had suffered at her loss, she had grown to love him more and more deeply. If Thor was the kindest and wisest man she knew, and Eric the boldest, Harrald was the most honorable.

What agony, she wondered, would it have taken to break a man of such honor? The sadness of it all overwhelmed her, and she clung to Leif, taking comfort as much as giving it. And then, in comforting her, it seemed that he regained his composure, until it was her weeping in his arms; he comforting her. When she realized this, she was ashamed, for this was his sorrow before it was hers. She forced herself to stop weeping, dabbed her eyes with her sleeves, and looked into his face, suddenly overwhelmed with the desire to kiss him. She looked at him and saw the same desire in him. Not the humble desire to comfort. Not the hesitant desire to touch. Not in him. Not in her. No, the angry desire to shout defiance at death by making new life. Let his mouth move one inch towards hers and she would offer no resistance. Indeed, she would have brooked no resistance from him, would have stripped him angrily and pulled him down upon her.

And he paused.

"But just because we fear it," she said, "does not make it true. He may be well. He may have suffered nothing. You can't collect ransom for a dead man."

Slowly their passions and their limbs began to disengage.

"That is what I try to tell myself every day," he said. "It is why I must keep working to raise his ransom."

"I'm sure you will raise it," she said. "I'm sure you will ransom him."

They were no longer touching now.

"But I hate the waiting," he said. "When I was at sea I felt I was moving as fast as I could. Now we sit idle on the beach and wait for the monk's letter to be carried by another."

"Heorot will carry the message as swiftly as he can."

"But he will not return tomorrow. Tomorrow it will be five days since we came. It is not right for a guest to stay more than three days. A dozen extra mouths is a burden on your mother's stores. We would eat our own provisions, but then we would not have enough for the journey home. We dare not go hunting and we did not bring nets for fishing."

"Father said you were welcome to stay as long as you needed."

"I am grateful. But we will be even less welcome among your people when they see we overstay a guest's welcome, and when they know the corn that feeds us comes from their own bellies."

She stood and took hold of his hand. "Come," she said smiling at him and brushing the tears from the corners of her eyes, "It doesn't help to brood on it. Walk with me and tell me tales of Orkney and the Faroe Isles."

He stood and followed her obediently along the cliff-side path, looking out over the calm blue ocean across which lay his home and his imprisoned father.

After they had walked together a few minutes, he blurted out, "Did you tell Drefan about the books?"

"He is not interested in books," she replied. She shifted the position of her head against his shoulder and the grip of her arms around his arm tightened slightly.

"But did you mention them?" he insisted.

"I don't think so. Why would I?" She couldn't remember, but somehow she felt like she might have done, in the heat of argument.

"If he knew I had them, he could say I stole them from Lindisfarne. He could use them to accuse me of taking part in the raid."

"He knows you didn't do it. He told me so himself. Besides, why would you raid Lindisfarne with a great fleet and then come and sail here all by yourself?"

"I would not. But Drefan does not need a reason. He just wants an excuse to spill my blood."

"He shook your hand. He drank with you. He is bound by hospitality to be at peace with you."

"While I am blameless, yes. But if I were guilty of this great crime, he would be free of the bond."

"But why would he want to?"

"Every warrior in Northumbria wants the glory of spilling vikingar blood."

"You're not vikingar."

"I am Norsk. To him, Norsk means vikingar."

"He knows you are my friend."

"He does not like that either, I promise you."

"It's not like we…" She looked up at him. Drefan had asked and she had said no. Leif had not asked, but if he did, her body said that she would lie with him. Her heart was uncertain, and her head was appalled, but her body was willing—no, more than willing—eager. Did the body know more than the heart and the head? The head knew that she would soon lie in Drefan's bed. Her heart was reconciled to it. But her body rebelled. Her body had shown its rebellion to Drefan.

"Thor is right," he said. "We should keep apart."

"I know," she said.

Yet neither made any move to separate, but continued, entwined, along the clifftop path.

They had not walked on much further before she felt him startle and he stopped abruptly.

"What?"

"Look to your right," he whispered.

They were at a place where a section of the clifftop jutted outward. The path they were on cut off the angle of this promontory, but there was another, narrower, path that followed the edge of the cliff. On that path, lying in the tall grass by the cliff face, looking down toward the beach where the ship lay, were three men: Drefan and his cousins.

Her eyes widened and her mouth opened to shout a rebuke. His hand clamped over her mouth before she could speak, and she looked up at him and understood. He released his hand from her mouth and they began to back down the path toward the village.

Drefan could hardly have heard them over the sounds of wind and sea, and yet some demon, or some native wariness, or some sense of shame, caused him to glance around and see them. For a moment they looked at each other, startled, silent. Both Elswyth and Leif were conscious that they were arm in arm, but they froze in that posture, feeling that to break suddenly apart would only make their touch look shameful. Words ran through Elswyth's head, but this time no perfect word, no flawless act of charm flew to her. She flushed and stared.

Leif, beside her, glanced around for an angle of escape. Drefan instantly read his intent and directed Drang and Earh to run to the two points where the small path they were on joined the main path. Leif's pause to consider, so salutary against the perils of the sea, was fatal here. Before he chose which way to run, Drang and Earh were already too close to the junction of the paths for him and Elswyth to reach either one first.

"Drefan," Elswyth cried, "what are you doing here?"

Drefan said nothing. Drawing a sword from his belt, he began walking after Drang, whose path to join the main cliff path was shorter and nearer to where they stood. Elswyth saw the sword and understood its purpose.

"You and Leif are both my father's guests," she shouted. "You have shaken hands and broken bread."

Drefan said nothing, but quickened his pace. There was a grimness in his face she had not seen before. He would be on them in a moment, but he had made one error in calculation. In choosing the path that led him to them quickest, he had placed himself and Drang on the path that led away from the hall, with only Earh guarding the path back.

"Run," she said, to Leif, and she set off at once, running as hard as she could toward the hall and the spot which Earh had now reached, where the paths met.

She heard Leif running behind her. She saw confusion in Earh's face as she approached him. His hand was on the hilt of his sword, but he did not draw it. He was not willing to meet his cousin's betrothed with raw steel.

"Let me by," Leif cried behind her.

They were almost on top of Earh.

"Let me by!"

She ignored him, throwing herself forward towards the frozen flummoxed Earh. But then there was a firm grip on her shoulder and a shove that sent her tumbling into the bracken and gorse.

There was a thump and a crash beside her. She struggled to free herself from the sharp clinging gorse and the slippery enveloping bracken. By the time she could see what had happened, Earh was down in the bracken close by and Leif was past him on the path, paused, looking back at her with anguish and sorrow on his face.

"Run," she shouted at him. She glanced back and saw Drefan and Drang running up the path. "Run, you fool. Run!"

Leif turned and ran toward the hall.

A strong hand grasped her by the arm and lifted her to her feet.

"You are safe from him now," Drefan said, enfolding her in a painful embrace and pulling her head down onto his shoulder.

28 A Promise to Love

Elswyth struggled out of Drefan's embrace.

"You leave Leif alone!" she demanded.

"He was going to rape you."

"He was not. He hates men who rape."

"You have no experience of men."

"Except a whole village full of them."

"A whole village who fear your father's vengeance. Have you not felt their eyes on you?"

She had, of course. But though she had begun to find it wearisome sometimes, never had it made her feel afraid. And he was right, of course, she did not fear because she knew no man on the manor would dare to touch her. But to suggest that Leif was capable of rape? The accusation was so monstrous, so strange. Drefan could not possibly have misread his character so badly.

"What do you think they would do if they did not fear your father's vengeance?" Drefan asked, looking down on her as if she were a willful child and he a scolding father.

"I don't know. Some of them might. But not Leif. He is an honorable man. We were just going for a walk."

"He is a heathen. There is no honor among heathens. He had his arms about you. He was carrying you away to a hidden place to rape you and kill you. Then he planned to sail away before your father found your body."

"That's stupid." She could find no other word for it. How could she find an argument against an idea as absurd as this?

"Then why were his arms about you?" he demanded. "Are you saying you willingly went walking out with another man, embracing like lovers? Are you telling me you are his whore?"

"I told you. I was comforting him. His father has been captured and Leif does not have the money for his ransom. He fears his father will be tortured or killed. Wouldn't you comfort a friend who was bearing such a burden?"

"I know what I saw."

"Apparently not. First you thought I was kidnapped. Then you thought I was whoring. You make up horrible things because you can't think anything nice about a Norsk."

"You cannot see harm in anyone. You are a child who has been protected and spoiled all her life. You don't think there is any evil in the world."

"If I didn't, I do now. What were you doing there anyway? I saw you leave this morning. You said you had business."

"This was my business. I could not go back to my father and tell him I supped with a Norsk. He would have had my hide. So I decided I would keep watch. If he kept the peace, and sailed away, I would never need to tell my father that I shook his hand. But now I see I was right not to trust him."

"All you saw was me comforting a friend in his grief."

"A ruse, to get you alone. I don't trust him. I never did."

"Why not? Just because he is Norsk? Don't Anglish raid Anglish? Don't Anglish raid Welisc and Pict? Do you not trust

234

any Anglish man you meet? I told you, we have traded with them for years."

"You said he has books. Where would he have got those except from Lindisfarne?"

Elswyth felt a sickening lunge of guilt in her belly. She could feel her cheeks burning. So she had let slip about the books. She feared she had when Leif had asked her, but she had not been sure. But obviously she had, and this was the fruit of it.

"I was on the road," he continued, "and I remembered what you said, and I thought, there is treachery here. These vikingar play the part of traders to sell their loot. But they are false friends. And then I remembered how I had seen him look at you. I was afraid for you."

"Well the books come from Aachen, not Lindisfarne. He traded for them. He didn't steal them."

"If he is not guilty, why did he run?"

'You were coming at him with a sword in your hand. Three on one. Wouldn't you run?"

"I'm no coward."

"Nor is he. Have you faced a storm at sea?"

"You know so much about him?"

"He's my friend."

"Do you love him?"

"What?"

They had been bellowing at each other over the rush of the wind, but now he stepped forward, grasped her by the arms and turned her, placing his back between her and Drang and Earh who had been standing by watching the quarrel.

"Do you love me?" he asked, bending close to her ear.

It was a question like a breaching whale, enormous and implacable, emerging sudden and terrible out of a calm sea. When had either of them ever spoken of love? They had an understanding, an acceptable arrangement, advantageous to both parties. Love, she had always been told, was the product of a happy marriage, not its cause. Even with her mother and father, she had always understood that their coupling was a matter of desire and advantage. Love came later. Love came over her cradle. That was the way of the world. And yet, why would her father have married a slave, if not for love? A matter of honor perhaps, when he found out Edith was with child?

"You just called me a spoiled child and a whore," she said, parrying the thrust to buy time.

"Alright, I am sorry for that. But do you love me?"

"You have never spoken of love to me."

"I speak of it now."

"Do you love me?" she asked him. Another parry for time.

"Yes," he said, immediately and fiercely.

She looked at him, saw the anguish and longing in his face, and believed him. But how long standing was his love? Had he discovered it yesterday, when he saw her arm in arm with Leif. Today when he saw them again? Now, when the word disarmed her in argument?

"I saw you last year, take Willa up on your saddle," she said.

"I am no virgin," he said.

"I am," she told him, gazing at him to be sure he believed her, and believing that he did. The hurt in him was genuine. The anguish in his face pleaded for a response. "I can't love you if you try to hurt my friends," she said.

"I can't help being afraid for you, with a bunch of Norsk camped on your beach."

"Like they have camped there spring and autumn since I can remember."

"It's different now."

"They're not different."

"They are more desperate. You said his father was held captive. Desperate men make poor friends."

She hated him for this. Hated him because he had managed to force a seed of doubt into her mind. No, no, she refused to think it.

"If they were planning something desperate, why wait?" She demanded. "They have been here four days. If they were going to do something awful, they would have done it and gone before they were found out."

"For that matter, why do they wait? What are they waiting for?"

"For the money to come for their cargo." She remembered then that her father had told him that they were waiting for his wool production to be complete. Did he remember that? If so, he gave no sign. His suspicion was all on her.

"You know all their business?"

"Yes. They are friends. I talk to them."

"Does your father know you walk out alone with him, without a guard?"

"If I needed a guard to come up here, which I don't, Father would trust Leif to guard me."

"Well I don't."

"Well I do."

"Do you love me?" He had circled round her defenses again.

"I'm going to marry you, aren't I?"

"Are you?"

"You don't want me?"

"I said I want you."

"Well then…"

"Do you love me?"

"Will you leave Leif alone? And Thor and the rest?"

"If you love me."

"Then I love you." But her eyes went to the ground as she said it. She bit her lip.

He put his hand under her chin and raised her face to his, lowering his mouth onto hers while pulling her into a gentle embrace. He was careful not to hurt her as he had done before. She could feel the restraint in his arms as they surrounded her. She surrendered to the kiss. What else could she do? He had out-fenced her in the end. To have said no would have imperiled more than Leif and Thor. It would have imperiled the whole of her future, the future of her mother and her sisters and all her Welisc kin. It would have broken her mother's heart. So she kissed him back, as ardently as she knew how, aware of her clumsiness, excusing it with inexperience.

She was rescued by catcalls from Drang and Earh.

"Shut it, you two," Drefan said, releasing her. "You will respect my lady or my sword."

His cousins reacted with mock horror.

Drefan tensed up, but Elswyth, her peaceweaving skills returning to her at last, threw an arm around him and hugged him to her side. She felt the anger go out of him.

"I think as Lady of Bamburgh, it will be my right to approve any girl these two want to marry," she said. "Is that not so?"

"It will be so if I make it so," Drefan said. She could feel the delight in him to have her as his companion in jest.

"I know some thin ugly girls of no fortune, with dispositions to match."

And then they made mock obeisance to her and begged her to find them better wives, and she charmed them, charmed him, becoming, in her time of need, the lady of the hall whose office it is to bring peace and good fellowship to all, lifting their spirits, making them forget their treachery and their defeat. Yet inside her, something wept.

29 To Lie Among the Dunes

It was Attor's belief that mead made enemies of friends and friends of enemies. He was aware that forcing Leif and Drefan to eat and drink together had done no more than bind them to the laws of hospitality. It had not made them friends, and, loving them both, thinking of each of them as near to a son, he welcomed Drefan's return as an opportunity to try to do with many cups what one shared cup had not accomplished. And so, overriding the protests of his wife, his daughter, and most of the prospective guests, he insisted on a makeshift feast that evening, though with none of the formalities of the feast with which he had welcomed Leif's arrival. It was storytelling and laughter in the glow of mead and fire that he was after, and after a fashion he got his will.

A bard had wandered into the village and Attor had promised him several days employment, both to provide some entertainment to the young men whose dispositions he was trying to improve, and to keep the bard from telling tales in the next town or village of a Norsk ship lying on Attor's beach.

The bard was a canny fellow. He knew who Drefan of Bamburgh was and did everything he could to praise him. The effect on Drefan was everything that Attor could have hoped for. With a cup in one hand and the other arm around Elswyth's waist, he became his old self, generous and boisterous, boasting of exploits, posing riddles, singing songs. He and his cousins talked more and more animatedly between themselves as the evening wore on, their laughter ringing through the hall. They became more and more generous with the bard too, challenging him with requests for obscure songs, which he never failed to know and which he never failed to adapt to add some praise of his patrons. Elswyth managed to stump him every time, by asking for Norsk and Welisc tunes, which Drefan and the bard both treated with great merriment.

Mead, alas, did nothing to loosen Leif's tongue. He deflected a few of Drefan's jests with simple words, and declined twice the request that he should sing them a Norsk song. When Drefan and his cousins kept challenging him, Elswyth disengaged herself from Drefan's arm, and said, "I'll sing!" She did with all her usual charm, so that even the bard seemed pleased to play for her, though the tip she offered him for his accompaniment was far less than Drefan was showering on him to sing his praises.

After a couple of hours, Leif rose and begged to be excused. He mumbled something about making sure the ship was secure, and being awake to see what weather the morning would bring, and then stumbled out of the hall.

Half an hour after this, Edith begged to be excused also, saying the baby needed its rest, and Elswyth insisted it was time for her to go to bed also. Drefan protested, but Elswyth appeased him with a long kiss, which Attor found hard to watch, and then rose from his embrace, allowing her hand to run the length of his outstretched arm so that their fingertips were the last point of parting. This physical affection between his daughter and his future son-in-law was something Attor had not seen before, and while he welcomed it, it troubled him as well, for no father can bear to see his daughter grown.

Elswyth and Edith walked together in silence to the sleeping house, each on the cusp of speaking, yet dreading what might be said. They were both clumsy-footed from the mead, and Edith complained, with a laugh, that the baby was tipsy too, and was stumbling around in her womb like a plowboy on midsummer's eve. This sole attempt at conversation drew no response from Elswyth, and so they went in silence to their beds. But having seen her mother to her bed, Elswyth found herself reluctant to go to her own. Though she was tired and muzzy headed there was too much stumbling through her heart and her head for her to sleep. She left the sleeping house again, kicking off her shoes as she did so, to feel the warm earth beneath her feet. She made her way towards the beach, guiding her unsteady feet half by memory and half by moonlight.

Her only plan had been to go down to the water's edge, to bathe her feet in the hope that the kiss and heartbeat of the sea would soothe her. But then she saw a form sitting on the same log that she had found Leif sitting on that morning. She turned towards him, moving silently, barefoot in the sand. His head was down between his hands, and he was unaware of her approach.

She walked up to him and kicked him in the shin, as hard as she could in bare feet, using her heel to dig into the muscle. She nearly lost her balance doing it, and staggered a little to keep her feet.

"Dumb ass!" she said.

He looked up at her, startled. If the kick had hurt, he gave no sign of it.

"I'm sorry I abandoned you," he said, looking wretched.

"Abandoned me? Why did you knock me down?"

"I told you to let me by. I had to get to Earh. I did not mean for you to fall. I was trying to clear a way for you."

"Dumb ass!" she repeated, and kicked him again.

He rose and stepped away from her, "You should have let me by," he said.

"Dumb ass. Fool. Idiot. It was you they wanted, not me. I was going to jump into Earth's arms. He would do nothing to hurt me! You would have escaped easily."

"Among my people, a woman caught in adultery is subject to vengeance as much as the man."

"There was no adultery. How could there be? I'm not married to either of you."

"You are promised to Drefan. If he thought you had lain with me, he would want vengeance on you. That is what I feared. I was trying to get you safe to your father's hall."

"I was trying to get you safe to my father's hall. Drefan would never hurt me. I was afraid for you."

"If that is true, he is a better man than I give him credit for. But I did not know that. I'm sorry for your bruises, truly I am, but I did not know what else to do."

"Dumb ass."

"Kick me again if you still have bruises to avenge."

"Dumb ass," she said again, stamping her foot and rolling her eyes to the heavens. "Do you think I mind a tumble in the grass? That was nothing. But I had to tell Drefan I loved him. Now he has his hands all over me, and I have to kiss him and tell him how wonderful he is, and hang at his heels like a puppy."

He stared at her.

She stared back, angrily.

"Do you?"

"Do I what?"

"Love him?"

"I hate both of you."

"But you are meant for him?"

"That was Father's bargain. Not mine."

"But you will marry him?"

242

"Ach!" she cried. "I do not want to talk about him. I have had his voice rattling between my ears all day. I am sore from where the jewels on his belt dug into me as he clutched me to his side."

"I don't want to talk about him either."

They stood in silence for a while, facing each other, angry.

"Will he tell your father that I knocked you down?"

"He won't tell Father that he was spying on his guest, then tried to kill him and made a mess of it."

"Will he try again?"

"Not as long as I keep telling him I love him and hug him and kiss him and—I thought you didn't want to talk about him."

"I don't."

Silence again, and then he said, "I am sorry you have to do that for me. It is not right, if you don't want it."

"Who said I didn't want it?"

"You did."

"Suppose I like it?"

"You should. He is to be your husband."

"Not if I don't want him."

"It is your father's wish."

"It is my choice," she said. "But who else will offer himself as a rival to Drefan?"

He turned away from her.

"I suppose you think I should be doing all that with you," she said.

"I don't think that. I know I should not do any of that with you."

"But you want to."

He turned back to her. "Do you want me to?"

She wanted him to. She turned away and walked toward the beach, her footsteps wandering on the soft sand, the sound of the sea filling her head, the rush of the waves, the eternal heartbeat of the sea, setting her own heart racing.

She heard his footsteps behind her. Her head reeled and her heart felt like a kitten chasing a sunbeam. She quickened her pace to keep ahead of him, but he took a few quick steps, grasped her again by the shoulder, halted her, turned her, pulled her to him. She was prepared for his mouth. She was prepared for his hands at the clasps of her brooches. She was prepared for him to lift her from her feet and lay her down in the sand. She was prepared to touch and to be touched, to open and to be entered.

And he paused.

He paused in the moment of embracing. He held her against him, and she was aware of each part of him as it touched each part of her. She waited. She had done all she could. The final push must come from him, or it would all be sand and ashes. She stood still, her arms around him as his were around her—she had made no conscious movement to embrace him, expecting to be borne immediately to the ground, but her arms had found their own way there. He looked down at her. She returned his gaze, steadily and indifferently, waiting for him to complete the journey he had begun. Did he wait for one more sign from her? What more could she possibly show him?

They were both drunk, both sad, both shipwrecked, both reckless. All this was clear to her. She was not so drunk that she did not understand. She was so sad and aching and angry that she did not care. But the last step over the threshold must be his. His peril was greater than hers. His duty was sterner than hers. She would not seduce him out of his duty. She would only stand and show herself ready to receive him if he chose it for himself.

She listened to the sound of the waves hissing on the beach, the distant rumble of the breakers that hit the rocks beyond the river mouth, the snuffling of animals in their pens, the patter of a dog about some private errand. Minutes passed, or hours it seemed, and still they stood in their half-consummated embrace. But she sensed that her will was stronger than his, or

244

perhaps it was simply that her pride was more stubborn. His surrender was upon him. She looked pleadingly into his face. She parted her lips and tilted her head back. But she knew already that his mouth would not bow down to meet hers.

He loosened the pressure of his hand upon her back, not releasing her, but easing his grip, as a man eases his grip on the steering oar to give a ship a little of her own head.

"Still bound by your father's rule?" she asked him.

"Yes," he said. "It is a good rule. A necessary rule."

"Dumb ass," she said. She broke out of his embrace, angry and sad.

He reached out a hand to her, tentatively, then drew it back.

"Last chance, sailor boy," she said.

He did not move. She curled her lip contemptuously and turned and walked back toward the hall.

In the darkness, she did not see the figure that stepped back into the shadows of the hall as she passed by.

30 Better Than Me

Edith could not fall asleep. She had never spent a more painful, awkward evening in the hall, never any evening in which neither her powers as peaceweaver nor Elswyth's (which she reckoned to be greater than her own) had sufficed to make any kind of peace. The poor bard had tried valiantly as well, and had surely earned his money. But she would not have been surprised if he left the hall that night fearing his own powers as a bringer of conviviality were waning.

The first object of her sympathy was Leif, who she held almost as a son in her affections, yet to whom she could not, before Drefan, show all the solicitation of motherhood. Had Drefan (who was soon to be her son) treated any natural born son of hers as he treated Leif that night, she would have taken him aside and twisted his ears. And yet, that Drefan had sat down and eaten and drunk and passed the cup with Norsk at all was something of a miracle. It was perhaps too much to ask that it should be done with ease and grace. And Drefan, however much an oaf he could be, was a man of honor. Having eaten and drunk with Leif, and shaken his hand, he would not quarrel with him. And perhaps that had been the trouble with the evening—that the quarrel that Drefan and Leif were heir to as representatives of their respective races had been bottled up and corked—this, it seemed, by Elswyth's doing more than any other. But quarrel it still was, and therefore no conviviality was possible between them, and every hour spent together in the hall must be filled with sullenness and resentment.

But as she lay awake fretting about it, she began to worry more about Elswyth. She knew that Elswyth had left the sleeping house again, and at first she resolved to let her be, hoping she had decided to go back to the hall and return to Drefan's side. Her daughter had been a picture of gaiety and affection all evening. She had doted on the man she was to marry—sung for him, laughed with him, drunk from his cup, eaten from his hand, rested within the compass of his arm. There had been something false in the performance, for her gaiety had been out of proportion to the tense mood of the room. That in itself was to be expected. That was the role of the peaceweaver, to make men merry by being merrier than they, to make them cordial by being more cordial than they, to shun discord as an unwelcome guest, and invite harmony though it must come from the ends of the earth. And this Elswyth had attempted, with all the art that was native to her, and such additional art as Edith had managed to teach her. It had been to little avail. Might the mood have been worse if not for her efforts? Perhaps. But no one would claim that either of them had succeeded in weaving peace in the hall that night.

But it began to seem to Edith, as she reflected upon it, that Elswyth's shows of affection and attention towards Drefan had seemed false even apart from the practice of the peaceweaver's art. More and more she came to suspect that Elswyth had not merely been trying to soothe the rancor between Drefan and Leif, but to conceal her own rancor towards Drefan as well.

To see that rancor continue for a second day was particularly troubling. Elswyth had such a gift for friendship that Edith had never known rancor to be sustained from one day to the next between Elswyth and anyone—excepting perhaps Hilda, but that was Hilda's doing. But here was that same rancor toward Drefan that had been there yesterday, not mended but grown worse. And if it continued, could Drefan, however much an oaf he might be, remain unaware of it forever?

The more this sleepless wondering dragged on, the more she became convinced that Elswyth had done what Drefan had asked of her, against her own desire, of necessity, and in doing so had come to despise Drefan, and her mother as well. And with that thought in her head it became impossible for her to go on without knowing.

She rose, therefore, and went in search of Elswyth. From the door of the sleeping house, she saw the form of her daughter crossing the compound before the hall. Elswyth saw her standing waiting in the doorway and stopped a few paces away. The message could not have been clearer, but Edith was seized by a heartache too strong to allow her to respect Elswyth's wish to be alone. She went to her, and Elswyth waited where she was, looking at the ground rather than at her mother.

"I thought you went to bed," Edith said.

"Couldn't sleep," Elswyth replied, her voice low and surly, her eyes still on the ground.

"Neither could I," her mother replied.

"I want to go to bed now."

"Where did you go?" The anguish Edith saw in Elswyth now was not two days old. It was of the very hour.

"I'm tired, Mother."

"You are not happy."

"I don't have to be happy all the time."

"But you have spent the evening with the man you are to marry, drinking wine, singing songs, telling tales. How can that not have made you happy?"

"Can't I just go to bed?"

"Where did you go?"

"Mother, I'm tired…"

"Did you go to him?"

Elswyth stiffened, as if with alarm, then turned away from her mother towards the sea.

There seemed only one answer. Only one thing to ask. "Has Drefan asked you to lie with him? Are you wandering about here waiting for him?"

Elswyth turned back to her again. "Why shouldn't I, if I want to?"

"Do you want to? Or is it because…"

"You didn't wait."

"I had nothing to wait for."

"Father couldn't have courted you without…"

"Hilda already thinks I am a trollop," Edith said. "Darling, please not you too."

"Weren't you a trollop?"

"One man. In all my life I have lain with one man. Your father."

"Well, if I was waiting here for Drefan, and I did lie with him tonight, I would only ever lie with one man as well."

"Is that all you want? To be no better than me?"

"Isn't that what you wanted of me? I don't need to be better than you, Mother. I'm not. That's Hilda, not me."

Edith went to her and grabbed her by the arm. "Oh, my darling. Please be better than me. I beg you, be better than me."

"Really, Mother? At what cost? What should I give up to be better than you? Whose safety? Whose freedom? So that I can be better than you?"

Edith could not keep tears from her eyes. "Darling. You don't know. You've never felt your belly pinch. You've never gleaned a field or lived on roots and dandelions. You've never been prey to plowboys or any young thegn that visits the hall. I need you to be a lady. Not half a lady like me, not pretending half the time and hoping no one notices, not Lady Cyneburg looking down her nose and pretending you didn't make a fool of yourself. I need you to be a proper lady, who knows the right things and says the right things and does the right things. I need you to embroider like your fingers were born to it, not like mine that were born to the broom and the quern and never did learn to make an even stitch. I need you to wear shoes on your feet, cover your head, and keep your dress clean."

"And what else, Mother? What else must I keep to be a lady?"

"Don't darling. Be kind to me. Hilda is right. I am a trollop. I think like a trollop. You don't know the difference. You will. A year in Bamburgh hall, and you will see what your grandmother saw, what Lady Cyneburg sees. Cyneburg forgives, because she is a lady. But she knows. She forgives it in me. But she cannot forgive it in you. You are to be Lady of Bamburgh after her, and you must be all she is and more. You must be better than me."

"Mother, why are you saying this now?"

"Because of what I see in you. What I saw tonight. You don't want to marry Drefan. You don't want to marry Drefan, and I don't know why. And I am afraid that it is because… I'm afraid I have made you hate me too."

"Oh, Mother, I'm so tired. I just want to go to bed."

Elswyth broke from her mother and began to walk toward the sleeping house. Edith turned and called after her, "You don't have to."

Elswyth turned back to her.

"You don't have to marry Drefan if you don't want to. Perhaps we can find another way."

"Don't be ridiculous, Mother," Elswyth snapped in return. "There is no other way." And then she turned and entered the sleeping house, leaving her mother standing alone under the harsh gaze of the summer stars.

31 The People Rule Themselves

The weather turned Anglish the next day. A grey bank of cloud crept in from the sea and coated the shore with a misty wetness that was less than rain but more than fog so that raindrops seemed to distill out of the air on anybody unfortunate enough to have to venture out into it. Haymaking was suspended and the hall was filled with the grating ring of men sharpening scythes and sickles and mending all manner of tools and implements while the fires tried vainly to drive the dampness out of the hall air.

The Norsk men were there as well, at Attor's insistence. They tried to be helpful in the work, offering to turn the grindstones or help hone the blades, but few Anglish took up the offers they made, and the Norsk spent much of the time playing Hnefatafl among themselves using pebbles for counters on a board that they scratched out on the dirt of the floor, ignoring the muttered complaints about their idleness that came from the very men who had refused their aid.

Thor sat on the floor and played with Daisy and Moira. Some of the other children of the village tried to join the game but were called back by their parents. Whitney ran around the hall, dodging the work with great dexterity but eventually, finding every avenue blocked, she disappeared outside, only to return half an hour later, mud-spattered to her eyebrows, soaked, and shivering, to be dried and laid down to nap by the fire by her mother.

Elswyth spent much of the morning sitting in uncomfortable silence beside Hilda as they worked on their embroidery. Hilda would glance over at her from time to time and then silently stretch out her work to show how much greater progress she was making, but other than this there was no communication between them. Late in the morning, Attor walked by and tapped Elswyth on the shoulder. This was his sign that they needed to talk. This held no terrors for Elswyth. Whatever her misdeeds, her father was always faster to excuse them than she was herself. Her father's indulgence was not boundless, but it was vast. What Elswyth had never guessed was that her father lived in terror of her running away again and was thus afraid to say any cross word to her. Her mother's reaction was quite the opposite. Edith would have tied a rope to the hall doorpost and the other end to Elswyth's leg if Attor had permitted it. Fear that his wife's tight hold might provoke another flight had loosened Attor's boundaries even further. The result was that no daughter in Northumbria looked forward to her father's talking-tos with less trepidation than Elswyth did.

Attor led her to the serving kitchen, a small partitioned area at the back of the hall where food from the kitchen was staged before being brought in for a feast. He shooed the slaves who were working there out into the rain and sat down heavily on a stool. Elswyth hopped up on the edge of the table. She had learned that it paid to have her head higher than her father's in these encounters.

G. M. BAKER

"I had decided that it was better that no one should challenge Leif at the feast," he said.

Elswyth said nothing. She had a full defense prepared, had rehearsed it in her head several times. But she did not expect to have to use it. Her father would find a way to excuse it himself if she only gave him time.

"I did not want to remind everyone of Lindisfarne again. You understand?"

"Yes, Father."

"I did not think Leif was up to answering the challenge."

"He…" she caught herself and stopped abruptly.

"What?"

"Nothing. Sorry Father. Go on."

"He is young. He has suffered a great tragedy. He bears a heavy burden. You understand?"

"Yes, Father."

"And his Anglish is not good."

"It's pretty good when he gets going… Sorry. Go on."

"So it was safest to say nothing about that ugly business."

He cocked an eye at her as if inviting her to speak, but she remained silent.

"I know it is the lady's right to challenge the guest…"

Again the cocked eye. Again she met it with silence.

"But it is the lady's first duty to ensure harmony in the hall."

"Yes, Father."

"Perhaps it was not right to put that burden on you, in the circumstances."

"Mother was tired."

"Your mother is never tired."

"Then why?"

"To test you. To train you. You will be Lady of Bamburgh one day."

"Not for ages. Kenrick and Cyneburg are both healthy as horses."

255

"No one knows when death may come. A fever, a cut that festers … And as heir, Drefan will keep his own table, from time to time, to entertain his friends, and to gain the respect of the people he will come to rule. Your role will be crucial on those days. Your mother wants to make sure you are ready. But perhaps she should have waited for another time."

"I'm to be married after the harvest. Unless the king suddenly decides to drop in on us, there won't be another feast until the harvest, and then my wedding feast, which will be in Bamburgh."

"Still, there was so much ill feeling in the hall that night. It was too much to ask of you. I should not blame you, really. I should have overruled your mother and had her do it."

"But…" She caught herself again. Stop. Don't make excuses. Let him make them for you.

"What?"

"Nothing. Sorry, Father."

"Not that it came out badly in the end."

"No, Father." No, that night in the hall had gone well enough. Better than any night since.

"But it might have."

"Yes, Father."

Here the conversation lagged. Her father sat pondering a while, but she knew his scoldings well enough to know that he had exhausted his line of attack, and, finding no resistance, was beginning to doubt the justice of his campaign—a lion embarrassed to be seen growling at a lamb. Now came the familiar shift, from scold to confidante.

"Leif acquitted himself well."

"Yes, Father."

"Perhaps the people were impressed that he had the courage to speak."

"I thought so."

"Not that they are exactly welcoming them. How did Leif get that cut on his temple anyway?"

"Just an accident, Father. I dressed it with honey so it didn't fester."

"Good. I am glad you are taking care of him. It is a good example to the people."

"Thank you, Father."

"Still, when a man offers to turn a grindstone for you, and you refuse him… Everyone in the hall is still sulking and the Norsk are off in the corner playing games Elswyth…"

"I know. It's so silly. They know perfectly well Leif did not raid Lindisfarne. Even Drefan knows it."

"It might not have been so bad if we had not rubbed their noses in it again."

By "we" he meant "you". But it was his way to take all faults on himself. Elswyth was adept at turning this to her advantage, but hearing it now, she had a sudden attack of conscience. It had been her act, which she had taken in knowing defiance of her father's will, because she had seen that his tactic was not working. It was a grownup act, and she suddenly realized that she could not bear to be excused for it as a child.

"I had to," she said, firmly. "I could feel it in the room. The question had to be asked and answered. There would have been no peace till it was asked. They may be sulking now, but they are not fighting. It would have been worse than boys throwing stones if I hadn't asked the question."

"Boys throwing stones?"

"That's how Leif got his cut. Sorry, I just lied about that. I don't know why."

"Which boys?"

"It was dealt with, Father."

"Which boys?"

"I'm not going to tell you. Leif and I dealt with it."

"Quite the rebel you have become, daughter."

"I'm not trying to be a rebel, Father."

"Why lie about it?"

"Because I knew you would ask which boys. And I didn't want to have to disobey you."

"Then why disobey?"

"Because when we dealt with it, it was over, and we said we would not tell you about it."

"What did you do to them then? There had to be some price paid."

"Not telling you. Sorry."

Attor gave a low growl under his breath. "You know what my father told me, as he was dying? He said the people govern themselves in secret. They only come to the lord when they cannot settle things among themselves. He did not tell me it was the same with children."

"Didn't you always tell us not to be tattle-tales?"

"I suppose I did. You are saying I trained you to defy me?"

"Yes, Father."

"So what happened in the hall is my fault."

"No. You asked me to be lady of the hall. I took the lady's part. I made the choice. I knew it was not what you wanted. But I also knew your way was not working. And Mother told me I did well. She said Drefan would have been proud of me if he had seen it."

"She said the same to me."

"So, are you proud of me too, or are you angry?"

"A father can be both. You'd be astonished how often a father finds he is both."

"I'm not sorry."

"You frightened the life out of me when you brought Snell forward to challenge him."

"Leif said the same thing."

"He gave a good answer."

"Yes, he did."

258

"If he had not…"

"If he had given no answer at all, because he was not asked…"

"We are steering a path very close to bloodshed, child."

"I'm not a child. See," she added, showing him the shoes on her feet.

He laughed. "I see, but Elsy, it is not you that should have to steer that path."

"Well I am," she said. "I don't want to be, but I am." She felt her chest tighten as she said this. Her father did not know the half of it, and it was best that he should not. The people govern themselves in secret, for how could the lord sort out this tangle with justice? "How soon will Heorot be back from Monkwearmouth, do you think? We will be off this path that steers close to bloodshed once he returns with the gold."

"Aye, but if all had gone as well as it could on his journey, he could not have been back before today, and he won't make much progress in this weather. The roads will be too slick. But remember, child, he had to cross the Tyne, and the Wansbeck, and the Blyth. Then wait on the abbot to agree to the price and collect the gold. Then cross those rivers again. It may be days yet."

"Poor Leif. It must be eating him up. He seems so calm, but I know he is suffering."

"Leif treads a lonely path," her father said. "The lord's path is always a lonely one, God knows, and Leif is new to it."

"He has Thor, and Eric, and the rest."

"He is their jarl, now. Thor is his mentor, and a mentor cannot be a friend, exactly. The rest must obey him, and the servant cannot be friend to the master either. I am the only one who bears the same burdens, but I am too old to be his friend. And too much a landsman, I suspect. But you love ships and the sea. And you love those monkish books as much as he does."

"Are you sure that's wise, Father?"

"Of course. It will cheer him up. I realize that once Drefan came you wanted to keep company with him. I had no idea you and Drefan had become … that you were so … so ardent."

"I'm still a maiden, Father."

"Aye, well, I've not seen the two of you sit so close before, nor kiss like that."

"I'll warn you next time, Father, so you can look away."

"Anyway, Drefan rode out this morning. God knows what could be so urgent that he rode out in this weather. Drang and Earh were not happy about it, I can tell you. Meanwhile, Leif sits alone in the hall, sharpening that knife of his hour after hour. He'll turn it into a pin before sundown. Go talk to him about ships and books and Spain, and all the places you keep talking about. He needs a sister, since he doesn't have a friend."

"A sister?"

"Aye. You can be a good sister when you put your mind to it."

"Do I have to?"

"Why not? Have you two had a quarrel?"

"Of course not."

"Two days ago, no one could hold you to your duties for you had to hear sea tales. Now I ask you to and you don't want to."

"But Father, I can never go. It is foolish to torture myself with tales of Orkney and Spain when I'll never go farther than York or Lindisfarne."

"You risked much for Leif's sake. You can do this little bit more for him. I'm right about this. Please don't defy me again."

"Very well, Father," she said, with a sinking heart. She hopped down off the table and kissed him on the cheek. The people rule themselves in secret, and only come to the lord when they cannot settle matters among themselves. And sometimes, not even then.

32 A Walk in the Rain

Leif noticed Elswyth coming towards him across the hall. When it became clear that she meant to speak to him, he put his knife and whetstone away and walked toward the door, plunging out into the mist without hat or cloak. He started to make his way down toward the beach, where the ship would offer a small degree of protection from the weather. He turned when he realized that she was following him. She kept coming toward him, so he turned and walked on. She fell in behind him, keeping a distance of several yards. He continued at the same pace, and she behind him, until they came to the edge of the sea. There they paused, neither looking at each other nor speaking. There was only a few yards of sea visible before it faded into the enveloping mist. All sounds but the waves were hushed by the mist. The waves were muted also, but what sound of them remained seemed to pervade the air with a gentle roar like the slumberous breathing of some unimaginable great beast. They stood together on the sea's edge, yards apart, soaked with the dew coalescing on their skin and clothes, relishing its damp chill.

261

Then Elswyth turned and began to walk north along the sea's edge. After a moment, Leif followed. He took a course a little more inland and hurried a little, until he was walking in parallel with her, a dozen yards off her larboard beam, keeping pace, but never trimming his sail to intercept.

They passed the ship thus, unnoted by the man on watch, huddled under his sealskins, and passed on down the beach, in silent distant company, growing colder and wetter as they went, until the pleasure of it faded into an oblivion, into a small grey world defined and given direction only by the line formed by sand and sea, each alone except for the constant beacon that kept pace beside them.

They walked on like this for half an hour or more until they reached the end of the beach, where the rocks intruded into the sea, impassable except at low tide. Elswyth began a long turn inland, and Leif, understanding the required maneuver without the need to speak or look for any signal, walked on a few feet further before he turned toward the sea, so that even in the turn they kept their distance. Her pace slackened until he had completed his turn and drawn up on his parallel course. Then she resumed her cruising speed, and he matched it, until, sodden and footsore, they came again to the ship, and there he stopped, letting her sail on alone, back toward the hall, with not a word spoken or a glance exchanged.

But, moments before her form would have been swallowed up in the mist, she turned and came back towards him, violating the zone of neutrality they had observed until then, but still stopping a few feet away. Her usually buoyant hair was plastered flat to her skull and her spring-flower complexion and autumn-berry lips were washed almost white. She was shivering.

"I told Drefan about the books," she said. "I didn't mean to. We were arguing and he asked why you were camped on our beach so long. I was angry with him and I didn't think before I spoke."

He looked at her in silence. The shame and hope he saw in her face made him want to weep. He felt neither anger nor dread. Why had he not kissed her last night, when she invited him to? There was no harm she could do him that he would not bear. He only wished to enfold her, to take the anguish from her heart, to champion her against all the world.

"He was bound to ask that question," he said. "He is to be your husband. You were bound to tell him the truth."

"I'm sorry."

"You did nothing wrong."

"Yes I did. Not that, maybe. But other things. I am sorry about all of it."

"Don't be. There has been no harm done yet. Tomorrow Heorot may come with the gold, and I can sail away without loss."

"Without loss?" she asked him.

"With no less than I came with," he said, with a shrug.

"No harm done," she said. Tears would have been superfluous in the mist.

She paused a second, almost as if in the end she would come to him.

"Father says you need a sister," she said.

"I have two sisters," he said, puzzled.

"I should have told him that."

She turned and walked away, making her way slowly to the village.

***

As Elswyth was passing the hall on her way to the sleeping house to change her sodden clothes, a large figure loomed out of the mist. Eric had been hunched under the slope of the hall roof, trying to keep a little dry while keeping watch.

"It won't do, Princess," he said.

"Go swivel, Eric," she said.

"It's not my swiving I worry about."

"Well you can sure as hell stop worrying about mine."

"When I see him leave and you follow?"

"None of your swiving business."

"My swiving life if your father finds out."

"Shows what you know. Father sent me. He thinks Leif needs a sister."

"Your father is a swiving idiot."

"I know. But I'm not. And I'm still a swiving virgin, so swivel out of my swiving way."

"Make sure you swiving stay that way."

"Mind your own swiving business."

Still Eric did not move, so she walked around him. He did not move to block her way again but turned where he stood to watch her walk away toward the sleeping house. When she was gone, he cursed under his breath and set out for the beach in search of Leif.

In the sleeping house, Elswyth dried herself with her lambskin and climbed into bed, quaking with sorrow.

33 Musical Chairs

The weather cleared the next day but the fields were too wet to work, and, every form of sharpening and mending having been completed the day before, Attor declared a holiday from the fields. He hoped, in part, that this would create the occasion for his people to go down to the beach and meet and talk with the visitors, whose presence they had, for the most part, sulkily ignored since the day they had arrived.

In all the days that Leif and his crew had lain on the beach, one thing above all others had marked the strain on their welcome—the absence of children. At any normal port of call, they expected to be overrun with curious boys and cheeky little girls, to be plagued with constant demands for stories and treats. They expected young men to come down to the ship to boast and to barter local wines and ales for silks and combs and trinkets to please their sweethearts. They expected young women to come, to flirt, and to be courted, and to disdain their courtship, and to win promises of gifts while promising nothing in return. But here there had been no children underfoot, no young women, no young men. They had been kept away, or stayed away of their own volition, held off by their parent's fear or by their own. It was not within the thegn's right to order other people's children down to the beach, but, determined to set an example, he ordered his own to go.

Hilda came and sat down on the sands near the ship without saying a word to any of them. She was carrying her work basket and she took out her embroidery and started on it, ignoring the questions and the admiration of her work that came from the curious Norsk sailors who gathered round to look. This expedition to the beach was an interruption of Hilda's private plans for the day, and, having fulfilled the letter of her obligation, she went on about her business as if she had never been interrupted.

Moira came, carrying Daisy on her narrow hip, and wishing to find someone else to take care of her. Thor's eyes lit up at the sight of the bairn in her sister's arms. The old man took Daisy from Moira. Daisy looked studiously at him, considered whether to cry or laugh, as if she were a young woman considering which dress to put on to please her lover, decided for laughter, and began to tug happily on the ends of Thor's mustache. Moira, relieved of her charge, began talking, going from man to man and telling everything she knew, or supposed, or hoped, without seeming to care that few of them had many words of her language.

Whitney came too, following Moira. Whitney ran. Poor, mad, blissful Whitney ran up and down the stretch of firm damp sand at the tide's edge, until she was exhausted, then lay down and fell instantly asleep with her head cradled on Thor's boots.

Seeing the thegn's daughters around the ship, the two boys who had made their peace with Leif came down also and were received enthusiastically by Leif and by the rest of the crew, who, lacking any other occupation, competed with each other to show the boys the workings of the ship and tell them sea stories.

Elswyth came too, a little while after her sisters, with shoes on her feet and a wimple covering her head and neck. Over this she was wearing a deeply hooded travelling cloak that enveloped her figure and drooped over her face almost to the end of her nose.

Thor looked up and frowned at Elswyth's approach.

"Father told us all to come," she told him. "He wants to show that he trusts you with his children, so the rest of the village will come down to the ship like they used to. Am I supposed to disobey him and stay away?"

"Aren't you warm in that thing?" Eric asked. He too had observed her approach with a frown.

"Since I have to be here, I want to look at the books. This is so that Brother Alun does not have to look at me."

Brother Alun was indeed on the ship. Kendra still breathed and a careful hand could still find a pulse in her, but she did not wake and looked sure to die without waking again. The monk had engaged a boy to sit by her bedside and watch her, for it was known that people sometimes woke from such sleeps when death was close upon them and might speak lucidly before their final end came. He did not expect such an event. He expected that her breath and her pulse would soon fade away and the body grow cold. But the boy was instructed to run and find him if there should be any sign of waking, and meanwhile he went to the ship to read the books that, once they were in the possession of the Monkwearmouth scriptorium, would be claimed by monks of greater seniority, while he would be sent back to copying.

Leif, who had been sitting in the ship listening to the monk reading, stood up when he heard Elswyth's voice. He looked at her and, feeling his eyes on her, she looked back at him under the drooping hood of her cloak. The understanding between them was complete now, though it had never been stated. Each knew exactly what the other felt, what the other wanted, and exactly what stood between them. Looking at each other was thus at once painful and comforting, for each had only the other to console them in their estrangement from the one they loved.

The monk's incomprehensible Latin—Elswyth had made no progress in understanding it, having no points of reference for anything he read—had a kind of hypnotic quality to it. There was a certain comfort in him, too, as a figure apart from her world. She felt set apart from that world herself, separated from it by the secret she kept. The monk seemed an apt companion in alienation. That he refused to look at her was an obvious obstacle to any kind of intimacy or fellow feeling in their mutual exiles, and yet his refusal to look at her, to participate in the world's desire for her, was so much a part of what set him apart that if he had looked at her as other men looked at her, he would have been part of the world, and therefore not a sharer in her current exile. And so she sat, out of his direct line of sight, sweating in her over-warm travelling cloak, separated from his words by the barrier of language, and yet warmly comforted to be in the presence of one who like herself could not express or indulge or even acknowledge the ordinary desires of life. And in this way she felt an intense friendship for him, one which she fancied he shared, a fellowship in exile, even if they were as exiled from each other as they were from the rest of the world. If it were possible for him to live so, surely it was possible for her to live so as well. Of course, he lived with others who lived as he did. He had companions in his chosen exile, companions with whom, she supposed, he could discuss all the trials and fears and hopes and joys of their exile. And this led her to an extraordinary thought, for one whose thoughts turned so often to muscled arms and calloused hands: if Thor could wish to be a monk, why not she a nun? And what, oh what, would her mother say to that?

Leif sat opposite the monk, in a position where he could not look at Elswyth without turning his head. The monk read on, aloud, his Latin alien to them both, but his emotion in the reading—here excitement, here sorrow, here delight, here puzzlement—were plain to hear. At length he came to the end of the book he was reading and paused to ask Leif for another volume. Leif took the volume from him and was about to return it to the chest, when he paused, turned, and laid it in front of Elswyth.

"Do you want to look at the pictures?" he asked her.

She looked up at him. They both knew that they wanted to look at them together. They both knew that it would be natural and innocent enough for them to sit side by side on the deck and look at them, talk about them, delight in them as they both wished. Elswyth knew that to do so would be to obey her father's explicit command. But both knew that such intimacy was perilous. Perilous, and painful also. If she were to look at pictures, she must look at them alone, and he must sit, idle in the sunshine, close, but out of communion, while she did so.

"Yes, please," she said.

He laid the book in front of her and then went and pulled the next volume out of the chest for the monk.

"It is strange work for a man, the making and reading of books," Leif said, as he placed the volume in the monk's hands. "I wish I understood where the profit in it lies."

"The profit is to know the mind of God," Brother Alun replied seriously.

"You have strange gods," Leif said. "Our gods are the gods of land and sea and air, the gods of forest and of harvest, gods of the hearth and gods of war. A god of words is a strange god."

"Indeed," said Brother Alun, as if struck by this for the first time. "Our God is a God of words, for the Gospel of John says, 'In the beginning was the Word and the Word was God.' All the

269

more profit in the study of words then, for to study words is to study God."

"Is it a hard study?" Leif asked. "I have studied many years to learn the handling of a ship, the reading of the sky, and the finding of harbors. I have many years to study still to learn all the ways of trade. How long does it take to learn the craft of bookmaking?"

"It is reckoned the study of a lifetime."

"Yet you can read the letters. You can make inks and pens, you can prepare skins for writing, and can form the letters. How long did this learning take?"

"I have studied ten years. Learning the letters comes easily, and the making of parchment, pens, and ink is a trade like any other. But it is learning Latin that is difficult. It is a language apart, wholly different from Anglish. And then there is the history to learn, and the scripture, for you cannot fully understand the meaning of a book until you know the history of the peoples who wrote it."

"Still, I do not see the profit in words, unless they work magic."

"We do not work magic," the monk said. "Magic does not work. Only the foolish and uneducated believe in it."

"What about miracles, then?" Elswyth asked. "Aren't miracles magic?"

"Magic is man's attempt to bend nature to his will," the monk said. "A miracle is an act of God. We may ask God for a miracle, and some men have the ear of God, and their requests are often granted, but the miracle comes from God and God alone. The proud try to work magic; the humble are granted miracles."

"No miracles for us then," Elswyth said.

"You are saying I am too proud to hear the miracle of prophecy? That I am not worthy to hear prophecy even if Kendra had any to utter?"

"I'm teasing. But if prophecy only comes to the humble, you can count Kendra out, believe me."

"Ah, but consider the Old Testament. The prophets spoke not to the humble but to the proud!"

"So maybe you are not proud enough for Kendra to speak to you. I think Kendra is too proud to speak prophecy and you are too humble to hear it."

"So I have wasted my days here?"

"No. Leif needed you to write the letter for him, and to tell him the value the books. If you hadn't been here, what would we have done? And what would have become of the books?"

"So you are suggesting that it was God's purpose to send me here to ransom the books?"

"And to help Leif."

"Why would God send me to help a heathen?"

"The good Samaritan, remember. It's your story."

"It's still the other way round. The Samaritan was the pagan."

"So it is right for Leif to help you, but not for you to help him?"

"The first help we must give the pagans is to tell them the good news. Not help them sell stolen goods. Goods stolen from Christians."

"Not stolen," Leif said. "My uncle bought them."

"Bought them cheaply, knowing them to be stolen."

"Bought them at the price the man who sold them agreed to."

"Because he was a thief and could not sell them for their true value without being caught and punished."

"That is not my uncle's fault, nor mine."

"Do stolen goods become rightful property simply because a thief sells them? If that were so, any thief would travel with a merchant in tow and sell him the goods as soon as he stole them, leaving their original owner without recourse. A merchant like you would sail an hour behind a vikingr and buy his booty as soon as he stole it. Would that be a just trade? Would the trader really be any different from the vikingr?"

"You know that I cannot give up the books."

"I know. It is your father's ransom. But if it were not your father's ransom, if your father was safe in his hall, would you give up the books, knowing that they were stolen?"

"What of the price my uncle paid for them?"

"What if that were returned to you?"

"And what of the cost of transporting them?"

"What if a fair price were paid for that also? Would you give up the windfall and return them to those who paid for their creation?"

"Why should I?" Leif asked. "If a man cannot keep possession of his property, that is no affair of mine. I did not rob him. My uncle did not conspire with the bandit."

"Still, obligation or no, would you do it?"

"Perhaps," said Leif, after a moment's consideration. "By doing so, I would make a rich man my friend, and thus I might win a share of his trade, and over a lifetime that might be more valuable than the books. But I do not have a lifetime to get my father's ransom."

"If the books belong to the Bishop of Utrecht," Elswyth asked, "will the Abbot of Monkwearmouth send the books to the Bishop of Utrecht after he has paid for them with his own gold?"

"I do not know," the monk replied.

"And if he did," she asked, "would the Bishop of Utrecht send back the gold that the Abbot of Monkwearmouth had paid for them?"

"He should, I suppose."

"Then he will have paid twice for them," Leif said.

"If he didn't," said Elswyth, "the Abbot of Monkwearmouth would have paid for them and had nothing."

"So it is clear," said the monk, "that it is unjust that a trader who neither made them nor paid for them should have the profit of them, no matter how dire his need."

"Without the trader," Leif said, "neither bishop nor abbot would have them. The trader earned his profit by recognizing the value, preserving them, and transporting them."

"It's like musical chairs," said Elswyth with a laugh. "The books and the gold are the last two chairs and Leif, the bishop, and the abbot are the players. Someone will be left without a chair when the music stops, and it mustn't be Leif."

"But why should it be the bishop or the abbot?" the monk asked. "They are surely innocent of all this."

"So is Leif," Elswyth said. "It is the Frisian bandit who stole them that is the guilty one."

"But how is it possible that we have three innocent men and only two treasures?"

"But there are not three innocent men," Leif said. "The Bishop of Utrecht failed to guard his property. That is his fault. I am not responsible for it. Nor is the Abbot of Monkwearmouth. He should buy the books from me and I should keep the gold for my father's ransom."

"But if the bishop is guilty for not guarding his property," the monk said, "is not your father guilty also, for not guarding his own property, for allowing his people to be killed and their goods looted?"

There was a nasty silence then. The monk blushed. He had spoken in the flow of argument, not thinking of the consequence. Now he hung his head.

"I don't like these monkish games of words," Leif said. He turned and vaulted over the rail onto the sand below.

Elswyth moved to follow him but caught herself. She turned back to look at the monk, a rebuke on her tongue. He raised his eyes and looked her full in the face, his face rueful. And then he realized where his eyes had fallen, and pulled his cowl down over his face. Elswyth wanted to hug him for sympathy as much as she wanted to scold him for his unkind words, but she realized at once that this would only add to his distress.

"I did not think before I spoke," he said, ruefully, rising to his feet. "I must try to make amends." He clambered awkwardly over the side of the ship and dropped clumsily to the sand below before hurrying after Leif who was walking northward along the margin of sand and sea.

Elswyth watched the monk follow Leif up the beach. Her first instinct was to vault over the side and go after him, obedient to her instinct to include herself in every conversation. But she restrained herself. She realized that she loved them both, in different ways, and wanted them to mend their old friendship, and that this was something that she must leave them to do for themselves. Besides, the day was growing hot and she was roasting in her heavy travelling cloak. Realizing that the two men from whose eyes she had wanted to shield herself were now walking away from her along the beach, she sloughed it off and sat with her chin on the rail, watching until the monk caught up with Leif, and the two walked on beside each other. She watched until she saw the tensions grow less in each of their frames, and then picked up the cloak, folded it over her arm, and made her way to the side of the ship and down to the sands. The wimple she kept on, however, despite finding it scratchy and hot in the sun.

"The bairn's getting hungry," Thor said, when he saw her. Daisy was trying to suck nourishment from her thumb.

"I'll take her," Elswyth said. She took Daisy from Thor's arms.

"Come on, kitty cat," Elswyth said, nudging Whitney with her toe. Whitney wakened, looked up at her sister adoringly, hugged her round her leg, and ran.

Elswyth started across the sands towards the village. Hilda took this as a signal that her own obligation was ended and packed up her embroidery and followed. Moira did not notice their exodus at once, but when she looked up from the story that she was telling Eric, she stopped mid-sentence and fled after her sisters.

34 Football on the Beach

That afternoon, Attor found a bladder and organized a team of Anglish to play football against the Norsk crew. Leif was certain that it would end in bloodshed. His fear deepened when Attor pulled off his shirt and made it plain that he intended to play for the Anglish team, and that he expected Leif to play for the Norsk. But as guests who had now overstayed by twice the customary three days for a visit, the Norsk had little choice but to agree to their host's request. The goals were marked out. The two sides took up their positions. The ball was thrown in, and the game was on.

Elswyth did not go down to the beach to watch. Edith knew where her daughter would be. She sighed as she looked at the steepness of the path—an easy walk when she was not carrying a child, but a trial in the latter days of a pregnancy—and started up towards the cliff top.

She had no clear plan of what she intended to say to Elswyth once she found her. She wanted reconciliation before any more concrete objective. She knew that every child must eventually suffer pains that no parent can soothe or take upon themselves, and she knew that this moment had come for Elswyth, that she might never fully understand what had so roiled her daughter's heart these last few days, however keenly she was aware of her own part in it. It was the peril of urging your child to be an adult that with that came an adult's reserve, an adult's privacy, an adult's right to suffer their own pain in their own way. She had sought Elswyth hoping that the sight of her daughter would let her know how to begin, but when she found her and looked at her back as Elswyth lay looking down at the beach, at the wimple that covered her hair, which should be flowing down her back in waves, teased by the wind, she had no inspiration, and stood still, watching her, hoping that something would come to her.

"I know you're there, Mother," Elswyth called, after Edith had stood silent for a minute or two.

"Can I come and watch with you?" Edith called back.

"Of course you can," Elswyth replied, not turning to look at her.

Edith came forward, dropped to her knees, and then awkwardly worked herself into a lying position beside Elswyth. She could not lie flat because of her extended belly, so she lay on one side, facing her daughter, but then turned her head to look down on the beach where the game was going on. They lay beside each other in silence for some time.

Play went back and forth, with much shouting and pushing, but little scoring. Then Califace collided with Hogni and went down in a heap and struggled to get back to his feet, stumbling and dizzy.

"That must have hurt," Edith said.

"They seem to be enjoying themselves," Elswyth replied.

"They always enjoy bruising each other," Edith said. "I suppose I can understand that. But they seem to enjoy being bruised just as much, and to come away better friends the worse they hurt each other. That is the mystery of it."

"Leif says no man want's a coward for a friend," Elswyth said.

"Ah, I suppose that must be it."

"I know I am supposed to be doing my needlework…" Elswyth began.

"Your father declared a holiday for the men," Edith replied, "so we should have a holiday too."

Elswyth turned and smiled at her. Edith felt a wave of relief come over her at that smile. She wanted to reach out and pull Elswyth into an embrace and weep with her. But she knew better and only smiled a little in reply.

"Of course," she added, "we only get a half holiday, for we shall have work to bandage them and feed them when this is over."

They laughed, and then they both said "Ow!" together as Lars' elbow met Attor's eye. Attor sat blinking on the sand while the game went on, then staggered to his feet and charged after the ball like a bull.

There was a crack as Oxa's boot met Leif's shin. Elswyth winced, and Leif hopped painfully on one leg until Garberend, running blindly for the ball, barreled into him and knocked him sprawling. Leif lay still for a moment. Elswyth tensed and did not breathe until she saw him stir groggily on the sand and get to his feet to run off the injury.

Edith's heart had also skipped a beat when she saw Leif lying there, so it took a moment before the meaning of Elswyth's reaction sunk in for her. She looked at her wonderingly, remembering Elswyth's definitive "Yuck!" when she had first spoken well of Leif's appearance. She reached out a hand and stroked Elswyth's hair.

"Drefan's upset," she said. "He was all shame and bad temper when he left yesterday."

"I don't care," Elswyth said belligerently.

"What has happened?" Edith asked gently, her heart in her mouth.

"He wants me to prove I can give him children."

"Do you mean he threatened to refuse the marriage if you weren't with child?"

"No. It wasn't like that. It was…"

"You don't have to tell me." But then Edith paused and said, "But if you want to…"

"It was just…" Elswyth was awkward, fidgety. It was painful to see her so unlike herself. "He ignored me for so long, and then he kisses me and an hour later he tries to lay me down in Foxton wood…"

"Did he hurt you?"

"No. Of course not. You know he wouldn't."

"But you refused him?"

"Yes." The word was so full of shame and hesitation that it near broke Edith's heart.

"Why?"

"I don't know," Elswyth said. "Perhaps I did not want my daughters to hate me."

"Was he angry?"

"No. He was upset. But he apologized afterward. He said he had been unkind and he was sorry."

"So it's all right then?"

"You think I should have?" Elswyth asked. "You and Father…"

"He asked no proof of me."

"Whatever happened to Elene of Hadston?"

"She married Halwende of Prendwick. She died last year."

"How?"

"Childbirth. She'd lost four before. Two at birth, the other two before they reached five. But I hear the one that killed her thrives."

"You never lost a child?" Elswyth asked.

"No. You are all living, bless me. I think the one after this will be a boy."

"After this?" said Elswyth, turning to her mother with an incredulous look on her face.

Edith rolled over onto her back. "I'm barely thirty-three, dearest. Not quite a crone. I've a few bairns in me yet. This one feels like another girl, though."

Elswyth made no reply but turned her attention again to the battle on the sands.

"Leif has grown to be a handsome lad," her mother said.

"His beard looks ridiculous."

"It will grow in soon enough."

There was a shout of triumph from below. The two sides parted. The ball was thrown in and they rushed together again, resuming the slaughter.

"Do you lie here to watch the game or to watch the man?" Edith asked, rolling back onto her side and lying close beside Elswyth.

"You can speak plainly, Mother," Elswyth said, watching as a long kick sent the ball bouncing towards the waves.

"You like Leif?"

"Leif is an idiot."

"Does Drefan know that you think so?"

"Drefan is an idiot."

"Drefan will soon be your husband. And Leif will soon sail away."

"I know, Mother."

Edith put an arm around Elswyth's shoulder, gave her a peck on the cheek, and laid her head against Elswyth's neck. They lay there for a few minutes, Elswyth unresisting. Was this a trouble that would pass? Was it Elswyth's wistfulness that had made Leif into a rival for Drefan, or her heart?

Oh, pray it is her wistfulness, her terrible fickle wistfulness. Please, God, don't let it be her heart!

Then Edith realized that Elswyth had tears in her eyes, and, in another moment, she was weeping and shaking in Edith's arms. And Edith had her answer, for the product of wistfulness is sighs, and the product of the heart is tears.

"Were you scared?" Elswyth asked, when she was cried out.

"When?"

"When you and Father…"

"When he laid me down under a haystack? I'd been working all summer to have him do that."

"But were you scared?"

"I was terrified. But I felt safe at the same time. Safe and terrified."

"I didn't feel like that."

"When? I thought…"

"When Drefan tried to lay me down in Foxton wood."

"What did you not feel, safe or terrified?

"Either one. Annoyed. He's had half the girls in the village out to that wood."

"Not half."

"Willa."

"Oh. The silly cow. Her father's got money. She could win a thegn's son standing up."

"But if she'd cropped? Do you think he would have…"

"God, no. He was just scratching the itch. He was waiting for you to come of age."

"He wasn't waiting, though, was he? And then all of a sudden he takes me out there like any kitchen slave?"

"I was…"

"I know. Sorry. But I'm not. All of a sudden he can't wait?"

"He saw you with Leif."

"I was fetching him for lunch."

"Hanging on his arm, laughing…"

"I'm not supposed to laugh?"

"But he was right, wasn't he? About you and Leif."

"No!"

"You're in love with Leif—or something very close to love."

Elswyth did not answer.

"You were with him yesterday? I could not find either one of you in the hall."

"We went for a walk."

"In the rain?"

"I like rain, and he's used to it."

"So you and he haven't…"

"God, no!"

"He will sail away when Heorot comes back with the abbot's gold. Tomorrow with the tide, I hope."

"I don't care."

"Good."

There was silence between them for a few minutes, and then Elswyth said, "Leif is the son of a chief, just like Drefan."

"Hardly. Drefan will be ealdorman of half the country north of the Tyne. Leif will be jarl over what, a small valley, a village, a couple of ships? Not much more than your father, really. Less, now that they have been raided and their treasures taken."

"But both are sons of noblemen."

"I suppose. Has Leif asked you…"

"He has his rules of trade."

"They are good rules. Men's rules. But among men, I think they are wise."

"I don't care."

"Leif scares you?"

"Leif would never hurt me."

"No but…"

"Yes."

"Things will be easier with Drefan once Leif sails away."

"I suppose."

"A Norsk ship on our beach is upsetting enough, these days, without all this."

Elswyth looked skyward. "I suppose."

"He has learned that he wants you. There won't be any more Willas now."

Elswyth looked into her face again. "Were you…"

"A virgin?"

"Were you?"

"I was. I told you, only one man."

"Was Father?"

"I never asked. He seemed so."

Elswyth paused here a while and then asked, "Is Father a fool?"

"A fool? No, love, he's not a fool."

"It was him who told me to go to Leif, yesterday. He said Leif needed a sister to cheer him up."

"I see. No, your father is not a fool. But he is an innocent, perhaps, especially where you are concerned."

"And where you are concerned?" Elswyth's words landed on Edith like a blow.

"Yes."

"So when you…"

"Yes, I knew he was an innocent then. Yes, I played on that. Your grandmother was not wrong about me. But you must never, ever doubt that I loved him, right from the start. Because I did. Always. I still do."

"So would you tell Mayda to find some innocent young thegn and take him out behind a haystack and get herself with child?"

"No."

There was a long pause then. Edith could feel the question coming, but even when Elswyth spoke it, it came like another blow. "Then why me?"

"Can you forgive me?"

The words of forgiveness did not come. But then Edith saw tears gathering in her daughter's eyes again. And then Elswyth said, "Can you forgive me?"

"Forgive you? For what?"

"Two nights ago, when you found me out of bed. It wasn't Drefan I was looking for."

A terrible apprehension gripped Edith then. But she made herself stay calm, made herself speak gently.

"Tell me," she said.

"I went to Leif."

"And..."

"I tried to get him to..."

"To lie with you?"

Elswyth nodded, bleakly.

"To lie with you, as I lay with your father, under summer stars?"

"Yes."

"I should never have told you about that."

"That's not why..."

"Did you?"

"Did I?"

"Did you lie with him?"

"He said no." Here Elswyth was striving valiantly to hold back sobs. "He wouldn't even kiss me. The rules of trade."

"Thank God for that. If you had cropped..."

"I know."

"Well, thank God for Leif's discretion. I hope you are as grateful to him as I am, though I suppose it would be awkward to tell him so."

Elswyth did not respond to this, but lay beside her mother with wretched sorrow in her eyes.

"It's not just that he turned you down, is it? You love him."

No motion of either confirmation or denial.

"You know he is promised to a jarl's daughter. Sibbe, I think Thor said her name was."

At this news Elswyth rolled over onto her back and stared at the sky. "I know," she said. "And Leif could not save you, or my sisters, or Mayda and the rest of our kin, if Father died."

There was nothing to say in answer to this. Edith reached out a hand and placed it on Elswyth's belly, stroking her gently.

"You needn't worry, Mother," Elswyth said, still looking at the sky. "I'm going to marry Drefan."

"You will forgive him then, for Willa?"

"The only difference between him and me is that Willa said yes and Leif said no."

"Oh, baby…"

"Don't, Mother. I'm not a child. Don't excuse it. I hate it when you and Father do that. If Leif had said yes…"

"Your father knows nothing of this?"

"Are you going to tell him?" She asked this dully, expressing neither desire nor apprehension.

"I should, I suppose. But I don't see how it would do any good."

"Because he's such an innocent?"

"Because there is nothing he can do. Unless I have to worry about you and Leif…"

"You don't. I'm going to marry Drefan. It's like you've always told me, Mother. He's a good man. He loves me. He wants me, anyway. Until a week ago, I loved him, or I expected that I would. By harvest time, I may be in love with him. I will try, anyway. You and my sisters will be safe. Granny will be a free woman. And Mayda and the rest. And I will get to travel. Not to Spain, but all over the district, when the ealdorman does his rounds, and to York, to the king's hall, when he visits there. And the king will come to Bamburgh, at least once a year. I will serve dinner to the king and give him his cup. My mother was born a slave, and I will host the king at my table." Here she turned and looked at her mother with tears in her eyes. "And you will be there with me, Mother. I shall insist. When the king visits Bamburgh, you will visit too. I will present you to the king. And Hilda and Moira and Daisy. Even Whitney. Whitney will meet the king and smile at him."

Edith leaned towards Elswyth, meaning to kiss her on the cheek. But Elswyth turned towards her suddenly, so that their faces were inches apart.

"Are you proud, Mother? Are you proud now?"

Edith pulled back in shock. "Must you be cruel to me? Do you hate me now?"

Elswyth's face softened from anger into wistfulness. "No. It's just… I know you now. All along you were my mother and I didn't know you."

"I'm sorry. I'm sorry that I ever…"

"Don't be. If you hadn't, I suppose I would be Mayda now, laying some innocent young thegn down behind a haystack and getting myself with child so I would not get sold off to some less innocent thegn for a concubine."

"Mayda wouldn't."

"Because she knows you won't sell her off."

"Perhaps. I don't know. I don't want to find out."

"But with me…"

"Now you are being cruel."

Elswyth said nothing in reply. She turned and looked down at the sands, where the pace of play had notably slowed and most of the players were hanging their heads in exhaustion when the ball was not near them. "I think the game is nearly over," she said. "We should go gather herbs and make bandages."

"Elsy…"

Elswyth stood and offered her mother a hand to rise. "I don't hate you, Mother. Everything will be all right now. Come on. We have work to do."

35 Man to Man

The game ended in bloodshed, of course, with the Anglish leading by four bloody noses to three. And then the bruised and exhausted men embraced each other like brothers and drank themselves insensible on the beach. The battered men woke with ringing heads in the morning, each Norsk a guest in one hut or another in the village, hosted by whatever man he had bested or been bested by in the game, where they were scolded by the wives and teased by the girls and pestered by the children as they ate their breakfasts and nursed their sore heads and other sundry cuts and bruises.

The Anglish limped back to their fields and the Norsk returned to the beach. They had offered to lend a hand in the fields, but Attor's ship had returned from its fishing expedition loaded with a catch that would help tide the village over until the harvest was in, and the fish needed to be cleaned and dried, and so the Norsk were asked to help with this, which they did willingly.

Kendra died in the night without waking or uttering any word of prophecy. Her family spent the day preparing her body for burial. The monk, thus relieved of his charge, asked Attor for food for the road, but Attor begged him to stay a day or two in case Heorot returned from Monkwearmouth with a letter rather than the gold they had asked for—something Attor feared since Heorot was now past due, unless he had run into difficulties either at Monkwearmouth or on the road. The monk was easily persuaded, for it gave him another day with the books.

The day was clear and hot, so Leif ordered the sail raised to provide shade to the deck and he, the monk, and Elswyth, embroidery in her hands, sat with their backs against the book chest, each facing a different point of the wind. Leif was hoping that his ear might begin to pick up something of the Latin tongue, for it occurred to him that if he could learn a little of it, he would be able to trade with any house of Christian holy men in any country, without needing to learn every local language. Elswyth was there because, though she must soon part from both of them, she found the company of each of them soothing. Her mood was wistful and melancholy, but the melancholy was sweet in their company and bitter apart from it.

It was in the middle of the afternoon that a cry of alarm from one of the men startled them.

"*What is it?*" Leif cried in Norsk, jumping to his feet.

"*There,*" said Thor, pointing down the beach, not toward the village, but northward to where a group of men had rounded the last of the headlands that intruded into the beach and were trotting in their direction, sun glinting on spearpoints. This was not the far headland to which Elswyth and Leif had walked in the mist, but a much nearer less intrusive point that provided the last point of concealment between the further beach and the place where the knarr was beached.

"*Anglish?*" Leif asked.

"*Aye.*"

290

Elswyth shaded her eyes with her hand and examined the approaching figures. "Drefan!" she said.

She vaulted over the side and started running towards the approaching men.

"Stop her," Thor said.

A hand grabbed her by the shoulder.

"Too late to mend it now, Princess," Eric said.

She twisted in his grasp, but could not break his hold. His fingers dug painfully into her shoulder. She turned to Thor, pleading, "I have to go and talk to him."

"Why did he come that way, where there is no road?" Thor asked her.

"He knew Father would stop him."

"So he is willing to break hospitality and murder your father's guests. Why? He thinks what Eric thinks, what I fear." He looked at Leif.

"No," Leif said.

"We never!" Elswyth cried, trying in agony to twist herself out of Eric's grip as he marched her back to where Leif and Thor stood. "If that's what he thinks, I have to go tell him it is not true."

"He's not come to talk," Thor said.

"I can convince him."

"We can't risk it," Leif said. "If he thinks what Eric thinks, he will want revenge on you as well as me."

Eric handed Elswyth over to Thor, whose grip on her was as firm as Eric's, but not so painful.

"We didn't, Uncle Thor," Elswyth said, a sob of panic rising in her throat. "I promise we didn't. Please believe me."

"I do. But you sailed very close to the wind, and now we are on a lee shore. But we'll waste no time on that now."

Eric ran to summon the men from the drying racks and break out the weapons chest on the ship.

"Best you can do for us is run and fetch your father," Thor said.

"No, I won't leave you. He's got twenty men with him, and Father won't be able to gather our men and get back here from the fields in time. I have to try to talk to him."

"I will go for the thegn," the monk said. "I'd be no help in a fight, and I doubt that young man is in the mood for a sermon." He set off running at once before anyone could say anything to him.

"You should go too," Leif said to Elswyth. "We are not enough to keep you safe."

"Why don't we all go back to the village, then?" Elswyth said. "We can barricade ourselves in the hall."

"Look again," Leif said. "What do you think they are carrying?"

"Spears," she said, but then her sharp eyes saw what he had seen. "Oh! Some of them have torches."

"They mean to burn the ship," Thor said.

"Can you get it into the water?" Elswyth asked.

Thor shook his head. The low tide that had let the Anglish come so far along the beach, had left the ship sitting high on the sand.

Eric thrust a sword and shield into Leif's hands and offered the same to Thor.

"Will you stay by me if I release you?" Thor asked Elswyth.

"Alright, but you let me talk to him when they get here."

"If he's in any mood to talk."

Thor released her and took the weapons that Eric offered him.

Without needing to be told, the men had armed themselves and formed a rough line in the sand, their faces to the enemy and their backs to the ship. Leif looked to Thor for guidance. He was out of his depth in a battle line.

"Let's put some distance between our backs and the ship," Thor said. "We can retreat back to it if they try to get behind us, but I'd rather keep those torches away from it."

"Move forward," Leif ordered. He led the men up the beach towards the advancing Anglish. They were getting near now, puffing and blowing. They were running through sand in heavy leather sewn with iron rings and it sapped their lungs. The Norsk line closed tightly together, leaving Elswyth standing behind them.

"If it comes to a fight, you run," Leif said to Elswyth. He said it with more command than she had ever heard in his voice.

"I will," she said. "But let me try to talk to him."

"Anything that will buy time for your father to get here," Leif said.

The approaching Anglish began to draw together into a tighter pack and slow their steps. Drefan called his men to a halt a dozen paces from the Norsk line. Drang and Earh were there. With them were more than a dozen men, dressed in leather, armed with shields and spears, some with helmets and some bare headed.

Thor had kept Elswyth behind him while they advanced, but now she stepped around him and took a step towards Drefan, Thor's hand descending on her shoulder to prevent her approaching nearer. Drefan was clearly startled to see her.

"What are you doing?" she asked.

"I don't explain my business to Welisc whores," he said.

Elswyth had planned on icy calmness, but at the word whore, she flamed. "Don't you dare call me that! I am a maiden. You are the one who lies with whores!"

Thor's hand tightened on her shoulder.

"You lay with a vikingr," Drefan said.

"I did not!"

"You were seen!"

Leif took a step forward. "I have not lain with any woman of this place," he said.

"You were seen," Drefan said. "Swiving in the moonlight among the dunes when you thought we were all in the hall."

The color drained from both Leif and Elswyth's cheeks, and they looked at each other, anguished. Drefan saw the look and saw in it only a confirmation of guilt.

"Dirty vikingr bastard! Dirty Welisc whore!" he screamed.

"If you saw anything," Elswyth said, "you saw an embrace, nothing more. We didn't even kiss. And yes, we embraced. I was drunk and I was angry with you and I wanted him. And he would not take me. You lay with Willa. I tried to lie with Leif and he would not, because he respects you, because he respects my father. So you can be angry with me if you like, just like I am angry with you about Willa. But you have no cause to be angry with Leif."

"I don't take the word of a whore."

"I'm not a whore."

"I don't take the word of a whore."

"She speaks the truth," Leif said, taking a step forward and standing in front of Elswyth. "She is yours. I make no claim on her. But I am bound to her as oath-kin. I will defend her against any man who threatens or insults her."

"I don't take the word of a vikingr."

"What have you come for, then?" Thor asked.

"To protect the people of Northumbria against vikingar and whores."

"You would make war on Attor's guests? On his own land? After you have eaten and drunk with them?" Thor asked.

"It is they who broke the bonds of hospitality," Drefan said. "He lay with my woman. No bond protects a man from vengeance who lays with another man's woman."

"They have both told you they did not lie together."

"They lie, old man. You know it. I can see it in your face that you do not believe them."

"I believe them. I am angry with them. That is true. They have acted like children, and I say this of my own jarl. But I believe they did not lie together."

"Then you are a fool or a liar, old man."

"We didn't," Elswyth shouted, struggling in Thor's grip, trying to confront Drefan eye to eye again. "Yes, we acted like children. I did. Leif didn't. I did. And I'm sorry. I really am sorry. But you have to stop this. If you don't want me anymore, fine. I'll go and marry a slave if you think that is all I'm good for. But you have no quarrel with Leif."

"You think I don't want you?" Drefan cried. "I defied my father, because I wanted you. I defied my mother, because I wanted you. I broke bread and shook hands with that vikingr bastard because you asked me to, and I wanted you. But I can't touch you now. You are polluted by this vikingr. You'll never get the stench of him out of you. He has ruined you, as vikingar ruin all they plunder."

"You think you don't reek to me of Willa? But I was still willing to take you."

"Did you still want me?"

"I was willing…"

"And there is the stench of him! There is only one way to blot it out." He gestured at the line of spear points and torches behind him.

Leif took a glance behind him at the empty beach, knowing it was too soon to see Attor coming, but hoping for it anyway. He took another step forward.

"If your quarrel is with me, fight me," he said. "Man to man."

"No," Elswyth screamed. "I don't want you hurting each other over me."

295

Thor put his hand on her other shoulder and pulled her back to him. Leaning down, he whispered in her ear. "Leif knows what he is doing."

"It's not fair," she said. "Drefan's a soldier. He's wearing mail."

"Useful in a melee, but a fight like this is lost by the man who tires first. Drefan's been running in that heavy gear on a hot day. He's still panting from the run. Leif is rested. He will keep Drefan occupied until your father comes."

Drefan took a step forward, his sword raised.

Leif held up a hand. Slowly he removed his sea jacket and his shirt and dropped them on the sand. They offered little protection against a sword cut. A cut through clothing was more likely to fester than a cut to bare skin. He shrugged his arms toward Drefan as if to suggest that Drefan, in sporting fairness, should remove the mail coat he wore, made from hundreds of iron rings sewn onto his leather jerkin, and the grim helmet that was on his head. Drefan shook his head, which drew catcalls from the watching Norsk.

"Anglish do not believe in fighting fair?" Leif asked, still not picking up his shield or drawing his sword.

"Did the vikingar at Lindisfarne wait for the monks to arm themselves before they began their slaughter?"

"You know we were not among the men who raided Lindisfarne," Leif replied. Still his sword stayed in its sheath and his shield rested against his leg.

"Defend yourself, vikingr, or I will slaughter your men as your people slaughtered the monks." Drefan took another step forward. Leif picked up his shield and drew his sword.

Drefan advanced. Leif stepped back and circled right. Drefan stepped after him, keeping the distance between them the same. Each time Drefan feinted forward, Leif stepped back and circled right, until their positions were reversed and Leif had his back to the waiting Anglish and could see Thor, with

Elswyth held fast by the shoulders in Thor's huge hands. He saw the look of fear on the old man's face, and the look of longing terror on Elswyth's, and in that moment felt the last of his defenses against her collapse.

Drefan surged forward. He had too many steps to take to catch Leif off guard, but this time Leif did not have a chance to dart back and had to stand to meet the blow. He took it sword on sword, the impact of the blow ringing down his arm and stinging shoulder, elbow, and wrist. His muscles remembered: a blow should be deflected along the blade, not caught all at once, metal to metal, where the force might stun the arm and make the hand lose its grip on the sword.

Drefan too was shaken by the force of the blow, and took a step back, flexing his sword arm. Leif swung his shield, hoping to knock Drefan off balance, but the Anglish met him shield to shield and now his left arm rang. Leif stepped right, up the beach, towards the softer sand. Drefan followed, swinging heavy blows that Leif met with sword or shield. He had expected more sophistication in Drefan's attack. It was not that he himself was trained to do more with a sword than to swing it like a club, but he had thought Drefan would be full of crafty tricks of swordplay, and that he would be working hard to dodge cunning thrusts. But the Anglish just swung and swung, his blade clanging sharply against Leif's sword or thudding dully against his shield.

Leif was content to receive the blows and turn them aside, knowing that Drefan was expending more energy than he was, especially wearing his heavy armor. Leif could almost feel the weight of it as it tugged on Drefan's broad shoulders. Leif was quickly warm and running with sweat and Drefan must be getting hot inside his mail and the woolen tunic beneath it. Leif kept moving into the softer sand, knowing that Drefan's legs would tire more quickly there. Whenever Drefan's attack wilted, he would go on the offensive himself, in part to show the

Anglish that he had courage, in part to show the Norsk that he was not beaten. Now that the fight was on, he did not want Drefan to have a chance to rest, for he was convinced that he could beat the Anglish by tiring him out. He did not aim for the body, still fearing that Drefan knew some subtlety of swordcraft that he was waiting for an opening to display. Instead he hacked at Drefan's shield, keeping his own shield up to ward off the counterattack when it came. If he felt the resistance weaken, if the counter did not come, then he planned to push Drefan backwards, hoping that he would lose his footing and fall on his back. Then Leif would be on top of him, with his blade to the Anglish's throat and force the surrender.

The desire to spill Drefan's blood was strong in him, had raged in him since Drefan first uttered the word "whore". But he pushed it back. He fought for exhaustion and surrender, or simply to waste away time until Attor would come and break it up. And with every blow he struck, his hatred of Drefan ebbed, for he came to understand, even as they fought, that their rivalry was over. Drefan had made a breach with Elswyth that could never be mended. No man can marry a woman who he has called a whore in front of his followers. His own cause was as hopeless as it had ever been, but he stood without rival, even if he could never claim the prize.

Leif was tiring. His arms and shoulders ached and his hands were numb and tingling. Was Drefan tiring? His blows seemed just as heavy, though perhaps there was a longer pause now between one blow and the next. Leif's legs were heavy and the sand beneath his feet felt as cloying as mud. He forced himself to keep moving, knowing that the sand must be wearying Drefan also, knowing that he would feel weariness in his own bones and muscles long before he felt it in the weakness of the other man's attack. How long had they been fighting now? How long till Attor came?

Drefan ceased hacking and stepped back, Leif followed and battered Drefan's shield, though it seemed like his right hand could barely raise the sword. He felt Drefan's shield arm weaken. The Anglish gave way before his attack. He pushed forward, ramming shield against shield, trying to force the other man off his feet. He felt Drefan stumble, but then the Anglish found his footing and stepped aside, deflecting the force of Leif's shield sideways. Leif stumbled but kept his feet. He brought his sword up to meet Drefan's blow, felt the weakness of it, stepped right, took the next blow on his shield. And then he felt the handle of the shield wobble and give way. Suddenly, he was holding the handle alone, while the shield fell toward the sand, rotating on the leather strap around his left elbow so that the rim swung down and bit into the side of his leg. He stumbled backward, trying desperately to free his arm from the shield strap. But the leather had twisted itself into a vice grip around his arm. He stepped into a tangle of seaweed, lost his footing, and was down, feeling the rough sand sting his back as he fell.

Elswyth screamed when Leif fell. But Thor said, "Don't fear. Let Drefan accept his surrender, and perhaps that will satisfy him."

With the immediate threat of his opponent removed, Drefan was suddenly staggering with weariness. He stumbled in the sand and almost fell himself. Then he took one staggering step towards Leif. Leif ceased struggling with his shield and dropped his sword.

"I yield," he said.

Drefan took another stumbling step toward him, and then another. Leif lay still, offering no resistance. Slowly, Drefan began to raise his sword.

"He yielded," Drang said.

Drefan continued to raise the sword, though from his movements it seemed that he could barely lift its weight. Elswyth was screaming and fighting Thor's grip. And then Eric rushed forward from the Norsk line and swung his axe into the side of Drefan's helmet, just as Drefan was about to start the downward stroke. Immediately the two lines of men rushed together. Elswyth felt herself lifted off her feet and turned away from the fight, then there was a grunt and suddenly the sand was rushing up to meet her and a great weight landed on top of her, knocking the breath out of her.

36 Fire and Death

Elswyth's face was buried in the sand and she was more than half dazed. She took several fruitless breaths, but her mouth and nose were blocked with sand and she could get no air. Fighting desperately against the weight that was crushing her, she twisted her face in the rough sand until she found a small space where she could draw breath. She could see no light and hear no sound except her own harsh breathing and hammering heart. Panic flooded her. Then she realized that one leg was free of the weight oppressing her and she kicked desperately, feeling the sand yield before the blows of her foot. But no one seemed to notice, and she had to wait many minutes, unable to understand what had happened, weeping and desperately trying to calm her panic before at last the weight was rolled away and her father was lifting her and cradling her and demanding to know if she was hurt.

"No, no, let me go," she cried, for as soon as she had been restored to the world of light, as soon as she could breathe again, she had realized what the weight that oppressed her must have been. Her father put his hand to her head, trying to stop her from turning and looking, but he was too gentle and Elswyth twisted in his grasp and saw the huge still form of Thor lying in the sand, a bloodied Anglish spear beside him.

But even this was not the first thing in her heart. "Leif, Leif," she cried. And he was there beside her and she struggled out of her father's arms and into his. She embraced him and kissed him and demanded to know if he was injured. And he embraced her and kissed her and told her he was not and asked the same of her.

And then, being assured of each other, they looked around them. Attor stood looking at them in confusion. The Norsk and Drefan's men stood with their weapons idle in their hands, with Attor's men between them. Drefan lay still on the ground, the monk bending over him and listening for breath. Eric stood with his shipmates, grim faced, leaning on his reddened axe. And Thor lay dead.

Attor walked across to Drefan. The monk looked up at him and shook his head. Attor's shoulders slumped and he turned again to look at Leif and Elswyth, entwined in each other's arms, weeping.

Then suddenly there were voices yelling: *"The ship!"*

Lars was pointing, and the other men had turned to look at the flames jumping up the sides of the ship, clawing up the mast, slithering up the tarry ropes, smoking in the furled sail. The Anglish torch bearers must have done the task that had been set for them as soon as the melee broke out, running around the outnumbered Norsk defenders and flinging their torches into the dry tarry heart of the knarr.

Leif released Elswyth and ran towards the ship, stooping to pick up his sea jacket from the sand. His men followed him, and some of Attor's Anglish also. Elswyth followed, with no thought as to what she might do—she followed because he ran.

Leif glanced back and saw her.

"Keep her away," he shouted at Attor, as if she were his to protect, and Attor was his to command.

He ran into the ocean, rolling around to soak his boots and trousers. He pushed his sea jacket into the water to saturate it and ducked his head to wet his hair and beard. He stood, staggering under the weight of the water, threw his arms into the sleeves of the sea jacket, ran back to the ship, and hauled himself aboard.

There was fire everywhere: fire in the ropes, fire in the sails, fire catching in the decks where the pitch-soaked torches had landed. Smoke billowed from the hold. The crew were beginning to scoop up sea water in their shields and fling it at the sides of the ship. Some of Attor's men were helping them.

***

Attor caught Elswyth in her headlong rush toward the ship. She struggled to break his grip, but he pulled her to him strongly.

"Stop him," she cried, "Stop him."

"It's his ship, girl."

"He'll be killed."

"Maybe, but that ship is his people's wealth, their safety. His life is promised to them."

"Let me help him."

"He has his men to help him."

"Let me go."

"No, child. You will stay safe with me."

She fought him, cursed him, struck him, but he held her, and her fury turned to tears, and he comforted her.

And even as they stood and watched, another figure came hurtling down the beach and threw himself over the rail of the blazing ship.

***

Leif's clothes steamed in the heat, and his lungs gasped in the arid breathless air. He saw a line of buckets standing along the rail and he tossed them overboard to the men toiling to bring water. But he knew it was hopeless, the fire had found the pitch-soaked seams and had run along them to every rib and bulwark in the ship. By a dock, with water all around the ship, there might have been a chance. But here on the beach, with the prow high and dry and the tide lapping only inches deep at the stern, there was no way to get water into the ship. There was only one chance to save anything now. He turned and looked for the books. The chest stood open on the deck. Beside it, a coil of tarred rope blazed and its flames were licking around the chest, looking for a place to catch. The deck was hot under his feet as he moved towards it. A cinder caught in his eye, stinging furiously and blinding him with tears. By the time he had cleared his vision, the chest had become obscured in a billow of smoke rising up from the hold. Darts of flame were beginning to lick up between the planks of the deck, and the air was filled with hissing and roaring. He heard men's voices shouting also, but could not make out their words or language. The smoke choked him and obscured his vision. He found the chest, as much by memory as by sight, and bent his back to drag it away from the burning rope. He heard a roaring crash behind him and guessed some piece of the rigging had come down. He bent to lift the chest, but one of its leather handles had burned through and it snapped in his hand. He tried to get his arm around it, but the chest was too awkward. He began to drag it across the deck, aware of a dreadful pain growing beneath his feet. He choked on the smoke, and had just decided that he must choose between saving the books and saving himself, when a hand fell on his shoulder. He looked up and through the smoke made out the face of Brother Alun.

"I'll take this end," the monk said.

Together they lifted it. The nearest rail was alive with flame. They carried it back toward the stern, seeking a way of escape. Just as they seemed to have found a way clear, there was a sharp crack overhead and the main yard crashed to the deck. The yard smashed the chest out of their hands. Books scattered across the deck and fell into the blazing hold. The burning sail billowed slowly down and enveloped the stunned monk. Leif ran to the monk, leaping over the smoldering books. The monk was screaming and flailing at the flames that bit into his back. Leif dug him out from under the burning sail, picked him up, threw him over his shoulder, ran to the stern, and tossed the monk over the rail into the shallow water. He turned for one last look at the books, but they were already on fire. At his feet there was a basket, brimming with bright thread and trailing half-finished embroidery. He flung it wide, then leaped over the side and into the water, rolling over to extinguish the cinders that clung to his clothing.

***

The first thing that Edith saw when she came down to the beach was the blazing ship, orange flame driven greedily by the onshore breeze that dragged a plume of black smoke across the summer sky. It crackled and it roared and there were loud snaps and cracks as the joints and seams gave way. The yard was already down, lying broken athwart the blazing ship, but the mast still stood, naked and black, pointing skyward in a last act of defiance.

A party of men passed her, bearing between them, the body of the monk. From their attitude she might have thought their burden a dead man, except for how he writhed in their arms and the mewls of agony that escaped his lips. They stopped as they came by her and she looked into the face of the wounded man, which was charred and matted with twisted flesh and bright blood. She gave the bearers some quick instructions to begin boiling wine in a brass pot and to send slaves to pick plantain and cut willow, and then hurried on.

She saw Elswyth, weeping in Leif's arms. She seemed to be unhurt, so Edith did not go to her, but hurried on to find her husband. Attor was standing with a knot of men and when she came to him, he tried to prevent her from looking at the scene they were gathered around. She pushed through his constraining hand, however, and looked. Almost at her feet, the huge form of Thor lay, vacant eyes staring up at the sun. There was no sign of any wound on him, and no sign of violence except for the bloodied spear that lay near his body. Yet the terrible vacancy of death was on his face and death's lumpen awkwardness beset his limbs.

Every death is unbelievable. No matter how many times one gazes on a corpse, the wonder of it never abates. The body seems as a castoff garment, and you expect to find the true form of the person standing in naked wonderment beside you, staring, as you stare, on the impossibility of their discarded flesh, and you wonder, uncomprehending, at the absence of that necessary spectre. But the absence of Thor's ghost seemed to Edith an impossibility of another order. Thor had seemed to her, as he had always seemed to Elswyth, a force beyond the world's touching. He was too good, too solid, too serene, too joyful, too solemn, to ever heed the call of death. And yet here before her lay the empty vessel, the abandoned husk, of Thor, and Thor himself was nowhere to be found.

She turned and looked at Attor, uncomprehending in her grief, but he indicated with his eyes another group of men gathered around another fallen body in a patch of bloodied sand a few yards away. She went to see, resisting again Attor's attempt to restrain her. At first she could make no sense of what she saw, for the face of the dead man had been gashed open from temple to eye. It was only when she looked into the faces of Drang and Earh that she realized that the cloven head belonged to Drefan.

She turned into her husband's arms, aghast.

"Where are the children?" he asked her.

"Hilda took them to my mother. When I heard the commotion, I didn't know what else to do."

306

"As long as they don't see this," he said.

"What happened?"

He tried to explain, but he did not really know himself. The monk had found him in the fields shouting news of a fight on the beach and he had run down with the men and broken up a battle between Drefan's men and the Norsk sailors, but by the time he had made them stop, Drefan and Thor were already dead.

They looked at Drang and Earh for an explanation, but both seemed mute, unwilling to speak of it. They went back to the Norsk gathered around Thor. Eric was leaning on a blood-ied axe, his face so grim that neither of them had the courage to speak to him.

Elswyth and Leif were still down by the tideline, wrapped in each other's arms, staring at the burning ship. Edith tugged at Attor's arm to start him walking towards them.

"Do you see this?" he asked, meaning the embrace between Leif and his daughter.

"Yes."

"Did you know…"

"That she was in love with him. Yes, she told me."

"You said nothing to me."

"I only learned yesterday. She said Leif rejected her, and that she would marry Drefan. So what was there to tell?"

"Did Drefan know?"

But before Edith could answer, Elswyth saw them coming. She broke from Leif and threw herself into her mother's arms. Leif, ashen faced, dropped to his knees and lowered his head, offering his neck to Attor in an act of contrition and surrender. Attor went to him, took him by the elbow, and pulled him back to his feet.

Elswyth looked into her mother's face, utterly desolate. "Drefan saw," she said. "He saw." Edith did not need to ask what he had seen. Another soul had been wakeful that evening when she had met Elswyth coming back from the beach. All now was explained. Nothing now could be mended. She simply drew Elswyth into a tighter embrace and held her as she wept.

"The question is," Attor said, after a while, "what are we to do with you now?"

"Count me among the dead," Leif said.

Elswyth broke from her mother's embrace. "What does he mean?" she asked, addressing her father rather than Leif.

"He means that he considers himself an exile from his people."

"Why?" she said, turning to Leif.

"I have lost my ship and my cargo," he said. "I have lost my father's ransom. Thor is dead. My family is ruined, and I am the cause of it."

"I am the cause of it," Elswyth said.

"No," he said, going to her, embracing her, stroking her hair as if they had been lovers from of ancient days. "They are my rules and I broke them."

"You did not lie with me," she said, muffled in the sheepskin.

"I caused Drefan to think I did. And that is what the rule is for. To avoid making any man jealous of you. I knew this. But I failed."

"My fault. You kept saying no. I didn't listen."

"I said yes as often as I said no. I wanted your company. I loved you from the first time we looked at the books together."

"I should have kept the two of you apart from the beginning," Attor said. "Cuthbert's bones! I sent you to him, told you to be like a sister to him, forbade you to disobey me."

But Elswyth turned on her father in sudden fury and struck him in the chest with her fists. "Don't you dare," she said. "Don't you dare try to take this from me. It is my fault. All mine. Don't you dare say it isn't."

Attor took a step back, stunned. Edith wrapped her arms around Elswyth and tried to soothe her. "This is not the time for this," she said. "There is work to be done, and little time to do it before nightfall. Next thing for you to do is to tend Leif's wounds and get some food into him. He is your responsibility now. You have chosen him, and now you must care for him. He is exhausted and has had no meat since breakfast." She turned to Attor then, and said. "We should go and tend to Drefan's body. The Norsk will tend to Thor, but Drefan is one of ours."

They went back together to the place where Drefan had lain, but the body was no longer there. His men had picked him up and were carrying him back the way they had come along the beach. The bloodied sand where he had lain had been covered with fresh sand, the spot detectable only by the crowd of boot-prints around it.

Edith looked after the retreating men. "Where are they taking him?" she asked. "Why not bring him to the hall?"

"They are ashamed. They broke hospitality, and they know it."

"Surely Drefan thought he had cause."

"I guess Drang and Earh thought he did not."

"Did he?"

"If he thought Leif had lain with Elswyth? Most men would do the same, even if Leif were not Norsk."

"He should have come to you, then. You would have the first right to revenge if Leif had defiled your daughter."

"Perhaps that is why Drang and Earh are ashamed. Perhaps they think Drefan stole my right. Perhaps Drefan knew that I loved Leif too well to be revenged on him, especially if Elswyth had gone to him willingly."

"She did. She told me. She wanted to lie with him, and he refused."

"What did Drefan see then?"

309

"I don't know. Enough to make him believe what he already suspected, I suppose."

"Enough to give him certain cause for revenge? Or was it an excuse because he wanted to spill Norsk blood for Lindisfarne?"

Edith sighed. "It cures nothing to find fault with the dead," she said.

"It might ease her heart a little."

"No. She's right, my love. She sat with Drefan in the hall, kissed him, talked of their marriage with him, and that same night offered to lay with Leif, would have lain with him, she says, if he had not refused her. There is no excusing that. She will not hear it excused, and that is to her credit, at least."

"Then how am I to save my child? Drefan dead. Thor dead. The ship burned. Harrald's ransom gone. How can she bear all that?"

Then Edith wrapped her arms around her husband and wondered how he would ever be able to bear that this was a burden he would never be able to take from his daughter's shoulders.

**

Leif had been stoic while facing Attor and Edith, but at last his defenses crumbled. Elswyth had become for him both the one for whom he most wished to be strong and the one before whom he was most willing to show weakness. He fell to his knees in the sand, tired beyond words, sad beyond hoping. Tears sprang to his eyes and flowed down his cheeks. She embraced him as he knelt, resting his head on her bosom, letting his tears soak into the fabric of her dress, taking her turn to be strong for them both. When there were no more tears in him, he raised his head and looked up at her.

"I do love you," he said, hopelessly.

"I love you," she said, stroking his hair.

"I have to go."

310

"I know."

"I can't come back."

"I know."

"What will you do?"

"I will take you to the hall and get you something to eat."

He was so weary that he stumbled twice as she led him across the beach and up the path to the hall. Each time, she supported him. As they walked, ordinary physical pain intruded upon his sorrow for the first time. The muscle in his back that he had pulled in the football game must have been injured again, for he felt like he had a dagger in his back. His left arm was bruised from shoulder to wrist from taking Drefan's blows on his shield, and there was an ugly and painful welt around his arm where the leather strap of the shield had dug into his flesh when the handle had given way. His right hand was swollen and numb and his right shoulder ached from wielding his sword, his legs above his boots were covered with burns, and there were burn marks on his face, neck, and shoulders where cinders had settled on him. One eye was grossly inflamed and his vision was blurred. He had twisted his right ankle when he jumped from the ship and now it was painful with every step. His breath was raspy from the smoke that had entered his lungs. By the time they reached the hall, he was dizzy and would have collapsed on the path if not for her assistance.

There was a table set in the hall, but he was too far gone to eat much. He gulped water, for he found that he was parched with thirst, but though he was hungry, his hunger did not seem to matter. Elswyth made him lie down in a bed in the guest house and then she washed his wounds, bound them, and salved his burns. She covered him with a blanket, and its warmth was like a drug. He closed his eyes. His pain was lost in an all-enveloping weariness. As he closed his eyes, he felt the brush of her lips on his cheeks and forehead, but not even that could rouse him from the sleep that came, like a wave washing over a crippled ship, wrapping it in the darkness of the sea.

37 The Night Watch

Elswyth emerged from the guest house, tearful, chilled with grief, and staggering from weariness. Night had fallen and the moon, which had looked down full-faced upon her tryst with Leif among the dunes, was now slowly averting its face from the squalor of earth, though it still gave much light to the world below. By that light she saw that two men, spears in their hands, stood guard outside the door of the guest house. They nodded to her as she passed, grim faced, but at first she did not question their presence. She was too weary to notice or to question. But as she walked away toward the sleeping house, the oddity of it at last penetrated her mind and she turned and looked back at them. Against what threat did her father set a guard tonight? Drefan was dead and his followers had fled, ashamed. Who else might come for Leif's life tonight?

She began to walk back towards them, meaning to demand an answer from them, but as she did so she saw that there were watchfires burning on the dunes along the path to the beach. Still half dazed, she turned and walked towards the fires, trying to understand their purpose. An armed man, clad in every bit of leather and iron he possessed, hurried by her towards the watch fires.

"Best be inside, Lady," he said, as he passed.

The word "why" was stillborn on her lips, for she understood at last. She turned and looked in the opposite direction, to the road that led inland. No fire was lit. No man stood guard. It was not against Drefan or his companions that her father had set his guard. It was against the Norsk on the beach.

She walked toward the watch fires, knowing that her father would be there, with his men. She knew him by his limp in the half dark as he paced back and forth between the fires he had set. He must be anxious. His sight was bad enough by daylight. By moonlight, he would be all but blind. And then there were the fires. They gave warmth and heart to the men, kept them from the creeping fear of dark and silence, but they ruined their sight also. Other men must be set further down the beach, to keep watch, their eyes not ruined by the firelight, but still, her father would fret that he could not see for himself whatever approached him.

He did not even see her until he almost fell over her in the dark.

"Good God, child," he said, when he saw it was her. "I thought it must be your mother, but she is in her bed, and so should you be."

"Why are you all out here?" she asked him. "Why have you set a guard against Eric and the crew? Why are there men guarding Leif? They are not our enemies."

"Oh child," he said. Then he paused heavily, as if expecting her familiar contradiction. But she did not contradict him. She had behaved like a child and she would not deny it.

"Kenrick will want blood," Attor said at last.

"But they will be gone by then," she said.

314

"And if they are gone, at my connivance?" he asked. "What do you think Kenric will do then? Whose blood will he seek to avenge his son?"

Her heart was very still and she was cold. "It should be mine," she said.

"No, child."

"It should. It is my fault that Drefan is dead."

"Not yours alone."

"He would not be dead if I had not done what I did."

"True. But I will not give your blood for this, child. Nor would Kenric take it. It is not his way to be avenged on a child. His quarrel is with the Norsk. And if I help the Norsk escape his vengeance, his quarrel would be with me."

"But what are you going to do, Father? You can't turn Leif over to Kenric. You can't let him kill him."

"Don't you see, child? If I don't give him Leif, and Eric—who struck the killing blow—and all the rest beside, then I am a traitor to my lord and he will have my life and my lands. And then what becomes of you, and your mother, and your sisters? The estate will go to my brother, and you know what he will do, especially if I am dishonored. He will sell you all for slaves. And what of Whitney? A mouth to feed who will never do any work? I love Leif like a son, but I cannot sell my wife and my daughters for his sake."

It was too much. She sank to the sands under the weight of it. She put her head between her hands and wept. Her father sat down on the sands beside her and placed an arm around her. For a long time they simply sat together, her weeping and heaving with sobs as he held her against his heart.

At last she looked up at him. "Is there nothing I can do, Father," she pleaded. "I love him. I would do anything to save him."

"There is nothing you can do," her father replied. "In the morning there will be men come from Alnwick and then I shall go down the beach and put the Norsk under guard, when I have enough men to do it without a fight. And then we will wait for Kenric to come. All you can do is go to your bed. You are dog weary. You must rest. In the morning you will say goodbye to Leif, and you and I will weep for him then, for we cannot show any love for him once Kenric comes. Do you understand, child. It must be this way, for your mother's sake, and your sisters."

"And yours, Father," she said.

"Well, I'll not think on my deserts. I am well scolded. I will not take your blame upon myself this time. But I have blame enough of my own. It would not be unjust if I were to bleed for it. But I will not see my wife or my children bleed, no matter what their guilt. But if you care for me, aid me now in what I must do. Go to your bed, where I know you are safe. Please, child, go."

He stood up and gave her an arm to help her rise. She rose, feeling very unsteady on her feet. She nodded her assent word- lessly, kissed him on the cheek, and then began to stagger back along the path to the village. It was hard to walk with the sobs boiling up in her chest, but she was resolute. It was such a slight thing, to obey her father's command and go to her bed. But it was a thing, a very small thing, to begin to set in the balance against the great weight of her crime, and all that had come of it, and would still come.

As she passed into the moon-shadow cast by the bulk of the hall, she heard a step behind her, but before she could turn to see, a hand was clamped across her mouth, a thick arm was thrown around her waist, and she was pulled off her feet, back- ward, into the deepest shadows beside the hall.

She knew at once that it was Eric. Her assailant was too big and too bold to be anyone else. She was not afraid. She expected that he would pull her into a dark corner, release her mouth, and whisper his errand to her. But he didn't. He pulled her clean off her feet and carried her along the wall of the hall, and then darted from the shadow of one building to the next down towards the bank of the river. Still holding her, Eric plunged into the river. He entered well below the ford, where the water was deep and the current smooth. She wanted to protest and tell him that he was going to drown them both, but it was too late. And then Eric was swimming, his hands still clamped around her, kicking only with his legs, as if he were saving her from drowning. And then the water began to grow shallow and he was on his feet again, carrying her out of the water, her dress heavy and streaming.

He carried her across the beach on the far side of the river, towards the hidden cove where she sometimes came to bathe. There, far from the village, and with the crash of waves to drown out any cry she might make, he at last put her on her feet and took his hand from around her mouth.

She turned and looked at him, not sure if she should be terrified or angry.

"Hello, Princess," he said, looking down at her. "You're a lucky find."

"What the hell, Eric," she said. "I could hardly breathe."

"You'll live," he said.

"Why? Why have you brought me here?"

"Out of earshot."

"But why?"

"I came for the boat."

"How? My father guards the beach."

"Swam it. Out to sea and up the river."

"Against the current?"

"Aye. It was a pull. But your father has the boat pulled out and four men to guard it. And I don't see spars or oars in it, so he's hidden those. If he weren't a damn fool, he'd have holed it or burned it to keep it from me."

"So why take me?"

"Kenric will come. If we are here, we are dead men. So I need your father's boat. And I need Leif back. If the boat had been in the water, with spars and sail and oars in her, I would have gone for Leif and taken him."

"He is guarded."

"Pftt," he said, dismissively, blowing air between his teeth. "But I couldn't get the boat. Then I saw you. So I will make a bargain with your father. Your life for Leif and the boat."

"My life? Eric, you wouldn't." She looked up at his stern face in the moonlight, unable to believe him. Her horror was not at the thought of dying. She merited death. But could she have made Eric hate her enough to spill her blood? That was a terrible thought.

"Ask your father if he will take Leif's life," he said.

She turned away from him and took a step towards the tide. "I already did," she said. "I already did."

"And what did he say?"

"He would not let his wife and children be made slaves. And they would kill Whitney, Eric. Poor Whitney, who never hurt a mouse. They would kill her because they can't use her."

"And Kenric will kill Hogni and Lars and Leif, and all of them, if we don't get that boat."

"You wouldn't, would you? You wouldn't really kill me?"

"I won't have to. Your father won't chance it."

"But then Kenric will come and my father will be a traitor in his eyes, and he will kill him."

"Aye."

"It should be me. It should be me. Do whatever you want with me. But let my father live."

"Should I die for him, then, and Leif, and all of them? Should they die, for your crime, so that your father may live?"

"Will he trade my mother and my sisters' lives for mine? All of theirs for mine, when I am the cause of this?"

"He'd swallow hot coals and put out his own eyes for you, girl, and you know it. He'll not weigh odds when he sees my knife at your throat."

"But if you kill me, like you killed Drefan, then my father has lost a daughter like Kenric lost a son. How could Kenric blame my father then?"

"He could not. But then your father would come for my blood. I would fight him and I would win. He would die. And still I would die by Kenric's hand. And Leif would die. And all the crew would die. The world is not just, Princess. It is your crime. If the gods were just, your blood should pay for it. But it is Thor's blood that has paid for it. And it will be your kin or mine who will pay for it. It would be just if Leif paid for it too. It was his crime as much as yours. But he is my captain and my blood. I am blood bound to save him."

"You talk so much of blood," she said.

"What is there that binds but blood? What is there that looses but blood?"

Sheer numb misery settled over her. "All this?" she asked, helplessly. "All this for one embrace?"

"You still say you weren't swiving, Princess?"

"He wouldn't even kiss me."

"Odin's other eye! Now I believe you. But there is no justice in the world. It is not what is done, Princess. It is what is seen, and what is thought."

She had no reply to make to him. She began to walk along the edge of the sea. She knew he would not restrain her. She could never outrun him, and no one in the village would hear any cry she made. He followed her, and walked beside her, side by side, almost as if they had been lovers, strolling in moonlight.

"When?" she asked.

"First light. Before there's time for any to come from Alnwick. Tide will be right then."

She walked on, and he beside her, in silence. The moon hung low over the sea. There would be true darkness for an hour or more before dawn began to redden the sky in the east.

"Would you have?" she asked him.

"Would I what?"

"Have taken me among the dunes and laid me down and undone the bands that bind my bosom?"

"You are Leif's woman."

"I wasn't then."

"The rules of trade."

"If not for that?"

"I'll have any pretty girl that's willing."

"Any?"

"There's been a few."

"So I am any pretty girl to you?"

"I am Thor's man. You were not any pretty girl to Thor."

"I thought I was your friend."

"Aye. But it changes nothing. Blood is blood."

He turned around. They were getting closer to the mouth of the river and to the village than he was willing to go. She turned around too and followed him. It was pointless to do otherwise. When they came back to the place they had started from, he sat down with his back to a rock, facing the point on the horizon where the sun would rise. She sat down beside him. She placed her head on his shoulder. His arm went around her waist to secure her. At once she was asleep.

38 Expiation

It seemed no time before he roused her, but the moon was down and the east was aglow with the promise of the sun.

"We go now, Princess," he said.

She stood and looked out across the sea, rippled pink and orange in the predawn glow. A deep longing came over her, a longing to take ship and sail away from all her shame, and all who knew of it and suffered for it. And then, in this most base of longings, she saw her salvation and her expiation.

"Eric," she said.

"Come on Princess. Shift yourself."

"If you could save my father, without losing your life, or Leif's, or the crew, would you do it?"

"He is oath brother to my jarl."

"Then yes?"

"It can't be done."

"But if I were lost to my father, as Drefan is lost to Kenric. Then Kenric could not blame my father."

"Men do not rage by logic, Princess."

"Men love other men who have suffered what they have suffered."

"Aye. So? Your blood does not secure my life, or Leif's."

"But my theft might."

"What do you mean?"

"You need a bargain with my father, to get Leif and the boat. I need a way for Kenric not to blame my father. If I am stolen by vikingar, then I am lost to my father and Kenric will grieve with him. But if I go with Leif, my father will know I am cared for, and he will make the bargain. You will get Leif and the boat. My father will live. My mother and my sisters will be saved. And I will be with Leif."

Eric stopped in his tracks and thought.

"Will it work?" she asked him, after a minute. "I don't trust myself anymore. I have done so many things wrong. Show me my folly, if you can see it."

"I'm only thinking if it makes my peril worse," he replied. "For your part, it could go wrong a hundred ways."

"Didn't you say last night, it is not what is done, it is what is seen, and what is thought. What will Kenric see? What will he think? A son killed by vikingar. A daughter stolen by vikingar."

"There are a dozen men who could give it the lie."

"Maybe there are. But it is something. It might save them. Let me try, at least."

He looked down at her, at the desperate pleading in her eyes.

"Oh, Princess," he said, "you will be the death of us all before you are done. Come then. We must talk to your father."

They swam across the river side by side. With the tide high, the current at the mouth was easy. They came up on the beach just behind the place where Attor's watchfires were guttering away their last fuel. Gloomy men sat, shifting and yawning, their spears upright in the sand beside them, looking down the beach the other way.

"I'll not give you a chance to play me false, girl," Eric whispered to her, and he took his knife from his belt, pinioned her hands behind her with one hand and put the knife to her throat with the other. "Careful not to trip now," he whispered, and he pushed her forward, the blade tight against her throat.

"We need to bring him away from the men," she said. "I can't shout the plan in front of them all."

"You will be the death of us all, girl," he replied, and he began to walk her forward towards the watch fires.

No one heard them come. No one turned to look. They were quite near to the camp before Eric stopped and whispered, "Call him."

"Father," she called, the sound of her voice sharp in the still morning.

One of the seated figures stirred. He gripped his spear and rose heavily to his feet. "Fetch us breakfast, girl," he cried, without turning round.

"Father," she called again. This time he caught the tone in her voice and turned.

"Who's that," he said, squinting at the figure that seemed too tall to be his daughter.

"It's me, father," she said. "Me and Eric. Come a little closer so you can see. But leave the spear please."

All the men were up now, their hands on their spears. Attor waved them back. Leaving his spear in the sand as she had instructed, he walked forward until he could see them clear enough. And then he stopped, frozen between surprise and fear.

"What are you doing, Eric," he said. It was hard for them to hear him, he said it so quietly, as if he feared that a raised voice might jolt Eric's knife into Elswyth's throat.

"Seeing to mine, as you must see to yours," Eric said.

"Don't hurt her," Attor said. "If you want a hostage, take me."

"No," Eric replied. "She serves my purpose. But come, I must talk with you, old man," Eric said.

"Let her go and we will talk."

"I know better than that, old man. Follow us or watch her bleed. But first, drop your knife on the sand."

Attor did as Eric instructed, dropping the knife and following as Eric drew Elswyth back toward the river.

"She has a way we all might live," Eric said, when they were out of earshot of Attor's men. "But until I have your oath on it, my knife stays at her throat."

"You would not hurt her," Attor said.

"No more would you hurt Leif. But if we must, we will. Listen to her. They may both live."

"Listen to me, Father," Elswyth begged him.

"Speak then, daughter. But for God's sake, man, you need not hold her quite so roughly."

"I'm all right, Father. Truly, I am. Please listen."

And so she told him her thought. She would go with Leif and Eric, and Attor would tell Kenric that the same man who had killed Kenric's son had also stolen Attor's daughter. And then Kenric and Attor would be brothers in their grief. Her father listened to all this in silence. If he saw in it the chance to save the lives of those he loved, it did not show on his face.

"Kenric will never believe such cock and bull," he said when she was done.

"He might, Father. He will want to believe it. You saved his life. He will not want to believe that you betrayed him."

"And if he does not, your mother and your sisters will pay the price for it."

"And you, Father. I know."

She was about to say more, but then Eric swore an oath, and she looked up from her father's face and saw that her mother was running towards them, as fast as her distended belly would allow, leaving a basket of bread and meat dropped on the sand.

"You let go of her, Eric," Edith shouted, running straight for him.

Attor grabbed his wife by the shoulders and restrained her.

"Hush, love," he pleaded. "Keep it quiet."

"What's going on?" Edith demanded.

Attor started to tell her, but stumbled over the words, so Elswyth repeated the story for her mother.

When it was over, Edith turned to her husband.

"What do you think?" she asked him.

"Leif's ship has been on our beach for over a week," Attor said. "Drang and Earh have supped with Leif and Thor in the hall. And they saw all that was done."

"And what will Drang and Earh tell Kenric?" Elswyth asked. "Will they tell him that they broke the hospitality of your hall?"

Attor frowned. "They'd not like to admit that," he said.

"Drang will tell Kenric the same story that Drefan told me when he caught me and Leif on the clifftop," Elswyth said.

"Caught you doing what?" her father asked.

"Walking. Talking. Nothing else, I promise. But Drefan said Leif had deceived you, that he really came here to rape and pillage. Drefan claimed he had rescued me just as Leif was carrying me away to rape me."

"Oh, how awful," Edith said.

"Yes, but he believed it. It made no sense, but he believed it because he wanted to. And Drang will want to believe that he was in a fight with a treacherous vikingar band, and Kenric will want to believe that his son died protecting us from vikingar."

"But why do you have to go," Attor asked, "if we can make him believe that?"

"Because we sheltered Leif," Edith said. "If she stays, we are allies of the vikingar who killed his son. If she goes, we are dupes of the vikingar who stole our daughter."

"Half the village knows this is not true," Attor said.

"Kenric won't talk to half the village," Edith said. "I could not even get Drefan to meet my mother, because she is a slave. Kenric won't talk to slaves."

"You think we should agree to this?" Attor asked.

"No. It might work. But there are so many ways it might fail."

"You forget that I have a knife to her throat," Eric said. "I'll give you a chance to live, if I can. But whether she comes with us or stays here, you will give me Leif and the boat, or I will slit her throat."

"You won't hurt her," Edith said, looking at him very steadily. "You would gain nothing by it. You would all die anyway. Why take her life as well?"

"You don't think I have cause for revenge on her, for Thor?" Eric said.

"I know you do," Edith said levelly and calmly. "But I have known you since a boy, Eric. You're a hard man, but you won't do this. And I know why."

"Mother," Elswyth said, "I don't know if he would do it. I know I deserve it. But if you love me, let me do this. I could not bear it if anyone else died because of what I did."

Edith looked at her daughter with the same steady gaze that she had focused on Eric.

"Please, Mother," Elswyth said. "It is the only chance for everyone to live."

Edith paused a long time. She turned and looked at Attor and then turned back and looked at Eric.

"You swear to me that she will come to no harm."

"I'll keep her safe as best I can."

"She must marry Leif then," Edith said.

"Mother, yes, I want to, but there is no time," Elswyth said.

Edith shook her head. "Until you are married, you are not one of them. It is all about kinship with you, isn't it, Eric? If she goes with you, and not married, then she is kin to none of you.

She would be no more than a Welisc slave to your people. I'll not have that. If she is married, though, she is kin to all."

"Aye, that is so," said Eric.

"We have to be away before anyone comes from Alnwick," Elswyth said. "There is no time."

"It's just the words that matter," Edith said. "Promises before witnesses. The rest is just a party. Go and rouse Leif now and tell him. But make sure your sisters do not wake. They should know nothing of this."

Elswyth looked up at Eric, who still held the knife to her throat.

"No," he said. "I would be a fool to let go of her. And you would be a fool to ask me to. You need me to be the Grendel of the piece. If that is the story you will tell, that needs to be what your people will see. We will go to the hall with my knife at her throat. She will marry Leif with my knife at her throat. You will tell your men to rig your ship and provision it, and all the while I will keep my knife at her throat. And then I will sail away with her."

39 The Widening Sea

Making Leif understand took some doing. He was groggy from sleep, in pain from his wounds, and still unbearably weary. When he first saw Eric with his knife to Elswyth's throat, he cursed him and ordered him to release her. Eric, reluctantly, did so.

But Leif was not the only one who awakened. They had also laid the monk in the guest house, after they had done what little they could for his burns. He had seemed dead to the world when they entered, and perhaps dead indeed, or on the edge of it. But now his eyes came open, bright and feverish, but awake and alert. He was terrible to look at, for his face and scalp were crossed with livid blistering lines where the burning pitch-soaked ropes had handed on him. He gasped with agony on waking, and Edith quickly poured a draught from a jug she had placed by his bed and helped him to drink.

"What is happening?" he asked, when the draught had dulled his agony enough to let him speak.

They looked at each other.

"We have to tell him," Edith said. "If he lives he will have seen us together, and he will know what happened after."

"And what if he tells what we have done."

"Then we are ruined."

"Simplest to kill him now," Eric said. "A mercy too, by the look of him."

"No," said, Attor and Elswyth, more or less together.

"Then we must tell him," Edith said, "and beg him to keep our secret."

They told him. Some parts they had to repeat, for he was distracted by his pain, but at last they made him understand.

"You want me to lie to the Ealdorman of Bamburgh?" the monk said, aghast, when the tale was finished.

"You owe Leif your life," Elswyth said. "Now you can return the gift."

The monk closed his eyes, his face drawn with the anguish of his burns. Awkwardly and painfully, he pulled his right arm out from under his blanket and made the sign of the cross and lay for a moment in contemplation. Then he opened his eyes and said, "I suppose the Jew must do for the Samaritan as the Samaritan has done for the Jew."

Elswyth knelt beside his bed. She took his hand in hers, and, seeing that the back of the hand was unburned, she kissed it. "Forgive me," she said. "This is all because of me. Your agony should be mine."

"I forgive you," he said. He looked her directly in the face, for all concupiscence had been burned from his flesh.

"No more time to waste," Eric said.

"We must get them married first," Edith said.

"But can she marry a pagan?" Attor asked.

Their eyes turned to the monk for an answer. "Of course," he said. "Marriage is a civil matter. And many Christian women have married heathen men. Had Bertha of Kent not married the pagan King Æthelberht and welcomed St. Augustine, Britain

330

might be pagan still. Perhaps your daughter will be an apostle to the Norsk."

Then Attor took his daughter's hand and placed it in Leif's. "I offer you this woman, my daughter, to be your wife. Will you accept her, protect her, provide for her, and for her children?" he asked.

"I will," said Leif.

"Leif," said Elswyth, "I take you for my husband. Now say, 'Elswyth, I take you for my wife.' There is more, but we don't have time for it."

"Elswyth, I take you for my wife."

Edith rushed to embrace them both.

"Granny said we would marry," Elswyth said. "It breaks my heart that I can't tell her."

"I'll make sure she knows before she dies," Edith said.

"And tell her I'm sorry. I'm sorry she will die a slave. I didn't mean…"

Here Elswyth was on the edge of tears again. But Edith came and embraced her and whispered, "Don't fret more on that. I will find a way yet."

Then Elswyth put her hand down to touch the round belly that stood between her and her mother. "I'll never know my sister," she whispered. "I'll never see her, ever, in my whole life. She will never know me. She will think Hilda is her big sister. You must tell her all about me, Mother. Promise." And then she grew very melancholy, and tears came into her eyes and she said, "She will never know what I look like. I will never know what she looks like. If you have another baby, I won't know about it at all. My babies won't know their grandmother. Or their grandfather," she added, pulling her father into the embrace. "Tell Hilda to have lots of babies, so you won't miss mine so much."

"You go to your husband's hall, as a daughter must," Edith said. "There were always to be tears at that parting."

"There is so much to say," Elswyth said, finding herself shaking and tears coming to her eyes once again.

"And no time to say it," Attor said.

"Say it to your pillow, every night," Edith said. "And I shall say it to mine. And we will know the other speaks, and strains their ears to listen."

And they hugged again, and kissed each other, and then Eric, ever anxious at the delay, took Elswyth by the arm and held the knife to her throat again, and said. "No more time. We go."

***

Attor ordered his boat to be rigged and launched. Edith ordered provisions to be gathered and placed in it. Among them she placed a bundle in which she had included the best of Elswyth's clothes and other small possessions, and the whole of her collection of jewelry and all the silver Attor could lay his hands on. Through all this, Eric stood with his knife again at Elswyth's throat. When the boat was ready, he forced Attor to help Leif over the side and then climbed in himself with Elswyth.

"Push us off, old man, or watch her bleed," Eric said.

Attor silently waved two men forward, and they pushed the nose of the ship off the bank until it floated. The ship rode the current down into the sea.

As soon as the ship was away, the people of the village rushed down towards the beach, many shouting that they would be avenged on the vikingar still camped there. Attor had to run hard and knock three men down before he made them see that attacking the other Norsk would cost Elswyth her life.

Once clear of the river, Eric raised the sail and brought the boat up parallel to the beach. The rest of the Norsk, confused by all that had passed, but seeing their chance, fled into the sea, swam out, and climbed aboard.

"You're away now, Eric," Attor shouted, as they had arranged. "Send my daughter back to me."

Eric took the knife from Elswyth's throat. "What, a fine young slave like this," he shouted back across the water, just as they had agreed he should. "A girl who can warm my bed and grind my grain. No. I'll keep her."

Then Attor screamed curses at Eric across the waves and wept and tore his hair.

There was nothing to do then but stand on the beach and watch the sail of Attor's boat—a small and fragile thing compared to the knarr that had burned—recede into the haze. Edith stood with Daisy in her arms, trying to form in her mind the whole of Elswyth's future life, the whole arc of her happiness, as if only her imagining it could ever make it real. Attor stood beside her, brooding on the fragility of his boat, its age, the strength of its planks, the soundness of its seams. He was holding Moira who wept into his shoulder, saying "I hate them. I hate them. I hate them," endlessly. Daisy bawled in Edith's arms. She knew not why, but she felt her mother's desolation and wept for it. Whitney, alarmed and confused, pounded along the edge of the surf with unusual fury. Everyone in the village stood beside their lord. Some wept. Some shouted curses at the disappearing boat. Some hurled spears wastefully into the surf. Some discovered the body of Thor, left behind when the Norsk fled, and began to mutilate it, greatly grieving and shaming Attor, who dared not command them to stop.

One soul alone was not convinced by what she had seen. Hilda had known more of Elswyth's heart than anyone. She stood, glaring across the sea at the retreating sail, muttering under her breath, "Liar. Liar. Liar."

***

Elswyth looked back across the widening sea. The beach where her family, her kin, her village wept for her was sunk now. Only the cliff remained in view—the cliff from which she had first spotted the coming of the knarr.

All knowledge of what would pass upon that shore in days to come was denied to her. She would whisper the joys and sorrows of each day into her pillow, as her mother had asked, not knowing if her mother lived to hear them, if her father lived to place a broad arm about her mother's shoulder and comfort her as she wept.

She glanced briefly at Leif, lying in pained half sleep in the prow. She loved him. She would bear his children. One day, perhaps, she would take ship with him and come at last to Spain. But on this coast, they could never be seen again, never while her father or her mother might still live. And so she must face a life in wistful melancholy, wondering always if everyone she had ever loved before him was alive or dead.

"We call it sailor's heartache, Princess," Eric said, seeing her look, and knowing it from of old. "Every trip begins with it the same. No man knows what shipwreck awaits him. No woman, child, or father left behind knows if or when they may return."

For the first time, she looked around at the other men, lying in the bottom of the boat. Their faces glared back at her and at once she realized what they saw when they looked at her. She was the shipwreck that had awaited them when they had set out on their voyage.

They hate me, she realized—she who had always been so easily and so universally loved—they hate me, they hate me, they hate me. St. Agnes, pray for me.

Historical Note

This book contains historical errors. Some I am aware of, some, doubtless, will be painfully obvious to scholars of the period, but most of them will remain unknown or at least unprovable. The Anglo-Saxon period lasted over 600 years and yet we have less data about it than we do about a single modern day. How the daughter of an ordinary thegn would have lived and thought and hoped and strived, we can really only guess at. The written records we have relate mostly to royal and monastic houses. The archeology is full of hints and suggestions, and a great deal of wonderful jewelry and art, but little to suggest the specifics of the life of what we might best describe as a middle-class young woman. An enormous amount of Anglo-Saxon scholarship has been done and is being done, but it yields little in the way of consecutive historical narrative such as we would associate with other periods of history. Rather, through the interpretation of scattered documents, excavations, and place-name studies, combined with analogies to other times and places, certain patterns of life and practice emerge, though tentatively at best. Reading histories of the period, one often gets the impression that one is reading a book made entirely of footnotes, since most books devote most of their text to discussing specific sources and their possible interpretations, rather than constructing what we might usually think of as an historical narrative.

Even where we do have written records, the meaning of terms is often hard to pin down. A "hide" of land seems to mean different things at different times and places. What "peaceweaver" meant does not seem entirely clear between the sources in which I have encountered it. I have interpreted it to suit my dramatic purposes.

For a novelist, this is in part frustrating and in part liberating. To assemble a whole picture of the life and thought of my characters, I have had to borrow elements from different times and places, select from various interpretations what best suits my dramatic purposes, and fill in the gaps with things borrowed from later times (the tugging of forelocks as a sign of respect, for instance).

Other than Twyford, I have chosen to use modern names and spellings for places. Many of these names originate from the period, and it is simply easier for the reader who cares to look them up on a map. Twyford, of which the sources record the synod that Brother Alun mentions and not much else, is commonly, if not certainly, identified with the current village of Alnmouth. I have taken certain liberties with the geography of the village. Elswyth's cliff is a hill, and today is separated from the beach by a golf course. The Anglo-Saxons did not play golf, so I have removed it and made the cliff steeper. Cliffs such as I describe do exist along that coast.

We don't know how the Viking raiders knew how rich a target Lindisfarne was. It seems reasonable to suppose that there was trade going on before the attack, and that such traders would have found themselves unpopular afterward.

The source and meaning of the word Viking are uncertain. I have chosen the interpretation that *viking* was a verb and that *vikingr* (plural *vikingar*) was a word for pirate, not because I think it most likely, but because it suits the story best. The term does not actually seem to have been in use at the time the story is set. They would probably have said something like Northmen. But *vikingr* is too good a word to waste.

Brother Alun's statement that marriage is a civil matter may come as a surprise, but the church did not come to regard marriage as a sacrament until sometime in the twelfth century. Weddings were not church affairs, though of the marriage customs of the minor nobility of the eighth century we know pretty much nothing. It does seem that the requirements of marriage were pretty simple. If a couple said they were married and slept together, they were married. Arranged marriages were no doubt common, but by law a woman could not be forced to marry against her will. Marriage between classes, however, seems to have been discouraged (as it usually is). Christian women did marry pagan kings, which sometimes led to the conversion of their husbands, and therefore of their people.

There was no parish system in the church in Britain at that time. Its religious foundations appear to have all been monastic in structure and there are records of complaints about the bishops and secular clergy failing to visit and instruct their flocks, so Twyford's lack of a church and rare visits from clergy is plausible.

The Anglo-Saxons were not a backward or illiterate society, though how far their culture extended beyond monasteries and royal courts is hard to tell. They were still very much a warrior culture though. The extent to which Christianity had affected the kinship structures of the earlier pagan warrior culture is hard to know for any particular time and place. Similarly, how completely Christianity had replaced earlier religious ideas and practices will have differed over the period. I have painted a picture of these things to suit my dramatic purposes, not to attempt to fix them accurately for the time and place of my story.

We think of the wimple as religious dress today, but they are common in the depictions of women that have come down to us from the period.

I know of no such edition of *The City of God* as described in the story. (This one was destroyed by fire, so of course it has not come down to us.) Whether such an edition would be worth a jarl's ransom, I have no idea.

Whitney's condition is pure literary invention, and mildly symbolic in its intention. It should not be identified with any real condition.

All of the above is based on what I remember from my reading over the period in which this book was conceived and written. It should not be mistaken for scholarship or cited as fact.

About the Author

G. M. Baker strives to write serious popular fiction: fiction that finds the truth of the human condition in stories of action, adventure, romance, and even magic and expresses them in a popular style using accessible prose.

For more on serious popular fiction and other matters literary and various, subscribe to his newsletter at https://storiesallthewaydown.com.

Read more at https://gmbaker.net

If you enjoyed *The Wistful and the Good*, please leave a rating and review on Amazon and Goodreads. It really helps. Thank you.

Also by G. M. Baker

St. Agnes and the Selkie (Cuthbert's People, Book Two)

Mother Wynflaed of Whitby Abbey rules a joint house of monks and nuns, and many layfolk besides. Her office forbids her to have favorites, but when a young woman appears on the doorstep, soaked from the sea and too terrified to speak her name, Wynflaed comes to see her not only as a potential postulant, but as a daughter. She names her Agnes, but before Agnes can become part of the community, Wynflaed must discover her secret.

Though Wynflaed finds it impossible to think ill of Agnes, Agnes herself keeps pulling down one penance after another on her head, as if trying to expiate some grave crime. As some in the abbey begin to fear her, Agnes becomes Wynflaed's obsession, upsetting the harmony of the abbey, and leading Wynflaed to question her worthiness to rule.

When Eardwulf, the young king of Northumbria, comes to Wynflaed seeking counsel, he too becomes infatuated with Agnes.

As Wynflaed unwinds Agnes's secret, she begins to fear that Agnes is a danger to both the abbey and the king. She plans to send her away. But Eardwulf has other ideas, and Agnes has other admirers.

Available here:
https://mybook.to/StAgnesandtheSelkie

The Needle of Avocation (Cuthbert's People, Book Three)

Hilda is the second sister, the plain one, the overlooked, the put upon. She is also the finest needlewoman in Northumbria, though she distrusts anyone who tells her so. Her mother, Edith, was born a slave and seduced and married a thegn's son, a fact which embarrasses Hilda greatly. Edith has tricked the local ealdorman into betrothing his only son and heir, Anfaeld, to Hilda, an arrangement unwelcome to everyone but Edith, and particularly to Hilda who would rather retire to a nunnery and spend her life in embroidery.

It is Hilda's right to refuse the marriage, but the future of her mother and sisters may depend on her making the match, a role that should have fallen to her beautiful older sister Elswyth who was kidnapped by vikingar three years earlier.

On the way to her wedding, Hilda meets a heartbroken king, his petulant child bride, an abbess who wrestles with a great torment, and the shy young man she is supposed to marry.

Feeling herself mistreated by them all, including her prospective mother-in-law, Hilda resolves to refuse the marriage and become a nun. But first she must solve the double enigma of what really happened to Elswyth, and why Anfaeld himself has not refused the marriage.

Lady Isabel and the Elf Knight

The Devil always begins by giving thee work that is just," Horrocks said. *"Then he tells thee, thou dost just work, therefore thou art just. And then he tells thee, thou art just, and therefore any work thou dost is just."*

When Isabel kills the Elf Knight and takes his horse, sword, and horn, she believes that she has done just work. She has broken his enchantment and has rid the twelve kingdoms of a great evil. Horrocks' advice to lay down the Elf Knight's tools falls on deaf ears.

But something old is waking in Isabel, something that longs for the gallop and the chase, for bright sun and the rush of wind against the cheek, for glimmering steel and bright blood and the dying of light in the eyes of the slain.

Without the Elf Knight's sword at her side, Isabel feels lost and terrified, but after almost murdering the man she is supposed to marry, she realizes that either she must put the Elf Knight's tools aside or exile herself forever. But already it may be too late, for Isabel is losing herself and within her the Elf Maiden grows in strength and fury.

Available here:

https://mybook.to/LadyIsabelandtheElfKnight

Printed in Great Britain
by Amazon